The New War

I0645653

Hope for real Justice

By

Roger Roberge Rainville

When two lawless punks chase down a sixty-two-year-old Vietnam veteran in his own neighborhood after witnessing a homicide and shoot him in the back four times, it sets off a whole "New War" for him and six former Nam vets he's proud to call - brothers.

The New War
(Hope For Real Justice)
The New War
Written by Roger Roberge Rainville
Copyright © 2024 by Roger Roberge Rainville

ISBN: 978-1-945423-67-3
Cover Artist: Diane Noody
Published by 5 Stones Publishing
www.ilncenter.com
Contact: randyjohnson@ilncenter.com

The New War

(Hope For Real Justice)

Boss **Clint** **Eh-Jax** **Lenny** **Boom** **Hap** **Bull**

The seven men in our group are veterans who were very active in Vietnam combat missions from the latter part of the war between 1970 and 1975. Here's information about the *"patriots"* you'll encounter in the story. Later on, you'll meet four Middle East War fighters that join our noble cause - the *younger squad*.

"I'm Steve Senco. My friends call me 'Boss.' I will be narrating the accounts of this story. I was a sniper in Army Special Forces taking out enemies as far away as half a mile. I also used tranquilizer rifles as part of numerous covert operations. I served three years Vietnam as a combat soldier, then, stateside as an MP for a year. After serving our country, I worked as a foreman for a specialty steel company and retired at age 62. I'm married with two grown married children and three grandchildren who are my life. I devote my time to family and veteran buddies. We meet at the local VFW where we socialize. I also help men from various branches of the military that are struggling with (PTSD) and other problems from their combat experience.

Billy "Bull" Flack - 64 also married. He did a stint in the Marines during the Vietnam era. He competed in weight-lifting competitions. He's really good with computers and electronics. He also has gadgets for surveillance, and communication - mini microphones and ear pieces to communicate when doing "covert ops." After his service, he used his skills at a large private investigation firm. He retired at 60.

Jack (a.k.a.) "Eh-Jax" Bodine - 62 - married but not getting along as well with his wife as he'd like to. He's strong, but has a real gentle nature until you mess him; then…watch out!!! He spent six months in a Vietnam POW camp. He has scars from the beatings he took. He's retired from the Post office with a nice pension. In Nam, he did his share of sniping and took out at least 45 enemies at around a quarter mile or more.

Jim (a.k.a.) "Clint" Gardon - 61 - married a while back and split up amicably. He rides a motorcycle… no tattoos, short hair, and reminds me of Clint Eastwood; you know, that "Go ahead and make my day" kind of attitude. He has some medical background as a medic in the Army as well as infantry training. He's an excellent marksman. He worked as an Emergency Room assistant and took an early retirement at 58.

Jack "Happy Jack" Mason or "Hap" for short - 57, ex-Army; served as a helicopter gunner in Nam; took a bullet in the left shoulder. After Nam, he became a cop and taught small arms and long gun use to new recruits at the police academy before retiring at 55. He lost his wife to cancer and has been doing the best he can to get through life. His kids and grandkids are all he's got. He's very upset with the way the neighborhood has turned out.

While he was a police officer, he'd seen just about every kind of crime a cop can see. He had seen enough vile things people do each other and the gross disregard for the law. Now that he doesn't have to deal with criminals as a cop, he smiles a lot; hence, "Happy Jack." He still connects with his old partners on the force, Sergeant Shawn O'Rourke.

Benny "Boom" Sorel - Ex-Marine - 63, who is hard as nails and was/is an explosive specialist. During his time in the field, he got to blow up a lot things and enemies. He also created a lot of "diversions" with smaller explosions to draw the enemy away from where his unit needed to go. He has scars from shrapnel damage to his right arm and leg. He's divorced with three grown children; maintains a good relationship with his ex-wife. They sometimes date. After his service, he drove large mail trucks to distance cities and retired at 60.

Lenny Shine (aka) "Lightening" as in Grease Lightning." He's 58, and ex-Army. Married with grown children, loves his wife. He's a top martial artist. His hands are so fast that he once saw some jerk mistreating his woman and decided to step in. He casually walked over, stood just a bit behind the guy, threw his bottle of beer against the wall as a distraction and when the jerk looked to see what happened, Lenny, quick as a blink, snapped off a punched to the guy's jaw and knocked him out. Before retiring at 55, he was the manager of a major heavy equipment outfit.

A special aid to the group: Sergeant Shawn O'Rourke - 63 years old. He's Hap's former partner on the police force of our fair city. He runs the front desk at Precinct 10. He should be retired but wants to stay active and took a front desk job.

YOUNGER PATRIOTS IN THE GROUP
from Middle East wars

Chuck   Angel   Dave   Mickey

Chuck Armand, 29 years old - a Middle East War veteran. His job in the war was like mine, that of a sniper. He took out several bad guys from distances of over 1,000 yards and had at least thirty kills. He's a dispatcher for a major tractor trailer truck company. He's into guns; side arms, rifles and automatic weapons. Never married - still looking for the right lady.

Dave Alamos, 37 years old - (Afghan war vet) divorced. He did intelligence work for the 42nd CA Bn. in the 90s. After his tour of duty, he was hired as to do intelligence consultation for various local law enforcement groups. His expertise resulted in many arrests and prosecutions of a host of criminals.

Mickey, (aka) 'Lefty' - 31 years old married with an eight-year-old daughter. He's another Middle East war veteran, involved in precision drone strikes. He works for a company that specializes in drones for commercial use; movies, law enforcement surveillance, TV news footage, commercials, real estate videos of properties, and private contractors.

Angelina (Angel) Cruz is a pretty thirty-year-old Latina of Puerto Rican descent. She served with Mickey (Lefty) Syms in the Middle East war. She did her share of taking out enemies, some at fairly close range. She was wounded; took a bullet in her right thigh and has scars from a roadside bomb on her right arm and face. Mickey trusts her with his life. Before her service with Uncle Sam, she spent 5 years training as a boxer under the name "La Fuerza" (The Force). She won 8 of her 10 fights with 7 knockouts and 1 TKO. She works as an office manager for the city's Records Department.

WARNING!

What follows might be a bit upsetting for the faint of heart. Remember, my men and I are all ex-combat soldiers and have seen the ugly side of war, some of it, very, very ugly! We've seen how harsh and cruel the enemy can be and how some of my men have had to be just as harsh and cruel out there on the battlefield. It's just the way war is. It's ugly! There's nothing nice about it. No one wins. Everybody loses!

In the sequence of events I'm about to share with you, some of the tactics we use are severe and cruel, but after you know the facts of each case, you might just agree with our actions. Although we would like to live in a *"Utopian"* society, we all know that's not possible in this crazy, evil world. As it says in the book of Ecclesiastes, chapter 3… there's *"…a time for love and a time for hate, a time for WAR, and a time for PEACE."*

We all fought for peace and came home in hopes of living a peaceful life. Well, that didn't happen, and now, we want to make drastic changes. All the men on my team were tough-as-nails soldiers. We're older now; we've all slowed down quite a bit, but haven't lost our combat knowledge and can still create "covert operations" to fit any number of situations. Some of the men were deep covert operators. They can be brutal if need be. Welcome to the "NEW WAR."

PROLOGUE

My name is Steve. I'm very angry about the part of the city where I live; about the way life in the neighborhood has become unbearable for some people because of the violence and criminal activity. The neighborhood is far from being what it used to be. There are way too many bad things going on here now; too many people doing whatever they want to do with regards to crime and degenerate behavior. They respect nothing and no one; not parents, not their neighbors, authorities, their elders, themselves or property. Most of them don't know what the word "RESPECT" means.

In Moses' days, out of control young people were dealt with harshly by parents and authorities. There was no need for youth detention centers for juveniles or jails for the older bad guys. They rid themselves of bad people; "…purging the evil among them."

In the book of Deuteronomy, chapter twenty-one and verses eighteen to twenty-one, it says:

> *"If someone has a rebellious son who does not obey his father or his mother and will not listen to them after they discipline him, his father will take hold of him and bring him before the elders at the gate of his town. They shall say to the elders, "This son of ours is stubborn and rebellious. He is a glutton and a drunkard." Then all the men of his town are to stone him to death. You must purge evil from among you."*

Something has to give! Things need to change! Good people shouldn't have to put up with punks and bad men that threaten them day in and day out! It's just not right, damn it! People are sick of it! Although I back and respect the cops, I realize they can't be everywhere to stop the robbers, the burglars, drug dealers, wife and girlfriend beaters, child abusers, rapists, home-invading perps, or drive-by shooters! There's got to be a solution to all of this insanity!

The following quote from the movie **"Network"** is my exact sentiment, and that of thousands of good people living in our neighborhood.

> *"I'm mad as hell, and I'm not going to take it anymore!!!"*

In one year, the area where I live had; 283 assaults, 10 murders, 44 rapes, 150 robberies, hundreds of scams, 550 burglaries, 2,045 general thefts plus 285 car thefts and climbing. When I was much younger, those numbers were extremely low compared to now. ENOUGH IS ENOUGH!

We're a group that formed to even things out.... no worries about retribution, just justice; doing it the old fashion way! Before lawmen were put in place to take care of unsavory characters, degenerates, murderers and all forms of low-life malicious perps, justice was taken care of by the locals banning together to bring peace and punish the cockroaches that made life miserable for good people. It was good people against evil people. We're the good guys and we're damn mad about the bad elements around us. Our plan is to do our best to make a difference. We know we can't clean it all up, but we can send a strong message. We see that we have a serious infestation of bad guys in our society that need to be removed. There needs to be a force in our neighborhood that will do that. We be them!

Chapter 1

How it all started

Let's start from the beginning. One night in late spring of 2010 as daylight just faded, I came out of a delicatessen at the corner of Richfield and Park and heard a gunshot! This guy came whizzing by and almost knocking me down. He was running like hell to get away from two punks holding what looked to be 9mm Glocks. I moved back quickly into an entranceway of the store to get out of their way. The street light allowed me to get a good look at them as they ran by and I know they got a look at me too. As they closed in on the guy they were chasing, they fired three shots. I took a quick peek to see if it was safe to get out of there; I only saw a glimpse of the guy being chased. He was face down on the ground with a gun laying at his side and the two shooters standing over him. One guy shot him again as he lay there. They both turned and began running toward me because they knew I could ID them. I ran as fast as I could, but this sixty-two-year-old guy could only move so fast. They got close enough to fire several shots. I felt pain in the back of my right thigh, left arm and left shoulder blade area. One more shot was fired before I went down and lost consciousness. I was hit on the side of the head. Fortunately, the bullet hit my skull at an angle and glanced off but left a very nasty gash in my scalp.

It wasn't long before I opened my eyes in an ambulance with guys tending to my wounds. They stopped the bleeding while making their way to the hospital. I couldn't help but feel a lot of anger; not sorry for myself, but EXTREME anger that this kind of crap happened in my own neighborhood!

What insanity! What cruelty! What makes these guys do this kind of thing without even batting an eye? Boy, I wish I had had a gun! Having had one would have at least given me a chance to defend myself. It's crazy! The bad guys have guns, illegal at that! Meanwhile, a lot of honest and upstanding citizens don't have, don't want, or can't get them. The average citizen doesn't stand a chance against hoodlums like these. They're getting more and more brazen. These punks have no conscience, no morals. It's a damn zoo out there! I was now a victim of multiple gunshot wounds with a very bad attitude toward the rats that did this to me.

The doctors did a good job patching me up. I was lying on my hospital bed thinking about assaults that are perpetrated on other innocent people and thinking how degenerate our society has become. I remembered a news item about an old lady walking down the street that was attacked for her purse. The punk punched her in the face and knocked her down. She only had a few dollars on her. Punks like that need a beating; just to give them a taste of their own medicine.

Another damnable attack I remember is about a burly moron beating up on his girlfriend. He dragged her by the hair out of the beauty shop where she worked. He continued to beat her in the street and dragged her to a house, down the driveway and plunged her head into a two-foot pool and drowned her! All the while, people were watching this and NOT ONE lifted a hand to save her. Even though I'm an older man, I wish I had been there. I would have done something. You can bet on it! It seems to me that two or three of the on-lookers could have ganged up on him or hit him with anything in sight that could have stopped him!!!

It's beyond idiocy to me that in our society, people can't under-stand that you sometimes need to get involved. I remember seeing a TV show hosted by Don Quiñones entitled, "What Would You Do?" The show had to do with getting involved when you see something wrong being done to innocent or defenseless people. One of the problems with getting involved is "retribution!" People are afraid that if they get involved, they'll get hurt if they step in to help, or that the culprits will come to seek revenge after they get arrested, then released. It's understandable. There are times when you just have to get in there and do something!

We as Americans have interceded all over the world and were called heroes. What the hell's the difference if it's against oversea tyrants or some local tyrants that we kick butt? Tyrants, or a better term, "cockroaches" are pests that need to be squashed! We have domestic war zones and not enough soldiers; meaning, law enforcement, to take care of the problems plaguing our cities and neighborhoods. What can be done? If this keeps up, the entire country where big cities are located and some small towns and villages will be out of control. As a society, we can't allow that to happen. You hear it so often, "Something has to be done!" I get that! But, what can the average man or woman do to change what's happening to our way of life? Things are getting worse, not better!

A vow of revenge

After several days in the hospital and being in and out of consciousness due to the medications, my six brothers in arms from the VFW were finally able to see me fully awake. They wanted to hug me, but knew the pain of the bullet wounds wouldn't allow that. Instead, they each took turns giving me a kiss on the cheek or forehead. These guys are great. Any one of them would lay down his life for me, and I, for them. Their presence brought a lot of joy to my heart.

The last to greet me was Clint. When he saw my condition, he walked over to me with tears in his eyes and said, "Brother, we WILL find whoever who did this to you. We'll get 'em, Boss!" The others all vowed to be part of the hunt for these cockroaches.

After their visit, I began thinking of ways to go after the scum-bags that did this to me. I know revenge at times isn't a good thing, but these thugs killed a man and were still out there running free. THAT'S NOT RIGHT!

My initial thought was; *find them, give 'em a beating and make them disappear!*

I wondered how many other people they hurt or killed. Just like in war when I was in Nam, we hunted the enemies and killed them. There were no trials with judges, lawyers and juries; no slap on the wrist, no plea deals and no reduced sentences. The crap that's happening in our streets is no different to me! We have enemies of good people all over the country and they need to be taken out. I realize we're not in Nam, but damn it, sometimes, it's a war zone in my own neighborhood! Something has to be done! The problems won't just go away. Somebody has to try and make a difference, but who?

Back home

It took a couple of weeks, but I finally got out of the hospital. Happy Jack, Boom and Clint came to take me home. I still feel a lot pain in my right thigh, left arm and left shoulder blade area. My head wound with the thirty plus stitches is still very sensitive. I don't like the reminders I have to live with. Maybe it's a good thing. It keeps the urge strong for what needs to be done; getting those punks!

My buddies don't stay long. They can see I need to rest. After about a half hour, they each give me a light hug and a kiss my cheek, and leave.

Putting the word out on the perps

As they drive back home after their visit, Hap says to Boom and Clint, "We have to find the rats that did this to Boss. With the news coverage, those punks know he's alive and can identify them. We can't allow them time to get to him. We can only hope someone on the street will come forward with the info. Let's put the word out."

"Sounds like a good plan to me," says Boom. "Once we do find them, you know that we'll have to go Redneck on them, right?"

"I know," says Hap. "That'll be just fine with me. People who want to kill me, you, Boss or any others in our family or friends, can't be allowed to be around. We'll talk to the other guys and tell them to put the word out on the street. Hopefully, we'll get names quickly."

Clint says, "When we do find out who did it, whatever we do will have to be done right. We're going to have to be really cool and slick about it. If we make the wrong move, one of us could wind up hurt or dead. We can't chance that. When we meet up with the others tonight at the Post, we'll toss around some ideas."

"Sounds good to me, my friends," says Boom. "I'm so looking forward to nailing these rats."

Four days later - got 'em

As I continued to recuperate at home, Boom, Clint and Hap came to give me some good news. I was lying on the couch watching *"Walking Tall."* I love that movie. The guys had something important and very private to tell me. My wife was out shopping, so we had all the privacy we needed.

Clint started by saying, "You know those two punks that shot you, we caught up with them. One of the young vets by the name of Mickey 'Lefty' Szymanski who comes to the VFW Post has seen our group there several times and knows about you getting shot up.

He came up to me and said; "I found out who the guys are that shot your friend."

I said, "This is really good news. Who are they and what did you guys do?"

Boom jumps in and says, "According to our source, Mickey, it was a twenty-one-year-old named Anthony Perkins and his twenty-year old buddy, John Baker; two really bad news characters, but not anymore. They're both gang-bangers that have been involved in heavy drug dealings and drive-by shootings."

Boss asks, "What did you mean when you said, not anymore?!"

Clint looks at Boom and nods for him to continue. "The man at the Post, this Mickey guy, told us that he heard from some younger gang members he knew on Central Avenue that it was Perkins and Baker. He said that he overheard Perkins bragging that he had capped a guy named Shaky because of a big drug deal that went sideways. He also heard that they ran down some older guy who saw them do the shooting and shot him too. That'd be you, Boss."

"Yep! That'd be me, alright. Okay, let's get back to what you said before about them being 'bad news characters, 'but not anymore.'"

Hap tells him, "We found out where they hung out and what they were into. They were two of the biggest drug dealers in the area and were under someone really powerful in the drug trade from the east side. Our source didn't know who that was. Boom and me had a meeting with Clint to figure out how to get these two rats and make things right."

"I can't wait to hear what you came up with. Knowing you guys, it had to be righteous."

Hap says, "You'll love this Boss. We got Mickey from the Post to talk to one of his street guys to set up a $10,000 drug buy with Perkins and Baker for an older dude he knows, meaning Clint. They always go together when they deal; you know - backup in case there's trouble."

"So, how did it go and how did you bag these killers?"

"We were slick about it," says Boom. "The deal was set up so only one of us would be present to make the buy. Clint in disguise, looking like an old hippy type, went in while I hid about two-hundred feet away with my trusty Henry .22 long rifle. Boom and me stayed out of sight and ready to jump in the game if needed. When it came time to exchange money for product, I took a bead on the backup and Clint was ready with a stun gun he palmed in his right hand to take down his mark.

As he approached the dealers, Clint waived cash he had in his left hand. The sight of cash is always a good lure. Perkins was the one with the drugs and Baker had his hand inside his coat, like he was ready to pull a gun. That was expected and easy to spot. They had no idea what was going to happen. Still holding the wad of cash, Clint asked to see the goods and as soon as Perkins raised a small, opened gym bag, he zapped him with his stun gun! Down he went. At that moment, I shot Baker in the chest area as he started to draw his gun. He dropped to the ground like rock. The mere fact that Perkins was drawing to shoot Clint made my shot the right thing to do. No remorse there. I hit him square in the heart."

"What did you end up doing to them or with them?" asks Boss.

It was Clint's turn to tell the rest of the tale. "Baker was out. I pinned Perkins to the ground with my knee on his chest before he could revive completely. As he recovered from being tased, he started swearing and yelling. I punched him in the jaw and knocked him out to keep him from drawing attention. Boom and Hap came quickly to drag the two to the edge of Ward's canal. We took the 9mm Baker had in his belt. I assumed that was one of the guns used to take you down, Boss. We also checked Perkins, and sure enough, another 9mm tucked in his waist. We can have one of Hap's former cop friends on the force check to see if they're matches for any of the slugs they took out of you. My guess is that they would be a match for the ones that took you down. We have them tucked away in a safe place."

"So... tell me, where are these two low-life now?"

My friends look at each other and Boom makes a hand gesture to give Clint the floor.

"Boss," he says, "Knowing these two actually killed a man in cold blood and almost killed you, we didn't hesitate to finish them. We did like we did in Nam with known enemies when it was either them or us. We hit them when we had the chance.

In this case, it was us against them. By all counts, you should be dead. We could have figured out a way to hand them over to the cops with the guns as evidence, but it would have meant, your name being put out there for Perkins and Baker's buddies to be able to zero in on you and your family for retribution. We couldn't allow that. Also, you'd have to go to court and have to deal with the press, lawyers, prosecutors, jurors and appeals! When we were in Nam, as ugly as it was, we, had to make decisions as to who lived and who died. With these two career drug dealers and killers, we felt it was the right thing to do. With the life they led, people will think it was gang rivals that took them out.

Good news though. Before we capped Perkins, Boom put his hand over his mouth, held his .38 to his head and told him to shut up. He then asked him who his drug source was. He was reluctant until he heard the gun being cocked and Boom telling him that he has three seconds to give up the name.

This Perkins rat was a real scared punk because he quickly said, 'My main source is the biggest dealer in the city. He goes by the name of Raptor and has a place on Division Street. He don't play man. He makes dudes disappear that don't do what he says."

After we got this great piece of information, Boom didn't blink and squeezed the trigger. Perkins just slumped down nice and easy. We then tied cement blocks around their waist and dropped them in the canal a little way downstream from the bridge where no one would think of looking. It's done, Boss."

I tell them, "I know it was a hard thing to do. You guys aren't killers, but these two punks had it coming. What you did was probably going to happen to them at the hands of some other gang members. People like that who deal heavy in drugs and kill anybody who stands in their way, make a lot of enemies. All you did was cut that time short. Knowing they're gone will help my mental recovery. They knew who I was after the TV news people covered the double shooting for a few days after it happened. It would have been only a matter of time before they'd try to take me out so I could never be a witness. And, I'm sure those two probably killed other unfortunates since my episode with them. They were killers, but killers, no more."

Boom says, "Glad we could take care of that for you, Boss. Now, you can continue living without having to worry about those two. But we'll have to come up with a plan to get this Raptor cockroach that's responsible for feeding drugs to all of the local pushers that are poisoning our neighborhoods. He's gotta go too!"

Chapter 2

My brothers - at the VFW

It's now May 7, 2010, on a cool spring night. I make my way to the VFW on Memorial Drive where my Vietnam vet brothers hang out, them, as well as Gulf and Afghan War vets; Lefty being one of them. There are only a couple of much older guys; one from World War II and about six from the Korean War that come in regularly. I have a lot of respect for those old timers; there aren't many of them left. God bless 'em!

Anyway, I meet up with my six friends who came to see me at the hospital. Again, one by one, they hug me and welcome me back at our old watering hole. We have a lot in common. Yes Nam, but also, a brotherhood that only an ex-soldier from a war could understand and appreciate. The seven of us are all retired or semi-retired and spend our time staying busy as best we can with chores, some volunteer work, and part time jobs for extra pocket money. The average age is late fifties to early sixties.

These are the guys I'm more than proud to call my "brothers." We're a real tight group and would do anything for each other … to the point of death. All we need to do is make a call and we're there to take care of whatever the need is.

Talk of justice - lighting the fuse

During our conversations at the Post, Bull asks, "Did you guys hear about the jerk that killed his girlfriend last week in front of a whole bunch of bystanders!?"

Pretty much in unison, we said, "WHAT?"

As Bull tells us the story about the brutal crime, I can see Boom getting really tight and tense like he wants to get the guy and just mulch him!

Bull says, "The guy got arrested, and that's fine, but all he'll get is jail time with free room and board; that's shelter and food for as long as he's in, with the tax payers footing the bill. Meanwhile, the girl's family and friends will forever bear the pain of having lost someone they loved."

Happy-Jack (Hap) wants the floor and says, "See men, there's no 'real justice' out there. I dealt with that kind of scum for years on the police force. That guy should have gotten the beating of his life and then…get dead!" He continues, "That kind of stuff just puts me over the edge! What we need is REAL justice to deal with scums like that. Real justice is not out there and it drives me crazy!"

It reminded him of a story of street justice that a friend of his told him about. It had to do with this guy who used to beat up on his girlfriend.

Hap says, "After this girl left her boyfriend, he kept harassing her with phone calls at all hours of the day or night, and even at work. Well, she got a new man in her life that had special friends; Hulk types. Anyway, she told her new boyfriend about the ex. He told her not to worry about it anymore.

That night, this massive guy showed up at his door and said, 'Are you so and so?'

The guy said, "Yah! What do you want?"

As soon as he said that, Hulk-man punched him square in the face and dropped him like a bad habit. As he tried to speak, BAM; he got a backhand to the face.

The hulk told him, 'Shut up and DO NOT say a word!' The jerk just couldn't shut up and tried to talk. That only got him another smack to the face.

Hulk guy told him, "If I hear that you harass your ex-girlfriend EVER again, I'll be back.'

He also told him, "If by chance the cops should pick me up because of this little visit, there are four more just like me who will come by to pay you another visit. If that happens, you won't be able to walk for a long, long time. They'll also break both your arms so you won't be able to feed yourself or wipe your butt for weeks!"

Guess what? The problem was solved. Now, that's what I call swift justice! No cops, no lawyers and no judges in a courtroom; just PURE justice. That's what's needed!"

Bull puts in his two cents and says, "You know, I'd love to see a group of guys get together and catch those kinds of people, throw them in a van, drive them to a secluded place somewhere, keep them there for a few days, give them a beating a day for a few days, tattoo their foreheads with something that would mark them as bad guys, then, put 'em back on the street."

Clint says, "Whoa Bull! You've done some thinking about this before haven't you? I mean the way you just threw that out! WOW!"

"Yah, I've had thoughts about cleaning up the neighborhood. Man, there's so much garbage out there and not enough is done about it!" He goes on, "Why can't somebody do something about the trash that just keeps piling up? I don't know about you guys, but I'm pretty upset about our neighborhoods being run down and ruled by scumbags. This area was a jewel at one time and these rats are turning it into a ghetto! I'm real angry about that, aren't you?!"

Well, that got an idea started that was going to bring about a whole new kind of justice in the neighborhood! The fuse was lit! We hung out at the post for a while; drank a few pints and chit-chatted some more, then, one by one, everyone went home.

A week later - the "New War," and our creed

It's a week later now. We all meet up in the VFW's backroom for our weekly get-together, and don't you know, the subject of "cleaning up the neighborhood" comes up again!

Bull brings it up. He asks the question, "Did any of you do any thinking on the subject of cleaning up the neighborhood we brought up a week ago?"

I tell him, "Yah, I did! Funny you should bring that up! After I left here last week, I couldn't sleep all night. The stories about some of the crap we were talking about bothered me and I came to agree wholeheartedly with you about doing something to get rid of the punks that have put fear in our neighborhood; especially after having been gunned down the way I was."

I could see Boom was eager to speak his mind and motioned for him to go for it.

"I'm a peaceful man basically, but I get really angry, more than angry, when I see some of the things these perps are doing to terrorize our people. Yah, I'd love to see a group of guys get together and end their sorry life of crime and terror."

Bull looks around at his comrades and can read their faces. He asks if all the guys are of the same mindset as me and Boom. All of them say, "YES!"

You have to understand that all of the men saw action in Nam and all of them had taken out some of the enemies - some, at close range. To them, if it came to spilling blood and guts again for the right reasons, they wouldn't have a problem with that.

The collective yes inspires Happy Jack to make the following statement.

"You know guys, we all went to war to fight enemies oversea, and now, we have enemies right here in our own backyard that are threatening our freedoms, our rights, our neighborhoods and our lives! These scums are the new enemies! They're no different to me from the enemies we fought overseas. We had no real stake fighting overseas in a foreign country; this is our home, brothers!

Our families, friends and way of life are at stake here. For these things, I'd go to war in a heartbeat. It would be a very honorable reason to fight and put order back in our neighborhood."

I pipe in, "I totally agree with you brother." Taking a brief moment to look at each of the men, I say, "Is anyone here thinking what I'm thinking?"

"What?" asks Bull, "Let's form a posse, kick some butt, bust a few heads and if need be, put a real bad hurting on a few dirt bags out there?"

"Yep, that's exactly what I'm proposing. This is serious business, guys!"

Boom says, "I love it!!! Let's do it; and real soon before I get too old."

He adds… "Every man, woman and child deserve to live in peace, and any cockroach violating this basic human right should be dealt with, with - EXTREME PREJUDICE!"

All the guys agree with what he just said.

I tell the men, "What Boom just said will be our CREED! We have a NEW WAR on our hands, brothers! The fact that all of us know the streets of the neighborhood around here should make it easy to nail down certain trouble spots and do whatever needs to be done to get rid of the trash.

One thought that comes to mind is that when we 'tune-up' some punk and warn him that he'd better not come around to cause any more trouble, surely, he'd get his boys and come hunting for us. So…, we have to plan things really well; all covert operations! Two things we need to get right; one, we need to get them in the dark, and two, we can't let them ever see our faces. We have to devise ways to do that every time. If any of our identities were made known to any of them, it would jeopardize the entire group."

To talk more privately, we move to a secluded part of the post to discuss ideas on how to plan this - New War. I tell the men that we need to be a well-oiled machine to make it work. We'll need to do things just right to deal with every perp we pick up. The premise is that these creeps are lawbreakers and must be stopped! We need to lay out plans to nab them one at a time, maybe two or three at a time if it's easy enough to do. If we have to abort a pick-up, we do it! There'll be no need in running any risks. There will always be another day, a better time and opportunity to get whoever we want to get. We have to have fail-proof plans to catch them by surprise. We'll need to use disguises for any up-close encounters. We also need a place to tuck away the rats we catch for a time while we process them.

Boom says, "I have a nice size warehouse that I'm not using right now. It's in the old railroad station area. We can put our POWs there. And, I have a few ideas on how to keep them separated. I'll work out the details and let you know by tomorrow."

With a smile on his face, Clint says, "Isn't that, like abduction, imprisonment, kidnaping… or something?"

Smiling right back at him, he says, "Why, yes, it is Clint my dear friend. But, do you think anyone will miss these miscreants?"

Bull looks at the men and says, "Hey, why don't we do a trial run as soon as we can?"

Boom says, "Good idea. Let's roll! But, who do we bag and where? Hey wait! What about that big dealer Raptor on Division? He's been supplying all the pushers around here and who knows where else? He'd be the perfect target for us."

Getting the Raptor

Eh-jax has an idea and lays it on the squad. "I've got a fifteen-year-old Cadillac in my yard that I've been meaning to fix up. It's been sitting there for about three years. I start it up now and then just to keep the engine lubricated. It has plenty of room in the trunk to load up a couple of bodies. We could use that to transport our catch."

He adds. "We can run it with bogus plates in case we're spotted. I'll also remove the VIN plate so that it's harder to trace.

Afterward, we can take it somewhere in Raptor's neighborhood and torch it. The cops will figure it was some of his own people that got to him. And, if by chance it is traced back to me, I'll tell them someone stole it and since it was so old, I didn't bother reporting it."

Hap says, "I like that idea. Let's do it. This rodent needs to disappear!"

After a bit of snooping around to find out exactly where he lives and what he looks like, a plan is put together to bag him. Hap, Eh-Jax and I will do the honors. Clint, Bull, Boom and Len will be close by to take down any body guards our target might have along. It shouldn't be too hard for experienced ex-soldiers like us. I tell the guys that I have a high-powered rifle with a scope and silencer that will be perfect; no close encounter, just one round at a safe distance resulting in a corps. It's only right that I be the trigger man to take down the rat that was indirectly responsible for my near-death experience."

It's time

Across from Raptor's house is a five-story building; perfect for a sniper shot. Eh-Jax parks his Cadillac several houses away from our target's house, while Hap and I make our way to the top of the building. We're wearing city-worker clothes with Public Housing tags on them. My rifle is hidden in a large PVC pipe; making it look like we're there to do some plumbing work. That makes it easy for us to get in, go up to the roof, and wait for our mark to come out. Word is, he heads out around 9 pm to make rounds to collect dope money from at least a dozen of his pushers.

Right around nine, we see Raptor coming through the door and heading for his $50,000 plus GS 450 Lexus. I take aim, and as he puts a hand on the door handle, there's a soft pop from my gun and our mark is down. It's a head shot. That takes him out of the drug game along with the two that Clint and Boom made to - swim with fishes. Eh-Jax rolls his Caddy up to where the creep dropped next to his car. Clint, Boom and Len, wearing hoodies to disguises themselves somewhat, scoop him up and toss him in the trunk. They hop in and drive to an abandoned silo area where they torch the car. The cops will figure that he was capped by rival gang members.

The precinct notified

The precinct is called about a burning vehicle and the standard crew of firemen and officers show up to check it out. The firemen put out the blaze and when they open the trunk, they find Raptor, nice and crispy. My men didn't take his cell phone or driver's license. This was done so the officers could I.D. him.

As the news comes out that Raptor got killed, it shakes up the drug-dealing community in the area. Good! The great thing about the killing of this kingpin drug dealer is that there was very little on TV news about him. And, the cops didn't fall over themselves to investigate the incident.

The only blurb on TV was, "A man known to local law enforcement by the nick-name Raptor was found dead in the trunk of a car that was set on fire. It appears that he was shot in the head. All we know about him is that he was known as a main source for drug dealers and drug users in the city. We will have more on that story as the investigation progresses."

The cops have been trying to nail him for a few years. The feeling among the Narcotics Unit is that Raptor's case is going to be one that will never be solved. They know the city is better off without this guy.

Chapter 3

Who's next?

At the next gathering at the Post, I tell the men, "It's good that we took out Raptor, but we still have a drug-distribution problems in our neighborhood. There are a couple of drug dealers that hang around South and Lake Streets. One of them lives on a nearby street. We could pick him up with very little trouble when he heads home. These guys do a little business, then go back to where they have a stash and pick up more stuff. They don't like carrying a whole lot of drugs while standing on the corners. It's easier to sell a small amount at a time rather than risk being caught with a bunch if the cops come around. We'll lay for him; put him in the car and go for a short ride to our - time out resort."

All the men laugh at the *resort* thing and agree that it'll be good to do another run. The war is on! Clint volunteers to be on that team and wants to know who else wants in.

Eh-Jax says, "I'm in."

Lenny tells them, "We should have a backup plan for this first attempt with guys who can step in if something doesn't go according to plan.

"Good idea!" says Hap. He adds, "So, exactly how are we gonna bag this snake? How do we take him out?"

I pause for a moment and tell them, "We could use a stun gun. The effects of getting hit with it can last up to 15 minutes. The only problem, the cockroach might yelp too loud when zapped and that could blow our cover. Besides, you have to be right next to your target to do that. I can see us using those on occasion; maybe a lot."

I tell the guys, "There is another way. In Nam, I used tranquilizer darts on certain enemies so we could scoop them up and interrogate them; dead enemies can't talk. We'd catch some of them alive and get valuable *Intel*. I fired darts from a special air-propelled rifle that could be adjusted for distance so that the dart wouldn't become a bullet and go too deep into the target. I could put a guy out easily at about a hundred and fifty feet or so. It worked great, like the drug they give you for a colonoscopy. You're out in seconds. No real noise, no scuffle, just a slight pop when I fired."

Bull asks, "Do you happen to have one of these fine dart-shooting thing-a-ma-jigs?"

With a grin, I answer, "It so happens I do have one in my arsenal. I've had it for a long time. I took down a dog that was tearing into the trash cans in my yard a few weeks ago. He went bye-bye for a few hours, woke up and walked away; no real damage done. Of course, the dose has to be just right. I'm still able to mix the knock out juice to fit the targets I want to take down. I have a contact at a drug company who got me the drugs for this. Would any of you like to be my trial target just to show the others how it works?"

Hap asks, "How fast does it work and are then any after effects?"

"It works really fast and there are no serious bad after effects. You just take a nap. Hap, you look like you could use a good nap. How about we test it on you just to be sure?"

Everybody laughs.

"Okay, I'll do it! But it won't make me sterile or anything like that, will it?"

Bull, who was taking a huge gulp from his bottle, ends up having beer shoot out his nose after hearing that statement.

He says, "Hap, that's a good one - sterile! That's funny! Man, look at what you made me do! I got beer all over myself! You shouldn't crack jokes when people are guzzling beer! Now, look at me!!!"

All the guys burst out laughing and Hap says, "Aw…dry up Bull! You just need to learn how to drink from a bottle."

I couldn't help myself and jumped in with my own zinger and say, "No, it won't make you sterile, but if you'd like, we could have Clint with his service medical background give you a rectal exam while you're on unconscious; just to check your prostate."

Well, all the guys lose it and laugh till some have tears in their eyes.

Hap says, "NOT FUNNY! Not funny at all! And you, Clint; don't even think about it!"

The guys lose it all over again. After the laughter dies down, Len looks at Hap thinking about the rectal exam thing and begins screaming with laugher; which it sets the rest of the men laughing. It takes a while before the guys pull themselves together and get serious. They finally settle down.

I tell Hap, "Once the dart hits you brother, you'll quickly be out and I assure you, you'll be just as normal as ever after you wake up, no worries."

"Where and when do you want me to be as your pin cushion? I just gotta know how this works."

"Come to my house tomorrow at about 7pm and I'll do the honors."

Next day - sweet dreams Happy Jack

The next day, everyone gets to my house to see the event. Hap is a little apprehensive, but figures, *"What the hell, I got shot up in Nam, I can take a little dart in the butt…. and take a nice nap to boot!"*

I have a large back yard with no neighbors around. Hap is a bit tense but still willing to be the *test lab rat* in order to get rid of the neighborhood cockroaches. And, he knows I wouldn't do anything that would actually hurt him. I set up the gun and tell Jack to just stand there. I'm about sixty feet from him. I adjust the gun for distance and ask if he's ready.

He says, "Let her rip, brother! I'm good to go."

I take aim at his butt and squeeze the trigger. The gun doesn't make much of a noise, just a nice soft "pop." The dart hits his backside and in about five seconds, he slumps down and is out cold. The other guys stand there in awe.

Bull walks over to him and says... "Hap, are you dead, man?!"

He's just lying there breathing real shallow like and doesn't move. Bull walks away and says jokingly, "Hap is in a nice place right now. Let's don't bother him!"

The question now is, how long will he be out? The dose wasn't too strong, but fast acting. They pick him up, prop him in a nice comfy chair and sit around drinking a few brews and do more planning on how they're going to get the cockroaches off our streets, and, what exactly should we do to them?

As the men sit around tossing ideas for picking up bad guys, Boom says, "You know, I have a whole lot of wire fencing, lumber and 4x8 sheets of plywood in my warehouse. We can build a bunch of separate little cells with a gate and tuck our prisoners in them till we do with them what needs to be done.

Now, here's the part where we get real serious guys! Like I said the other night, I have a few ideas about what we should do with these damn misfits! Take for instance a guy we catch who's been beating up on his girlfriend, we hurt him! I mean, we give him a taste of his own medicine. We beat him a little for a day or two; not necessarily heavy beatings, just ones that fit the crime. Then, we'll figure out what to do with him so he never does it again."

Boom sees Eh-Jax wince a bit, like - it might have been a bit much. He looks at him and says, "Maybe you've ever seen a woman that got a real bad beating, but I have. She was never the same, just because of some PUNK! Believe me, a guy like that deserves to feel pain like the kind he's dealt out. To ME, that would be righteous justice!"

Eh-Jax responds, "Hey Boom, I didn't mean to object to what you said about putting a beating on a dirt-bag like that. I made a face because I was thinking, 'Man, I wouldn't want to be the looser that's gonna get beat down!' I'm all for it. Let's get us some bad guys!"

The conversation shifts to the question of, how many perps can the warehouse hold? Boom says he thinks he could easily build seven little cubicles inside his warehouse. He figures that as a group, we could deal with that many. And, by the time we process out a few punks, it'll make more room for the next cockroaches we catch.

We know the cops can't use the tactics we're going to use to catch and extract information from creeps we get because of due process and police brutality lawsuits; but, we're not them. We're going to be a special unit. We need to make it bad enough so the perps won't EVER come around again to mess up our neighborhood with their lawless antics. We need to take back the streets and give the folks in our neighborhood peace of mind and a pleasant, safe place to live.

Chapter 4

Setting up for our first mission

Thinking ahead, I remind the guys that we'll need to be extra careful to not get caught in a trap or be surprised by anyone. You know; that *unforeseeable factor*. We can't afford to miss a step, not even one! Everything will need to be thought out very carefully. We'll need to snatch up our targets really quick and be off with them before anyone can figure what happened. It's gonna have to be at the right time and place for every pick up.

Also, when we catch one of these neighborhood enemies, we need to address each other as *Bufford* in their presence. I chose that name in honor of "Bufford Pusser from the 1973 movie, "Walking Tall." What he did was very fitting for the war he fought against the bad guys that controlled his hometown. I came up with that so that when perps are interrogated, they'll only hear one name mentioned. So, when we release any of them, the only name they'd be able to connect us to would be - Bufford.

Hap ads, "We'll also need to use a vehicle that isn't too conspicuous. You know, like we can't use one that's like Eh-Jax's 1984 Caddy when we got Raptor. It'd be too easy to identify if someone saw us drive away. I think we should use the van I haven't used in about six months. It's an old 1987 Ford. It runs real good. It would be the perfect *paddy wagon* for getting our fishes to our holding center. We'll can call it the - *Fish Tank*. It's sitting in a friend's barn in the town of Barney. There are a lot like it on the streets; it's plain, nothing special about it. We can get paint-spraying equipment so we can do quick paint jobs on it to change its look after we pick up a few roaches. And, I also have a few magnetic business signs we can put on it to change its look. That way, people won't be seeing the same van going around the neighborhood as we do our thing. What do you guys think?"

Everyone agrees that it would be a good idea. Boom tells the men he has spray paint set ups and a several gallons of primers and different color acrylic paints. Changing the color of the van would be easy to do.

I tell the men that Clint, Eh-Jax and I will be in the van and the rest of the crew can spread out in the area as backups. I'll fire the dart and we'll scoop up our catch, put him in the fish tank and bring him to the lockup.

Happy Jack says, "Boss, you think you might need a driver?"

"WOW, missed that! That would be a great idea, Hap. It's your van. Are you up to it?"

"Absolutely Boss. I'd be totally bummed out if I wasn't the driver on this first mission! Let's start, Operation Clean-up!"

Boom says that he was going by South and Lake Streets last night and spotted the same drug dealers Boss saw.

I tell them, "Perfect! That'll be our first target. We'll get one of them after dark."

Right now, it's four in the afternoon. Me, Hap, Clint and Eh-Jax are psyched for our first pick up and will get together at the warehouse after supper to get ready to do the job.

I'm thinking, *"This should be interesting. Our first try at this and we don't know if everything will work out like we planned. We've got nothing to lose and much to gain if we can get rid of some the degenerates in the neighborhood."*

The posse mounts up, and the lockup

It's eight-thirty and darkness has come. Everybody's in place. Hap parks a couple of houses past our subjects on the corner. I'll be able to shoot from two angles, either the side sliding window of the van, or the blown out rear window. Bull is one of the back-up men and has hidden himself between two of the houses on the same side of the street where the perps are and Boom is a couple of houses past where the van is parked. Lenny is in the shadows across the street from where the pushers are doing business. This way, no matter where the cockroaches run to if they're spooked, someone will intercept them. Each man has a stun gun and will simply zap him.

We see a few customers come by. They do the handshake drug/money exchange thing and off they go. We know these rats are really dirty, and because of them, a lot of people live in misery; with drug addictions, yes, but also, the wasted money spent on the drugs. People would rather feed their habits before they feed their kids or themselves. That's a rotten deal all the way around. Well tonight, at least one of these rats is going to be taken out.

Since the pushers have been there for a while, one leaves to go somewhere; probably to pick up more drugs, or just going home. That leaves one dirt-bag alone. It's time for me to fire away. It finally happens a little before nine o'clock. We target the one who left. As he gets about ten houses away from his partner-in-crime, Hap rolls the van slowly alongside him, I aim, shoot – and, right on target! I hit him in the right buttock. The drug goes quickly to his brain; he goes down, and in several seconds and passes out!

Clint says to Hap, "Stop the van!"

As he does that, Eh-Jax and Clint jumps out, scoops up our prize and off we go to the "lockup." We tape his hands behind his back, blindfold him and tape his mouth. The blindfold assures us that the perp won't be able to identify any of us when he wakes up, that should take a while. When I tested the dart on Hap, it took an hour before he came to; and groggy for another hour or so. Maybe I put a bit too much knock out juice in the shot.

We have our first prisoner in hand, and now, the experiment will tell us how well the whole thing went and how everybody feels about, *the catch*. The great thing about today's pushers, and most people, is that they all have cell phones. That's a really good way of seeing who their friends are as well as their drug contacts. Now that we have a perp, his cell phone, driver's license, and address. That's a nice plus! It will prove to be a big help later. Hey, we even get a few hundred dollars from his pocket! Thank you very much Mr. Cockroach! This will help our cause. Any cash we get from the guys we nail will to be used to equip us even better. We're going to need specialty gadgets.

Hap drives to the warehouse where everyone meets up. He says to me, "Hey Bufford, "That dart really did the trick. It was perfect. Man, that dude went down fast. *Das ist sehr gut!"* (That's very good!)

"Yah, when you went down for the trial-shot I did on you, you had no idea how fast it actually worked. Glad you could witness it for yourself, Bufford."

Prior to getting our first bad guy, the men had been busy preparing Boom's warehouse by building seven 4 by 8 foot-cubicles to hold the inmates. They worked a whole weekend putting them together. Each one was simply built. They are rectangular frames wrapped with chain link fencing for the walls and ceiling, with chain link gates and padlocks. On the inside, the floor is a sheet of plywood with a blanket for a cover at night; a five-gallon pail and toilet paper. That's it. There are no niceties! The guys we catch will know the meaning of doing "hard time." We were going to make them as uncomfortable as possible. After sleeping on a wooden floor for a night or two, it will add to breaking any strong-willed captives. Guys in Nam prison camps had it much, much worse than that.

Each catch will be put in a cell with a special blindfold helmet we came up with. It won't allow them to see any light. If anyone tries taking it off, it'll trigger a switch and give him an electric shock. Bull tested it and got buzzed really good! That alone will mess with their minds. It was a take-off idea from the dog collars that shocks dogs when they bark. I could only imagine the torment the prisoners will go through; caged, wearing shocking blind-folds, and hard floor to sleep on. Oh yah! I can't forget the beatings; that'll be part of the justice they'll get. Also, each cell is rigged so that if a prisoner tries to open the gate, an alarm will go off. I'd say it's pretty secure.

Gathering information from our P.O.W

A couple of the men put our sleeping POW in cell one. Lenny gets the perp's driver's license and reads off his name. "Fellas, meet low life, cockroach, Reese Blount. He's only nineteen years old!"

We also find out where he lives. His phone is a big plus from this snag. Our boy has a whole bunch of names and numbers. A lot of them have nicknames, probably his close friends and most likely, some of his drug customers. Another big bonus is the text messages he has. This will help us in nailing a few more pushers.

One message is from a guy named Slam. It says… *"Yo Reese, got yo stuff ready to go c u at the gig tomorrow 10pm you know where."*

The word *"stuff"* is obviously drug product, the *"gig"* is the meeting and *"you know where,"* only our captive Reese knows that. When we interrogate him, we'll need to persuade him to explain the text.

We have an area in the warehouse set aside for interrogation with a special chair Boom came up with. It has clamps for the perp's hands and feet to make sure he's secure. The plan is that no one will get a real bad beating at first, but as in war, the objective will be to break the captive down and get as much information from him so that we can find some of his buddies and take them for a ride to the lock up too. The idea is that anyone we pick up will give us all the info we want. If we feel a captive isn't cooperating enough, we have ways of making him crack. We're pretty confident that it won't take much time at all. We're going to want names of drug suppliers, phone numbers and addresses.

Having Reese's cell phone with names will be a good way to ask him about his acquaintances. The idea is that we'll get him to make a call and set up a meet with this Slam guy. Our hope is that we'll get Slam, bring him to our fine facility and get the name of his supplier; hopefully, his main source.

I'm in the interrogation room with some of the other men, Reese is blindfolded and hands cuffed. He's really freaked out. Clint sits him on the chair, straps him in and removes the tape from his mouth. Reese starts talking, but Lenny tells him to shut up and listen. He tries asking a question, and BAM! He gets a backhand across the mouth; his lips drip blood.

Lenny says, "I told you not to talk! If you want to get beat, go ahead and talk!" Reese understands and stays quiet. This is a very wise move on his part.

I come in and say to him, "You don't know me but I know who you are, where you live, and - I have a whole lot of phone numbers of your customers, suppliers as well as your mom's name and phone number. You are a cockroach infesting the neighborhood with your drugs and whatever other crimes you've committed! Hey, maybe you beat up on your girlfriend too, uh? I'm sure you have her phone number in your cell phone. Maybe I'll call her and ask if you ever beat on her. If you did, you're going to know what if feels like to 'hurt!' Now then, I'm not a cop, but I intend to keep you locked up for a while, and if need be, maybe even kill your sorry ass just because you're useless to society! You're a cockroach that should be crushed! You hurt and even caused the death of a lot of people. You've destroying lives! You need to be put out of commission, you sorry little worm!"

You can see that Reese is scared out of his mind. One minute he was walking home and the next thing he knew, he was a prisoner. I think the part about *killing your sorry ass* got to him. I know it would get to me.

Just to make sure, I get his attention by giving him a fairly solid backhand across his right cheek and say to him, "Now you can talk to me!" I ask him if he liked the backhand. He shakes his head to signify "no." I tell him that it could get so unpleasant that he'll wish that he'd never been born.

I tell him, "You will help me contact the guy you were with tonight! What's his name!

Reese says, "He'll kill me if I give him up! I can't do dat, man!"

BAM! He gets another backhand across the mouth and begins tasting blood. I tell him that he has no choice and that I might just kill him if he refuses to cooperate.

Reese blurts out, "His name is Rodney, Rodney Chandler, okay?! Can I go now?"

"Can you go now? No, I don't think so. I'm going to need a bit more information than that... like, where does Rodney live? Does he have a gun? Who are his friends? You need to talk to me son, or I'll make your first night here really bad! I don't have time to waste. So, to answer your question; 'Can you go now?' The answer is NO! I'm sorry but you have to do time and I have to check things out. Once you've done your part and it works out, you'll be released."

He's asked where Rodney lives. He tells me that he's on Pierce Street in the lower apartment. I then ask if Rodney carries a weapon.

Reese says, "Yah, he always carries a 380 pistol and a knife."

Then, I ask him what the names of some of his closest friends who deal in the neighborhood. Reese is real hesitant but gives up; Joe Saunders, Alex Martinez, Jimmy Luca and Deshawn Howard. Hap writes down all the names for future use.

I say to him, "Now then, we saw a text message you received from a guy called Slam. I want to know who he is and what this message means: *"Yo Reese got yo stuff ready to go c u at the gig tomorrow at 10pm."*

Reese tells him that he's one of the main guys on the street. He says, "He's a huge supplier. I get all my products from him,"

I tell him that he has to make a phone call and tell this Slam dude that he'll make that 10 pm meet. Reese doesn't want to do this but knows that if he doesn't, it's going to be real bad for him.

I punch in the number from the phone list; activate the speaker and wait for Slam to answer. Hap set up the phone with a device connected to a recorder through a computer so we can tape the conversation and run a trace all at the same time.

Slam answers and Reese tells him, "Yo Slam, this is Reese; got the message about the meet. I'll be there at 10 tomorrow night."

Slam simply says, "See you at the meet."

That's all he could get in before Slam hangs up. The trace didn't work out. That's one of the problems with cell phones; people are mobile and it's hard to pin point a person sometimes. Anyway, we got the meeting set up for a "big catch." This will be very good.

Bull tells Reese, "I'm going to put you in your cell. The hand cuffs will be taken off but the blindfold stays on. If you try to remove it, you'll get a shock that will hurt…like, a lot!"

With the special blindfold secured to his head, Reese is put into his cage. He's told that he'll need to feel around for the pot and toilet paper to take care of his bathroom business, and that he'll be given food and water.

Back in the interrogation room, Lenny says, "Oh yah! The fishing was good!" He wants in on tomorrow night's, Slam catch. I tell him to go for it; to enjoy himself. The same team that picked up Reese would go again. They already have the practice. Lenny wants to go along as back up and to see what it's like from the van.

It's now 10:30 pm. Reese is in his cell in complete darkness. Not being able to see anything scares the hell out of him! Just the thought of having to sleep on the floor in that place all night makes him half crazy. That's only one of the problems he has. He's thinking about tomorrow and what he'd have to do to get freed. He thinks about the guys he's had to give up. That scares him big time because they too can hit his family for the betrayal. He's going nuts! He can't think of how to get out of this so that everything can be alright. He doesn't know what he's going to do. He figures he's a dead man either way… *"I give up names and my own people will kill me. I don't give up anyone and these guys are going to kill me."* Now, he gets prison religion and prays to God for help for help.

Chapter 5

Impromptu pickup of an injured Girl

While Reese is trying to sleep in his crude cubicle, some of the men go out into the neighborhood to check on things. Len, Hap and I spot some snake pulling a girl between two vacant houses and starts beating on her. Hap stops the van. The rat backhands her real hard repeatedly across the face then punches her in the stomach! She drops to the ground. She's between sixteen to eighteen years old. The punk beating her is big and looks to be around twenty.

Lenny says, "We have to get this guy!" The girl is in real trouble. Now, he's kicking her!"

We get out of the van. I've got pretty good cover of night and am able to approach quietly; wearing a hoodie and fake beard. The guy's back is to me. I walk over, and with one punch to the jaw, he's out cold! I bend down to check on the girl and see what a mess she is. The guy put a very nasty cut over her eye. It's bleeding profusely! There's also a deep gash on her cheek bone and her lips are split wide open. She's moaning really bad and holding her stomach!

She says, "My baby, my baby! He hurt my baby! Help me, please!"

I tell her to stay calm and that she needs go to the hospital right away. I ask what her name is and where does she live. She tells me her name is Chantal and her house is on the next street over.

As I care for her, Hap backs up the van, gets out, and helps Lenny throw the dirt bag in. They cuff and blindfold him, then duct tape his mouth and feet. The girl is badly beaten. I'm frantic! She hurts really bad and needs immediate medical care. I pick her up and hand her to Lenny in the van. As Hap makes his way to the hospital, Len cradles Chantal and does his best to calm her as she holds her stomach, crying bitterly, and shaking from the pain.

The roach is laid out in the back of the van and is motionless, still unconscious. That's good! We don't need for him to wake up and start thrashing about. We arrive at the hospital and see an orderly standing outside having a smoke.

Still in my disguise, I yell to the guy, "We found this girl in an alley. Get a gurney as quick as you can!"

The orderly comes out with one; Chantal is put on it and is wheeled off toward the emergency room. He can see how badly she's hurt. As he rolls away with her, he tells me that I need to come in and fill out a report. I tell him that I have to wash the blood off my hands and that I'd be there in two minutes. The orderly hustles to get the girl to the emergency room. As soon as the medical staff takes one look at her, they signal a "Code Blue" and rush her into an elevator to get her to the X-rays. In the commotion, I slip away and get back to the van. Off we go to *time out*. We now have two cockroaches in lockup. It was a good night.

Looking at our prisoner, I say to the men, "This guy is going to feel pain. This is a bad hombre, man! Yah, he's gonna hurt!"

As we head to the "Big House," as one of the men likes to call the warehouse, it's time to find out who this punk is. I feel the guy's pockets to find his wallet and cell phone. Just then, he wakes up and starts to thrash around like he's trying to get out of the van. I put an arm around his throat from behind and tell him to settle down or I'll snap his neck. Apparently, the neck hold feels threatening enough that the lad settles down. Lenny looks through the wallet and pulls out his driver's license. He read off the name so we all hear it. "Hey gentlemen, let me introduce you to Daniel T. Connors from Hill Street. According to his license, he's twenty-one years old."

Hap speaks up and says: "Well, hello Daniel C. from Hill Street. I'll just call you D.C. It's NOT nice meeting you! You will NOT like this trip and you'll wish you NEVER touched that girl!"

Danny gets a real empty feeling in his gut. He never expected anything like this.

He thinks, *"Man, who are these guys and what the hell are they going to do to me?"*

He can't imagine who would have come up on him and bagged him the way they did? He wonders if they're going to shoot or beat him to death and leave him in some field, or throw him off a bridge somewhere. He's so scared that he starts breathing really heavy and feels like he's going to pass out.

I speak up, "So Danny, you like to beat up on young girls, do you?"

I backhand him on the side of the head. He falls over from his sitting position. Lenny sits him up and tells him that he'll need to do a little stint in their prison for bad guys. He's going out of his mind; he can't talk and can't see anything. He can only listen to the threats and wonders what we're going to do with him. He's in for a rough night!

Reaching the warehouse, we take our boy out of the van, bring him into the room with the special chair and strap him in. Just as soon as he's strapped in, BAM! I give him a backhand across the mouth. I just thought the pain should start as soon as possible for this maggot. He's really scared. He can't see anything and can't move. He doesn't know how many men there are and has no clue how this is going to end. The blood from his split lip behind the duct tape has nowhere to go but in his mouth. He's forced to swallow it. Gross yes, but fitting! The girl he beat up I'm sure tasted her own blood as he beat her like a dog!

Bull gets his turn backhanding him and says to him, "Doesn't feel very good, does it, you mutt? So, you like beating up on young defenseless women, eh?" BAM, a backhand on the cheek! Lenny gives him one on the other cheek. It seems each man wants a piece of this creep. They imagine the girl could have been one of their own, you know; a daughter, granddaughter or a niece. They just don't like this guy at all and want him to hurt.

Lenny gets really close to his ear and says, "You know what? I'm going to do this to you for a whole week. I hope you're as tough as you think you are! A punk like you deserves to die, really! You're one of those useless sorry excuses for a human being! Danny, this is you're very unlucky day! You are a criminal and you're going to do a little time and receive pain for what you did!"

They take the tape off his mouth. Daniel wants to talk. While crying he says, "Please don't hurt me no more! I'm sorry! I'm sorry! I'm so…. sorry! Please, please, please… don't hit me no more!"

Len says, "No you're not sorry! You're NOT sorry you beat that girl like an animal. You're sorry that we have your sorry white trash ass and we're going to make you pay for what you did to that young lady."

He punches him in the stomach the way he did to the girl. Danny groans real low and can't catch his breath. He heaves like he's going to throw up.

Len continues haranguing him, "That girl you beat is supposed to be someone you care about and you treated her like a dog! Well, you're the dog and I like to beat bad dogs that hurt people."

Since he witnessed him beating the girl, he's really angry and gives him another backhand. Blood is dripping out of his mouth and down his chin. He's crying like a little child.

Bull tells him, "Why are you crying? Big bad guys like you don't cry, because you're tough! Yah, you're tough when beating on helpless girls. Well, Danny boy, how tough do you feel right now?!"

I nod for Boom and Bull to get him up and into a cell. They fit him with the special helmet, loosen the straps, walk him over to a vacant cell and take off the cuffs. Bull turns him toward the door, helps him get in by shoving him in with his foot. He stumbles in and falls to the floor. As the men turn to walk away, Daniel tries to remove the helmet and they hear him screaming like a girl! They just happened to forget to tell him that he shouldn't try doing that! He got the idea real quick as he sat there waiting for the pain to ease.

Happy Jack shoots back, "Oh yah, by the way, don't take the helmet off." He walks away with the others laughing and says, "Actually, that was pretty funny." He tells Danny to just sit there or lie down and sleep; that it's going to be a long night, even longer if he acts up.

Bull yells, "Just be cool dude! You've got no choice!"

As the men gather in the meeting room, they want to find out how the girl is before continuing with Daniel's tune-up sessions. Hap (the former cop) knows an intern in the ER and calls him.

"Hey Owen, it's Jack! I just heard a young girl from our neighborhood was brought in. How is she doing?"

"I'll check and call you back in a few."

Jack waits and after about fifteen minutes, he gets the call. Owen says, "That girl is only seventeen. Her face is a mess and will need lots of stitches. She also has a lot of internal bleeding." He adds, "Get this, she's seven months pregnant. She'll make it, but they needed to take the baby. They told me the baby was no longer alive. Whoever did this is looking at a manslaughter rap; maybe murder!"

Hap is really peeved now! This becomes a whole new ball game. We have a perp who not only beat up a girl really bad, but killed her baby. Tomorrow is going to be a real ugly day for Daniel C.

With Danny in his own cell for the night, away from Reese, some of the men, including myself, go home to get some sleep. Boom tells the men that he'll keep watch for the night. There's a bed in a room at the center of the warehouse that is pretty comfortable. The guys in the cages won't be a problem. He thinks they're too scared to start anything. He believes they get it. After everyone leaves, Boom checks on the two inmates. They're both huddled on the floor on their flimsy blanket. He goes off to the comfy room to sleep.

Chapter 6

Day two with Reese and Daniel

I'm up bright and early knowing that we have to check on Reese and Daniel to see how they're doing. The perps are locked up at extreme opposite ends of the warehouse so they can't communicate. Once there, I go to Reese's cage. He's sleeping and I make sure he gets a rude awakening. I take an empty fifty-five-gallon steel drum Boom has near the cages. I lift it over my head and slam it to the concrete floor right next to where our boy is sleeping. Not being able to see anything and being asleep, the ground-shaking noise this thing makes totally freaks him out. He jumps up, and in his confusion, he runs three feet as if he can get away and smashes right into the chain-link, bounces off and falls to the floor. I notice that he also just peed himself. Well, that's going to be uncomfortable for him! Sorry, no change of clothes here. He's going to stink, but that's going to be part of what he'll have to endure while he's with us. We'll leave Reese in his cage until we're done with Dan.

Eh-Jax gets Danny out of his cell and brings him to the interrogation room. He sits him down and back hands him. This is just a little of what he'll get as punishment for what he did to that young girl. Now, you may be wondering why all the "backhands" rather than straight-in punches to the face. The reason is that we don't want to bust the perps too badly right away. The backhands are still a lot of punishment though.

Anyway, Eh-Jax says to him, "You have no idea how bad you beat up that young lady. BAM! - another backhand. You don't like the taste of blood uh punk? Too bad, because you're going to taste a lot more of it in the next few days …you low life!"

Dan cries out again, "Please man, I won't hit her anymore, I promise, I really promise!

I say to him, "Oh for sure you'll never hit her again. You will never see her or go anywhere near her ever again. As a matter of fact, Danny you'll do time here and then you'll do time in a real jail with men who will know what you did. Guess what? The beatings will continue there. You're a cockroach and should be exterminated!"

Danny says in a weeping voice, "I didn't mean to hurt her so bad. I swear. I just lost it, man! I told her that she couldn't keep the baby; that we weren't ready for this! When she told me she was going to keep it, that's when I lost it and just went crazy on her! Please, I promise I won't do it again! Just don't hurt me no more! Please, I beg you!"

Eh-Jax says to him, "You didn't mean to hurt her so bad?! What the hell did you think you were doing while you were punching and kicking her?! Did you think those were just "love taps? You idiot cockroach! Are you right or left-handed?"

He responds in a weeping voice, "Right, why?"

Dan, still blindfolded and unable to move, hears someone light a plumber's propane torch. The flame from them is incredibly hot. Anyway, he feels the heat near his right hand strapped to the chair. The flame gets closer until he feels the burn and screams to high heaven.

As this is going on, Reese, the other inmate sitting in his cubicle in total darkness, hears the scream and shivers. He doesn't know what's going on. The only thing he knows is that someone is getting hurt real bad! This scares him out of his mind, because so far, he's only gotten a few backhands. He wonders what they're going to do to him when it's his turn. He's totally freaked out!

Dan's hand is badly burned. It's going to take a long time for it to heal. And, it will leave a very nasty scar. Clint's service medical training comes in handy here. He patches up our girl-beating punk so that an infection won't set in. It's not that the group doesn't want him to die; it's just that they're not done with him yet. Daniel is crying and in great pain. They release him from the chair, and Boom takes him back to his cell and locks him in.

He says to young Connors, "I know you're in a lot of pain and that's too bad! As you sit there dealing with that pain, think about what you did! You don't even deserve to live. One of our guys here wanted to cut off your manhood, that's how angry he is about want you did. So…. just sit there and hurt! You've earned that!"

He's still whimpering - half crying. He feels his way around to find his blanket on the floor and lies on it. The pain is still excruciating. He can barely stand it. He settles down and wonders what they'll do with him next time. This works on his mind and he sinks into a very deep depression, not knowing what else he'll have to endure and for how long. He's almost wishing that they would just kill him and end the torment.

Still day two,

Reese's turn in the chair

It's now 11am. I bring Reese out of his cage and get him into the special chair for a bit more interrogation and punishment. Clint smacks him on the side of the head just to get things started. I want to get some information about his drug-dealing activities on the corner of South and Lake. I ask him how many customers he has on any given day. He tells me he doesn't know.

I tell him, "Take a guess! I want to know how many people you deal to a day. And this time when you answer you'll need to come up with a number. Do you understand me?"

Reese says that it's different every day. And with that answer, Lenny lets him have one in the gut. Reese begins to heave from the blow and spits up a little puke. He can't catch his breath.

I say to him. "Remember I just told you that I wanted a number and you come up with that! No good Reese! Now then, a number - or you get hurt and the next hurt will be worse."

Reese says, "About twenty-five to thirty people; sometimes more and sometimes less. A lot of people want the stuff, you know."

I come back and say to him, "Now see, you could've saved yourself that little beating." I continue by asking him how much money he takes in from the poor drug addicts. This time, he's real quick giving me an answer because he knows he'll get beat some more.

"Some days I take in around four of five hundred dollars. I've done as much as a thousand with the right dudes wanting a big supply for special people they want to turn on. You know, like folks with money and power."

Clint says, "Oh yah? Who for instance? What big names can you give us?

Reese doesn't want to give up anyone that's too high and starts to cry, saying, "Please don't make me name those guys! They got people all over that will get to me or my own friends will get me! I give them up and my life is over! Please let me go and I'll never deal again in the neighborhood!"

I tell him, "If we let you go, you can't deal in ANY neighborhood. You'll need to disappear from this city. And now, we want a name of whatever big shot you deal with. It'd better be a good one or you will know what extreme pain feels like."

He tells us that a detective in the precinct is one of his best customers, that his name is Detective Ronnie Coates. He tells us that he scores about a couple of thousand dollars at a time for special events. He also gives up a councilman by the name of Ashton Clarion from the south district.

Hap tells him, "You did good with that bit of information, son."

With a smile, he tells him. "Hey, we might give you a 'star' on your report card for that."

Boom asks him if ever gives it any thought that he's ruining lives by peddling that shit; that it destroys families and mothers get hooked on crack and end up delivering crack babies.

He says to him, "Have you ever seen a crack baby you son of a bitch!? Do you care if the babies of these mothers grow up to have brain damaged and have learning difficulties? Do you know the pain and torment these little ones go through and may have a lifetime of problems? And, how about those young women who need to sell themselves to get their fix; some as young as four-teen years old. Do you care at all? Their lives are ruined. They have no future, you lousy rat, you!!!

Reese comes back with a bit of an attitude in his response. He says, "Man, I don't force this stuff on nobody. If they get hooked, that's on them. It's not my fault. It's them that want the stuff, man!"

With that, Eh-Jax loses it and gives him a backhand to the side of the jaw that sends him toppling over. The guys set him up again and he asks him how he counts the money he collects from all the sales. Reese asks him what he means. Eh-Jax gives him a shot to the stomach.

He tells him, "I want to know how you count the money, you know, with your hands. You hold the money in your left hand use the thumb of your right hand to count, right?"

Reese says, "Yah, that's how I count my money, why?"

Having been in a POW camp, Eh-Jax knows what real pain is. He wants to make a real big impression on this maggot. Being that he mentioned the word *thumb*, most of the guys kind of know that he's going to either break, smash or cut off Reese's thumb.

Eh-Jax faces Reese, grabs his right hand that's strapped flat on the armrest and gets right close to his hear and says, "This is for all the crack babies, young girls and mothers you've ruined, and all the other addicts, dead or living. People are dead because of you and your kind. This is for all your victims that live each day, and never, EVER have a good day!"

Holding a good size ballpeen hammer, he winds up and smashes his thumb. It split wide open and bleeds like hell. Reese screams to high heaven and cries like a baby. While that's happening, Danny, in his cell, hears the blood-curdling screams and shakes. He has no idea what just happened, only that some guy got hurt really bad.

Reese pleads in a weeping and desperate voice: "Oh God! Please don't hurt me no more! Don't hurt me no more, please, please, PLEASE...no more! I beg you, man!" With the pain and the fear he feels, he just sits there and weeps.

Eh-Jax says to him, "Now then, all the pain you feel, that's not even close to all the pain you've caused to all those strung-out people! I'd like to smash all your fingers AND both of your hands! That's what you deserve for all the misery and pain you and all the other rotten, low-life pushers have caused. But - you're so convinced that *'They want the stuff. That it's their OWN fault!'* You feel justified by being, WHAT, a good citizen who provides medicine for these poor addicts? Is that what you think?!"

He adds, "Would you like to count some money now, you worthless rodent? Hey Reese, do you think I'd be okay if I got your little sister hooked on dope? Would that be a good thing? I'm sure you wouldn't approve; you rotten low life! But, feeding the habits of other young girls, mothers and all your other customers, you have no problem at all with that, do you?! Perhaps you think like some of the people in the Godfather Movie... *'It's not personal, it's only business.* Well, we're making it, REAL PERSONAL!"

Reese is in so much pain that he can't respond to Eh-Jax's admonitions. The pain is so great that he just moans and cries. His thumb is crushed and bleeding. I'm sure he wishes he were home sitting on a nice, comfortable couch. Too bad! He doesn't know that his ordeal isn't over with yet.

Eh-Jax says, "Someone get him out of here before I go to work on his other fingers and hands!"

Bull and Clint loosen the binder on his bad hand, pour a bunch of hydrogen peroxide on his thumb and wrap a towel around it. That'll help keep it from getting infected and will catch the blood oozing from the split skin. They get him up out of the chair and lead him to his cell, leaving him there to meditate on all that was said and what he just experienced. Reese is holding his hand, writhing in pain and whimpering. He gropes around for his blanket and sits on it, hoping that the pain will subside. It doesn't. As long as he doesn't move his hand, the pain is lessened, but still throbbing a whole lot.

He can't see, but can hear them. He says, "I'm sorry, I'm sorry! Please let me go home! Please! I beg you!"

Lenny shoots back, "Let you go home! This IS your new home, son. And, saying 'please' isn't going to get you out of the mess you're in. You need to sit there and shut up! We'll see you again tomorrow."

I say to him, "This is going to be a very bad day and night for you Reese. With the pain you're feeling, you probably won't sleep much, if at all. Just think of what might be next for you in the days to come. Like Bufford said, *'you're only feeling a little of the pain you've caused.'* I want you to think REAL hard about the lives you've screwed up. Now, your life is screwed up. How do you like it?"

Reese says nothing. He's in too pain and too freaked out to respond.

The men spend the rest of the day planning the next pickup. Around 8:30 pm, the guys get ready. Bull says he'd take the watch tonight. He goes to the small room where the bed is to wait for Slam's arrival. He checks on the other two prisoners from time to time. They just sit there trying to cope with their pain. He'd like to feel sorry for them, but his sense of justice won't allow it. He feels the pain they're experiencing is well-deserved. They've had all day to think about their situation and what got them there in the first place. It's one of those, *"You reap what you sow moments."*

As Reese goes to lie down on the blanket, he cradles the hand and winces as the pain hits him. He settles down feeling like he's never going to get out alive.

He figures, *"These guys are eventually going to kill me"*.

His mind is reeling. He doesn't know what to think. He's in serious pain. He's very afraid, and is close to wishing he were dead. If he were dead, there'd be no need to worry and there'd be no more pain. He spends a lot of time thinking about all he's gone through in the short time he's been a prisoner. It blows his mind.

Chapter 7

Getting set up for the "Grand Slam"

It's 9:00 pm and the team going to get Slam needs to be in place by 9:30. The spot where Reese is to meet with Slam is at the edge of Stone Bridge Park. It's pretty secluded with a lot of space all around so he can see people, like cops, coming from a long way off. That would give slime boy Slam a chance to get away. Well, the men have a surprise for him. Being that Clint is really close to Reese's size, they do a switch. He has Reese's hooded coat on and in the dark, Slam won't know the difference when he comes to the spot where Clint will be waiting to meet him. He'll have a stun gun ready to drop him. This thing puts out 150,000 volts. That'll stop Slam in his tracks. If he should get spooked by something he sees out of place and takes off, we'll get him, whatever direction he runs off to. The plan is that all available men will be in on this takedown. We'll cover all the exits.

Everyone is in place, wearing ear pieces and sleeve-mics. Clint walks to the meet site and waits. In the dark, and from a distance, you can't tell it's not Reese. Slam won't know it until he's face to face with Clint, then, good night cockroach!

Here we go! Slam spots where his contact is standing and makes his way towards him. He has no clue that there could be a trap since he spoke to Reese himself to do the pickup. As he gets closer, Clint has his back to him with the stun gun ready.

As Slam gets close, he says, "Yo Reese." Clint turns and, Zap! The rat goes down and the van pulls up. The men put the package on board.

"WOW!" I'm thinking. *"This is very cool."* No hassle at all. We now have our third catch and he's a huge fish. We have his license and cell phone. This is great!"

I say to the men. "I bet there are a bunch of names on this guy's phone that may need a trip to the Big House. We'll see. And 'YES,' this thug is carrying a gun and a nice sum of money for our cause; at least $5,000. He must've made a few pickups from some of the area pushers before this meet."

With Slam in the van, handcuffed, mouth taped and blindfold-ed, off we go to the warehouse. According to Reese, Slam pro-vides all the drugs for the entire south side. Anyone else who has tried to deal products got hurt really bad and a few boys wound up in the river. Well, it'll be a great time with Slam when he wakes up. I can see that the other men can't wait to hear what comes out if this rat's mouth as we persuade him to talk to us. Slam comes out of his shock treatment and wants to say some-thing. He can't, and we won't take the tape off until we reach the warehouse.

As we enter the place, we take our new client to our interroga-tion room and strap him in our special chair. We can tell this guy has a real bad attitude. He's probably used to having punks at his disposal to go *jack up* people who get in his way. In his simple mind, he thinks he's still got power. He's completely delusional and we'll see to it that we bring him back to reality.

Clint gives me Slam's I.D. and cell phone. I look at the license and say to the boys, "Hey lads, I want you all to meet Derrick Little. He lives on the east side. And, here's a nice picture of him and his main squeeze. She's probably wondering when her man is coming home. Slam, wouldn't you like to call your woman, or, do you refer to her as your bitch?"

Just for the fun of it, we want to hear him speak, just to see what he'll say! We take off the duct tape from his mouth and sure enough, he starts right off by telling us that...

"We're all dead men, and that his guys are coming for him!"

With that comment, we all laugh, except Bull, our computer specialist. He realizes that this roach could be smart enough to have had some computer geek install a tracer in his phone or somewhere on him in case this sort of thing happened. Jack quickly checks the phone and, lo and behold, the phone is tricked out so that his soldiers can trace him if he disappears. He removes and destroys the tracer.

It was very fortunate that Bull thought of this. Just to be safe, with Slam's eyes being covered so he can't see, Jack scans the rest of his body to make sure there isn't a backup up. What do you know? He finds a homing microchip in his right sneaker.

Bull thinks *"Real smart, punk!"* He takes Slam's shoe, rips out the chip and destroys it. That leaves our young thug with no way to be traced.

He then interfaces his cell phone with an *extracting device* he got from a friend of his that works for the intelligence section of the police department and copies the information onto his own high-tech laptop. It should come in real handy, just like we did with Reese's cell. We'll use Slam's phone to set up more bad guys.

Since he knows nothing about what Bull found, this poor demented soul is still convinced that his guys will be coming for him. What a shame for Slimy Slam. It's going to be a bad time for him too. Clint is the first to initiate pain. He backhands Slam and tells him that he shouldn't be making idle threats.

Slam swears at him and says, "Man, you are going to be sorry you ever messed with me!" Still feeling sure his men are on their way, he says to the men, "When my guys find you, y'all gonna die; and your families too!"

BAM! Bull hits him on the other side and tells him. "You don't know who you're dealing with here and what we have on you punk! Your man Reese told us a lot about you and your business. Guess what? You are closed for business! As far as your customers go, they'll come to find out you disappeared. So, before you say anything else, I strongly suggest you listen to me and maybe you'll live. If you refuse to talk to us, we will make this part of your life really bad. I mean, really bad!"

Before we rough him up too much, we want information. He WILL comply; of that, we're very sure.

Loosening up Slam's tongue

Slam is now looking a little worried and sweating a bit. I walk behind him and say, "So Derrick Little, you feel confident you're going to walk out of here and that we're all going to die, uh? You must be some kind of powerful, big-time dealer who has killed a few people and made other people very afraid of you. You are slime. You're one of the lowest forms of life there is. You hurt and destroyed a lot of people and it seems to me you don't know what pain is. Guess what, son? You're going to know pain here!"

With that, I back hand him so hard that he falls over with the chair. He's out cold. The men set him upright and wait a while. Clint throws some cool water in his face to wake him up. I motion for Bull to hand me the ballpeen hammer. I take aim and smack his left knee cap. He screams like a girl and puts a bunch of curse words together, still threatening that *"We're all going to die!"* He tries to be tough but it doesn't work. Now, we let him know that no one is coming for him because we found the tracers in his phone and shoe.

Slam is still moaning and understands that he's in a real bad situation. Being used to being *"the man,"* he could never imagine finding himself in this situation. His mind goes wild. He doesn't know what to think. He has no *wild card* to play, so to speak. He realizes that he's alone now, with no one coming to save him; that we have him and that we're going to hurt him; maybe even kill him. He starts losing his tough-guy attitude and wants to make a deal.

Clint says to him, "Man, there's no deal to be made here. You're here to do hard time and pay for your sins! You and your kind have caused a lot of people a whole lot of pain, torment and misery. YOU'VE RUINED LIVES!!! What we offer here is some of the same pain and torment, just for you, because you need to get some of what you've dished out. You can consider yourself to be in a real dark place here, my man! You're a slimy little worm Derrick Little!"

He's really hurting but gets up enough energy to say, "Hey man, I'll do anything you ask, just don't hurt me no more. I'll cooperate with you, I promise. Please don't hurt me! Please take me to a hospital, my knee hurts so bad, please, I'm beggin' man! Please!"

Hap tells him, "Hospital! HELL NO! We don't think a hospital is in the cards for you punk! You're going to suffer through the night and for several nights to come. You'll get really good at hopping on one leg. Then, we might tap that other knee so they match. Have you ever had two busted kneecaps, cockroach?! It might be neat watching you crawl around the floor like the snake that you are. The thing is… you don't know what we are capable of doing."

He says to another man in the room, "Hey Bufford, don't you have a friend who has a couple of real mean dogs on his farm? Maybe we can take old Slam over there, lock him in the barn, and see what the dogs will do to him. What do you think?"

Hap answers, "You know what Bufford, that's not a bad idea! This guy is a rat and dogs like to chew on rats. Let me think about that."

Slam gets this real sick feeling in his stomach and says: "Man, please don't do that! I swear to you that if you let me go, you'll never see me again. I'll never deal in this neighborhood, no more."

Lenny shoots back, "Man, what the hell are you smoking?! Do you really think we're going to let you go back to the street where you can group up with your crew and continue your wretched life of ruining lives and killing people? You're dreaming, man! We're fixin' to make you pay for all the evil deeds your miserable life has produced so far. That means we may just have to kill you dead!"

I step in and motion for a couple of the guys to take Slam to his cell for the night. We'll deal with him some more tomorrow. As they unstrap him, he asks if he can have the blindfold off.

I tell him, "That's not going to happen, and by the way, DON'T try taking it off! If you do, you'll get a real bad jolt to your brain, and we wouldn't want that. We need your brain to work well until we're done with you."

Slam's knee is killing him. He can't walk. One man on each side, holding him up, they drag him to his cell and set him down on a blanket. He's told that he's not to be heard all night; to just be quiet and try to sleep.

He sits on the blanket holding his knee and feels it throb. After a good long while, he lies down and eventually drifts off to sleep. During the night, about 2 am, he wakes up due to the pain he's in. He begins to freak out. Not being able to see, because of the blindfold/helmet, he tries taking it off. All of a sudden, he screams like a banshee from the jolt. He quickly realizes what he's done and sits there breathing really heavy waiting for the sting to subside. It doesn't take long. He lies back down on the blanket and tries his best to deal with both the pain in his knee and the bad situation he finds himself in. The other two that are locked up in the warehouse are aware of the new prisoner but don't dare talk to him.

Like Reese and Danny, Slam too, thinks about what might happen the next day. It freaks him out really bad! He's used to being the guy who puts out the order to hurt, maim and kill people. This guy is a real *enemy of the good people* and should not be allowed to get back into society. In time, we'll make a decision on him. We have to see just how dirty he is.

Chapter 8

New man involved in "The War"

The next day, Happy Jack gets a call from his police buddy Sergeant Shawn O'Rourke at the 10th Precinct and begins talking to him about some creep who beat up a girl in our neighborhood. O'Rourke is still about seven years away from retirement and worked the same precinct with Hap. He tells him he heard about that and asks if they caught the perp. Shawn tells him they haven't found him yet.

He says, "They say the guy disappeared and no one has seen him in a couple of days."

He tells Hap that he'd like to get his hands on him and serve him his own brand of justice. Jack can't resist the opportunity and asks him what he'd do with him?"

Shawn says, "Man, he hurt that girl BIG TIME! He killed her baby! He's a KILLER and he's out there somewhere! Off the record Jack, I know I couldn't do it, but with this perp, I wouldn't bother with a court case. I'd put a whole lot of pain on him first and then take him out somewhere and shoot him! You know how many of these guys who hurt girls get to walk free and don't EVER get what's coming to them! Seriously! I'd love to find him and do it the *'old west way.'* You know as well as I do Jack, there are too many guys who are never caught and the victims go on suffering for years, some, for a lifetime. It's not right, man! I'm really angry about this! Every time some punk walks, I could go berserk on him and put aside due process. Anyway, that's the way I feel. How about you, what would you do?"

Jack says, "You and I my friend have seen a lot of the injustice on the force and it's not getting any better. It seems that it's getting worse every day. You gotta wonder how bad things will get before someone does something about this social disease? I'm with you as far as nabbing this guy and giving him swift justice, 'the old fashion way.' You're right, about 'no trial.' And, I too would like to see him hurt, then end his sorry life! Let me ask you! Would you really do him the way you said?"

Shawn answers, "Jack, I'd do it in a heartbeat. That guy has no business being alive for what he did. He brutalized that poor girl. He could've killed her, and don't even get me going on the dead baby! That put me over the edge! I'm so sick of light to no sentences for so many bad guys that come through the court system. Seriously, I'm at a point where I'd like to quit, but it's my job; I took an oath. I just wish we could have real and swift justice instead of dragging cases on and on, and then, seeing judges slapping too many of these perps on the wrist instead of giving them their just dessert!"

Jack comes back and says, "What would you think if a group of guys got together and nailed any bad guys they catch, and let's say, get them in a place to rough 'em up a bit and even hurt them bad?"

Shawn replies, "I'd say that would be a great idea and a great service to society; not to mention saving tax payers a lot of money in court fees to put away the scumbags!"

Jack asks him, "Have you ever thought of doing exactly that?"

Shawn tells him, "Me and two other guys on the force who were the arresting officers did exactly that with some rats who got off on rape and murder charges. They got rounded up, went to court, but the witnesses all disappeared. They got off for lack of evidence and witness testimony. We let some time pass then lured those punks to a back-alley storage unit and nailed them all. No one ever saw them again. We discovered all of them had weapons. Knowing that, we figured most, if not all, had taken part in shootings. After we took care of them, we checked the guns and saw that all the serial numbers had been filed off …all illegal guns! No surprise there, huh Jack?"

He continues, "This group had been involved in a lot of robberies, home invasions, and drive by shootings. That means; murders for which they were never caught, until the rape and murder of that one girl. This was a righteous thing to do, Jack. We got it done and never told anyone about it. You're the only other person who knows this. So, if it ever got out, I'd know it was you. So, keep this real *close to the vest!"*

"You know me better than that, Shawn. I'd never repeat anything you and I talk about. Besides, you know some things about me that were a bit shady when I was on the force. By the way, if I told you I heard about a group of guys who are doing pretty much what you just told me, what would you say?"

"Man, I'd love to meet them and shake their hands. Again, off the record, that's what every big city with runaway crime needs… a strong vigilante group or individuals like Bernhard Goetz who shot a few punks on the subway in New York when he was being attacked by four African American men from the Bronx December 22, 1984. You know damn well the cops and the courts will never be able to eradicate cities of the criminal element. But, if word got out that some perps are being abducted and punished, and some are never seen again, it would make a lot of the bad guys think. Hell, I'd even let one go free after he got the beating of his life; just as an example. And for sure, the word would get out on the streets. Now then, let me ask you; do you know of such a group?"

Jack hesitates a bit before he speaks and tells him, "Yah, I heard of a group that's doing that, but I can't tell you who they are. I heard they got a few guys in a secure place and are getting very good information from one guy in order to nail several others. As a matter of fact, they got a couple of big names, a detective and an assemblyman who are dirty."

O'Rourke says to him, "Out of respect for our friendship, I won't press you to divulge any names or give me any more info on the group, but I'd love to help out by giving you names of criminals in need of 'swift justice.' Tell you what. I'll call you later and give you a name and address of a guy who needs a real good attitude adjustment. This guy, Fred Bissel has beat up his wife Paula and kids for about seven years, and the law, so far, has not dealt with him properly. His wife is too afraid to press charges. During her seven years with him, he broke her nose, gave her several broken ribs, a concussion, a bunch of split lips and black eyes; and, who knows what sort of evil he's done to her in the bedroom. I'm sure it boils down to rape every time. He's a major rat, this guy. As for his children, he backhanded his three-month-old boy a couple of years ago. That broke his nose. The baby had to be rushed to Children's Hospital. His eldest boy has been beaten severely with a belt and the middle one as well. These poor boys and his wife don't EVER have a good day! Day in and day out, this SUPER JERK dishes it out. Man! It makes my blood boil! I'd love to see him get what he's got coming to him. What do you think?"

Jack says, "Shawn, I think the group would be very interested in tuning up this jerk."

Getting Bad Freddy

The next day, O'Rourke calls Jack and gives him the name and address of the abuser. He's Fred Bissel, a thirty-eight-year-old criminal husband and father. This bad guy needs to be taught a lesson he'll never forget. We won't keep him long and won't hurt him really bad, but bad enough. He'll know the meaning of pain and abuse when we're through with him.

According to Happy Jack, this moron has gotten away with beating his wife and children for way too long. No woman or child should have to endure a creep like that; terrorizing his own family. This familial terrorist is about to be terrorized himself. I can't wait to get this animal in *the chair*. His worthless life is about to get really hard for a bit of time. Maybe two days in *the chair of pain* ought to do it.

I think Eh-Jax would like first crack at him. He has a sister who was abused by her ex-husband. When he found out, he acted really quick and busted up his former brother-in-law. The guy left and never came back. Eh-Jax broke his jaw for starters, broke his right arm and cut off his right earlobe. He told him that if he ever saw him again that he'd cut off both his ears and his manhood! It's been three years and the guy hasn't reappeared. Eh-Jax did swift and righteous justice on this creep. It may seem cruel and crude, but it worked.

Let's go fishing!

Friday night, 6:30 pm. Besides Lenny, Eh-Jax, our driver Happy Jack and Bull, is also on this fishing trip. We wait patiently and see Fred leave the house. He makes his way to his favorite bar, the Drop Inn. After a couple of hours of drinking, we use the van to back into the side of his car and put a slight dent in it. Lenny is in disguise; long hair wig and a Fu Manchu moustache.

He goes in the bar and asks people, "Who owns the black Dodge SUV out in the parking lot." One guy points to Fred, Len walks up to him and says, "Hey man, I just backed into your ride. I'm sorry, man." Old Freddy flips out and cusses him out.

Lenny pretends to be upset and afraid. He tells him, "I'm sorry man. It's my fault. I'll pay for the repairs. Let's go and check out the damage and swap vehicle and insurance information, okay?"

Fred tells him, "Get your ass out there and show me what you did to my car, you idiot!"

Lenny's thinking, *"Man, this moron has NO social skills! He's just rude and crude. I'd love to give him a 'popeye' right here, and now!"*

They get to the car and the guy goes nuts. At that time, Eh-Jax (also disguised) walks up and says that he saw the whole thing and says to Fred that he'd be a witness. Eh-Jax positions himself so that Fred has his back to the sliding side door of the van. Just then, he hits him with the stun gun. Bull, who is inside, throws a bag over Fred's head and the men load him in. Old Freddy is stunned and bagged. Nice catch! Len takes the guy's wallet, cell phone and car keys. He gets in the guy's SUV, and as planned, follows our paddy wagon to Fred's neighborhood so he can leave the car near his house.

Before he gets in the van with the others, he uses the moron's cell phone to call Fred's wife, Paula.

He tells hers, "Mrs. Bissel, I'm calling to let you know that your husband won't be home tonight. He's going out of town for a couple of days. He's going to a conference to get his *'domestic abuse problems'* adjusted. You and your sons won't have to fear him anymore after he gets back home. We'll make sure he's cured. Also, your SUV is parked a couple of houses down your street with the keys left under the driver's side floor mat. Take care of yourself and the boys. I'll be in touch."

Back in the van, the sting from the stun gun has lost its effect; and although Freddy has a hood over his head, he tries to shake himself free. Bull has this nice cut-off ax handle and hits him in the head and tells him to "be cool and just sit there." No - old Fred doesn't want to cooperate. He acts up again and Bull hits him in the right shin while Eh-Jax puts a choke hold on him from behind. He gets the message and chills out. At this point, he's still isn't blindfolded, bound or gagged; he only has the hood over his head. Bull ties his feet together while Eh-Jax handcuffs him. He's told that if he acts up again that he'll get a bad beating. He doesn't make a move. Usually, women-beaters are punks and are only tough against women and don't mess with guys that can hurt them! He's told to lie flat on his stomach with his face to the floor. They take the bag off his head and put the *special blindfold helmet* on him. Since his mouth isn't taped yet, he wants to know what we want with him.

Eh-Jax pipes in and says to him, "How are your wife and kids, Freddy? Do you love them? Do they love you, OR are they afraid of you? We hear you're a real bad ass at home and have been for quite a while. Seems the courts don't want to give you what you have coming. You're a fat rat Freddy and like a lot of rats, you need an exterminator. You know what you sorry ass-moron, we're the exterminators. You dished out pain to your family and now, it's your turn to get some! How does that sound to you?"

Freddy wants to try and impress us with, "people he knows." He says, "Man, you need to let me go. I know a lot of high-ranking people at city hall and they'll get you guys. So, let me go and I'll forget this ever happened."

Bull says, "Hey fellas, what do you think? Should we let him go?"

"Oh sure," says Hap. "But first, we have to introduce him to the special chair. Then, we'll let him go - maybe!"

Fred has no clue what the *"special chair"* is and isn't too spooked at this time. They finally get to the warehouse, drive in and get the *new fish* out of the tank (van). Bull escorts him to the chair, Clint and Len strap him in, and right away, it begins. BAM! I let him have his first taste of what he'll get for a couple of days. His mouth is bleeding. He just puts his head down and says in a whimpering manner, "Please don't do that! Don't hurt me. I DON'T know why you're doing this. I didn't do nothing man! Why am I here?"

With that, Clint says, "WHAT? Here's why you're here." BAM! He backhands him on the side of the head and Lenny fires off a thrust-kick to his gut and knocks him over. They put him back in a sitting position and Bull takes a shot at him too. He takes his belt and lays a strike across his face. It stings like hell and Freddy grits his teeth and groans.

Bull says to him, "You didn't like that did you, you rotten bastard! NOW, you know what your wife and boys have had to put up with for all these years each time you went animal on them!

With that, Bull gives him another swipe on the other side of the face and says to him, "It sting really bad, huh moron?

You need to savor that pain a while and feel how bad it is. Your problem is that you don't know right from wrong. Well, you're in the right place. We're going to educate you really good! You should know full well that you DON'T beat defenseless women and children. Actually, we should just kill you. That's what you deserve. You created a hell hole for your family, full of misery day in and day out, you rotten maggot!"

Eh-Jax says to him, "You know Freddy, we have fifty more guys here, and all of them want to punch your lights out for what you've done to your family. Let's see, as I hear it, you've been a dictating tyrant to your wife and kids now for about seven years. I figure you should get at least four beatings a day, one beating per person for the next four days…maybe longer. How's that sound to you, you stinkin' degenerate?!"

Freddy's in pain and can hardly talk but manages to say, "I'm sorry man, I won't ever hit my wife and kids any more. Please let me go! I promise I'll do right. I'll change? Please let me go, I beg of you" Please!"

I speak up and say, "My, my, my gentlemen, we have another guy who is sorry; won't do it again and is willing to change. What'd you think of that Bufford? Do you think he's sincere and should we let him go?"

Boom says, "You know what guys, I think Freddy here is a LIAR! He's a weasel and is too much of an animal to be set free to go out there again and hurt the ones he's supposed to LOVE! What kind of a RAT are you? You're not a man! You are one of the lowest sleazes in the world! Instead of being a husband and father who protects his family, you do like the people in Superman's Bizarro World; you do the exact opposite! Instead of protecting them and loving them, you hurt them bad, and so …it's your turn to feel pain."

Freddy cries out again, "Please don't hit me no more, I've learned my lesson. I want to go home! Please let me go home!"

I backhand him on the side of the jaw and tell him to keep his mouth shut. I signal to a couple of the men to take him to his cell. They put him in and tell him to go to sleep. Like Daniel, he tries to take his helmet off and… ZAP!!! He screams like a girl and runs like he's trying to get out. He bounces off the fencing and crashes to the floor.

The men laugh… and Clint says to him. "We forgot to tell you! DON'T take off the helmet! It's wired to shock you. Now then, lie down, shut up and go to sleep! We've got more fun in store for you tomorrow. The other forty-five guys might want a piece of you. That's just to give you something to think about."

Old Freddy is hurting and freaked out just like the others in the lockup. He can't imagine what they'll do to him tomorrow. He's scared out of his mind. Right now, both sides of his face and jaw hurt as well as his ribs; two of them are broke. As he breathes, he can feel the pain from the cracked ribs moving back and forth with each breath.

Things start going through his mind about his wife and kids, and the verbal zingers Boom threw at him when he said, *"What kind of a rat are you? You're not a man! You are one of the lowest sleazes in the world. Instead of being a husband and father who protects his family, you do like the people in Superman's Bizarro World, you do the exact opposite. Instead of protecting them and loving them, you hurt them bad, and so… it's now your turn to feel pain, you weasel!"*

He lies down on half the blanket and covers himself with the other half and does his best to go to sleep, but sleep doesn't come. As he deals with the pain, he finds himself thinking about his family. He gets flashbacks of the beatings and verbal abuse he'd given his wife and kids.

He thinks to himself, *"If I get out of here, I'll change. I'll get help, but I don't know how this whole thing is going to end. These guys didn't believe me when I told them I'd change. How can I persuade them that I will?"*

He knows that they're going to beat on him again tomorrow. After all, they know that it's been seven years that he's been abusive and he realizes that if he were the one dishing out pain on someone like him, that he'd be merciless too.

He has a moment of clarity and thinks, *"I'll talk to those men in the morning and beg them to let me go home to make my apol-*

*ogies and get treatment for my drinking and abusive behavior.
I'll tell them that I will leave the house, leave my wife and boys
alone, and that I'll support them financially and hope that they'll
forgive me for what I've done to them."*

It didn't take a long time for this guy to come to reason. But,
like so many incarcerated offenders, it's a common thing for
them to *see the light* and get what is called, *jailhouse religion.*
He's aware that all his freedoms have been taken away and he
doesn't have a thing to say about it. When the law convicts a
criminal, it means he loses all privileges for the dirty deeds he
did and needs to pay a price. Freddy's anxieties overwhelm him.
He breaks down and weeps bitterly. After a long time of reflec-
tion, he drifts off to sleep.

Chapter 9

Setting up for the Rodney pickup

Like we did with Slam, we got Reese to call up his drug-dealing partner Rodney and set up a meeting. The meet is to happen behind Milt's delicatessen on Chicago Street at 10:30. It's been a popular place for them to do this kind of business. Should the police charge in for any reason, the site allows for several escape routes. He told Rodney that this is a huge score and that they needed to talk some serious business. That got our target real excited.

He thinks, *"Man! A huge score would mean I could make a ton of money instead of doing these nickel and dime deals for chump change."*

Time to go

The time has come to snag Reese's buddy, Rodney. The van is parked so that the back end is facing in the direction our prey will be coming from. He shows up in time and makes his way toward the back of the van. Lenny, who is hiding in the shadows near the van, zaps him with the stun gun. Boom and Lenny throw him inside in a split second.

We now have Rodney. The men get his cell phone and $400 in cash from his pocket. Thank you too Mr. Rodney for the very nice contribution. Hap drives off nice and easy. Away they go to the lockup to deal with their new vermin! (*A vermin is a destructive insect such as a cockroach or a rat.*) Rodney and the rest of the guys we have in custody are definitely vermin, rats and cockroaches!

As usual, we blindfold and gag him. With tie raps, we bind his hands and feet. On route, he comes out of his stunned condition and starts to go wild like a trapped animal! Bull gives him a punch to the forehead and knocks him out cold. He won't be a problem for the rest of the way back.

Boom says, "Hey, we're going right by Freddy's place. Let's stop there. I want to leave a little gift for his family. I went by there today and the house looks like hell, very trashy. Freddy is not only an abuser, but also, a real white trash moron. Look at that squalor!

Apparently, old Freddy drinks up any money that could be used to fix things up. Seeing that, you gotta know that his poor wife and boys don't have much. Let's give them a little Christmas in June." He grabs an empty McDonald's bag and puts in the $400 they got from Rodney.

When they get to the house, Boom tells Lenny to go to the door and hand the bag to the lady. Just tell her, "It's a gift for you and the boys."

Lenny is in disguise and does his good deed. It's done very quickly. Paula doesn't even have time to thank him. Len is at the door, says what he needs to say, then… gone! That's Lightening Len.

Back in the van, he says, "Hey guys, it's really pitiful inside that house. She looks terrible; like a woman totally deprived of any physical and emotional care. I also got a glimpse of the boys. Just looking at their faces, you can tell they've been through some very hard times. They're all looking pretty emaciated too. That rotten bastard is going to get a little something special from me tomorrow."

Our squad of avengers is into its fifth day of picking up trash from the neighborhood and depositing them in their respective cells. So far, we've got three drug dealers and an abuser.

Chapter 10

A New Lead

Later, Hap gets another call from Sergeant O'Rourke to tell him that some rat just beat the rap on a brutal rape and murder case and wondered if the guys he knows would like to have a shot at this weasel.

Hap tells him, "What specifics do you have on him?"

"This degenerate raped a thirteen-year-old girl and beat her to death on Stanislaus Street. They got him, but there were no witnesses or enough evidence to make a solid case. He had one of those high-priced lawyers to represent him and the judge cut him loose due to lack of evidence. His alibi, although we know was bogus, was accepted by the judge. We know without a doubt that he did it! He's a gangbanger and has done the same to at least one other girl that we know of. Anyway Hap, his name is Darnell Hawkins and he lives at 500 Hayden Street with his mom and two sisters. Tell your guys that he's very dangerous. He's got a long rap sheet! He's had eleven arrests, mostly for assault, theft and drug deals. He's already done a couple years in lockup. Now, he needs to be taken off the streets for good! We're certain he's been on at least two drive-byes, but we don't have solid proof to charge him with that. This last criminal act of the beating, rape and death of the girl was really bad! Good luck with this perp and let me know the outcome when he's off the street."

"As soon as I hear how things turn out, I'll certainly pass that info on to you, my friend."

Shawn is pretty bright and has figured out by now that Hap is part of the group. He's more than okay with that and he's very happy that real justice is being served up to some of the rodents in his city. He'd love to have such vigilantes in all of the neighborhoods. It would make his job and the courts' much easier. And, it would send a huge message to the other rats, cockroaches and worms slithering through our streets.

He thinks, *"If that happened, then, maybe our city would get better and the good people would feel safe about living here. As it is, some people don't even want to sit on their own front porch or take walk in their own neighborhoods. THAT'S WRONG!"*

Hap is also smart enough to figure that Shawn knows he's in the group of men doing the neighborhood cleanup. He knows that he'll never divulge what he knows and as a matter of fact, he has indirectly become part of this little army of *do-gooders*.

The lead hits pay dirt

It's Monday night and Hap calls to tell me we've got another *fish to fry*; a major punk by the name of Darnell Hawkins who beat a very serious charge and that he's out on the streets with his gangbanger friends. He gives me all the info he has on this rodent. I tell him that I'd get the phone chain going right away. We set up a phone chain for the purpose of letting everyone know when we have another perp to pick up. I make a call to Boom, and he in turn calls another; that person calls the next, and so on.

The next day at 8 am, all the men meet at the warehouse to get things figured out as to how and when they'll go fishing for this guy.

I tell the group, "Men, we have another real bad guy needing our justice. This Darnell is a twenty-five-year-old gangbanger, drug dealer, rapist and murderer. Let's set up the pickup for this rat."

With the information we have on the perp, me and Clint will stake out Darnell's place tonight and see what he does and where he goes. We plan on picking him up the following night.

Night comes, the surveillance

It's now 9 pm. Four guys volunteer for the mission in four separate cars to follow our subject. We set it up so that if he looks around to see if he's being followed, he won't see the same vehicle. The guys will take turns tailing him. Lenny plans on parking his car near Darnell's house and go on foot in case he should go into an area where cars can't follow. With upgraded surveillance capabilities; ear-pieces and mini-microphones, everyone will be able to stay in touch. This will make coordinate things really easy.

Clint and I (in separate cars) are parked near Darnell's place to see when he leaves. The vigilante gods are with us, for lo and behold, after only twenty minutes; here comes the rat. We stay a good distance from him and let everyone else know we're moving. The pursuit has begun.

As it turns out, we don't have to follow him too far. He only goes a couple of blocks and meets up with several of his boys. This could be a problem in snatching up Darnell if he's always with a group of guys. The question is; how to isolate him? Hap says that he'll call Sergeant O'Rourke and see if he has Darnell's cell phone number. If he does, we'll use that to call him and drop Slam's name in the mix to get him to a location of our choosing. Then, do the pickup. Hap makes the call and sure enough, Shawn has it. It was part of the info on Darnell's arrest file. The dummy kept the same phone number. Now, we too, have it. This is working out nicely.

I make the call to head back to home base and start working on our plan. We need to speak to Slam. Bull gets him out of his cage and I ask him if he knows Darnell Hawkins. He tells me he does; that he's supplied him and other gangs with drugs so they can sell on their own separate turfs.

I tell him that he needs to set up a meeting with Darnell and tell him to meet him under the bridge in the park at 9:30 tomorrow night. Eh-Jax dials up Darnell on Slam's cell. He does as he was told. Those two have done ton of business together resulting in more lives destroyed! This will be another righteous catch.

It's all set. We go fishing again, *mañana*.

Chapter 11

Another round with Daniel

Danny, the baby killer, has been with us now for three days and nights. The burn on his hand is still hurting really bad, as is his jaw and split lips. He has a hard time even drinking water, let alone, chewing anything. He has a cracked jaw and his ribs are killing him.

He feels really sorry for himself and would love to hear, "Okay Danny Boy, you're going home today." But that's not going to happen just yet. I made the decision to keep him with us a bit longer and make him a deal.

He's taken out of his cell and brought to the interrogation room. We sit him down, strap him in and begin to smack him around a little more. Not too hard, just hitting the same targets we zeroed in on him before. The blows are just hard enough to rekindle the pain in his jaw, his cheeks, his ribs, and, we even light up the torch and bring it near his hand. The blows we dished out are very painful, but when he feels the heat from blow torch near his burnt hand, he totally freaks out. We don't burn him anymore since the wound he has is going to ooze for a long time, and the scar will never go away. It'll be a reminder to him of what he did. We figure that one burn was enough.

Clint says, "Danny needs another reminder. I feel that the foot he used to kick Chantal in the stomach should get some attention."

He picks up the hammer and zeroes in on Dan's right instep. It's a crushing blow! Danny screams and cries like a child. He pleads, "PLEASE don't hurt me anymore! Please! I beg of you, no more, NO MORE! PLEASE!

Clint tells him, "Dan, I hope that pain stays with you a long, long time. That's the foot that hurt your girlfriend and KILLED her baby."

Bull says, "For me, I'd like to bust up his right shin and knee cap as well so his whole leg and foot ache for days. What he did deserves that!"

Boom tells him, "Dan, you have two choices as to what's going to happen to you. One, we keep you here for a month, beat you every day and then kill you, or two; you turn yourself in and never tell anyone about this place or how you got so beat up. If you do, we will find you and kill you! What do you think?"

With a cry in his voice and in much pain, he responds, "Man, I'll turn myself in and I won't say a word about you guys, I promise, I really, really promise I won't tell. Please, let me get out of here! I'm begging of you, please!"

I tell him that he'll need to place a call to the police and tell them who he is, what he's done, and give the name the girl he beat up. He's to say that he'll let them know when and where they can pick him up. This will be a good test to see how one of the perps we set free, does. Will he do the right thing or will he need to get bagged once more and never see daylight again. This is very serious! He's a woman beater and a murderer. He'd better do the right thing!

It's all set. We plan to take him to a vacant building right near the precinct, tie him up to a post in the building, put tape over his mouth, remove the special blindfold from behind and duct tape his eyes so he can't see any of us.

Letting Dan go

The next day comes. Clint and Eh-Jax do the honors, with Hap driving. They get to the building we picked out for his release; the men secure Danny to a steel girder. Hap dials the precinct and Daniel tells the officer on the other end what he did to Chantal and that he'll be in the vacant building at 589 East Babcock Street to give himself up in half an hour.

With that done, we leave him alone. He starts weeping out of gratitude that his ordeal is over. He is also freaked out knowing that the cops will have him. He'll go to court and end up doing a long time in prison for his crime. Just to make sure the cops get all the details right, we put a note in his back pocket. They'll search him and will be able to read the details of what he did. Hap told his police buddy Shawn about the plan and that he should try to be in on the arrest. He told him that he could make that happen.

Hap, Bull and Lenny, park the van a little-ways from the drop off site to observe what the officers will do. After about twenty minutes go by, the cops arrive. They're a bit early. That's okay. Our men cleared out right after the call. They go in with guns drawn and in about five minutes, come out carrying Daniel who is still crying. The cops had taken off the duct tape from his mouth and eyes, and when he finally sees the outside, having been in complete darkness for the past few days. It's a *feel-good treat* to his eyes as he's able to finally look around and see people and things. They hustle him off to the precinct for processing.

Once they arrive at the precinct and empty his pockets, they find the note that reads…

"I Robert Connor beat Chantal Simmons and caused her baby to die when I punched and kicked her in the stomach. I admit to the crime and am ready to receive the penalty for my actions."

After one of the officers reads it, looks at Danny, and wonders what happened to him. He asks him what happened. He tells him that a bunch of young guys did it. He was told before we took him to the vacant building that he'll need to tell the police that story and ONLY that story.

The officer in charge says, "Okay, book him and then let's take care of his wounds. It seems we have a solid case on this perp."

He tells Danny, "So you're the monster who did all that damage to that young lady eh? You're going to go down hard for this."

Dan says nothing. He just puts his head down in shame and weeps.

After processing him, Sergeant Shawn calls Hap and tells him that punk will go through due process and will get a lot of years for what he did.

He says to him, "Oh, by the way, you can tell your guys, 'Thanks' for me."

Hap tells him, "I'll try to relay the message, Shawn. Take care, my friend."

Chapter 12

Sixth catch - Darnell Hawkins

Next day, it's Darnell Hawkins' turn to meet the boys. We can't wait to get this trifecta criminal for; murder, rape, and drug dealing.

We gather together and plan to pick him up at the agreed 9:30 pm meet under the bridge. When Lenny scouted it out, he noticed that you have to come down an embankment and then make a sharp left to get under it. That's perfect! Clint plans on getting there way before Darnell is due to show up and when he does, as soon as he makes that left under the bridge, ZAP! He'll go down. Along with Clint is Bull and Eh-Jax. They'll help carry the lad to the van. This should be an easy catch.

The time is at hand and Darnell shows as planned. He makes his way down the path, makes that left under the bridge and surprise! He's hit with the stun gun and goes down. The men are quick to gag and blindfold him. They cuff his hands behind his back and call Hap on their headsets in the van. He drives up to the path and the men put their new fish in the tank. Off they go to the warehouse which, by the way, is only a couple of miles away.

In the van, they pick Darnell's pockets. They get his license, cell phone and a nice little .22 caliber pistol; no surprise there. They take his cash; only $250. For one of the main dealers to dealers, Darnell is poor compared to the other two drug-dealing jackasses we already bagged. At any rate, the money will still fund some of our needs. The guys also find a few bags of heroin and a needle. It seems that this drug dealing, rapist, murderer not only deals, but is a user himself.

As Hap starts to drive to warehouse, he comes out of his stunned state but stays still. He has no idea what's going on. All he knows is that he got knocked out and somebody had him tied up in a van. He figures it might be friends of the girl he raped and killed and that they're going to kill him.

They arrive with their prisoner and put him in the chair. The rough treatment starts really quick with him. Hap backhands him and nearly knocks him over. I slap him on the other side of the face with enough force to snap his head sideways.

I say to him, "So besides being a major drug distributor and part of the rats that ruin people's lives with narcotics, you're also the punk who beat the rap on that girl you raped and killed, eh? Well, since the courts couldn't do the right thing and put your butt in jail, guess what? We're going to deal out the punishment you missed out on."

The tape is removed from his mouth and he says, "Man, I didn't kill that girl, it was somebody else. The judge let me go! I'm innocent! You need to let me go. You got the wrong guy! I swear it!"

"No, no, no! You did it, and you know you did it!" says Bull, "Now then, if you're going to lie to us, we'll castrate you; tie you to a tree in the park till somebody finds you in the morning. By then, you'll will have bled out and be dead. What do you think of that, you miserable scumbag?"

In a weeping voice, he says, "Man, I told you the truth, I didn't do it! It wasn't me! You gotta believe me! I'm not the guy you're looking for! Please, please, believe me!"

"So, you insist on lying to us," says Clint. "Hey Bufford, get the straight razor! Stand him up and someone pull his pants down. We're going to neuter this pervert!"

They stand him up and begin to undo his pants. He cries like a child, "NO! Don't do that!!! Okay, I admit it! I did the girl, okay?! There! I said it. I did it! I did it! Now, please don't cut me that way. Please!"

I backhand him and say, "We knew you did it, Darnell. According to police evidence, your DNA was all over her. The cops had you dead to right but you had some sleazy lawyer get you free by getting someone to lose the DNA evidence. We just needed you to admit it and be a man about it. But, you're not a man, are you? You're a rapist and murderer who thought he got away with something. And, you thought nothing of it. Killing someone was no big deal. Well Darnell, this is the day you get dealt with."

BAM! Lenny lands a solid punch to his stomach. He loses his breath and begins to heave. As he recovers a bit from that, Bull backhands him and over he goes along with the chair. He has a nasty cut over his right cheekbone and Hap hits him on the other side after they set him up straight again.

He steps back and says, "There, I wanted to match the facial arrangement a bit. Now, the cheeks match just right."

Darnell's cheeks are bleeding as well as his lips. He begs for the guys to stop. I tell him that we'll stop for tonight but that tomorrow could be a much worse day for him. I signal a couple of the men to take him to his lockup. No one tells him about not trying to remove the special headgear/blindfold. They want to see if he'll try taking it off. The boys put him in his cell and tell him that there is a blanket in there where he can lie down, and a chamber pot for him do whatever toilet things he has to do.

The men walk away and go to another room to talk about Darnell's future. He can't hear them talk and figures they've left, but they can see him and the other roaches through a large window.

After about two minutes, we hear a really loud scream! Ah… poor Darnell tried to take off his blindfold.

Boom goes out and yells, "Hey Darnell, don't you try taking off that helmet! You'll get a shock. Now, lie the hell down and behave yourself!"

He is freaked out like the other prisoners, about the pain, yes, but also about the shock he just got and the fact that he can't see a thing. Imagine yourself being in a hostile environment, in great pain and total darkness. It's gotta be a really bad trip! He gets the message and settles in as best he can. And, there's not a peep from any of the other caged punks in the warehouse.

Chapter 13

Catching a cop
and councilman Also,
freeing Wife-beater Freddy

We go back to talking about the rats we've picked up so far and come to the decision that we'll need to release the perps we have. Our hope is that they'll be put away for a long time, or for good. We also need to capture the two big names; Detective Ronald Coates and Councilman Ashton Clarion. We'll have Reese make a phone call tomorrow and tell those two that he broke his cell phone and that it took time to get another phone to contact his main supplier to get their numbers.

We pull Reese from his cell and have him use one of our untraceable phones. He sets up a call to Detective Coates as planned and tells him about his broken phone and asks him if he's in need of *products* (drugs). Coates chews him out and tells him how this gap in time screwed up his partying, that people depend on him for fresh goods. Reese tells him that he'll meet him tomorrow at 8:30 pm in back of the church where they normally meet, at the corner of Meriden and Cumberland; it's a perfect spot for them. It's very dark there and away from street traffic. Coates tells him he'll be leaving the precinct around 7:00 and will be on time. He tells Reese to not be late. He assures him that he'll there with the stuff. It's all set. Coates is going down! We plan on running the same body switch gag we did for Slam with Clint wearing Reese's gear.

It's been a busy first week so far. We have four bad guys who shouldn't be part of society, let alone, part of our neighborhood. The question is; who do we release next? Danny's gone to jail and will be with some men who will give him more bad times. Women beaters and baby killers don't do well among men whose sisters or mothers have been beat or killed by some cockroach. He will not have good days in prison.

While we're talking about nailing Detective Coates, I ask the men, "How about cutting Freddy 'the wife-beater' loose? What do you guys think? He's a real bad man, but from what I can see, he could turn things around after we give him one more round in the chair and promise him that he'll be a cripple for the rest of his life if he doesn't change his ways. We'll let him know that we'll be watching him every day and the cops will be by his house at any given time to check things out."

The men agree. It's a bit late, 8:30, but he's brought out of his cage and placed on the chair. Since Boom has the harshest voice, we let him read Freddy the "riot act" to drive the point home. Boom backhands him with two strikes, one on each side of the jaw and grabs him by the throat. He puts enough pressure in his grip to make Freddy's throat real uncomfortable.

He tells him, "Freddy, you'd like to go home to your wife Paula and your boys wouldn't you?"

He does his best to nod "yes" and blurts out what he thought of saying to them about changing.

"I promise if you let me go home, I will apologize to my wife and kids, and get counseling for my drinking problem and the way I treated them. I promise! I'll leave the house and won't bother my wife and boys until I can do things right. I'll support them financially, and in time, I hope they'll forgive me for all the pain I've caused them. I promise! I promise, so help me God!"

I tell him, "That sounds really nice, Fred. Here's the deal. We'll let you go home, but you'll need to be the very best husband and dad you can be. You don't blow your money on booze anymore! You definitely DO NOT beat your wife and kids! If you do, we WILL get you and this time, we'll break both, your hands, arms and legs. We will make you a cripple for life. And, you WILL clean up you house! You have your family living in a rat hole. It's a disgrace. You need to do a complete 180 toward your family! Is THAT understood?!

"Yes! I understand. I won't drink anymore and I won't hurt my wife and kids. I promise. I understand what I did was wrong. Thanks for letting me go."

The men get Freddy out of the chair, get the blood cleaned up off his mouth and chin and place him in the van. Hap drives. Lenny and Bull go along to get him back home. They go a bit passed the house where he lives, and stop. Lenny tells him that he has a gun with a silencer ready to shoot him if he acts up when they take off the cuffs. Len tells him to lay flat on the floor of the van with his face down. He does as he's told and Bull takes the special headgear/blindfold off and wraps duct tape around his head to cover his eyes. When he's let out of the van, he'll be able to undo the head duct tape so that he's able to see.

It's 9:30 pm. The street is dark and there's no one around. Bull and Lenny lead him out of the van and walk him a few houses away from his own. He's told that they'll leave and that he is to stay there for a count of 30 before taking off the tape from his eyes. He's told to not look back once the tape is off. The duct tape is wrapped around his head only once around. It'll take him about minute before he can take it off.

Now then, he doesn't know what kind of van the men used. Hap parked down the street a bit after he dropped off Bull and Lenny who are standing in the shadows to see what he does. They can see that it looks like he's counting. That's good. Then, they see him struggle to get the tape off. When he does, he doesn't look back, like he was told. He runs towards his house while Bull and Lenny keep a good distance back; far enough to keep him in sight until he gets to the house.

As the boys left the warehouse with Freddy, I placed a call to his wife and told her that her husband was coming home. I told her that he got a beating for what he had done to her and the kids and that she should not be afraid of him anymore. I assured her that if he did anything at all to her, or the boys, that he would be picked up again be made a cripple. I told her that I had a man to man talk with him about his drinking and abuse, and that I'd be watching.

Freddy gets to the door. It's locked. Len and Bull see him knock. His wife opens it. He steps back, and gets down on both knees.

The men can see him weep and hear him say to his wife, "I'm so, so very sorry for the way I've treated you and the boys. I promise I won't do that anymore. I Promise. I really promise! Please forgive me!" The boys are also at the door. He says to them, "Boys, forgive your dad, please! I'm sorry I've been such a bad daddy. Forgive me!" He weeps bitterly.

His wife and the boys see how sincere he is. They approach him and say they forgive him. Freddy stretches out his arms to motion that he wants to hug them all. They come together in a "group hug." All of them are now crying. But, it's a good cry.

Bull looks over at Lenny in the dim light and can see the glitter of a tear on his cheek.

He pats him on the back and says, "Come on Tonto, our work here is done. Let's get back to the ranch and tell the others about this happy ending."

Bull is also very moved by what just happened, but he puts on his *macho* front. That's just the way he is; big hearted but tough as nails.

Chapter 14

TV news flash – and, two new targets; Detective Coates and Councilman Clarion

We're into our sixth day of removing trash from the streets of our neighborhood and lo and behold, the TV news guys get the word that some boys from late teens to early twenties have disappeared. That would be Reese, Slam, Rodney and Darnell.

One newscaster put it this way. *"It's come to our attention here at WGRK that several men from the south district area have simply disappeared from the face of the earth. Families of the missing men are at a loss trying to figure out where their sons are. There are all sorts of speculations that perhaps rival gang members or individuals seeking revenge have had a hand in those disappearances. One mother said that her son has not come home for three days now; that he sometimes stays away for a couple of days, but he usually calls to let her know he's okay. Our call to the police to find out if they know anything about any disappearance of local men produced no answers to the mystery. We'll keep you posted as we get more information on this story.*

Meanwhile, at the mayor's office ..."

With this new development, I tell the men that we need to make some things happen sooner than later. I'm talking about our drug dealers. They have customers who depend on them to be around and two of them are Detective Ronald Coates and Councilman Ashton Clarion. We need to get those two before they get spooked!

It's 7:30 pm. I say to the men, "Let's gear up for Coates' pickup and hope that the newscast didn't raise any red flags with him that one of the missing guys may be his drug supplier. Guys, we'll need to be extra careful with this one. We have a dirty cop who deals drugs and who knows how many backups he might have. We'll need to get him as fast as we can and disappear fast."

Everyone is in on this pickup except the Boom. He'll babysit the inmates while the six of us get Coates.

We make our way to the site and each man takes a position to make sure no one can interfere with our fishing trip. A half hour earlier, Hap parked the van nearby. Clint has Reese's gear on and waits in the shadows.

Coates pulls behind the church at 8:25 in an unmarked car and shuts off the headlights. Clint makes his way towards him with a bag that looks like a good supply of drugs. As he approaches, Coates lowers the window and stretches out his hand with an envelope to make the payment, and ZAP! He's frozen in shock from the stun gun. Right away, Bull and Eh-Jax rush to extricate him from the car. They move fast and drag him to the van. In he goes, and Hap takes off. We have him! We're all relived that it came off without a snag.

Everyone was a bit nervous with this catch. After all, he is a detective. I tell the men via headsets that we have the "Big Fish" and that we're on our way home. As with the other fish we caught, we bind his legs, cuff his hands behind his back, blindfold him and tape his mouth while we're in transit. We empty his pockets to get his badge, gun, cell phone, wallet and money. By the way, in that envelope, there's $10,000. That's a hefty donation for our cause. Thank you!

The scary part about this catch is; how do we handle him? I mean, do we put a hurting on him or what? He's not our typical hoodlum, he's a cop! Well, first thing first, we'll get him to the warehouse and get him settled in. He's not a big man, about five foot eleven, so he won't be hard to handle, especially with big guys like Eh-Jax and Clint.

Detective Ron, now out of his stunned state, is really freaked out. He thinks to himself, *"Who the hell would dare do this to me, a detective?!"*

He can't imagine who, but knows he's in trouble. Just the way he got taken tells him that whoever pulled this off did it in a well-organized manner, like pros. He'd like to talk but can't because of the tape. It really freaks him out that he can't see. He can hear, but the men are all quiet. Coates figures he's on route to some out of the way secluded place where they'll eventually talk to him, and, he in turn, will be able to talk to them.

About ten minutes from the pickup, we arrive and bring Coates to our interrogation room. The plan is to run a scam to trick him in making self-incriminating statements. That way, we'll have taped evidence that he's tied in with Reese and Slam. The good cops know both these rats and have been trying to nail them. Well now, they'll have another rat to put away; one of their own.

We sit him down in the chair and Clint tells him that he'll need to keep his mouth shut and only answer the questions he's asked. Bull removes the tape over his mouth, and Coates wants to talk.

As he utters the first word, Clint smacks him on the right side of his jaw and says, "Detective Coates, didn't you hear the directions you were given? Don't talk! Just listen, and when it's time to answer, then you'll talk to us. Is that understood?"

He has that hard guy attitude and says, "Yah!"

Hap runs the tape recorder and I start right in with, "You're probably wondering why we picked you up and brought you here. Well, you see, we want to move in this area and do business, the kind of business you were going to do tonight with Reese and Slam. Now then, if we release you, will you do business with us?

Coates says, "Sure, why not? One source is as good as another as long as you can get me what I want. What do I care who I do business with as long as I can get the goods I need for my people."

"That's a good choice detective." I ask him how much stuff he'll need or want each week.

"I have a lot of high-level friends who count on me to supply them with whatever they need. I could use at least ten thousand dollars-worth a week of mixed drugs; heroine, grass, cocaine and crack as well as a good supply of ecstasy. From time to time, I'd be good for a $5,000 buy for a single special occasion. The people I deal with don't want any connection with run-of-the-mill drug dealers. They need someone like me, someone from their own social status. They don't like and don't trust the scumbag street dealers."

I continue the questioning, "How long have you been buying from Reese and Slam?"

"I've been doing business with them for at least four years."

"Who do you supply drugs to?" I ask.

"You name them; I do it for lawyers, cop friends, politicians like Councilman Ashton for one, TV people, several big businessmen, a bunch of bar owners; anyone I know who want to party and get high on more than just cocktails. Several of my high-profile customers are hooked pretty badly! They're very steady customers and a source of great cash flow in my pocket."

I ask him to name some more people. He's very reluctant and tells me that he'd rather not. I tell him that if he's unwilling, then we'll have to get down and dirty and that will entail physical pain and maybe a few broken bones. With that said, he gives us a string of names. All of it is on tape.

I ask him if Reese and Slam have done any work for him, like hits on other gang members.

Coates says, "Oh yah! These two and their boys knocked off at least six or seven guys, maybe more. As a matter of fact, they capped three guys just last month who wanted to be my suppliers. They wanted me to drop Slam and Reese and take them on as my drug source."

Feeling that we have plenty of information that the Newspapers, TV stations and the District Attorney would gobble up...

I say to him, "You know what Detective Coates? I've not been very honest with you. Actually, we're not drug dealers, we're a special undercover group that was put together to get rid of dirt bags like you and a host of others plaguing this city. All that you said is on tape. You're DONE! We're going to get you back to your car, now. You'll still be blindfolded, cuffed and gagged. We'll put the handcuff key in your front shirt pocket so you can free yourself. That'll take you a couple of minutes. You'll be free to go and do what your conscience tells you to do. We'll keep your badge, gun, cell phone and wallet. We can drop everything off to Internal Affairs, and hand over a copy of the recording to them and the media if you don't do what you need to do to make this right."

Coates has nothing to say. He knows he is totally screwed, or will be as soon as the D.A., TV stations and newspapers receive the incriminating information. Not a word. He just sits there like a man who was given the death penalty; knowing full well that he's guilty as hell and that there's no way out.

I motion for the men to take him out. They re-tape his mouth, put him in the van, bring him to his car and leave. It'll take a bit of time to get the duct tape unwrapped around his head before he can see to use the key for the hand cuffs. By then, like shadows in the night, our men will have faded into the darkness in the roving "fish tank."

It takes a bit of time, but Coates gets free of his restraints and makes it home where he walks the floor most of the night trying to come up with a way out of his predicament.

Next catch - Councilman Clarion

When we get done releasing Coates, it's 9:40 pm, and I tell the guys that we should see about snatching up our cocaine-snorting Councilman Clarion as soon as possible.

I tell them, "I once heard on a newscast that Clarion is a steady patron of Harry's Bar on Amber Street where he likes to rub elbows with many of his financial supporters. It isn't too far from here."

I ask the men who would like to go fish him out, and without skipping a beat, Bull, Eh-Jax, Clint and Boom volunteer right away.

Bull says, "I would love nothing better than to jack up a crook-ed public leader. Imagine that, an elected official doing drugs. You gotta ask yourself, what good does this rat do for the city? Nothing! He's a leech…just another cockroach! I'm gonna enjoy this catch a lot."

He continues. "And another thing; buying cocaine costs money and for sure, he must have some crooked deals going to fund his drug needs. As a city councilman, he's not doing this strictly on a salary of maybe, $50,000 to $60,000 and change. As always, the question is, how can we lure him into a trap?

Hap says, "A lot of politicians are always looking for campaign donations or have some other crooked deals that benefit them financially. We have his phone number in Coates' cell. I'll call Mr. Clarion and tell him that I'm a huge supporter of his and that I must leave on business early tomorrow and need to see him tonight at Harry's Bar to give him $10,000 cash donation toward his re-election.

Hap, makes the call, and as luck would have it, he's able to set up a meeting with him at Harry's for 10:15 pm tonight. The men don't have much time left. It's already 9:45. They have about a fifteen-minute ride to the bar and they need to get there ASAP. The plan this time is to have Clint drive his own car, in disguise, and wear a shirt and tie so that he looks like a businessman while the other three ride in the van.

Both vehicles arrive and park in a lot across the street from Harry's that is reserved for his customers. At 10:10, Eh-Jax who is in the passenger seat of the van spots our target.

Clint can hear Eh-Jax's voice in his earpiece, saying, "Yo Buford, your man is at your thirty." …meaning, behind him.

He says, "I see him. I'll get out and walk over to where he parks and get him in a position behind his car so that you can pull the van right next to us."

The councilman parks and as he gets out of his car, Clint walks over to him and says, "Mr. Clarion! How are you? So glad you could meet with me at this late hour. I was asked to deliver a special gift of $10,000 from my employer and some of his influential friends for your next election."

As he engages in a conversation with Clarion, Hap slowly drives the van over; Clint puts his hand in his suit pocket as if he's going for the money and pulls out his stun gun. In the blink of an eye, the councilman is zapped and drops to the ground. Bull and Eh-Jax are quick to scoop him up and dump him inside. They're gone with their prize in thirty seconds.

The next thing Clarion realizes is that he's in a vehicle, completely tied up, blindfolded and gagged. Being a person of some importance and accustomed to being pampered, this kind of treatment is shocking to him. He's terrified and doesn't know what to make of it. He'll soon find out. The men make it back to the base and bring our non-illustrious councilman to the interrogation room. They sit him in the dreaded chair of pain.

I get right to it; "So Mister Councilman, I hear you're good friends with Detective Coates and obtain recreational drugs from him, and, in turn, you supply some of your friends. Is that right?"

He's a bit hesitant, but answers, "Yes, I know Coates and he does provide me with drugs. I only sell a small portion to close friends; most of it is for personal use. I'm not a dealer; I would never do that! What do you want with me?"

Boom jumps in and says, "What we want is for you to resign from your councilman position and go away. You were elected by the good people to represent them in this district and be their voice on a number of social issues. But, by being a drug user and involved with other users, you've shown yourself to be unfit for the job. Therefore, you need to put in your resignation, right away!

With an emphatic tone, he says, "I can't leave that office! Although I do some drugs, I'm still able to do my job. People depend on me! And besides, I'm not the only one in public office in this city who gets high occasionally. There are a whole lot of others in power doing the same." He throws out a dozen names we can follow up with and get them really spooked! We'll play the tape to them with Clarion's voice on it. Hopefully, that'll scare them enough to fly right and think about their careers.

Everything Clarion said is taped. Bull replays it for him and says, "Now, I want you to listen to another recording." He plays what Detective Coates said when he was interrogated.

After hearing it, he can see that we have enough information to bury him, if we want.

I tell him, "Councilman, we're going to let you go, but before we do, we'd like to leave you with something."

I hit him with a firm slap to the face, hard enough for him to feel a good sting. This scares him. In a whimpering voice, he says, "Please don't hit me again! Please! Let me go and I'll resign tomorrow."

I motion for Lenny to unstrap him and take him out. He and Hap put him in the van and drop him off near Harry's Bar. Len cuts the tape that is binding his wrists. By the time he can get the tape unwound around his head, they'll be a few blocks away.

Now, we wait and see if the councilman will follow through and actually resign tomorrow.

Chapter 15

Detective Coates' demise at the precinct, and Councilman Clarion's resignation

At 9 am the next day, Sergeant O'Rourke sees Detective Coates come into the precinct house and notices that his mood is very sullen. He looks extremely troubled about something. He sees him going into his office, shuts the door, sits in his chair and turns it toward the window. He just sits there and stares into space for the longest time.

O'Rourke, knowing that we picked him up, figures that he's pretty shaken up about having been tagged. Coates is worried that everything will come out and that his twenty-eight-year career will end. The disgrace he'd have to endure plus the loss of his position weighs heavy on his mind. He knows that he can kiss his pension good-bye. He becomes more and more despondent as he sits there contemplating what he should do. He is at his wits end.

Shawn is working on some of the arrest files at the front desk. After about forty-five minutes, he walks down the hall toward the break room and as he passes Coates' office, he sees him motionless and slumped down in his chair! He goes in and sees a needle stuck in his arm and an open bag of white powder. Coates shot up with heroin. His heart stopped! Quickly, he finds a NARCAN injector in the precinct medicine cabinet; comes back and injects him. It's no use. It doesn't work. Too much time has passed and Coates must have taken too big a dose for the antidote to work. He's gone.

O'Rourke surmises that Coates thought it better to "check out" now than to have to go through all the mess with Internal Affairs, the media circus, lawyers and the court process; and worse yet, jail time! That wasn't going to be an option. He chose the easy way out.

Of all the perps we picked up and processed, Coates ended up being the easiest to find a solution as to how we'd have to conclude our dealings with him. It isn't pretty, but it'll do just fine. At least, it's one less high-profile dealer out of business. We're sure that when Councilman Ashton hears of the overdose/suicide, he'll get really shaken and may consider the same option.

Having the incriminating information on tape with Coates' voice will be really useful in dealing with Ashton if he doesn't resign. It'll also be a huge help in putting Reese, Slam and Darnell in the jail for a long time. We'll deal with that after we have a meeting to see what the consensus will be concerning turning in those three.

Councilman Clarion hears about Coates

As the precinct chief receives the news from Sergeant O'Rourke about Coates' suicide, he in turn, passes that information on to the Police Commissioner and the mayor. They follow the usual protocol for something of this nature with regards to contacting the family, internal affairs and the media. They want to hold back putting out any statements to the news outlets until they do a preliminary investigation.

Since the detective works out of a precinct that is in Councilman Clarion's district, he is also told about Coates' death. He's extremely shaken and doesn't know what to do. Then, he realizes that we might turn over the recordings the Commissioner and the news people. This puts him in a position where he needs to do what we told him to do or everything will go public.

He gets set to write his letter of resignation but pauses to think about his career. He knows there is no way he can talk his way out of this situation. The thought of having to face his family, friends and constituents is overwhelming. He chooses wisely and does exactly what we told him to do - resign!

It takes a good half hour to write the letter, and when it's done, he asks his secretary to come in; hands her the hand-written copy and tells her to type it right away and get it over to the party leaders. She does as she's told. When she finishes typing it, she summons an office courier and has him hand-carry it to the officials who will read it and proceed with preparing a speech for the public and news media announcing Councilman Ashton Clarion's sudden resignation.

While this is going on, he busies himself packing personal items from his desk. He wants to make a quick exit before anyone can ask him the dreaded question…why? If there's an upside to this, it's that he is single and won't be dragging a wife and kids through the humiliation of the usual media circus something like this brings on. He's mortified! He just wants to fade into oblivion, at least, for the time being.

After several minutes of packing, he sits down and thinks about how he's going to move forward and what he'll do to survive. He's a forty-year-old man who has done nothing but politics since he graduated from college.

He thinks, *"Now what? How am I going to survive and will all my friends abandon me?"*

He thinks about his drug supplier buddy Detective Coates who he partied with, and how he was able to lead a secret life with regards to drug use. Now that he's dead, he has no more trusted drug supplier with clout. He's on his own and he knows that none of his political friends will want to associate with him; especially since Coates can be tied to street gangs and criminal activities that include drug dealing and murder. This is serious and he's fully aware of all the ramifications. He knows that we'll turn over the information to the authorities and news media and that he'll be implicated as an active drug buyer and user.

The thing about a lot of officials, they often have an "out." For Clarion, his solution is to move out of town and connect with a brother in Erie, PA who has a very successful restaurant and bar business where he can make a living. As he's working on gathering as much as he can from his office, he makes that his immediate plans.

Once back at the house, he calls his brother Ralph and explains his situation. The good thing about this deal is that it was Clarion who gave him money to start the business. Ralph is both sadden and disappointed with his brother but agrees to make him a partner; he owes him that much. This solves our ex-councilman's problem about having to face all the people he'd have to explain why he resigned.

The next day after Clarion's political party had a chance to process everything, they let news people in on Councilman Ashton Clarion's resignation; without the gory details. The information the news people get is short and sweet.

They're told, *"Councilman Clarion made a decision to leave his post without giving any reasons for his quick departure; just that it was a personal matter."*

That was it …over and done with. Basically, he packed up and left town.

Now, on to more "crime-fighting!"

Chapter 16

Next night, turning in our prisoners

Now that we have closure with Detective Coates and the councilman, our next step is to turn in murderer Darnell Hawkins along with gangbangers, Slam and Reese, with taped recordings on Hawkins as well as Slam giving up Reese and all of the cockroach dealers connected to them. They being; Derrick himself (aka Slam) Little, Reese Blount, Rodney Chandler, Joe Sanders, Alex Martinez, Jimmy Luca and Deshawn Howard. Darnell won't be able to find any loop-hole this time. He'll be spending the rest of his life in jail.

Hap contacts Sergeant O'Rourke to inform him that there will be three bad guys tied up at a certain location with tape cassettes taped to them that will clearly ID killer Hawkins, Detective Coates, Councilman Clarion as well as Slam and Reese as prime suppliers. Also on the tape is the admission that the two dealers were involved in several killings. For the moment, Hap holds back the location until we're ready to place our catch there.

On this drop, we have Hap as the driver, along with Clint and Boom. Len and Eh-Jax want to follow in a car just in case there's a kink in the drop. It's always good to have backup. One can't be too careful.

It is 9 pm and dark out; perfect for the drop. The men put Darnell, Slam and Reese in the van and roll out of the warehouse. They head to a different abandoned building, not wanting to use the one where Danny the *baby killer* was dropped off, just in case it's being watch. One never knows. This is part of our M.O. We can't use the same drop off location twice for fear of being found out.

Len turned us on to that vacant building on Roland Avenue that is easy to get into at the backside. Hap gets there in about twenty minutes and drives to the back. Darnell, Slam and Reese are unloaded and brought in. Before they were taken out of the warehouse, their special blindfolds were taken off and had their eyes and mouth duct tapped. Now secured to a post, Hap makes the call and tells his police buddy Shawn, where to pick up the next bad guys.

Since O'Rourke is off duty at home, he calls the night shift sergeant at the precinct, Sergeant Miller, and fills him in on a collar his men need to make right away. Miller dispatches a couple of squad cars with lead officer Lieutenant Scott Landry and three other men who arrive in about five minutes. The men find Darnell, Slam and Reese tied to a post. As they shine a flashlight on Slam, they can see there's a note tapped to him.

One of the cops removes it and reads it... *"Search his right pocket and you will find two tapes that will be very important to prosecute these three and their associates. It will also shed a light on Detective Coates and Councilman Clarion"*

The officer retrieves the tapes and gives them to Lt. Landry. Two other cops cut their prisoners from the post and search them. They are then handcuffed, loaded in a patrol car and taken in for booking.

Once back at the 10th Precinct, Lieutenant Landry hands over the note and tapes to Commanding Officer Captain Xavier Mendola. He reads the note and promptly plays the tapes to hear what's on them.

After hearing the taped conversations, he smiles and says to his officers, "Seems we have some vigilantes helping us clean up our city. That's very good! *¡Eso es muy bueno!* We've been looking to get these guys and have a confession from Hawkins. Now, they've been handed to us on a silver platter. Any way we can get 'em is fine with me. Lock 'em up! Even though it's not according to the law, this vigilante group has handed us a few bad guys who deserve exactly what they're going to get.

Background on Mendola's dead son

O'Rourke isn't surprised that the captain feels the way he does. He told Hap that Mendola's own son was beat to death by a group of six punks from an inner-city high school after a basketball game. He was only fifteen. They were all caught, but because they ranged between fourteen and sixteen years of age, they were charged as minors. All of them were only given two years in a "youth detention center." The captain never got over it and always wanted to exact a more proper punishment. So far, he has never acted on that. Had he done so, for sure, he'd be a prime suspect. So, he figured that down the road, his boy would get the justice he deserves.

As for the group that was just handed to him, Mendola gives the matter some thought. He's glad he was given these bad guys to put away but wonders how far this group will go with their methods of extracting information from the perps. He wonders if he's going to have to go after them for taking the law into their own hands. He figures he'll see what else comes up before he does anything.

Right now, being an old school cop, he's more than okay with what's turned up and thinks, *"Since this city's law enforcement can't possibly be everywhere, where crimes happen, maybe this is just what we need, 'vigilante groups' or 'auxiliary cops' that can fill in the gap and help me rid my city of criminals."*

For now, he puts it on the back burner and will wait to see what the group does next.

With the information on the tapes and O'Rourke having become a strong ally to our team of "avengers," we're certain Mendola will make the convictions stick when Darnell, Slam, Reese and the rest of the rats are brought to court. With that done, our incarceration unit (warehouse lockup) is empty…but not for long.

Chapter 17

Jake (The Snake) Toolie

Eh-Jax calls me and says that we have a new cockroach to deal with. He says that a certain white trash moron is seriously harassing some good folks a few blocks from where he lives. He said he heard a woman talking to a friend that she *"can't take it anymore;"* that her neighbor Jack Toolie, a hefty guy in his late forties, is driving her family nuts because of verbal abuse and a number of other things he's done to harass her and others. She said that he's been doing this for a long time and that it just keeps getting worse.

I told him that we'll deal with him tonight; that we can do this quickly enough. I said I'd make a few calls and gather a couple of the men. Eh-Jax gives me the name and address of this rat and some other specifics, like; who lives in the house with him? What kind of car he drives; does he live in a downstairs or upstairs apartment? I get all the info and make a plan to get this jerk at around 10 tonight. My thought is to get Clint, Boom and of course, Hap as the driver, to take this one.

It is nine-thirty and the guys are set to go. They pull up a couple of houses past Jake's place and walk to his door. They have on plastic masks that are almost clear but are still a good disguise. Boom knocks at the door. Jake opens it and the first thing he sees is a .357 magnum in his face. He's pushed backwards, away from the door and told him to SHUT UP and to get on the floor face down! Clint quickly duct-tapes his mouth and head to cover his eyes.

Boom keeps the gun to his head so he can feel the barrel and tells him, "Don't you move, you stinkin' sewer rat! You are one of the lowest forms of white trash people I know and you're going to be sorry you EVER screwed with the neighbors. Listen very carefully you weasel! You WILL clean up your act; that means, your house, your property, your garbage mouth, your lousy behavior toward your neighbors and - you'll even clean up the way you look! You look like a BUM. You're a disgrace to the neighborhood! Your house and property are a mess and your entire attitude is totally unacceptable. You WILL apologize tomorrow to anyone you messed with and promise them you won't do it again. Just so you know that we mean business, here's a taste of what you'll get if you don't do as we say."

He whacks him on the head with the gun (a la pistol whip) and Clint stretches out his left arm so that his hand is lying flat on the floor. He stomps on it. Yep! It's broken! We can hear the muffled scream through the duct tape. He's in serious pain. That's good. He gets the message. Clint sits him up and backhands him across the mouth with a solid blow. Old Jake tastes blood. Like all the other perps we've backhanded with a taped mouth, he can only swallow it. That's become the "norm" with the smacks to the mouth of our perps. Too bad!

Clint tells him, "That's for all of the foul language and really nasty things you've been saying to the good folks around here. From tonight on, you JERK! ...you WILL no longer do that or we'll come back and cut out your tongue."

After having said that, Clint backhands him across the face and knocks him out. We take the tape off his mouth so he doesn't drown in his own blood from the busted lips. We place him on the couch and leave. He's got a broken hand, bloody lips and a very sore jaw; maybe, broken. We'll keep an eye on him and make sure he behaves. If he doesn't, we will be back. Eh-Jax says he'll follow up on him in a couple of days to see if there are any changes in his behavior, his property and the way he looks.

So as to not be suspicious, he'll talk to the people across the street from Jake about the house next to his that's for sale. He'll ask about the neighbor just to see what they have to say about him. If they hear good things, like him apologizing to the lady next to him and others he's been a creep to, that'll all go in his "well-done column." If he's still abusive, he can expect HELL to come knocking really hard on his door. We hope he'll do the right thing. We'll see.

Chapter 18

Old Sparky/New Sparky

A couple of days go by, we're at the warehouse and Happy Jack tells us he just saw a program on TV about a Texas prison electric chair where they electrocuted bad guys with 2,450 volts of electricity. The chair was nicknamed "Old Sparky. It was used between 1926 and 1964 to electrocute 361 prisoners on death row. That 2,450-volt level was set in Nebraska. It became the standard for electrocuting prisoners."

OLD SPARKY

Eh-Jax says, "And, did you have in mind to electrocute some of our guests, Hap?"

"No, but what if we had our own version of the electric chair; one that would put out a lot less current that we could use to wise up some of the bad guys we pick up. We could give them a much lower dose; a level that would shock the hell out of them, but not kill 'em. We could call ours the '*Attitude Adjustment Sparky.*'"

Everybody busts out laughing.

Bull jumps in the discussion, "Not a bad idea, Hap. We could use something like that on lesser offenders, just to teach them a lesson. This way, instead of smacking them around and leaving bruises, cuts or broken bones, we would certainly drive our point home."

He looks at the others in the room and asks, "Anyone else think this could be useful?"

Len says, "I like it. They won't bleed, their bones won't break and the bad boys will NOT want a repeat trip to our own 'Old Sparky.' But… I still want to break a few bones and split a few lips on those who deserve it. That way, they'll have something to take along with them when they're out of here. Speaking of 'taking something along,' I wonder how Daniel's crispy hand is doing. I'm sure he's still in a lot of pain and the scar will be a constant reminder that he doesn't want to see us ever again."

Then he gets back to the topic at hand and says, "Hey guys, what thinks thee about Hap's idea of a special chair, the New Sparky?"

No one objects to using a little electricity to adjust a few bad attitudes. Boom tells us that he has all the equipment to put together a makeshift electric chair. He walks the guys over to the materials he has in his shop and shows us how easy it would be to make such a contraption, one that would be able to deliver as little or as much voltage as we want.

He tells the men, "When I was young, our family visited relatives in Fort Erie, Canada and they took me and my cousins to a huge amusement park called Crystal Beach. In the middle of the Magic Carpet Fun House building, there was this bench you sat on, and it triggered a small transformer or something and gave people a jolt that shot you right out of there!"

I tell him, "Okay Boom, put it together. We'll try it on the next bad guys we catch; just to see how well it works. Boom goes to work and in about three hours, he has the chair/bench ready to go. It was simple enough. He placed metal plating on the seat, back and arm rests; hooked up a transformer that will regulate the amount of juice he wants to zap our bad customers with. The bench could easily fit a couple of guys at a time.

While he was putting finishing touches on the chair with leather restraints, a couple of the men took care of cleaning out the chamber pots in each cage and readied them for the next residents.

Boom comes over to the room where we take turn sleeping to watch the perps. Happy Jack is there.

He says to him, "Hey Hap, would you like to give Old Sparky a test drive?"

"NO, I would NOT! The knock out dart was fun enough for me! When I woke up, I had a nasty headache. How about we just have the next inmates we get, test it? There's no need for one of us to suffer. That is, unless YOU'D like to give it a try, Boom."

With a laugh, he says, "No, not me! Thank you. My batteries are all charged up. But you Hap, you look like you could use a little boost. You've been looking a little sluggish lately."

"Not funny, Boom! Let's just wait until we get new guinea-pigs that could use a little spark in their life.

Chapter 19

Eh-Jax follows up on Jake "The Snake" Toolie's progress

Three days later, around 3pm, Eh-Jax heads over to the bad neighbor's street and walks up to a man working in his front yard. He introduces himself and asks about the house across the street; the one next to Jake Toolie's house that's for sale. He tells him that he's interested in buying it. He asks how the neighbors are.

The man looks up at Eh-Jax, grins - and says, "If you'd come to me a few days ago, I would have told you to not bother even looking at that house; the man in the house next to it was a real piece of work! I say was, because all of a sudden, he changed overnight! It seems that he got 'religion' or something. Three days ago, he came out, talked to all the neighbors and apologized for his foul language, insults, and over all bad behavior. This guy swore like a trooper and constantly taunted the family next door; always yelling at kids playing in the street or near his house. He'd give dirty looks to anyone passing by. Today, he's a model citizen. I don't know what happened, but I'm glad he changed. Tell you what. People around here were just about to take care of this problem the old fashion way, if you know what I mean."

"WOW," says Eh-Jax. He was that bad, and now, he's completely changed, you say."

"Yep! He's completely changed. I haven't heard a bad word out of him. I saw him cleaning up his entire yard with four or five teenagers, perhaps, his nephews. His appearance is even better. He used to walk around like a bum; wearing raggedy clothes, unshaven with his hair all scraggly. He was just one of those people who had no self-respect and no respect for others around him. He was a white trash, low life! I'm glad for the neighborhood that he decided to change."

Eh-Jax thanks the man for talking to him and gets in his car. As he leaves, he looks back at the house to see all the work Jake did. He smiles and thinks to himself, *"It just goes to show what a bit of persuasion can do to make people change their behavior. So much for using kind, soft words to get people motivated. Jake needed an old fashion attitude adjustment. There was no need for multiple chats with a social worker or sessions with a psychologist. We did it in one fell swoop! He's cured. We done good! Now, let's hope he doesn't relapse."*

Chapter 20

Bad boss mistreating his workers

A couple of days after checking up on Jake and his behavior, Lenny comes in and tells us that his wife Denise's CEO boss at an electronics company is mistreating all of his employees and making inappropriate advances to young females in the office. She says that the women reject his advances. It's been going for a long time. He's fifty and married. Len says Denise told him that her boss is overbearing and is making life miserable for the workers. She said that he fired seven plant workers in the last month; three of them were women.

She said, "He doesn't need a real good reason to get rid of a worker, he just tosses people out like they're garbage. One of the men he fired, Roger Rundell, was with the company for eighteen years and got canned because he took three days off. The poor guy worked two days sick as a dog then took the three days off because he could barely stand on his feet. He was vomiting and nearly passed out last Tuesday afternoon."

Len says the idiot's name is Rudy Sacks and that he has a picture of him from his wife's cell phone. He printed a photo of him to show us. According to Denise, he gets to the company a little before 9 am and usually leaves at 6 or 7 pm. He drives a burgundy BMW that is worth about $300,000!

I ask Clint if he'd do a little surveillance to see if he goes anywhere after work for a cocktail. He agrees and plans on checking him out today. It's a quarter to six. Clint makes his way to observe Rudy. He parks his car outside the gates of the company to wait for him. He sees Sacks get in his car. He's about five foot ten, 200 pounds and slightly balding. He drives past the gate and heads for the gentlemen's club on Smith Street. It's seven-thirty when he arrives. Clint goes in and sits way over at the other end of the bar to observe this cockroach. He sees him talking to a few men and notices that he gets out of line with the young cocktail waitress serving them. That's a sure sign he's in the habit of having his way with the ladies.

Around quarter to nine, Clint notices that Rudy is getting ready to leave. He's near the door and goes out quickly in order to get to his own car before Rudy reaches his. He follows him home. Our new target lives in a very nice gated community. This tells Clint that we'll have to get to him before he reaches home. With that bit of information, he heads home and calls me to say what we'll need to do. We plan on getting this malfeasant tomorrow night.

Chapter 21

Young thugs at a delicatessen

On his way home, Clint needs to stop at a corner delicatessen to pick up milk, bread and a six pack of Molson Ale. As he nears the store, he notices a group of teens, between fifteen and eighteen-year-olds bothering a young girl (Sandy) as she walks by with her mother (Mrs. Annie Lewis). One young punk, Pete, is bold enough to grab the girl's butt. She turns around and slaps him in the face.

As she tries to give him a second slap, he blocks it and tells her, "Back off bitch before I slap you silly!"

Her mother sharply chastises him. The guys all laugh and Tommy, who seems to be the leader, says, "Shut up and take your little whore home where she belongs!"

The guys laugh again and the mother approaches him. She's eye to eye with him and says, "Tommy Sanders! You need to apologize to my daughter and to me! How can you THINK that it's okay for Pete to do what he just did and for you to say what you said to me? You're nothing but trash, the both of you!"

This bold punk's response; "Just shut up and go home you old broad! I don't want to hear you preaching at me, especially since your little whore got knocked up by Jerry Bogart last year."

Annie is livid! "Why you insensitive little worm! You're a real low life for saying something like that! You think your family is better, right? How about your older sister who is strung out on drugs and sells herself to take care of her habit? Don't you dare attack my daughter that way, you bastard! You got dirt in your own family!"

With that said, all the guys in the group say, "Wooooo!" in unison, as a way to say to Tommy, "She got you really good, dude!"

That really fires him up and says to her, "You need to shut your mouth before you get hurt, old lady!"

"What? You're going to hit me, Tommy?" You're that much of a low life that you'd beat up an old woman? GO AHEAD tough guy! DO IT! I DARE YOU!"

Tommy shoves her and tells her, "Just go home!" He turns away from her. She glares at the group, takes her daughter by the hand and walks away. Sandy is completely distraught and in tears.

Mom moves her along and says, "Come on sweetie. They're idiots with no brains. Someday, someone's gonna make them pay for being such rotten morons!"

Clint thinks, *"What can we do to these boys to get them to show respect to people? What this Tommy did was really stupid! He needs to be taught a lesson; him, as well as the other idiots he's with. Now, here's a case of 'group mentality' behavior. One guy starts something and the rest join in. I'm sure a couple of the boys didn't approve of what Tommy did, but, none of them objected to the cruel words he unloaded on the mother and her daughter. The question is, how do we straighten out a group of five all at the same time? I need to call the men and see if we can't take care of this tonight if these little hoodlums are still here."*

He watched the whole thing from his car across the street. The lads have no idea he saw and heard everything. He calls me to let me know where he is and what happened; that we need to get the guys together ASAP! It is nine forty-five now and he'd like to get them all before anyone leaves to go home. I tell him that we'll be there in about fifteen minutes or so. He tells me that he needs to move his car around the corner and park about ten houses down from the corner.

The car is positioned so he can look directly at the delicatessen. He still has on his disguise and makes his way to the store. The boys are blocking the entranceway. Clint is nearly six feet tall and most of the boys are almost his height or a bit shorter.

He gets near the group and says, "Excuse me, can I get through, please?"

All the boys move over a bit, except one. Six foot-two Richie doesn't budge an inch. Clint grabs him by both shoulders and moves him, gently, but firmly.

The teen has the nerve to tell him, "Hey man! Don't you touch me! Who do you think you are messing with me like that?"

"I'm sorry! I mean no disrespect, son. I politely asked to get through and you didn't move. I just needed to get by and you were blocking the door."

All the other guys are looking at him with their game-face on. You know, that tough-guy look, like two boxers facing off before the fight.

Richie is still uptight and says, "Who do you think you are? You got no right to handle me that way, man! I WAS gonna move!"

Clint apologizes again and goes in the store to get his things. While he's in there, the elderly owner, Salvator Marini, who is hidden from view, talks to him and tells him that those boys are constantly harassing people and blocking his doorway, and that people have to fight their way in and out.

He tells Clint, "My customers feel threatened every time they come to my store when those boys are out there! They have no respect! They pushed an old man around the other night and slapped another in the face a week ago when he asked them to move so he could get by. They're bad guys! They have no morals, no manners and respect nothing and no one."

"Have you called the cops? Clint asks.

"I've done that in the past. They come by and tell them to move along. They do, and then come back ten minutes later. I can't keep calling every ten minutes and they certainly don't want to be bothered coming back over and over again to get them to stay away. I've lost a lot of business because of these guys. I have no proof, but I'm sure it was them that broke my windows a year ago after I closed up one night. Hey, I've been here for thirty years, way before they were born. It's not fair that I have to live this way! I don't know what to do any more. This used to be such a great neighborhood. Not anymore. It's been going downhill for the last ten to fifteen years. I sure wish something could be done to fix this problem."

Clint pays for his groceries and tells the man, "Hang in there, sir. Things will change." He walks out of the store. The boys are all standing there, still, with their *game-face* on. They're blocking the doorway, again!

He tells them, "Hey guys, I really don't want any trouble. I just want to go home. Can I get through... please?"

They don't move and Clint asks again, "Can I get through?"

Tommy says, "Yah! We'll let you through, but if we ever see you around here again old man, you're going to get hurt! Dig it?!"

They make a small path. Clint needs to bump each punk to get through. He walks across the street and heads toward where he parked his car. As he fades into a dark area to a point where the boys can't see him and calls me to say where he'll be.

He says, "I'm hidden behind a tree ten houses from the corner on Stevenson. You'll see my car. I'll be waiting"

The wait isn't too long. We arrive within fifteen minutes after I hung up with Clint. Me and the other men make our way to where he is. We're all equipped with stun guns and ready to *"rock and roll."* The plan is to have Clint go to the corner and taunt the boys so they'll come after him.

He goes there and gets their attention by staring at them and wearing a smile that says, "Come and get me, punks!"

Richie sees him and tells the others, "Hey, hey, check it out! Look who's back! It's the old man who needs a beating." He yells across the street. "Hey old guy, do you want us to bust you up? You better be on your way before we come over there and take you down dude!"

He says, "I just want to memorize your faces so me and my boy can come back and kick your asses!"

That did it! Here they come! Clint turns and jogs toward the spot where the rest of us are waiting. As they get near, Clint stops and turns toward the punk that's closest to him, stun gun in hand, and zaps him. The rest of us are only a few feet from him, we swarm them and each man has his own target. All of a sudden, there's a series of zaps from the guns! Almost simultaneously, they're all hit and go down. We got us another fine catch.

Hap drove the van with Bull and Eh-Jax on board. The other men drove their own cars. We figure we can't take them all, but we can take at least three of the five boys. We take Tommy, Richie, and Pete for sure and leave the other two punks. We move them aside and prop them up against a tree and duct tape them to it. It'll be a trip for them when they come out of it to find the others gone - vanished!

Okay! It went smoothly and we have three little maggots in need of a lesson on how to be human beings. It's 10 pm. We're on our way to the warehouse. Hap notifies Officer Shawn at home to tell him about three young men from the neighborhood won't be home tonight; that they went to a "pajama party." That's all he tells him. Shawn understands.

We get to home base and unload our captives. All the boys are blindfolded, mouth and hands taped. We march them to the interrogation room and sit them down. We place Tommy and Richie on the metal bench so "Sparky" can do its job in a little while. We secure Pete to a regular chair. He was one of the guys who grabbed the girl's behind. That's why he was taken along.

Richie was the one who wouldn't move for Clint as he went into the Deli, and Tommy, well Tommy's the one who went way over the top with Mrs. Lewis and her daughter. He has the, *"engaging mouth before brain,"* problem. We're going to fix that.

I walk up to Tommy and Richie sitting on the bench and give each one a not too heavy backhand across the face.

I say to them, "Howdy tough guys! How are you? I'll bet you never dreamt you'd find yourself in a place like this, uh? Don't you just feel so helpless right now like the people you harassed and taunted every night in front of Mr. Marini's delicatessen? What? Do you guys think you own that piece of the street? Is that what you call, *your turf*? You are morons who need to be taught a lesson in proper behavior, respect and common sense. Surely your parents didn't raise you to be STUPID!" That's YOUR choice; a very, very bad choice."

All three get a backhand. They're all crying and looking real scared.

Hap has their IDs and cell phones. He tells us. "Gentlemen, we have here, Tommy Sanders from Orchard Ave., Richie Morrison from Archer Street and Pete Durkin from Benson Street. Boys, you're in for a bad night for the way you've been traumatizing people around here."

Hap, Len and Clint take the tape off their mouth and the group mentality kicks in. Almost in unison and weepy voices they say, "We're sorry! We're sorry! Please don't hurt us."

Eh-Jax says to them, "Boys, you're way too late to say you're sorry. You're sorry because we have you, not because of what you've been doing to the good people in the neighborhood. You want to be bad boys, tough guys? Okay! We'll treat you like bad boys and then we'll see if we can't make you change your mind about treating people better."

I motion Clint to turn up Sparky to 20 volts. He does, and the two lads tense up and scream like death has come to get them. Pete Durkin sitting in the regular chair hears the screams and breaks down and cries. He doesn't know what we're doing to his buddies, but he knows they're in a world of hurt and that he's next.

Boom says to the two who just got zapped. "You didn't like that, did you boys? That's too bad, because you're going for another ride."

Clint turns Sparky on again for a couple of seconds. It seems a lot longer. The boys' bodies tense up again and they scream even louder this time. Pete is going nuts not knowing what we're doing to his pals. His turn is coming for at least one Sparky session. We want to make sure the two leaders of this *little rascals* group get the worst punishment. We take Tommy and Richie off the bench and put Pete there. We give him his turn in the *hot seat* for two seconds also. He mentally goes through the ceiling and screams like a girl in a very high shrill that could break glass. When the session is over, he's breathing very rapidly; like he just ran a mile. I guess it took his breath away. While Pete is regaining his composure, Tommy and Richie are both in tears and fear they're going to get more of Sparky.

After the effect subsides, Pete just sits there weeping like a child and says, "Please don't do that again! I beg you please!!! No more, no more! Please! I swear on my mother's life that I will never stand in front of that store! I promise! Please don't hurt me anymore. It hurts bad! Please don't hurt me, don't hurt me! I beg you!

I believe blind people are much more perceptive than people who can see. They don't have all the visual distractions. This frees their mind to use other senses more and more. In the case of the boys being blindfolded, maybe it'll open up the common-sense area of their brains. Just maybe, they'll realize the errors of their ways. I'm sure the pain we gave them was a real attention-getter. Being in the situation they're in, the hope is that they'll straighten out when we release them. It'll be interesting to see the result of their time here.

I step in and tell all three boys, "We're going to let you go, but if you EVER bother that storekeeper or any of his customers or people passing by, we will bring you back here, beat you first, then, put you back in this electric chair till you catch fire! What's more, you three and the other two morons who were with you tonight WILL go and apologize to Mr. Marini and any of his customers you've either insulted or assaulted. And, you will tell him that from now on you will guard his store. If any other idiots want to make the front of his store a 'hang-out,' it will be your job to not let that happen."

Hap adds, "Also, if you're hanging around the front of the deli and elderly folks want to shop there, it'd be really nice if you opened the door for them. And, since you have nothing better to do with your time than just hang around, we'd like for you to make sure you wash his windows once a week. What do you say?"

Pretty much in unison, they all say, "Yes, we'll do that."

I come back and tell them. "One more thing you BETTER do! Go to Mrs. Lewis' house and apologize to her and her daughter Sandy. It'd better be a sincere apology. We're going to check up on you to make sure you've done all that I told you to do. I want you to remember that we have your I.D.'s and cell phones. We'll keep them and make copies of your I.D.'s. In about a week, we'll mail your stuff back to you. Big warning guys! Don't fail in what we told you to do! You've proven you can be complete asses, now; prove that you can be the kind of good sons your parents would be proud of."

I motion the men to tape their mouth and take them away. The same team that brought them to our little *rehab center* will take them near the place we picked them up and let 'em go.

The men get to the neighborhood and park the van. Their boys' hands are duct taped in front. This way, they'll be able to undo the tape that's wrapped around their eyes. Once they can see, they can help each other un-tape their hands. Too bad for them, the duct tape that's stuck to their hair is going to be an added punishment. That stuff is really sticky. I imagine they'll lose a lot of hair. I'd love to be there to watch it all. We'll follow up with a phone call to Mr. Marini, Mrs. Lewis and her daughter Sandy in a couple of days.

Chapter 22

Plans to Get CEO Rudy Shacks and Captain Mendola's inquiry

It's Friday night and the decision has been made to capture our abusive CEO, Rudy Sacks. According to Lenny's wife Denise, it's his habit of finishing the work week at his favorite bar, the one Clint followed him to. She said that he works a bit late on Fridays then goes to the bar and spends a fair amount of time before heading home. We figured we'd run the same scam on him that we did with our wife and child beater, Freddy, you know, doing a fake fender bender thing to get him out to the parking lot.

Boom would have that *executive* look if he put on a suit and tie. I ask him if he's up to it. He agrees, goes home to dress up then makes his way to Rudy's factory to wait for him to leave his office.

Meanwhile, back at the station, Captain Mendola is still wondering who's been playing cop and prosecutor for the recent batch of bad guys they've brought in. He's very intrigued and would like to talk to one of them. He puts out the word once again to the officers at the station by saying…

"I'm asking again; if anyone of you has any idea who's doing this vigilante work, let me know. You can slip me an anonymous note if you want. That way, you won't have to show yourself.

I just want to talk to whoever it is that's doing this. Maybe we can combine forces. I'd appreciate your cooperation. Be safe out there."

Sergeant O'Rourke calls Happy Jack after his shift and tells him what his captain said.

Hap asks him, "Is he looking to arrest the men doing this or does he just want to talk?"

"I don't for sure Hap! But, if I were to guess, knowing him like I do, he probably just wants to talk. He'll be working tomorrow night (Saturday). He likes to work that schedule because of the elevated criminal activity happening on weekends."

"Okay Shawn, I'll pass along the info you gave me and we'll see if they'll contact him."

Hap tells me about the conversation he had with the Sergeant. I tell him that I'd call Mendola tomorrow night.

I tell the guys, "I knew that it was just a matter of time before we'd have to talk to someone in charge at the station. We're at that point. I'll let y'all know how it goes."

Time to sack, Sacks

Now, it's time to snag our CEO. Boom calls me to let me know that he's in place and that the rest of the team should get over to the bar to do their part. I get the men rolling. Hap, Bull and Eh-Jax go together. Lenny takes his car so he can use it to back it into CEO Sack's car to create the scam to get him out to the parking lot. It's all set.

Boom sees Sacks leave his office and get into his car. He follows him to the bar and lets the perp go in first. After about ten minutes, he goes in wearing a disguise; tinted glasses, and seventies-like mustache and goatee.

He makes his way toward him; Sacks has his back to him. He taps him on the shoulder, Rudy turns and Boom says to him, "Hey man! They told me you drive a grey Beemer, is that right?"

A bit annoyed that this character from the 70s is interrupting his cocktail hour, he says to him in a snobbish tone...

"Yah! Why?"

"I'm really sorry, man! I was backing up in the parking lot and creased your car door on the driver's side. I didn't want to just leave you a note, so I came in and asked who owns the Beemer. They pointed to you. I wanted to do the right thing. Let's go out and we'll exchange insurance information. I'm really, really sorry, man!"

Rudy's looking really upset and angry that his "big boy toy" got damaged. He's also real perturbed that he's got to deal with something like this on his night out.

He asks Boom, "How in the hell did you do this? What's the matter with you? Don't you know how to drive? There better not be a lot of damage! Do you know how much that car cost me? It was specially made! People like you shouldn't have a license. You must be some kind of idiot, man!"

Boom apologizes and just lets him rant. He knows he's going to get his chance to humble this jerk. They go out to the parking lot. Lenny put a nice crease in the BMW's door. He backed it in just enough to push in the larger part of his door a bit.

The two get to the cars and are looking at damage. Rudy gets in the passenger side to get to his glove box to dig up his registration and insurance card. As he bends over to open the glove box, Boom zaps him with the stun gun. He's down. The men in the van pull up quickly, scoop him up and toss him in. Bull and Eh-Jax do the usual securing bit; blindfold with duct tape and secure his hands, feet and mouth. Len gets his car keys. Off they go to the Big House. One more rat to deal with. This one is going to be different. He's got money and is educated; educated yes, but an idiot at the same time. It's interesting how some educated people can be so dumb!

Lenny moves Beemer down the street to hide it while they take their catch to our holding center. Before he leaves, he places a tracer and another device under the car to be used later; in case we need to make a LOUD impression on this weasel. He thinks he's got damage now, but if it becomes necessary to deal with him again, his precious car will go - BOOM! …compliments of one of Boom's explosive concoctions.

He makes his way back to his own car and heads for the warehouse so he can join the others in straightening out the big shot looser.

On the way to the warehouse, Rudy comes to and is beyond freaked out. This is his worst nightmare. Actually, not yet! Wait till he gets the special treatment in the interrogation room. Then, he'll go right out of his mind! Oh, this is going to be a real pleasure straightening this guy out. Way too many big shots have this air of superiority that make them think of themselves as though they're extra special; above the rest. Old Sacks is about to get humbled.

They reach home base and take their catch to the room. He's strapped in, still has tape over his mouth and of course, he's been fitted with our unique shocking blindfold helmet as well.

Boom has a need to take the first shot at him since he was the one that Shacks chewed out in the bar about the accident. He lays one right across his mouth. As it happened to the other boys, Rudy's lips are bleeding and he too, finds himself tasting blood. It's a pretty gross experience for Mr. Upper Crust. Too bad!

Bull takes the tape off his mouth and tells him, "Listen carefully! Don't talk until you're asked a question, Rudy!"

With the tape off, wouldn't you know it, right away, this educated fool wants answers.

"Why did you guys abduct me? Is it money you want? I'm rich and can give you money."

Bull cuts him off by laying a heavy slap across the face and says, "Weren't you told not to talk until you were asked a question? DON'T TALK!"

Lenny steps in and begins to let him know why he finds himself in the situation he's in.

"Rudy, we have your wallet with all your identification and we also have your cell phone. So, we know where you live and for sure, we know where your company is. We know you're married. The reason we have your pompous ass here is because you shouldn't be allowed to lead a company where you treat your workers like crap. And, you think that being a CEO of a large company gives you the right to intimidate and abuse certain women and other workers in your employment. You're a weasel!"

Clint is near Sparky. I motion for him to light him up a bit. He turns it on for two seconds and Rudy grits his teeth and does his best to muffle a scream! But, he can't, he screams like a man that just dropped a fifty-pound weight on his toe! After the power is turned off, he sits there breathing heavy and looking very angry that, that was done to him. He doesn't say a word.

I say to him, "We don't want any of your money. Our job is to straighten you out. You have a very bad attitude toward people in your employment and we mean to change the way you operate. If you don't change, we will get you back here and make you wish your mommy had never had you! Now then, we'll take you back to your car. You'll have to free yourself from the mouth gag and the blindfold of duct tape around your head. When you go to work on Monday, first thing you do is call Roger Rundell, apologize to him, and tell him he's got his job back. You will also make sure he gets back pay from the time you fired him up to now! Then, you will have a meeting with your office and plant workers so you can apologize to them. Oh, and those women you've been abusing and tormenting, you will give them a bonus of $5,000 each and will never disrespect them again. Do you understand?

"I understand. I promise, I understand! I'll do exactly as you said; to apologize and treat my all my workers right and the women in the office will each receive $5,000. I won't ever be abusive again. I promise. Don't hurt me anymore, please! I beg you, don't hurt me!"

Just to make sure our boy Rudy is really on board with what he has to do, I motion Clint to give him another dose. He gives it to him for another second and cuts the power. Rudy shakes like a leaf in high winds for about twenty seconds, then, his body settles down.

I tell him, "I know you didn't want any more pain, but do you have any idea the huge amount emotional pain and misery you've caused your hard-working employees? They're the ones who make your company productive and stable? They don't owe you anything you miserable twerp! Without good help, you wouldn't be as successful as you are. That second jolt you got was to make sure you 'get it!' GET IT?"

"I get it. I swear to you I'll do the right thing,"

"I hope so! We'll know very quickly if you do it or don't honor your promises. If I were you, I wouldn't screw up! Your wife might like to know how you've been behaving. Think divorce! Think alimony, and having to give your wife half of all you have - company and all! Just do the right thing and make a new beginning for yourself."

He says, "I promise I'll follow through. I promise!"

Hap and Eh-Jax take him back to his car and leave him there to untangle himself. Once that's done, Sacks goes home and makes plans to right the wrong he's done.

Chapter 23

Apologies to Mr. Marini and Mrs. Lewis

A few days after dealing with the three hoodlums that made the deli store owner's life a living hell, Boom makes a phone call to Mr. Marini to see if the lads came by to apologize and offer their services as "guardians" of the store.

He says, "Why yes! All the boys came in and apologized like you wouldn't believe. It was almost nauseating. You should have seen the way three of the boys shook as they made their apologies. It was a thing of beauty; especially the way that group has tormented me. Now, they're like angels. They open the door for my older customers, and, I can hardly believe it, they even washed my windows yesterday.

Whatever you said to them did the trick. It's simply amazing! One day they were little devils and the next, angels. I sure hope they stay that way. Thank you whoever you are. I owe you."

"You owe me nothing. It's was pleasure educating those boys on how to behave. I'll be keeping an eye on your store. If they get out of hand, I'll know. I have their addresses and phone numbers. Take care and God's best to you!"

"Thanks again for your help sir. You have no idea how relieved I am that I can run my business without fear every time I come in to work. God bless you! God bless you!"

Mrs. Lewis

Boom made another call to Mrs. Lewis to find out if all of those nasty boys made it over to her house to make things right, especially Tommy Sander, Richie Morrison, and Pete Durkin; the three who got to meet "Sparky." They were the ones who were the most abusive.

Mrs. Lewis says, "I don't know who you are or what you said to those boys, but they all came by yesterday like little gentlemen and sincerely apologized to me and my daughter. I was pleasantly amazed by the change in their attitudes and manners. They were all so evil when they insulted me and my daughter the other day. They promised to never disrespect either one of us again. Thank you so very much for talking to them."

"You are most welcome Mrs. Lewis. I wish you and Sandy God's best. Take care."

Chapter 24

Girlfriend Abuser

George Como

Okay! Mrs. Lewis and her daughter Sandy got the apologies and now, it was time to see about another idiot thug at the high school by the name of George Como who's been tormenting his ex- girlfriend Noëlle. She's sixteen and he's seventeen going on seven!

Along with Como's bullying, we also got word two young ladies at the same high school Como goes to have been doing their own bullying of a nice timid girl. Her name is Sherri Bloom. She's fifteen, pretty, very intelligent and outgoing. Apparently, the two bimbos, Peggy and Karen, feel that it's okay to pick on nice girls. They'll be getting a lesson soon.

Back to Como's case

First, we need to deal with Georgie Como. He used to verbally and physically abuse Noëlle while she went out with him for a while. She had the smarts to end the relationship before it got way out of hand. Now that she dumped his sorry butt, he won't leave her alone and is constantly harassing her with phone calls and tries to humiliate her in public. He's another young misguided soul in need of a lesson.

We found out that he likes to go by Noëlle's house in the dark of night between 9 and 10pm to see if any other guy is calling on her. The word is that he might be carrying a high-powered CO_2 pellet pistol. This makes things even more serious in dealing with him. We're going to act quickly on this. I suggest that we follow him tonight and see exactly what he does. Bull wants this creep. His own daughter had a similar problem with some punk. He fixed that by sending a couple of his friends to pay him a visit with a baseball bat. No more problems!

Bull goes out with Lenny to scout things out. Just as we were told, Georgie makes his way down Noëlle's street near 9:30 pm. He walks by slowly. The trees on that street create a cover that hides him well. He gets in the shadows, pauses in front of the house, and looks through the windows hoping to see her, and maybe, just maybe, another guy. He walks past her house and ducks into the neighbor's yard where he hides under a willow tree that acts as a canopy. He stays there for about a half hour then makes his way back home. Alright, tomorrow night will be "pain night" for Georgie.

The next night

Again, it's Bull and Lightning Lenny who make their way to snag the catch of the night, and deal with him on the spot. A third man, Clint, is acting as backup with a couple of M-80 firecrackers in case our guys need a distraction. They're wearing disguises and carrying a bat. Their plan is to hide near that willow tree, wait for Georgie to hide there, take him down with a stun gun, then bind his hands with zip-ties and duct tape his mouth and eyes. The men will have to be very careful to not make noise.

Here he comes! Bull and Lenny are in place. Clint isn't far away to do his part if need be. George does his routine, and just as predicted, he goes under the willow tree. A few seconds later, ZAP! He's down. The men secure his hands with zip-ties, duct tape his mouth and eyes. Bull takes his cell phone; he'll look through it later and find his phone number for future contact. He also has his wallet and takes his license. We have his address and guess what else? - Lenny finds a loaded pellet gun tucked in his belt. This boy having a pistol has the potential of causing someone serious pain.

He comes out of the shock from the stun gun. Once they feel he can understand what they need to say to him, Bull holds him down while Lenny gets really close to his ear and tells him in a quiet but stern whisper that he'd better never harass Noëlle or any other person again. He's told that he's never to walk by her house again or call her. Also, that he's to not even say a single word to her in school - EVER!

Len tells him, "We have your license and cell phone. In a few days, we'll mail your stuff back to you except the gun. We'll be keeping tabs on you and if we hear that you messed with her or her family at all, we will get to you and make you hurt really bad! Do you understand me?"

He's scared to death and shakes his head vigorously to signify, "yes!" He understands.

With the job done, Bull zaps him again and while he's in the state of shock, Len hits him with the bat on each shin to lump them up really good! Both men head for the van where Hap is waiting to take them home. Georgie still has the duct tape over his eyes and mouth. His shins aren't broken, but for sure, they're severely bruised. He might even have a slight fracture in one or both legs. He will have a very hard time walking for the next few days or so. That's a shame! He got a little of what he deserves. We were kind, actually.

As he comes to from the second round of being zapped, he wants to scream in pain but knows that if he does, even with the duct tape over his mouth, he'll be discovered by Noëlle's parents. While still in a sitting position under the tree, with a lot of effort, he's able to take the duct tape off his mouth. He has a really hard time undoing the tape around his eyes and head. He tears out a lot of hair in the process. He can't do anything with the zip ties binding his hands. He needs to get from where he is and figure out a way to free his hands.

He does his best to get to his feet and walks home. His shins are in terrible pain. He can barely walk. Now home, he goes in the garage where he finds a utility knife to cut off the zip-tie. It's a good thing his parents have gone to bed. He limps in quietly and heads to his room without his folks noticing. He goes to bed and lays there in agony. Sleep will not come tonight for this bully. There's "Karma" for you.

We're hoping to get a report in a few days from our source about Georgie's conduct concerning the *hands off Noëlle* policy. Then, we'll place a call and tell him that he's either in the clear, or, he should be afraid of more retribution for breaking the agreement.

A report on Georgie

A couple of days later, after school, we get the report about Georgie, his badly bruised shins and how he's behaving at school. The word is; he looked really humbled as he walked from class to class, he limped along the hallways. We're told that when he saw Noëlle coming toward him in the hall, he ducted into a classroom until she passed by so as to not take a chance of being seen near her. It looks like we have another goofball straightened out.

To make sure he knows that he's being watched, Bull makes a call to his cell. He tells him…

"We got word you behaved well today and are staying away from Noëlle. Good boy! Keep it up! If you screw up, we'll make sure both your legs will be casts for a long time! Remember, we've got people watching you."

Bull can hear George's voice shaking as he says, "No sir, I won't screw up."

The call ends by the lad saying, "I will stay away from Noëlle. I swear to God!"

Now that we know Georgie will be a good boy, we're pretty sure this *tune-up* of a bad boy will hold.

CHAPTER 25

Now, the other bullies

Peggy and Karen

On to the next task; high school bullies Peggy and Karen, who take pleasure in tormenting poor Sherri Bloom. They're not aware that what they're doing can lead to very serious emotional problems and things can turn incredible ugly. It can also lead to suicide. That's very scary, and very wrong! The question is; what can be done to straighten them out? Eh-Jax tells us that if we can isolate them somehow, we can put *"the fear of God in them."*

He says, "Hey guys, how about we 'tar and feather them? You think that'd be too harsh a punishment?"

Bull makes a face, gives him a quizzical look and says, "Eh-Jax! For real, man?! I'm sure you can get tar easy enough, but feathers?! Where the hell you gonna get feathers? I've never heard of anyone ever saying to me;

'You know what, I gotta get me some feathers so I can tar and feather this feller that's been giving me a lot grief.'

Boom says, "Eh-Jax, you gotta double up on your meds, man! You're too radical!"

All the guys roar with laughter!

To keep the shenanigans going, with a smile on his face, Hap says, "Hey, I know a farmer in Eden that's got him a chicken

farm. He plucks his own birds and has a ton of feathers for anyone that wants 'em. And, I have a friend who works at the tar pit
in Lancaster where we can get us a nice bucket of tar."

Eh-Jax just sits there smirking at his pals sling zingers at
him. He says, "Well, well, well, aren't you guys so special the
way you beat down one of your own."

They all bust out laughing again and Eh-Jax can't help but
crack up himself. Oh, the camaraderie!

At this point, before things really get out of hand, I jump in and
get everyone back to earth.

I tell the men, "Although it would be very interesting to tar
and feather these two wayward young ladies, I don't see that as
the way to go. We have to come up with something that won't
have us go overboard. In anything people do to rectify problems of this sort, there's always that 'fine line' that shouldn't be
crossed. We have to remember that they're young teenage girls
who should know better than to bully people, but don't. They're
just a bit dumb. We'll have to think of a sensible but sure way to
impress them that it's wrong to treat folks that way.

The next question is; where can we isolate the girls so we can
deal with them? According to Boom's source who was talking to
him about the bullying, the girls go to a nearby park to drink beer
and smoke grass on weekend nights. That's where we'll need to
be.

Being that today is Wednesday, we have a couple of days to
make our plan and take a walk in that park to see where the girls
will most likely be. Hap and Eh-Jax say they'll go check it out.

At dusk, they make their way to the place they were told the
kids party. As they walk through the area, they notice beer cans
and lots of cigarette butts on the ground. They also see discarded
empty plastic bags; those used to hold marijuana and cigarette
paper for rolling joints. They figure that this must be the spot
where the teens come to do, *their thing.* It's very secluded and
dark. Just a few feet away from that area are bushes that would
be perfect to hide behind to wait for their targets. For now, the

men can pretty much take the night off to rest. Tomorrow at the warehouse, we'll plan exactly what we'll do with the girls.

Chapter 26

Lenny reports on CEO Sacks

A bit after the meeting about the two bullies, Lenny calls me to give a report about our playboy CEO, Rudy Sacks. He tells me his wife Denise told him that yesterday, Rudy made good on his promise to the people at his company. He went on the plant P.A. to apologize to all of the employees for the way he's been treating many of them. He also requested that the office ladies who were mistreated or offended by him come to his office so he could talk to them face to face. As it turns out, he made sincere apologies; handed each one a $5,000 check and told them that he would be a different boss from now on.

Len tells me, "Hey Boss. That makes me feel like we're making a difference in some people's lives. It's a good feeling. Let's keep on keepin' on!"

"Yes Lenny. We are making a difference. It's all good and we'll surely keep on keepin' on my friend!"

Chapter 27

Peggy and Karen bullies (part 2)

F riday night is here and it's time for a social lesson; "People Skills 101." We meet at the warehouse and gather up our two-way communication gear and make our way to the park. Once there, we hang back until we get word that the girls are on the move toward the park.

It's now 9:00 pm and dark outside. Me and Boom, wearing transparent masks, make our way to the area of the park where the party site is located and disperse so that we can surround the girls. After about fifteen minutes of waiting, they arrive and go to the party spot. Each one has a can of beer in her hand. We watch for the right moment to move in. As they sip their beer, Peggy pulls out a joint and lights it. Boom and I sneak up on them from behind; I grab Peggy and Boom has Karen. Immediately, we put a hand over their mouth so they can't scream. They're told to not make a sound and they won't get hurt. They're frozen with fear; both are hysterical, but cooperate. Quickly, Eh-Jax steps in and duct tapes their eyes and mouth, and sit them on the ground.

Even with their mouths taped, we can hear them crying and see them shaking like leaves in the wind. We can imagine them thinking...

"They're going to rape us and then kill us!"

And, along with that, they're probably reaching way down in their souls praying for God to help them. Understandably, their fear is extreme and maddening at this point. They don't know what's next.

Boom tells them in a soft and caring voice; "Girls, I want you to calm down and listen very, very carefully. First of all, we're not going to harm you. You just need to listen to what I have to say and then do what I tell you to do, okay?"

Peg and Karen do their best to get control of their emotions and nod to signify they're ready to hear what I'm about to say.

Just looking at them, they don't look very intimidating, just typical teenage girls that you wouldn't think could do what they did to Sherry Bloom. Well, they did and we have them. Now, it's time to straighten out their heads and hopefully get them turned from the - *dark side*.

As usual, with all of our detainees, we get their cell phones and look for personal IDs. Only Peggy is carrying a driver's license. Obviously, she's at least sixteen. Although we'd like IDs on both girls, this will do. Looks like Peggy will be our contact person if we need to take this matter any further.

I say to them, "The reason you've been targeted for this is because you are bullies and have done something terribly wrong to one of your classmates. I'm sure your parents didn't raise you to be like this. You chose to be bad girls. Now, we're bullying you. How does that feel? Not good, right? How would you like to be picked on the way you pick on Sherry Bloom? Think hard about all the times you made her suffer; not only at the moments you attacked her, but even at night when she couldn't go to sleep because she knew she had to be confronted by you each and every day! It got so bad that she wanted to drop out of school and has even contemplated suicide! This is really serious, girls! Your behavior toward an innocent girl has been criminal!"

As they heard what I had to say so far, both girls are now weeping in a remorseful way. I think we made the right impression on them. I surely hope so.

I tell them, "Here's what you'll do. You will go home and tell your parents about the bullying you've done, but you won't tell them anything that happened here tonight. Most importantly, you'll need to apologize and be a friend to Sherri. She has nothing to do with what we did to you tonight. Another school mate of hers gave us all the information. So, don't even attempt to implicate her! If you do, remember, we know who you are and where you live. You don't want to know what we'll do to you next time if you don't follow through. Do you understand?"

They both quickly nod their head to show they understand. The men set them on their feet and are told to count of fifty before taking the tape off their mouth and eyes. The men fade into the darkness. Both crying and still shaking. That will pass soon enough. After they count to fifty, Karen is the first to remove the tape from her mouth, and then, her eyes. Peggy is really freaked out and can't find the edge of the tape to remove it. Karen helps her and finally manages to get her freed. They're still shaking. This is the most traumatic thing they've ever experienced. They hold on to each other and just weep. After a few minutes, they make their way home.

It's 9:50. Peggy gets home first and enters the house through the side door and goes upstairs to her bedroom. She needs to get herself calmed down before telling her parents what she needs to tell them.

Her mom yells up to her, "It's about time you got home. You still have the dishes to wash."

Peggy yells back, I'll be down in a little bit. I need to do a few things in my room first."

She sits on her bed and tries to figure out how she'll tell her folks about her and Karen bullying one of their classmates. It takes her a while to get up the nerve and have the right words to say. After about a half hour, she's ready. She makes her way down stairs, approaches the living room looking pitiful, and stands there quietly. Her mom can see that something is wrong.

"Okay." She says, "What's wrong? What have you got on your mind?"

Her dad can also see that something isn't right. He shuts off the TV and waits for her to speak.

She begins, "Mom, dad, I need to tell you something I did that's very bad. Karen and me have been bullying this girl Sherry Bloom for a long time at school and caused her a lot of pain. I just need to tell you that someone made me see how terrible that is and that I needed to tell you about it. I'm sorry! I won't do it again, I promise. What Karen and I did is wrong. We'll apologize to Sherry and somehow make it up to her for all the terrible things we did."

Her mom frowns at the fact that her daughter stooped so low as to bully one of her classmates and says,

"It makes me really sad you did that, but I'm glad you share this with us. We appreciate it, and I'm sure it'll never happen again, right?"

"It won't. I promise you guys, it won't."

Her father says, "As a dad, this is very disappointing to me, Peggy. I didn't raise you to be like that. You're still the little girl that I love very much. You have to know that as my daughter, part of your job is to do things that make me proud of you. Okay! I believe you're sorry and that you'll do the right thing going forward. In doing that, you'll do your mom and me proud! Your mom and I love you want the best for you."

She says, "Again, mom, dad, I'm so sorry for disappointing you. Thanks for understanding. I love you both."

She hugs them both, leaves the room and walks to the kitchen to do her chores.

As for Karen, she too told her parents pretty much what Peggy told hers. They were very disappointed and told her to make things right with Sherri on Monday, or else! Karen promised them that she would apologize to the girl and do her best to befriend her.

The reconcile

The weekend is over and on Monday, the report comes back that both Karen and Peggy did the right thing. They found Sherri Bloom outside the school building; approached her and Peggy spoke for herself and Karen.

She said, "Sherri, we want to apologize for the terrible things we said to you and incredible pain we caused you. Please forgive us. We were wrong and won't do it ever again. Forgive us for doing so wrong."

Sherri broke down and wept. Both girls took turns hugging her to console her. As they did that, they too cried. To show Sherri they were sincere and wanted her friendship, they asked her if she'd go to the school's football game with them this coming Friday. She accepted.

Another situation rectified. That's always a good feeling. It's strange, but some people need to be taught a lesson, regardless of age or social status. Like Boom, I feel good knowing we are making a difference.

Chapter 28

Jerry Mack, and an Order of Protection

We had taken care of two bully situations, but the neighborhood still has a lot of other ugly situations that could use our intervention. For instance, Hap got another tip from his cop buddy Shawn about some creep who has an "Order of Protection" against him with regards to his former girlfriend; that she's reported him to the police at least fifteen times. Shawn tells him that she's a twenty-five-year-old young lady named Jane Spears. And, the punk that's tormenting her is Jerry Mack. He's made her life miserable. He has beaten her many times and had a strangle hold on her life for two years. She couldn't leave the house without him knowing where she was going and with whom. He treated her like a dog.

This is what we talked about before; *cockroaches in the neighborhood making life hell for good people.* Jane doesn't have any good days. This miscreant, Jerry, sees to it that she doesn't. He makes her life as miserable as he can. He won't stay away; and by doing that, he's violating the Court Order.

He's sneaky and bold at the same time. Example! He knows her routine and he'll purposely follow her to the supermarket and makes sure that he checks out at the same time at the checkout counter next to her. The question here is; should he be able to go to the same grocery store where she shops? Of course! But if he should find himself in the same line his ex-girlfriend is in, does the law say he has to move to another line; distancing himself from her? That's where the order of protection might have gray areas. The jerk also has one of those cell phones you can't trace. He makes phone calls to her house and hangs up as soon as he hears her voice. He does this on a daily basis. Jane is at her wits end. She doesn't know what to do. It's time to get this fool and wise him up!

Hap gave us the details as to where he works, where he lives and where he goes out to have a few drinks with his buddies and hopefully meet women. He thinks he's some kind of Casanova! He's just a goofy guy who is delusional. He hangs out at a bar called Molly's Place and is there most nights; a typical booze-hound. We'll be there tomorrow night to observe him and if the conditions are right, we'll bag him.

Time to rock-a-bye Jerry

At nine-thirty Tuesday night, Jerry finds a spot in Molly's lot and makes sure he's in a safe parking space for his tricked-out Mustang. He loves that car more than life itself. He sees to it that it's parked on an angle so no one else is able to put their car too close to his. Old Jerry fears somebody will pull next to his car and when they open the door, they'll put dings or chip the paint on his precious baby.

Hap, Clint, me and Eh-Jax are waiting patiently to make our move. We're all in disguises. Hap and Clint are in the van, I'm with Eh-Jax in his car. It's time! Just as our goof-ball is parking, Eh-Jax backs up and bumps his back fender. He puts it in park and gets out to deal with the situation.

As expected, Jerry goes ballistic and begins screaming and spews out all sorts of profanities.

He tells Eh-Jax, "Look at what you did to my car! I can't believe this, man! Do you know how expensive this car is?! Are you STUPID, man! I ought to kick your ass."

Jerry is about six foot two and Eh-Jax, five ten. He makes like he's cowering to the loud mouth man-child and tries to calm him down. As Jerry goes on ragging on Eh-Jax about the accident, I get out of the car to join in the conversation.

I tell Jerry, "You need to calm down! It was an accident. It's not like he did this on purpose, you know! We don't need to have this minor fender bender escalate into something you might be sorry for. Just exchange IDs, car insurance information, and let the insurance companies handle the details."

With a very bad attitude, Jerry says, "I'll get my papers, and you, you do the same!"

He sticks a stiff finger in Eh-Jax's chest, poking him hard and says, "You really ruined a good night, man! I'd love to kick your butt and ruin your night, too!"

Eh-Jax says to him, "Again, I'm sorry. I don't want any trouble. Let's just exchange information and be on our way, okay?"

Jerry is still fuming. As he turns to go into his car for his papers, I motion for Hap to pull the van near the scene. He positions it so that when we tag this punk, it'll be easy loading him in.

Clint gets out of the van and says to Jerry, "Hey, dude, we saw the accident from across the street. If you need witnesses, we got your back, man."

Just when Jerry starts to respond to that, ZAP! He's hit with a stun gun and goes down. We load him into the van and secure him like all the other fish we caught so far. We get his wallet and cell phone and make our way to the warehouse to process yet another "dirt bag."

Jerry slowly comes to and Clint tells him to relax and not get rowdy. He's freaked out and the survival instinct in him or something makes him go wild. He can't see or speak and it makes him go crazy. Clint hits him with another dose of the stun gun. He tenses up from the jolt and goes limp.

After he comes out of the chock, Clint tells; "If you want to get crazy, we'll just zap you over and over again until you settle down."

He doesn't make a move. I guess the second jolt really got his attention.

Hap arrives at the warehouse and the men bring Jerry directly to the interrogation room. Boom takes the tape off his mouth, and Jerry, breathing like he's hyper ventilating, asks, "What do you want from me?"

Before he can say another word, BAM! BAM! Clint gives him a couple of hefty back hands; one on each side of the face. And, Len gives him another right on the mouth. His upper lip is bleeding.

Lenny says, "What we want from you is for you to wise up! You're an idiot who needs to learn the meaning of, *Court Order of Protection*! You were told to stay away from Jane Spears and you thought that court order didn't really mean what it said. That makes you a super idiot! Now look at you! How do you feel, us having you here, bound, blindfolded and beat up? It doesn't feel good, does it? Your unwillingness to follow the law put you here.

Len looks at me and nods towards Sparky. I signal Clint to turn it on. Jerry gets the usual two second dose. He screams; tenses up, and convulses wildly.

I say to him, "How would you like to get this every day for a week, or for a longer period of time; let's say, like five seconds instead of two?"

He's nearly in tears and breathing really hard as the effect of the shock subsides; taking about thirty seconds. We give him time to settle down before he answers.

Finally, he does and says, "Please don't hurt me no more! Don't shock me anymore! I'll do anything you say. Just don't hurt me! Please!"

Bull steps up and tells him, "Hear me well Jerry. That poor girl you've been tormenting will never see you around her house or hear from you ever again by phone or any by any other means. If you mess up, we'll know it and we'll bring you back here and keep the voltage running through you till we see smoke! And, we'll even put a cherry on top of that by torching your precious car! You only got a little taste of the pain this thing can give you. Now then, we'll take you back to your car; you'll then go home and continue living your life like a normal human being without bothering Jane or any other lady. If you screw up, you'll wish you were dead! Is that understood?"

Jerry says that he'll never bother her again. Knowing the pain our little contraption gave him, we're pretty sure he'll do the right thing. We plan on calling Jane to give her a number she can call in the event Jerry bothers her again.

The next day...

It's Wednesday morning. Hap calls Jane.

"Hello Jane! You don't know me but I know the situation you were in with regards to the Order of Protection you had against Jerry Mack. I just want to tell you that he shouldn't be bothering you any longer. If you ever see him near you at all, call the number I'll give you, day or night, and we'll deal with him. He's been warned and should know better than to trouble you any longer. Now, enjoy your life, as you should."

Before he hangs up, he gives Jane a phone number to call if Jerry ever bothers her again.

As a group, we're confident Jerry won't be dumb enough to go back on his word; especially after we told him we might kill him and trash his precious Mustang.

Chapter 29

Garage rip-off artists

Chuck Ludel, 42 years old, has a car repair garage on Reed Street. His garage is the only one in the area that has multiple bays for repairs of all kinds; tires, break jobs, mufflers, tune ups and engine rebuilds. If something goes wrong with your car, they'll do good work there. There's one big problem though. They've been known to rip off women and older folks. A friend of mine said they con customers into having unnecessary work done. It's all about beefing up repair bills.

Lenny says, "That's interesting! Me and Bull came across a situation Saturday when we heard three women talking at a Jim's Diner in a booth next to us about Chuck's garage. The youngest woman, a single mom of two was in tears because she was told by one of Chuck's mechanics that she needed an entire break job for her car to pass state inspection; at a cost of nearly $500! She cried to the other women there that she just couldn't afford it and that she needs her car to go to work."

I turned to her and said, "Excuse me, but I couldn't help overhearing your conversation. I'm a fair mechanic. Would you allow me to look at your brakes to see if you really need new brakes or if they're trying to rip you off?" Her name is Ana.

She looked at me with tears in her eyes and said, "Would you do that for me? I am so broke. Even working two jobs, I can't afford that kind of a bill right now!"

I told her, "When you're ready, you can follow me to my house where I have the tools that will make it easy for me to get a good look at those breaks."

After the ladies are done, Ana signals that she's ready. They leave the diner and follow Lenny and Bull. Once there, Lenny notes that it's a two years old Nissan with only 13,000 miles on it. He removes one of the tires to check the condition of the calipers, break-pads and the rotors. You can see him getting angry.

He stands up and says to Ana, "There is absolutely nothing wrong with your breaks. Those bums are trying to rip you off! Chuck's people are not nice! They're rats! Here's what I want you to do. I have a friend who has a garage on Clinton Street. You can go there to get your car inspected. I'll call him and set up an appointment for you for tomorrow after you're done working. You won't need any work done to your car. It's in great shape."

Ana tells him, "Thank you so much! You've made my day! How can I ever repay you?

"There's nothing to repay," says Len. "Go and have a great day and God bless!"

After Ana leaves, Lenny and Bull talk about her experience and decide they're gonna call Chuck's garage to mess with him. Bull makes the call. It works out well! Chuck himself answers.

"Hello! Chuck's Garage! This is Chuck. How can I help you?"

"Hello Chuck! Listen! I checked out a couple of cars of people you gave estimates to."

"Yah! What about them?"

"Well Chuck, you see, I'm a very good mechanic and I'm here to tell you that you're a CROOK! You tell people they need work they don't really need! You're a bad man and need to stop doing that!"

Chucky is taken aback and yells, "WHO IS THIS?!

"It's not important who I am. If you continue ripping people off, you can expect the police at your door, or maybe, just maybe, a visit from some guys you really don't want to screw with."

"Are you threatening me?"

"Absolutely! You see, you don't know who I am, but I know who you are and where you live and work. You need to SHUT UP and listen! We've got our eyes on you and if we find out that you've ripped off one more person, your life is going to get really miserable! There will be no second warning. You'd better run your business on the up and up! You've been warned. Don't screw up!"

Bull hangs up. He already has a plan. He'll send his twenty-four-year old daughter Janet to Chucky's garage on Monday to complain about a noise she hears; just to see what happens. She drives a five years old Ford Focus.

Monday morning

Monday morning, Bull loosens the muffler's heat shield so that it rattles as she drives. When Chuck's people do the test drive to see what they hear, they should be able to find the problem easy enough. To tighten the heat shield should only take ten minutes and cost no more than a few bucks. Bull will get the report on Chuck's inspection in a few hours.

Later

Well, well, well! Guess what? Janet takes the car in and is told that her catalytic converter will need to be replaced at a cost of $600 for parts and labor. Chuck tells her that it's rusting and won't pass state inspection when it is due at the end of the month. When Bull loosened the heat shield, he also examined the muffler and converter and saw that they looked to be in really good shape. Nothing needed replacing.

After looking at the estimate Janet brought back to her dad, he looks at it, smiles and says, "Some people, you just can't reason with."

Then, quoting a great line from the movie *Cool Hand Luke*, he says, *"What we have here is the failure to communicate!"*

He then thinks to himself; *"Okay! This is another job for our crew."*

He retightens the heat shield under Janet's car and sends her on her way.

Later at the VFW post, he tells me what happened.

I grin and say, "Interesting! I've heard complaints about old Chucky for a while now. Let's do what needs to be done. Methinks this idiot needs his own *tune up* and to be introduced to Sparky. Let's see when the best time will be to snag him. He's made a lot of money off good hard-working people. It's time we convince him of ending this scamming!"

Bull says that he opens the garage at 7am every morning to get things turned on and operational; and that his two mechanics don't arrive until 8. Since the place is located on a main street, it'll be difficult to snatch him up in broad daylight. Since Chuck will be alone for a while, it'll be perfect for doing what has to be done.

The call is made and Bull tells Chuck that he has an emergency situation with his van. He explains that his battery doesn't seem to hold a charge. To entice this greedy creep, he says he'll pay him double if he can accommodate him at the earliest time possible, and that he'd need to have it fix by 9:30 am so he could get to a job site by 10:00. Chucky tells him to come in at 6:30; that it would give him a two-hour window to fix the problem and get him rolling on time.

The next day, Hap in disguise, drives his van to the garage with Bull and Lenny hidden inside. Once there, he parks so the side sliding door of the van is interfaced with the garage's man-door. He goes in and tells Chuck to come out and check the battery cables to see if they're good or not. Chuck tells him that he'll meet him outside in a couple of minutes.

The guys in the van position themselves to nail the rat. He gets his coat on and makes his way outside to the van. As soon as he's close enough, Hap zaps him. Bull and Len open the side door, hop out, toss him in the back and do the usual restraints.

Now then, we're dealing with intelligent men here. Bull had the foresight of preparing a note to post on the office door of the garage telling the mechanics that he (Chuck) wouldn't be in today, and that they, need to open up the shop. Bull tapes the note to the door and the men roll out of there with their catch. As with all other detainees, they get Chuck's cell phone and wallet as well as cash from his pants pocket. Since Chucky likes ripping off people and raking in a lot of extra money, it's not surprising that he's carrying a substantial wad of dough.

Bull counts it out, smiles really big and says, "WOW! This guy loves carrying a lot of cash! He's got… let me rephrase that, he HAD $1,800 on him. Well, not any more. He doesn't know it yet but he just donated it to our cause."

He's still groggy from being stunned. A little bit into the ride to the warehouse, he comes out of it. Like most of the perps we've knocked out, he thrashes about as if doing that is going to set him free somehow.

Lightning Len lifts him to a sitting position, puts him in a rear choke hold and says, "Settle down Chucky! If you fuss at all, we'll just stun you again, and I know you don't any part of that. So, just be cool!"

Chucky and Sparky

Hap pulls inside the warehouse; we unload our Mr. Ludel, proprietor of the *Rip-Off Repair Shop* and bring him directly to our interrogation room. He's seated in the much-disliked chair of torment, "The New Sparky."

Since it was Bull's daughter he tried to rip off, he gets to have *first dibs* on this creep. Chuck's mouth is still taped, so, he can't speak. That's good, because he'd probably just interrupt anything Bull is going say to him. First thing first; the usual back hand to the side of the face to get Chuck's attention and for him to know right away that he's deep trouble.

Bull says to him, "I'm sure you have no idea why you've been brought here. Well, let me tell you why. You're a thieving rat that targets unsuspecting good people, mostly women and the elderly, and steal their money by telling them they need unnecessary repairs. Some of these poor folks barely get by from paycheck to paycheck and you have no trouble at all taking what little they have! That makes you one of the lowest maggots in town!"

Bull gives him punch to the stomach, which makes him lose his breath. He's still blindfolded but the tape is taken off his mouth, just in time to see him *up-chuck* the coffee and bagel he had earlier.

Once he's done regurgitating and is able to catch his breath, he yells out the same kind of plea all the other inmates did… "Please don't hurt me no more! Please! I swear I won't rip off any more customers if you let me go! I'll do the right thing, I promise!"

Bull looks at Clint who is closest to Sparky and nods for him to turn it on. The dial goes from 0 to 10 and Clint cranks it up to 3. As Chucky feels the current hitting him, he stiffens right up and lets out a blood-curdling scream that could wake up the neighborhood.

After three seconds of this torment, Bull leans in close to Chuck's face and says, "You miserable wretch, I'd like to break both your hands and arms so you can't do anymore car repairs. And, just so you couldn't go back to your garage, I'd like to burn it to the ground and close you up permanently. But, I'm a reasonable man, I'm going to let you go and you will pay back anyone you know you took advantage of, and any new client that comes in for repairs, you WILL be on the up and up with them; no more unnecessary repairs. Do you understand me?!"

"I understand. I understand! I won't do that anymore. I'll be honest with my customers. I swear to you, I'll do the right thing! I promise!"

Bull says to him, "I'm glad you get the message Chucky, but just the same, here's this." He gives him a slap across the face and nods for Clint to give him another taste of Sparky.

After the current is turned off, Chuck sits there trying to come down from the shock; whimpering and hyper ventilating. It's amazing how pain and fear can reduce even the toughest of men to a sad and helpless mess.

As Chuck deals with what he's just gone through, we hear…

"No more, please, please! I can't take no more of this! Please don't shock me anymore! I beg you! I BEG you!"

I step in and say, "Chuck, we're done with you here for the moment. We'll get you back to your garage shortly. Now then, the very first thing you'll need to do is have a meeting with your mechanics to tell them about the changes you're going to make. From now on, you will provide your customers with good car care, honest repairs and fair pricing! We will be watching you real close and if you slip up even a little, we'll destroy your business and bring you back here to make sure both your hands never work right again."

As sincerely as he can, Chuck says, "I promise I'll do everything you told me to do and won't cheat the customers."

"That's good Chuck. Now sit still for a few moments. I'll be right back."

Before I tell the men to release him from the chair, I motion for all of them to come to the outer office so we can plan how to drop Chucky back at or near his garage.

Hap says, "Hey Boss, I noticed a vacant building a couple of doors away for his garage. We'll simply drive around the back and dump Chuck there. We've got a good amount of duct tape around his head to cover his eyes. It'll take him a while to take it off. By the time that happens, we'll be long gone."

"Sounds like a good plan to me, Hap. Okay men, get the rat and take him back. Again, great job in collaring this sorry wretch."

Chuck is dropped off and left to deal with the tape around his head. Having to do that is no easy task. It'll just add to the punishment he deserves for hurting good people's pocket books. We'll wait and see how he does once he gets to his shop.

Career criminals don't learn!

The very next day, Bull sends his daughter Janet back to the garage with the $600 that Chuck said it would cost for her repairs. Bull loosened the muffler shield again so it would rattle. We want to see if Chuck will do the right thing. Actually, the money came from the $1,800 we ripped off of him when we snagged him. We also gave her an extra $200 for missing work for the day.

Janet pulls in and is approached by Chuck. He greets all the customers. He walks over to the driver's side of the car; Janet opens the window and says…

"I've got to get that converter fixed! The rattling noise is driving me crazy!"

Chuck tells her, "Well little lady, if you'll get out and go sit in our waiting room, I'll drive your car into one of bays and we'll get you straightened out right away."

He pulls the car in their third bay, the farthest one from the waiting room so Janet can't see what the mechanics are doing.

Chuck speaks to one of his men, "Get a new catalytic converter from the stock room and show it to the young lady in the waiting room so she can see that it's a new one we're going to install. You can save her old one; it's still in real good shape. We'll kill two birds with one stone, so to speak; sell her a new one, and put her old one in some other dope's car. You'll get a double commission that way."

The mechanic does as he's told; shows Janet the converter, then goes to work on her car. It's a fairly simple job. Forty minutes later, it's done. The man pulls the car out and brings the worksheet to Chuck. She pays the bill, gets in her car and heads out. She pulls over and calls her dad to tell him that the garage did the work on the car and charged her $589.00. When she gets home, Bull checks under the car to make sure they actually installed a new converter and accompanying pipes.

After doing that, he calls me to tell me what Chucky did. He's pretty angry at this garage man and wants to get a meeting going to see how we should proceed in dealing with him.

Boom's incendiary device

Chuck hasn't physically hurt anyone, but it's like the drug dealers; they hurt people indirectly by dealing drugs, which eventually ruins a lot of them. Chuck hurt a lot of people really bad financially. For some of them who live from paycheck to paycheck or are on fixed incomes, this is a major setback and we can't let him slide. We need to make a lasting impression on Chucky.

I make a few calls and tell the guys to meet at the warehouse at about 5pm this afternoon. The last man I call is Boom. I did that on purpose because I need for him to use his expertise in explosives.

Five o'clock rolls around and when all the men show, we start our meeting. I start it off by letting everyone know exactly what's going on and that we need to deal with our last detainee, Chuck.

I also state, "I know his mechanics will be out of work, but they too are part of the scams. Loss of employment will be their punishment. Hopefully, they'll also get the message. We need to close Chucky down!"

Boom already knows what he wants to do. He explains, "Three sides of the garage are solid brick and the three bay doors are its weakest points. I intend to take a twenty-pound cylinder of propane gas, fish a tube into the backside of the building through a small hole in one of the cement blocks and turn on the gas.

Propane is heavier than air and it will spread over the floor area. Once it has spread to a good portion of the inside, I'll slide a two-minute wick into the hole, light it and take off. We'll have enough time to get out of there. Since the building is far enough from the street and other buildings, only the garage will sustain damage when it blows. What do you guys think?"

I tell him that it sounds like a decent plan and that he should go with it. It's on. Hap will drive the van. Boom will set up the explosion while Bull acts as look out and back up in case someone comes by that could be a witness. He can distract him, or them.

Chuck's mechanics leave between 5:30 and 6pm. My men get there at 8:30 as planned and Boom does his thing. He floods the interior with propane, lights the wick; everyone boards the van and take off at normal speed so as to not draw attention. As they get a block and a half from the site, they stop and wait to hear the blast. Hap circles back so they can see what kind of damage it did. To their surprise, it went well. There is smoke and fire but not too much projectile debris outside the building except for some glass that blew out of the bay doors. It's an older garage with overhead doors that have eighteen-inch windows at eye level. That was good! It limited the risk of having an excessive amount of glass being sent air born.

Bull calls me from the van and says, "Boss, the package was delivered successfully. We're gonna park nearby and out of sight to see what happens when the fire department and police get here."

One of Chuck's mechanics lives just down the street from the garage and heard the explosion. He looks out his front door in the direction of the shop and can see right away that there's smoke. He calls Chuck and tells him about the fire at the garage. Chuck is quick to realize why his shop got torched. He flashes back in his mind what we did to him before we released him. He's shaken because he knows that we'll try to bring him in again and perhaps maim him for life; by breaking his hands.

As Hap, Boom and Bull in the van keep an eye on the garage at a distance, they spot Chuck driving in like a mad man to check things out. He parks his car about two-hundred feet away. The men see a couple of fire engines pull up, followed by three police cars. They keep an eye on Chucky to see what he's going to do. They see him approach one of the police officers, more than likely, to let him know that it's his garage. From the van, my men can see how horrified Chuck is. As he's watching the fire department put out the flames, the roof caves in. He can't even get in the building to salvage anything. He knows he's done!

Hap says to the others, "I think Chucky got the message loud and clear. But we still have to get him in our base for another *attitude adjustment*. Apparently, the first time around wasn't enough to convince him to do the right thing. Let's get back and talk it over with the Boss."

They head to the warehouse where I'm waiting to sit down with them and talk about snagging Chuck again for another go-round. The ruse this time will be Clint, in disguise, acting as a detective that is doing a follow up investigation on the arson.

Next day - Detective Clint

The next day, Hap calls his police friend O'Rourke at the station and asks if he's heard anything about a garage fire. He tells him that he heard about it and that the owner didn't have anything to say other than, 'He didn't know what happened.'

"From what I heard, Hap, he just stood there looking like man completely demoralized. The business is destroyed. It sure looks like someone wanted to get even with him for something. Since this is an obvious arson case, he was asked to come to the station to file a formal report. He didn't want to do it last night and said he'd be in the following day before noon to take care of that. That's all I got."

Hap says, "Thanks my friend." And, in a nonchalant manner, he adds, "What's this neighborhood coming to, Shawn! It used to be so nice around here. Oh well, we'll keep doing the best we can and keep a good thought, old buddy."

Knowing full well that he and his crew have become the *Equalizers* for the community, he simply responds,

"That's about all we can do, Hap. We'll keep a good thought and keep doing the best we can to live the best we can. Take care. And you, be careful out there."

"Will do my friend. I'll be in touch soon."

With the information he got from Shawn, Hap gets back to me about what he was told concerning Chuck. The plan now has to be that we'll get him today after he comes back home from filing a police report. He's fairly confident that they don't suspect that he had anything to do with the fire.

Later that day

After Chuck returns home from the station, Clint knocks on his door flashing a detective badge. In order to get him out of the house voluntarily, he's asked to accompany him to the garage so they can survey the damage and talk some more about the case and hopefully clear him of any wrong-doing. Chuck knows he didn't do this crime and is very willing to go. He gets his coat; the men leave the house and Clint motions for him to get in.

Chuck settles in the passenger side and locks in his seat belt. Lenny, being the smallest the man on the team, is able to hide on the floor of the back seat. Just as Clint starts driving off, Len reached up with a stun gun and knocks out our unsuspecting passenger. His eyes, mouth and hands are taped. Once again, off to the warehouse they go.

This is becoming somewhat of a routine; snagging perps, bringing them in and interrogating them. And, here's Chuck once more, strapped in Sparky, waiting for the pain to begin. He's the first perp we've let out, and then, brought back.

Again, it's Bull who wants a piece of him first since it was his daughter he ripped off. Chuck is blindfolded and his mouth still taped.

Bull starts by telling him, "Boy, you have to be one of the dumbest people on the entire planet! Why would you even think of screwing up knowing we'd get your sorry ass back here?!"

Hap backhands him and then punched him in the stomach. Chucky heaves as if he's going to throw up – again! The men wait till he catches his breath and Eh-Jax gives him another slap across the face. Everyone wants to backhand him till he loses consciousness. But we want him awake so we can bring closure to the mess this guy's put himself in. We can't allow him to be free to start up another rip-off garage. We need to make sure he never resurfaces to continue that kind of business. The big question is, what to do?

I rip the duct tape off from his mouth so he can speak. It tore a whole bunch of whiskers off his scraggly mustache. OUCH! That hurt. Good!

Chucky is scared to death. He figures the men will hurt him really bad and says, "Please don't hurt me anymore. I'm sorry I didn't keep my promise. My garage is gone and I'm in serious debt. I have nothing left. Please let me go and I'll leave town and never come back; but please don't hurt me! I'm begging you!"

This guy is such a loser! I step in and tell him. "You've got two choices here; either you go to the police tomorrow and tell them you torched your own garage, OR... we'll beat you really bad; pass an electric current through you on and off for an hour and then break both your hands, arms, and all of your fingers. What's it going to be?"

Before he can answer, Boom turns on Sparky for just a moment. This is to give Chucky some incentive to make the more sensible choice; turn himself in and take the rap for blowing up his repair shop. Actually, the fool that he is, did just that by "screwing up!"

As the effect of the shock from Sparky subsides, Chucky says, "Please don't hurt me anymore! I'll go tomorrow and turn myself in to the cops and take the blame for the fire. I promise."

I tell him, "Good choice Chuck! Now then, we have to put you out on the street so you can make your way to the police station. If you should get the bright idea that you can run somewhere, don't forget, we have all of your ID info and we will find you. If you force us to do that, then, we'll just shoot you. Now then, you go and do your time for this crime, which by the way, should take care of the numerous thefts you've done when you exaggerated repair bills on who knows how many people. You do that like a real man, not like chump! Are we clear here?!"

"Yes, we're clear. I'll do that."

We unstrap him. Hap and Clint take him in the van and drop him off just like before, right behind his garage; this time, the ruins of his garage. Like before, it'll be a while for him to take off the duct tape wrapped around his head. We'll keep an eye on him tomorrow to see if he goes to the station to turn himself in. To make sure the cops know, Hap says he'll have a note dropped off tonight to Sergeant O'Rourke that will tell him; "Chuck is responsible for the fire."

Whether he shows up or not, the cops will at least have something on him and keep hounding him till he confesses. Besides the cops, he's got us to worry about. We believe he'll do what we told him to do. Another thing, he won't be able to collect any fire insurance. This will ensure that he wouldn't have any *start-up money* to get another repair shop going. All he's got to look forward to now - jail.

Chuck does the right thing

The next day, Hap and Bull stake out Chuck's house and wait to see what he does. Around 10am, a car pulls up, the driver honks the horn and two minutes later, here comes Chucky. He gets in and we follow at a safe distance so as to mot be detected. I guess the last session did the trick. We follow them right to the precinct house. Chuck gets out, waves bye to his driver and goes in the station.

Since it's the day shift, Hap's friend Shawn is tending the front desk. Chuck tells him who he is and that he wants to speak to a detective. Sergeant O'Rourke rings up Detective Smardz down the hall from him. He was one of the precinct men first on-scene two nights ago. He tells Shawn to escort the guy to his office.

Chuck wastes no time in confessing about the arson. Det. Smardz gives him a yellow legal pad and tells him to write down the details. He sits down and writes as much information as he can that will lead anyone reading it that he did the dirty deed. When he's finished, the detective has a uniformed officer take him for mug shots, finger prints and placed in a cell until he can be transferred downtown to the lockup for prisoners awaiting arraignment.

Later in the day, Hap gets a call from O'Rourke, "Hey buddy, guess what? The guy whose garage went up in smoke the other night turned himself in today and will go to court tomorrow to plead guilty. Just thought you'd like to know. Glad he developed a conscience and that he's done ripping people off."

"Well, what do you know," says Hap, "Will wonders never cease? I appreciate the call my friend. And, I'm glad this crook will no longer be around to take advantage of honest folks. Hey, if you hear of any other rats that need a good "tune-up," let me know."

"As a matter of fact, I heard of some home repair contractor who took $15,000 from an elderly couple living on Social Security and barely making ends meet. The guy did a quarter of the work in their kitchen and hasn't returned. It's been two months. The contractor's name is Doug Martin. He works out of an office on Hills Street. Maybe someone could persuade him to return the money to those folks or finish the job. What do you think, Hap?"

Hap asks Shawn, "Do you think Mr. Martin could use a visit from certain concerned citizens?"

"Hey, it couldn't hurt. I'm sure he's burnt a lot of other people. It's something we see every construction season and so often, we hardly ever catch up with the creeps that swindle the elderly and unsuspecting folks."

"Okay Shawn, I'll keep Doug Martin on Hills Street in mind. Take care."

Hap hangs up and puts a call to me to let me know that we have another rat we need to set a trap for. I tell him to meet me at the Post tonight.

Chapter 30

Meeting about the construction guy

I get to the Post at 7:30 and along with Bull, I see Lenny and Clint. For tonight, it'll be only the four of us; enough of our team to put some thoughts together about getting our "contractor crook" and make things right or go for the worse ride of his miserable life.

Lenny knows exactly where Martin's office is located. It's in a seedy part of the city where there are a lot of shuttered buildings, empty lots, and the remnants of charred houses waiting to be torn down.

"I'll take a ride by his place after we're done with our little pow-wow tonight and see if I can get a phone number off the building or a work truck. If I can, we can set him up to come by a house to do an estimate. We can suck him in by stating that this would be a HUD project worth $75,000. That should bring him out. Sound good to you, Boss?"

"I like that plan, Lighting. As soon as you get a number, you can place the call and have him come to an abandoned house at 76 Peach Street. There aren't many houses there. Most are burned out or boarded up. It'll be a perfect place to get him inside, bag him, and put him in   Hap's 'Fish Tank' for the ride to our base."

After spending a couple of hours at the post, mingling with the guys and Clint talking to Chuck, an Iraq vet, Len takes off to do recon on the contractor's office on Hills Street. It's about three miles from the Post. When he gets there, he can't see any phone number on the building, but can make out a sign on the front door with a business logo and a phone number. It reads, "For a free estimate, call Doug at 969-0011. Office opens at 8 am." That's all he needed. He makes his way home and since it's already 10:30 pm, he figures he'll call Doug in the morning.

The call...

The following day, Len is up and at 7 am. He takes time to shower and shave, then, have his breakfast. He figures that by 8:30 Doug should be ready to receive calls from potential clients. He dials the number and gets one of Doug's workers.

He tells him, "Hello, is this Doug?"

"No, this is Vinny. Hold on, I'll get him for you. He's outside loading up his truck."

Doug gets on the phone and Lenny tells him about a HUD project with the dollar amount, and that it needs to be done ASAP! To draw him into the deal even more, he tells him that HUD is willing to give the contractor half of the money up front and the rest when the job is completed. That means that he'd get $35,000 right away. That's a very good chunk of money for a greedy, scheming guy like him. Upon hearing Len telling him about the "up front" money, he doesn't pause for a moment and tells Lenny that he can do the job. Len gives him the address and says to meet at the 76 Peach Street at 5:00 pm. The trap is all set for the vermin. Now, a few calls to get our team together to bag and gag Mr. Martin.

The Meet

Around 3:30, Clint, Bull, Lenny and I gather up at the ware-house where the van just got a different paint job and put on one of those magnetic business signs Hap talked about. One that says *"Sid's Plumbing,"* another has an official-looking county logo, and the third just says, *"Livery."* They slap on the county logo sign.

Our squad rolls out at 4:00. That'll give us enough time to set things up to capture the crook. The plan is that Clint and I, in disguise, will be waiting on the porch of the house for Doug while Bull and Len stay hidden in the van.

Not surprising, Doug is late. He drives up at 5:15 and gets out as quick as he can.

When he's just an earshot of us, he says, "Gentlemen, I'm so sorry for being late. Another estimate kept me longer than I expected. Anyway, I'm here. Let's see what this old place is going to need."

Clint shakes his hand and introduces himself as Mike Crato and I do the same - using the name Tom Crelly. I open the door and give Doug a little time to look around. After about five minutes, Clint hits him with the stun gun. He drops to the floor. We duct tape his mouth, his eyes, and secure his hands and feet. I signal Bull and Lenny in the van to come and help us put our catch in the five foot long by three-foot wide tool gang-box we placed in the house the day before. Once he's in there, we roll it out and put it in the van. The next step is to get him to headquarters to have a life-changing conversation that will include, "adult corporal punishment."

Once again, Hap drives into the warehouse; the men pull out the gang box and get Doug out and sit him our tricked-out chair. The creep doesn't know what's going on; he's totally dumfounded. He has no idea why he's been handled that way. Being taped up the way he is and unable to see or speak, he panics!

I start in on him, "Listen carefully Doug. The reason you're in the predicament you're in is because of the scams you've been running on a lot people. I don't know how many people you've swindled, but I imagine it's quite a few. You've pocketed a ton of money from good people who expected you to fix their homes. You're a miserable lowlife who needs to pay for those crimes."

I backhand him and Len who is nearest the controls for Sparky, turns it on. It's set for level three; not too high. As the current surges through his body, Doug lets out a scream that is muffled by the tape across his mouth and tries to say something.

Eh-Jax walks over and rips off the tape and says, "Sorry, we didn't hear what you said."

Doug says, "I'm sorry! I really am. Please don't hurt me anymore!"

Clint tells him, "You're a very bad man who needs to be put out of commission. You robbed people of their hard-earned money; for some, it was all they had saved for fixing up their homes. That makes you a real low life rat! For that, you're going to pay."

I tell him to sit there and not say anything, then motion to the men to head for the outer room. We need to figure out how we can make things right for the people Doug ripped off.

Boom says, "We should see how much money he has at home, at his office or in the bank. If it's substantial, we'll figure a way to get it and pay back the people he stole from. Let's go see what he's got."

We re-enter the room and as I make my way in toward Doug, I turn on Sparky and give him another dose. His whole body goes rigid and he screams to high heaven.

I get close to his ear and say, "Doug, you need to pay back those good people you screwed. That'll take a bunch of money. The question is, how many people did you scam and how much money do you have tucked away?"

He says, "I don't have much put away, only enough to pay my alimony, my men and my bills."

I think to myself, *"Alimony! I'm not surprised this rat is divorced."*

I'm not satisfied with the answer and give a nod for Clint turn on Sparky. Not expecting it, Doug goes wild! His body shakes like a leaf in a hurricane and screams like a girl. It takes a couple of minutes for him to regain his composure.

When he does, I tell him, "Doug, the next thing out of your mouth will be the REAL amount of dough you have tucked away from the thieving you've been doing."

"Okay, okay! I'll tell you, just don't hurt me anymore! I can't take it! I have just a little over $175,000 at my house."

"That's good," says Lenny. "We're gonna have to get our hands on all of it and pay back the folks you robbed. That means we'll also need your business record book so we can find each client you robbed."

He says, "If you let me go, I'll get all the money and bring it to you along with the names of the people I stole from."

Clint backhands him and says, "You gotta be real stupid to think that we'd let you walk out of here and trust you to come back with the names and the money."

The side of Doug's face feels like he's been hit with a two by four. He's a bit dazed but conscious enough to say, "Please don't hit me anymore. I'll tell you where the money is at the house. You have my keys and can let yourself in. The names of the people are in my office in a special ledger in my desk."

"That's what we wanted to hear," says Clint. "Now then, according to your driver's license, you live at 321 Huntley Street. All we need is, where in the house do you have the cash?"

He tells us that it's in a safe in his bedroom closet. Eh-Jax asks him for the combination. For fear of getting zapped by Sparky again, he gives it up without hesitating.

It's 8 o'clock. I nod to Hap and Eh-Jax. They know what to do. They take off and make it there in about twenty minutes. All the while, Doug is left alone strapped to the chair while Clint and I go in the next room to figure what we should do with our prisoner after we take care of the people that are owed the money.

Clint says, "We should talk to Hap and see if we can get Sergeant O'Rourke involved. After we get Doug's money and ledger, we can put him in O'Rourke's hands so he can be prosecuted."

I tell him, "Funny, I was thinking along those same lines. This guy needs to stand before a judge, go through due process and be given the right amount of jail time. Once Eh-Jax and Hap get back we'll make the arrangements to turn him over to the sergeant."

As Clint and I continue our discussion, Hap and Eh-Jax arrive at Doug's house. They go in and find the safe in the bedroom. Hap gets busy dialing the combination and gets the safe open with no problem. He opens the door and both men look at each other and smile. Hap starts passing the money over to Eh-Jax to place in a small gym bag they brought along.

Eh-Jax sees there's a .38 caliber pistol in the back of the safe. He says, "Hey Hap, take the pistol. We'll have your sergeant buddy check it out to see if it's legal. If it isn't, Doug will have another problem besides the charge of grand larceny; possession of an illegal gun. That should be good for additional time added to his sentence."

Hap grabs the gun and hands it to Eh-Jax who puts it in the bag. Everything takes place within fifteen minutes and off they go. They make their way to Doug's office to pick up his ledger book. After a short ride, they arrive, go in and find the desk. As Hap opens the top drawer and finds what looks to be a business book, the ledger, hopefully. He opens it to confirm it is what they're looking for and can readily see; dates, names, addresses, phone numbers, monetary figures and work to be done. They've got what they came for. Now, back to the warehouse to meet up with me and Clint and I.

When they arrive, it's 10:15 pm. They get to the outer room, away from the interrogation room and are eager to show us the loot, the gun and ledger. Eh-Jax is carrying the bag and dumps everything on the table. I'm anxious to count it to verify how much is actually there. Hap and Bull each take a small pile and begin counting. It's all in different denominations; fives, tens, twenties, fifties and a few hundreds. Doug was not very organized in sorting the money. We have to go through every wad and separate the bills. This will take a while. Boom volunteers to help. After getting it all counted, we come up with $200,250. Doug said he had around $175,000.

Hap says, "Doug was a bit off on with the amount he told us was in the safe. And, his ledger will be a big help for reimbursing the people he scammed. What's next, Boss?"

"Clint and I were talking about what to do with Doug and the money." He turns to Hap and says, "Clint mentioned that we should see if you could speak to O'Rourke so he could get our crook jailed and prosecuted. We could hand him over along with the money and ledger and leave it up to him to get the money back to the people that got swindled. What do you think?"

"I think O'Rourke will be very happy to hear we've got the whole package for him. After all, it was him who brought up the matter. I'm sure he'll do what needs to be done to get our Mr. Martin put away and the money returned to the victims."

It's done. Hap calls O'Rourke and tells him that Martin will be tied up and ready to be picked up at his office at 1284 Hills Street in about an hour. As for the money and ledger, he tells him that he'll have a messenger drop them off at the precinct early tomorrow and given to him and him only. Also, there'll be a note in the bag explaining everything.

Hap says to him, "If your officers wonder what to charge Martin with when they go to pick him up, just tell them that he's a construction guy who scammed people out of money and that one of them caught up with him and tied him up at his office. And, when the money and ledger arrive, you can tell your boss that they were delivered by someone who just came in, dropped a duffel bag and left."

We all go in the interrogation room. I tell Doug, "We're going get you out of here and turn you over to the law. Now then, you will not fight this in court with some slick lawyer. If you do, we will find you and bring you back here for a series of shock treatments and beatings. You're going to plead guilty and do whatever time the judge gives you. Do you understand?"

Doug is reduced to a frail and defeated man. He says, "I understand. I won't fight. I'll do the time."

Hap and Eh-Jax unstrap him and walk him to the van. They load him in and make their way to his office. At 11pm, Hap pulls in front of the door so that when they take him out through the van's sliding side door, it'll be less likely that anyone can see that Doug is blindfolded, gagged and has his hands tied. The transfer from the van to the front door goes smoothly. Hap walks him in and has him sit where they can't be seen from the outside. Eh-Jax is ready with a roll of duct tape and secures him really well in the chair.

As they get ready to leave, Hap tells him, "Doug, I hope you're not feeling sorry for yourself. You hurt, and maybe even destroyed a few people financially because of the scams you pulled. The cops will be here any minute to pick you up and take you to booking. Have a great time in jail."

Hap and Eh-Jax want to make sure the police pickup will go as planned. They role the van a short distance from Doug's place and wait for the cops to show up to see how Doug will behave.

After a half hour wait, O'Rourke's men finally arrive. Two officers enter the office and find Martin. From what our guys can see when the three exit the building, the officers got all the tape off Doug. They put him in cuffs and place him in the back of the squad car and head for the precinct.

Once the men see the squad car pull away, Eh-Jax calls me on his cell to tell me all went well and that the *rat* is on his way to jail. It's nearly midnight; everyone is tired. It's time to head home for a good nights' sleep.

I tell the men, "Good job you two. Much appreciated."

Chapter 31

"Instant karma" at a restaurant

It's amazing how many stupid and ignorant people there are in our society. No matter where you find yourself, there's always someone who just can't behave normally and needs an "attitude adjustment."

Lenny is at a restaurant with his wife Denise and hears a man belittling his girlfriend a few booths behind him. He's about twenty-seven; a goofy-looking guy that you know is a dominating bully. Len sits there and listens while the moron keeps going on and on. And then it happens! He hears the sound of a slap and the woman weeping. She's around twenty-one. He looks up from his dish, looks around and can see that no one in the place is saying anything or making a move to confront this putz!

Len tells Denise, "Pick up the check, pay it and then go wait for me in the car. I won't be long."

She knows him. She can see it in his eyes that his blood came to a boil. The woman-beater just woke up the fighter in Lenny. Denise picks up the check and goes to the register, pays it and exits. After Len watches her through the restaurant window getting in the car; he gets up, makes his way past the couple to the men's room. After a minute, he walks back toward the couple. The guy has his back to him and as he gets close enough, he hits him in the jaw with a jack-hammer punch that is a blur. This was a case of "no time to get the gang together to deal with the situation." It's one of those *"Instant karma"* moments. The guy needed to be put down, now! The rat is slumped in the booth and Len gets his wallet, takes out his license and looks at it. He sees the name Aaron Fuches.

He tosses the wallet on the table and gives the woman a card with a phone number she can call if her idiot boyfriend hurts her again.

He says to her, "When Aaron wakes up, tell him I have his license with his name and address. Tell him that he'll be visited by men who will hurt him real bad if he touches you again. You need to leave this bum; the sooner the better."

He walks out and can hear people applauding. He goes to his car and heads home. Meanwhile, back in the restaurant, our bad boy Aaron wakes up. His jaw is broken and can barely talk.

Another good size guy who was ready to jump in to intercede says to him, "Hey stupid! You had that coming. The man who put you down just left. You're lucky he didn't beat you to a pulp. You should know better than to talk down to your woman like that, and even worse, hit her! I was one click away from jumping in when he hit you. I might have gone a little further than just one punch. He's got your number. He knows who you are and where you live. If I were you, I'd be really scared! The way he hit you, you can bet he's someone you don't want to EVER see again!"

Aaron looks around and sees all the people looking at him. He holds his jaw and motions his girlfriend with his head, *"Let's go!"* He has that look of a guy who has been humbled. Lenny plans on following up on this creep to see if he's going to need further convincing that he needs to behave.

It didn't take long! The next day, at 9am, Lenny gets a call from the woman who was abused by her boyfriend at the restaurant.

She says, "Hello, my name is Michelle. I need help! Aaron beat me up pretty bad after we got home. He was mad that he got knocked out and that his jaw was really sore. The bastard took it out on me! I don't know what to do! I should have never moved in with him. PLEASE help me!"

Len asks what time he gets home from work. She tells him that he gets together with his buddies at a bar on Clinton Street after work and is usually home by 6pm for supper. He tells her that he went by the house in the afternoon to see the layout of the house.

He says to her, "At about 8 o'clock tonight, take out the garbage, then, get to the back door and yell to Aaron that some kids are messing with his car. Once he comes outside, he won't be coming back for a couple of days. During that time, gather any of belongings you need and go to your parents' house or to a trusted friend, and stay there. We'll give you some money so you can start a new life. I have your phone number and will call to check on you tomorrow. Your bad boy, punk, boyfriend, won't be hurting you anymore. Just do what I told you to do and things will be fine. Have a good day."

At 7pm, Hap our driver, Len, and Bull are on their way to rescue Michelle and snag Asinine Aaron. The guys make their way to 67 South Legion Drive; park the van just past the driveway and set up to nail Aaron. Len and Bull hide around the corner of the house; only about five steps from the back door. It's perfect for when the moron comes out. It'll be easy to stun and bag him.

At 7:50, Michelle comes out with an armful of trash, walks over to the garbage can, dumps it in and walks to the back door. Len is close enough and can see her as she stands under the door light. He can see how bad Aaron beat her. It looks like she has a fat lip and a very bad bruise on her left cheek; and, who knows if she has any broken ribs or other bruises on her body.

She opens the door and yells to Aaron, "Aaron, kids are messing with your car! You better come out here and see what they're doing!"

He bolts from his easy chair, storms through the door and just as he makes it outside, ZAP! He goes down; the guys secure him. Len whistles to signal Hap to pull the van into the driveway. Aaron is loaded on board. They head for the warehouse and are there in about fifteen minutes.

While they're in transit, Aaron wants to go wild. Len remembers which side of the jaw he punched him in the restaurant. He grabs him from behind and puts heavy pressure on the jaw. He screams through the duct tape covering his mouth.

Len tells him, "Hey STUPID, you would do well to just be real still or we'll shoot you right here!"

That got his attention. He calms down.

The men arrive at 8:40 and bring the punk to the interrogation room. He's seated in our "special attention-getting chair" and strapped him in. I'm there too and wait for my three amigos to go to work on him. Len gets the first shot at him since he was the one that saw the rat in action in the restaurant. He slaps him on the mouth which begins the blood flowing, then, backhands him on the cheek bone to puff it up real nice, just like Michelle's cheek. Bull turns on Mr. Sparky for a couple of seconds and the shock sends our bad boy through the roof! He screams and begins to breathe really heavy. He's probably thinking he's going to die.

Bull tells him, "Hey Aaron, how you feelin' man? Not too good, huh? Do you have any idea why you're our prisoner?"

Len removes the tape from his mouth and Aaron pleads right away. "Don't hurt me! PLEASE! Whatever I did, I'm sorry! Don't hurt me anymore! I'm BEGGING you!"

Len jumps in and says, "You're a low life, rat Aaron! You hurt Michelle pretty bad at that restaurant and when you got home, you put another BEATING on her?! I wonder how long you've been beating her."

He gives him a solid punch to the gut. This takes his breath away and he feels like puking. Bull picks up the hammer and gives his right hand a solid whack. For sure, he's got a couple broken bones.

Len continues, "We broke the hand you used so many times to beat on Michelle. You had that coming. Hope the pain lasts a long time. You deserve that."

Without skipping a beat, he adds, "Here's the deal I'm going to make with you. We're going to keep you here a couple of days so you can get your head straight and Michelle can clear her things out of your house. After that, we'll let you go and make sure the cops know who you are and what you've done. If you EVER make contact or bother her at all, you'll be back here and we'll make you a cripple for life."

With that, Hap turns on sparky; just for a couple of seconds, to make sure he gets the message. Our boy Aaron screams and stiffens up like a rod.

He blurts out, "I promise I won't bother Michelle anymore. I swear it on my mother's soul! I promise! I'll stay away. I won't go near her ever again!"

Len says, "That's good Aaron. Now we'll tuck you away for the night. I hope you take that time in your cell to really think about how much of a scumbag you are! You don't deserve to be this society. You're a cockroach that should be squashed!" Lenny leaves it there.

Hap and Bull take him to one of the cells. They put the special head gear on him and tell him about the bucket and blanket, then, leave him to deal with the trauma we put him through.

The following day, contacting Michelle

With Aaron safely tucked in one of our cells, Len contacts Michelle late in the day to see how she made out getting her belongings out of Aaron's house. He gave her a thousand dollars to help her get resettled in town, another city, or state. She tells Lenny that with the help of a couple of good friends, she was able to gather what she wanted from the house and made arrangements to leave the city and go live with her folks in Hollywood, Florida.

That's perfect! She'll be about 1,200 miles away from that cockroach of a boyfriend she sadly hooked up with. She tells

Len that she's taking a plane around 8pm tonight. That part of this episode is ending well for her. As for Aaron, well, he'll be released tomorrow with a little going away present. Len tells Michelle to tell her friends never to divulge where she went. One never knows about a moron like Aaron if he'll ever get the idea of chasing her down. We'll throw him off by feeding him bad information concerning her whereabouts.

Next Day

Around 9am the next day, Len calls Michelle to find out if she made it to her parents' place. He was happy that she answered. It saved him time trying to reach her if she wasn't available right away. First, she thanks him again for the thousand dollars; that it made everything so much easier.

She tells him, "My folks were so happy to see me and that there's no problem for me to stay with them. They saw the bruises on my face. My dad wanted to load up a gun and go find Aaron! I told him not to do anything. It took him a while to calm down."

He said, "That S.O.B. better NEVER come down here! If he does, I'll kill him!"

"I told my dad that the guy doesn't know where I went and that my rescuers dealt with him and will give him misinformation as to where I went. This made him feel a lot more reassured. He felt better and told me that I could stay with him as long as I needed.

She continued, I plan on taking a couple of weeks to heal, then, find a job and begin living normally."

Len tells her, "I'm so glad your relocation worked out so well. Now, take time to heal, both physically and emotionally. Good luck in whatever job you get, and one more thing, don't ever hook up with a looser like Aaron. Find a gentleman and have a good life. You have my number. Stay in touch so you can give me a progress report in a few weeks, okay?"

"Okay, I will. And, thank you again for everything. You saved my life. I was trapped and dying being with that monster!"

"We were glad to help you out. Be safe and be happy in your new surroundings. Bye for now."

They hang up, and now, Len and the others are ready to release Aaron the jackass!

The men get him out of his cage and bring him to the interrogation room for one last *special treatment*. Besides Lenny, I'm there with Boom and Bull. We sit our guest down. He doesn't say a word. He just doesn't know what to expect. Len fills him in as to what will happen.

He tells him, "Aaron, just looking at you, I want to take a hammer and beat the hands to a pulp that beat up Michelle so many times. But I'll be nice. You'll only get a little 'going away present.'"

Boom throws the switch on *sparky* and lights our bad boy up for a couple of seconds. Again, he tenses up and screams like a dying banshee.

We let him calm down and Len tells him, "You're a lousy little rat that should not be living among good people. Michelle has left the country. We have friends in Canada and made it possible for her to go live with them and start a new life. If you ever think of going up there to bother her, guess what, we've already alerted the Canadian authorities to 'flag' you if you try crossing the border. We gave them all the particulars of your woman-beating history and they will turn you over to the American authorities."

With that said, he gives him a solid backhand and says, "We're going to let you go in a few minutes. Just remember, you don't know who we are, but we know who you are and where you live. We'll be watching you to see if you abuse any other young lady. Don't EVER let us hear you've done that to another woman. The next time, we'll make you disappear."

Aaron is still whimpering and says, "I won't hurt anyone else. I promise. Please let me go home, please!"

Boom and Lenny release him from the chair. They lead him out to the van and take him to a vacant lot where he's set free. They leave the duct tape covering his eyes but cut loose the tape that secured his hands. The van rolls away nice and easy and the men can see Aaron struggling to free his head. They look at each and smile as if to say, "Another bad hombre bites the dust."

Chapter 32

New Guys and a gal join the action

It's 7 pm on a Friday night, and the men meet up again at the post. Mickey 'Lefty' Syms and some of his Middle East War veteran buddies happen to be there too. Lefty walks over to Hap and asks him if he can talk to him privately.

They go off to a side room and Lefty says, "I have to let you know that me and my friends know about the activities of your group."

Hap asks, "What do you know about our group?"

"Well, since I'm the one who dropped a dime on the punks that shot Boss and know that those two rats are no longer around, I figured you guys took care of business. What do you think about us joining force with y'all? Being part of the younger crowd, we're probably more in tune with what goes on out there on the streets and can be your back up whenever you need us. What do you think?"

Hap says, "Let me run that by my friends and see what we come up with. In the meantime, I need for you to be EXTREMELY COOL about what we just talked about here! You take this to the grave, you hear?!"

Lefty nods his head and says, "Got it, to the grave. Oh, and by the way, we have a lady, a Middle East veteran that served with me who would be an excellent addition to the group. Her name is Angelina Cruz. We call her Angel. She did her share of taking out enemies and was wounded. She took a bullet in her right thigh and has a few scars on the right arm and side of her face and neck from a roadside bomb. She hides that well with makeup. In dimmer lighting, you hardly notice it. I know we could trust her with what we know. She did boxing and archery before serving. She has a great boxing record and won awards in archery competitions. What do you think?"

"How sure are you she can be trusted to be brought into our operation? What we do is very serious! We can't have any weak link."

"Sir, I trust her with my life. That bullet she took was meant for me. We were out on a mission and when she saw the enemy aim at me, she pushed me aside just before he fired. I owe her."

"If Boss oks this move, you can bring her aboard. I look forward to meeting her. I'll trust your judgement about her character. Just make sure that she knows what we do is serious business and she is to NEVER speak to anyone about it, EVER!"

Lefty ends the chat with, "You have my word she can be trusted and will be a great asset to our cause. I'll bring her around so you can meet her and feel her out to see if she'll fit in."

Hap nods as if to say, "good." He turns and rejoins his brothers to tell them what he and Lefty talked about.

Clint says, "I suspected those boys knew something, what with us meeting up and looking serious when we discussed our business separate from the other men in the post." He looks at the men and says, "Not a bad idea having some of the young bloods backing us, and a lady to boot. That could be very useful. What do the rest of you think?"

Len pipes in and says, "If we can trust them to keep it all 'top secret,' we could use them when the need arises. We should get them over here and feel them out."

Hap walks over to Lefty and asks him and his two friends to join his group for a chat. Mickey, along with Chuck and Dave, walk over. Everyone is introduced.

They have a seat and Boss asks, "What do you guys know about our group?"

Mickey says, "We figured out why some of the bad characters around here have either disappeared or wound up turning themselves in to the law"

Clint asks, "So...where are you going with this?"

"Looks like you guys are taking care of some of the bad elements that are plaguing our neighborhood. We'd love to be part in whatever you've got going. This is our neighborhood too. I was born here. We all grew up here and can see the crap that's going on. We've been to war overseas and dealt with bad guys there. We killed a lot of our enemies and saw a number our buddies come home in body bags and others, maimed really bad. That's why you only see us three here. We share the same past experiences. We understand each other. We're more than ready to go to war with locals that want to be enemies of the good people around here."

I tell them, "Brothers, it was great making your acquaintance and we appreciate you stepping forward to offer your help. How about we get back to you real soon and see how we can work together?"

Lefty nods and says, "Whatever you guys need, we're here to do for you what needs to be done. No questions asked."

With that said, the men take turn shaking hands and the new guys get back to their spot at the Post to continue their little get-together and mingle with others there.

Chapter 33

Basketball-court Hogs

Man, bad people are everywhere! Our neighborhood basket-ball courts just have to have idiots in need of being wised up! I'd like to be positive, but when I hear of jerks causing hard-ships for good folks, it makes me go a bit ballistic!

Seems that there's a group of older guys between seventeen and twenty that think they're potential "pro" basketball players and hog the only two courts in the park. And, anyone who dares say anything either gets threatened or gets roughed up! That came to my attention Saturday through Hap from our younger warrior named Dave. His twelve-year-old nephew Josh told him that there are days the younger guys can't get on the courts until late afternoon. By then, they can't organize any kind of five-on-five games because it's near supper time for a lot of the kids his age that have to get home to eat.

After Dave called to tell Hap about that, he got a hold of me and we made a few phone calls to give our guys a heads up on this neighborhood problem. We told the guys to meet up at the Post Monday night.

The next day, Sunday, I figured I'd take a ride to the park and check out the action. I got there, parked my car, stood a slight distance from the where the older teens were playing and saw what Dave's nephew said went on there. I could see younger kids hanging around the sides of the two courts in hopes that one of the two sets of ten older guys would vacate one of the courts. They were indeed hogging them. I stayed there for about an hour taking mental notes. It didn't look like they were going to give up their turf any time soon. As a matter of fact, as one group took a break, other older guys would step in and take over; this denied the younger boys the chance to play.

I thought to myself, *"This ain't right! Time for our squad to do something about these bad boys!"*

I got back in my car and went home thinking about all that I had just seen. The poor boys were missing out on so much enjoyment a simple basketball court could bring them. I say to myself, *"This will be remedied!"*

Monday night

Fast forward to Monday night, all the guys show up, minus Angel, Lefty's lady soldier. Man, this is an awesome group. It's great that I can depend on them to be there. Anyway, we get our drinks, sit down and I tell them what Dave told Hap.

Clint says, "So, there's a group of about twenty older guys hogging the courts, eh? It's gonna be a problem rounding up that many! Do you have any ideas, Boss?"

I tell him that I didn't, that we'd have to really think hard on this one; that it'd be really tricky.

Lenny jumps in and says, "There's got to be a leader in that bunch. How about we find him, snag his delinquent butt and bring him in for pow-wow?"

Hap says, "That makes sense. They're probably not criminal types, just misguided souls that need to be educated on the finer points of, *proper comportment*; using corporal actions to make them see the light."

Lenny laughs and asks, "Hap, what the hell is *"proper comportment*, man?! You need to speak American!"

The guys look at Hap and snicker; a couple of them let out a few …ooos!!! …to let Hap know Len just tossed him an in-your-face comeback!

Hap tells him, "Let me rephrase that my poor ignorant but lovable friend. Proper comportment means, *'proper behavior.'* How's that Lenny?"

That's nice Hap. Thank you for clearing that up for me. Now, tonight I can sleep knowing that I know what *proper comportment* means. I love you man!"

All the guys get a good laugh. This kind of cutting up between the men goes on all the time and keeps things on the light side. It's just a guy thing.

I step in and ask Hap to speak to Dave to see if he can find out who the leader of that rat pack is. Once we know, we'll figure out how we can isolate him, bring him in, and do what we have to do to straighten things out so he and his cohorts adopt (looks at Lenny) - *better comportment*! Again, all the guys get a big laugh at this little running joke.

The next day, I get a call from Hap and he tells me that Dave has the name, address and phone number of the leader of the group from the basketball courts. He's seventeen years old Jerome Smith who lives a couple of blocks from the park. After I write down all the info, I tell him to get a couple of the men and meet at my house.

An hour passes and Hap comes rolling in with Boom and Eh-Jax. We sit down and Boom tells the guys that he did some thinking about getting all of the b-ball hoopers in one fell-swoop.

He tells us, "We need to get the leader; snatch him up, bring him in and get him to use his phone to get a good number of his crew of misfits in one place. Once there, we'll drop a net on the entire bunch and secure them to the ground."

I ask, "Secure them to the ground? HOW?!"

He says, "I know of an empty warehouse where there's a thirty-by-thirty-foot cargo net made of one-inch ropes. We can hoist it to the ceiling and once they're all there, we drop it on them. It's really heavy and will flatten the group all at once. We can stun just one guy to show the rest they will be next if they don't cooperate. At that point, we'll tell them to hand over their I.D.s, wallets and cell phones."

Eh-Jax says, "That's an okay plan, but what do we do with them once we have them? Our lockup isn't big enough to house over a dozen guys?"

I tell them, "The net can be their prison for a short time. We need to give these low life punks a chance to straighten up with regards to the problem they're causing at the courts. If they choose to continue in their wayward ways, well, it'll be beatings and 'Sparky time' for them."

All the men agree. Boom says that he can set it up with Hap, Bull and Eh-Jax. The men hit the road and go get it done while I set up a con to trap Jerome.

Isolating Jerome

We need to isolate Jerome. With the number we got on him, I make the call and tell him that he needs to come alone to the neighborhood law office on Woodlawn Street at 4pm to sign papers to release $5,000 in cash a little old lady from the neighborhood left for him in her will. He's told not to tell anyone.

Jerome is excited that he's going to get that kind of money. The trap was set. Now, how can we grab him without making any kind of scene in broad daylight? This was going to be much trickier than night abductions.

I run it by Clint and he says, "Lenny and me can be in disguise and dressed up to pass for detectives; intercept Jerome as he gets near the law office, flash badges and tell him that he needs to come quietly to the station for some questioning about robberies in his neighborhood. We'll lure him to the back of the law office, and bag him there. Since we'll be more or less hidden from any street pedestrians and traffic, we should be able to pull it off without any problems."

I like the idea and tell him and Len to put everything in motion.

Next Step - Picking Up Jerome

At last night's meeting I volunteered to be the one that'd sit outside of Jerome's house to let the guys that will do the pick-up know when he's on his way. It's Wednesday, 3:15 pm. Jerome comes down the front porch steps, to the sidewalk and heads toward the law office. The game is on. Everybody's in place and in a few minutes, we'll have our prey.

As he arrives at the law office, just like we planned, Clint and Len approach him before he gets to the door.

Lenny flashes a badge and tells him, "I'm Detective Lawrence. We need your help to solve the rash of robberies that have been going on in the area. Please come with us to the back of the office so we can talk privately. We don't want any of your friends seeing you speaking to men dressed like us; they might get suspicious."

They walk Jerome to the backside of the office and stand next to the van's sliding door side. When Len begins talking to him, Clint zaps him, he drops to the ground, the van door opens and he's tossed in. Off they go to our life-changing processing center. Our young man is bound; eyes and mouth duct taped; courtesy of Boom and Eh-Jax who came to assist. In a short time, they reach home base.

After Hap backs into the bay inside the warehouse, Boom and Eh-Jax bring Jerome to our interrogation room. This time, no need for back hands to the face. This isn't a real bad guy, just a simple-minded young man that doesn't know how to share public facilities. However, Mr. Sparky will be involved in straightening things out in his delinquent mind.

I start in on him by saying, "So Jerome, the reason we have you here is because you and your low life friends continually hog the basketball courts pretty much every day for hours and threaten anyone who says anything to your group about giving them up. You guys can't cut loose one of those courts so the younger boys can play, huh? That makes you and your buddies, terrible human beings! What do you have to say about that?"

Bull rips off the duct tape from his mouth and Jerome says in a very shaky voice; "I'm sorry, man! Please don't hurt me! I promise me and my friends won't hog both courts no more! I promise! Please let me go home! It won't happen again!"

Boom says, "You may not do it again, Jerome, but how do I know your pals won't keep depriving the younger boys and others the use of the courts?"

After hearing several different voices, Jerome knows there's more than one person there. He starts to get really scared and says, "I'll make sure the older guys only use one court. I promise you for real, man! I promise!"

I put one fingers up to motion Bull to turn on Sparky; he does so for one second, and Jerome is totally caught by surprise. He screams like hell and begins to breathe really heavy. I guess it took his breath away.

"Jerome, that's just a little taste of the pain we will unleash on you and your guys if you all continue to cause trouble at the park. As a matter of fact, you and your pals will cater to the younger boys and be their guardians. Do you understand!"

He's still breathing heavy and whimpering but manages to say, "Oh man! Please don't do that again, please don't hurt me, I understand! I understand! We'll share the courts, I swear it!"

I jump back in say, "It's ten after five. Here's what I want you to do Jerome. You'll use your phone to dial up the guy that is second in command in your bully group and tell him that some guys in the neighborhood grabbed you and hung you up in the Cargill Building on Pratt Street. You'll tell him he'll need to get a bunch of the guys to come help get you down."

After he gives us the guy's name, Boom finds his phone number on Jerome's cell and dials it. He hands it to him and says exactly what he was told to say. It'll take at least a half hour or more for his buddy to gather his troops and more time to get to the grey building. By then, we'll have Jerome hanging and all the men in place with stun guns and baseball bats at the ready for whatever we'll need to do.

Forty minutes pass, and seven of Jerome's guys arrive. They enter the place and can see that he's hanging about twenty feet above them; hands tied in front and tape over his eyes. Me and the rest of the men are well hidden and observe what's going on. One of Jerome's bigger guys goes over to where the rope holding him up is tied to a steel beam. He unties it and begins lowering him. The others standing below are ready to catch him in case he drops too fast. As he gets to about seven feet, we release the net which flattens and traps the entire gang, except the guy that let Jerome down. Eh-Jax comes from behind, stuns him, and ties him up.

Although the light is dim in this building, we're able to see the young lads squirming, trying to escape the heavy hemp net. They're not going anywhere. They're all screaming until Boom yells, "SHUT UP AND LISTEN!"

He tells them to hand over their cell phones and any IDs they have. Everyone frantically hurries to get them out of their pockets, except one. Bull zeros in on him; steps onto the net, making his way to the lad and hits his right shin with a bat. That gets his attention. The boy can't get to his phone and ID out fast enough.

Now, we're all out there in the open with opaque masks on. That's all part of our *M.O.* (*modus operandi*). We need to make sure we're always covered. After all, we're from the same area and the chance of actually crossing paths with one of these kids on the street or in a store is a real possibility.

I tell the boys, "LISTEN VERY CAREFULLY! We are a new kind of law enforcement that will keep track of you. We have your IDs and phones. We'll know all of your names, where you live and people you call on your phones. With them, we will have access to you anytime we want. You'll get your property back through Jerome. We've spoken to him and he will tell y'all what you WILL do! He'll also tell you want we did to him. You won't what he got!"

With that done, Boom signals four of the men to ready themselves to release the four corners of the net that are tethered to steel anchors attached to the floor.

Before that happens, he tells the trapped boys, "We're going to release you. It'll take you a bit of time to get this net off of you. Once you are loose, pay very close attention to what Jerome tells you!"

Boom and the rest of our troop ease their way out of the building. Once the boys see the men leave and the steel door shuts, they scurry to get the net off of them. It isn't easy, but they manage to get free.

Everyone hurries out of the building and make their way back to their neighborhood where Jerome speaks to the boys and lets them know that if they don't share the basketball courts with the younger guys that the men who did this, will grab 'em and put a hurt on them! He tells them about the electric chair and the pain he felt when the electricity went through him.

He says, "Man, you don't want any part of what I went through! Trust me! I thought I was gonna die! We're gonna do what we gotta do so we don't EVER get nailed by those dudes again."

Gary, one of the guys that was caught in the net asks, "Jerome, do you have any idea who these guys are?"

He simply says, "I don't know and I - DON'T want to know! Those men scared me to death! We gotta share the courts so none of us gets hurt!"

Sharing the courts is going to greatly cramp their style, but they all agree that they'll allow the younger boys to play without hassling them.

Basketball Courts Follow up

Friday morning, I tell Hap, "Hey Hap, contact our young troops and have them meet us at the post at 7pm tonight. I'd like to see if we can use them to do a follow up on the basketball players' *comportment* status. This will be a small trial run for them."

A little before 7pm, Chuck, Dave and Mickey show up and we get right down to business.

I tell them, "Okay, you guys would like to help out in the cleaning up of our neighborhood; well, we're going to get you involved. Here's what we have in mind. There's a problem at the basketball courts at Case Park. We've already tagged a bunch of them and want you to go check things out to see that the older boys are letting the younger ones have their own court. Seems the older boys hog both courts and have gotten rough with the little ones. Tomorrow is Saturday; lots of young basketball players will be there. Just go see what's going on and report back."

Mick and his men are up to it and Chuck says, "We can handle that. Hey, we're still young enough to go man to man on a court; maybe we can see about jumping in the game and see how they treat us; that is, if they let us play. If they get stupid with, we may even have a chance to wise-up a guy or two."

I tell 'em, "None of you can afford to have them know who you are or realize that they've seen you at the park. When we need you to step in and give us a hand for future operations, it's gonna be a must that you've remain as unknown as possible. Just go out there, make it a *covert operation* and report back to us. Oh, and take a few photos of the boys on the court in case we need to tune-up any of them. Photos will help zero in on any bad guys."

They signal that they understand and promise to only be in the shadows.

Dave says, "We'll take Angel with us. It's an easy enough job. She can take the photos with a long lens. She did some of that in the service."

"That sounds good to me. Keep an eye on her and see how well she handles her part. It'll be a nice way to see how she does.

Saturday in the Park

Saturday 10 am, the three men and Angel meet up to get to the park. As they arrive, they can see older boys in a five-on-five game on one of the courts, and on the other, younger boys have their own game going on the other court. To Mickey, it looks good until, the ball from the younger players' court inadvertently gets bounced into the path of an older guy and trips him up as he's making his way to the hoop. He gets up off the ground, gets the kid's ball, walks over to him and throws it hard into his stomach; knocking the wind out of him and making him cry. The boy looks to be only about eleven or twelve years old.

He says to the kids, "You boys need to keep your ball on your own damn court or get the hell out of here!"

Chuck, Dave and Mickey stay out of sight so as to not be seen while Angel snaps a few pictures. They hold back from moving in and man-handling this guy named Eddy; to exact street justice right away. They know they need to keep a very low profile, and do just that.

Jerome saw it going down and jumps right in. He goes over to the injured boy to see how he's doing. He's on his knees trying to catch his breath and crying. Jerome squats down and tries his best to console him and yells over at Eddy to come on over. He tells him to apologize to the kid.

Eddy still has his game-face on and tells the kid, "Sorry I hurt you, but I could have gotten busted up when I fell!"

With that kind of attitude and tone in his voice, Jerome stands up, backhands him, and says, "You need to man up and do it right! You hurt this boy! Now be like a big brother to this kid and make us proud!"

Eddy settles his emotions down and tells the boy, "Listen. I didn't mean to hurt you.   I was wrong doing what I did. I'm really sorry."

The boy nods his head to show he accepts the apology. Eddy extends his hand and lifts him to his feet; pats him on the back and says, "Go ahead and play. Have fun. Everything's cool."

With that part of the drama being over, all the boys, big and small, go on playing. Our young vets separate and take a walk a fair distance from the basketball courts, just to observe for a while longer before reuniting at the car to head home. It looks like Jerome will be keeping his promise. That's nothing but, good!

Chapter 34

Porch Pirate

On their way back home, Dave tells Mick to Stop at the Seven-Eleven on the left so he can pick up a couple of twelve packs for the game tonight.

Mick pulls over. Dave gets out and goes in to do his thing. While the other two are in the car talking, Angel spots a UPS delivery man putting a fairly large package on a porch; she's not really focusing on the guy, just a casual observation. The next thing she sees is a van pulling in front of the same house; a guy in his mid-twenties gets out with a package under his arm, goes to the porch, puts down the box he's carrying and snatches the package the UPS guy left. She quickly points that out to Chuck and Mickey; the three look at each other with a look of - *are you kidding!*

Angel says, "We need to tag this punk!"

Chuck says, "I'll bet this is the game; the guy from the van makes like he's delivering a package that probably has nothing in it and takes the UPS box. That's pretty slick."

They see that Dave is at the counter of the Seven-Eleven paying for his beer and comes out directly. As he gets in the car, Mick sees the van moving and makes his way out of the parking lot to follow the creep. Dave sees that he's going the wrong way to take him home and tells him he needs to turn around. Chuck and Angel understand why Mick did that and tell Dave about the porch pirate.

He says to Mick, "Stay on him! Let's get this slime! This is OUR neighborhood! It pisses me off that we have one of THOSE rats doing this to our people! We need to follow him to see where he goes."

Mick stays back far enough so as to not be detected. They can see the UPS van make another stop, and the thief does the same routine; fake box in hand to make the switch at the house and grabbing the goods. They follow for a few more drops on that particular street and watch this brazen hoodlum steal a few more packages. Finally, he turns off in a different direction than that of the UPS guy.

They follow him for about four miles until he turns onto Gavin Street; goes down past several houses and turns in a driveway. As he does a slow roll in, he hits the automatic garage door opener. Before he gets in, Angel gets his license plate number, AXE-3271. They all notice that he has quite a few boxes lining the back and the sides of the garage. She also got the number of the house, 172.

Dave gets on the phone to me. He says, "Hey Boss, you'll never guess what me, Chuck, Angel and Mick just saw! After our basketball *Covert Op* job, on our way home, we spotted a porch pirate. We followed him home to Gavin Street and saw that he has a bunch of UPS packages of all sizes in his three-car garage."

I tell him. "Great work! You know what, I'd like for you four to come up with a plan to nab this weasel and bring him to us. We'll have you come to our headquarters to see the set-up we have to deal with the criminals we've fished in so far. For now, I want you to run your idea by Hap. He'll tell you how we grab these cockroaches and what we do to keep our identity a secret. It's a very important part of how we operate."

Dave says, "No problem, Boss. Hap already shared with me the routine; disguises, surprise drop on perps, duct tape to secure hands and feet, and duct tape over the eyes. He made sure we knew to only call each other Bufford. He also told me about some of the ways your men tweaked some of the rats and then got them to turn themselves in. We'll come up with something and get back to Hap by seven tonight."

Dave gives me the perp's plate number and address. I tell him that I'll get Hap to rundown the owner through his cop friend at the precinct. Dave tells his friends what I proposed. They're really up for it; their very own fishing expedition in our - NEW WAR.

It's 2:30. The guys toss around a few ideas as they ride along. Chuck tells Mick to head for his house. Since he's not married, they'll have the privacy they'll need to put their plan together. Dave is also single. On the other hand, Mickey will stay to plan the "snag" but will get home by five to eat supper with his wife and teen daughter. Angel is free for the day and night. She's up for the planning. The four can't wait to come up with the right con to get this thief isolated and bagged.

Chuck says, "We'll need a van of our own to do this."

Dave says, "How about we pose as Natural Gas Company guys? That way, we can pull right into his driveway, go knock at the door, gain entrance under the pretense that one of his neighbors reported the smell of gas in the area and that we're checking all the meters on the street. We'll tell him that one of us, with a gas-sensing meter needs to check his meter in the basement to make sure it's okay."

As we're discussing our plan, Hap calls Mick and tells him that the plate number checks out for the van and that the guy's name and cell phone number; he is twenty-seven-year-old Kevin Vanick. He also tells him that this guy has done time for burglary and drug dealing.

With that information, the four feel good about going after this criminal. They figure they'll be ridding society of both, a drug dealer and a pretty serious thief. The packages he's stolen may contain people's life-saving medicine or other health equipment, or very important items that people absolutely need.

Mick tells Hap what the plan is and gets the green light to make it happen. It's set, except for the fake Gas Company van.

Dave says, "My brother has a white van equipped with several flashing lights that give people the impression that it's an official van. He uses it to do home repairs on the side and hasn't used it in a few months. I'll get that and meet you guys here at 6:30 tonight."

The fake gas guys

At 6:30 the three meet up at Chuck's house where they planned the operation. They get going right away. About fifteen minutes later, they're at Vanick's house - 172 Gavin Street. Dave is driving and Mick will be the gas man coming to check the meter. They want Angel to just observe for tonight and be ready to help secure the rat when they get him in the van. Part of the plan is to have a small propane tank inside the van with a hose sticking out of the back window and have Angel open it just enough to put a scent of gas in the air. This way, old Kevin will be convinced there's a gas leak.

As Dave stops by the side door of the residence, he and Mick, wearing blue hard hats, get out of the van; Dave has a clipboard in his hands, and Mick has the fake gas-sensor gadget. Mick rings the doorbell and waits for Kevin to answer. Angel does her thing with the propane tank. When he opens the door, he can see the caution flashing lights on the van and right away wants to know that the problem is. Mick tells him about a report of gas smell in the area and that the gas company is checking every house. He's asked to step outside and stand by the van until he checks his meter in the basement with the gas sensor meter.

Kevin can smell gas and stands next to the van. Just as he settles there, Chuck opens the door and zaps him. He's down and loaded in. Chuck and Angel do the binding and gagging. Dave calls Hap and is told where to meet.

They arrive at the designated location where Hap is waiting. He walks up to the van and tells Dave to follow him. As they arrive, Hap beeps his horn for one of the men open the overhead door and the vans roll in.

I walk over to our young team's van and say, "Let's see what you have there."

I see Angel inside and motion with a finger to my lips for her to be quiet! I don't want our prisoner to know there's a lady in the group. She nods to show me she understands. She can be our - *ace-in-the-hole*. No one would suspect a woman is part of the group that is taking down bad guys in the neighborhood. She'll be a special asset. Chuck grabs the thief, eases him out and stands him on his feet.

I tell him, "Okay Bufford, bring him along! It's time to have a little chat with this pirate."

Besides me and our young warriors and Kevin the perp, Hap, Boom and Clint are also there. We enter the interrogation room, sit our new catch down on the *hot seat,* strap him in and get ready to extract information. Just to get his attention, I look at Hap, wink, and put one finger up to signify giving him a one second dose of Sparky. He turns it on - ZAP! This poor fool screams loud enough to be heard across town. Well, our new young soldiers see that and look at each other, a bit astonished, but half smiling at the same time. They're impressed. This shows me they approve. Even Angel has a look of approval. I can only imagine what kind of atrocities she saw in the Middle East in combat. That's good! It shows me she'll fit in just right.

With Kevin's mouth still taped up, Hap begins; "So Kevin, you seemed to not like that very much. That's just a little of much more pain and discomfort you're going to feel if we don't get the right answers from you. Okay?"

Kevin is breathing heavy but manages to nod his head vigorously to say, "*Yes!*" At this point Boom takes the tape off his mouth, but not his eyes.

Kevin says, "Man, please don't hurt me! Don't do that again, PLEASE!!!"

Clint starts off by giving him a fairly hard backhand to the side of the face and tells him. "Hello punk! You know, those packages you stole from people's houses may contain life-saving medicine or medical equipment, even a little girl's birthday present sent from her grandma. Also, many other things that were specially ordered and cost hard-working people a lot of money. To you, it may seem like nothing, but to those folks, it means a whole lot. You're a scumbag and need to atone for what you did. Now then, we're going to ask you questions and if you cooperate, we won't hurt you anymore. But if you don't play ball, you're going to be in a world of hurt."

Right away, Kevin says, "Don't hurt me, please! I'll tell you anything you need to know. But, please don't hurt me anymore!"

I ask him, "How long have you been doing this porch pirating and, do you work alone or with others?"

Still breathing heavy and whimpering, he says, "I've been doing this for about nine months. I'm part of a group of seven guys with vans on the south side that are connected to an older guy who coordinates everything. He's about fifty years old and goes by the name Roscoe. We bring our stuff to him at a large building at 180 Dingens Street. We drive in and each guy empties his van and opens the boxes on eight-foot tables to see what's in them. Once Roscoe sees what's there, he pays us a small percentage based on what he thinks it's going to bring him. Most guys get about $100 to 150 a day. Some of the stuff is really expensive. You can bet he makes a ton of money from what we bring in."

"Okay. That's good information, Kevin. How many men does he have in that building that we need to be aware of?"

"He's always there with three of his guys who oversee everything. He only receives new scored goods from 5 to 7pm. This gives those of us who do the pickups enough time to work the daytime UPS delivery hours and get as much stuff as we can."

I want to know when this Roscoe might be alone.

Kevin says, "He's set up living quarters in an upstairs apartment in the building. He's there all the time. His men get there about four-thirty to get ready to meet the drivers so they can look over the goods and see what they have and figure out where they can fence the merchandise. They usually leave around 8pm."

I signal for the men to go outside the room. With the door closed, we walk far enough so Kevin can't hear our conversation.

First, I turn to Angel and introduce myself. "Hi there, welcome to our headquarters. I'm Bufford and these men are also called Bufford. I'm sure your friends explained the reason for that."

"Yes, they did, and I think that's a very smart idea."

I tell her, "We gladly welcome you to our group and believe you'll be an important asset as we deal with the scums that are hurting our great neighborhood."

"Thanks for allowing me to be part of your unit. I'm really happy to join you guys and anxious to take down bad guys."

I wink at her as a sign of approval and all the guys give her a - thumbs up.

With that formality out of the way, I tell everyone, "Okay. We have all the info we need to bust up this group of creeps doing criminal business in the neighborhood. All we need to do is grab Roscoe and when he's in our custody, we can get him to give up his gang members. It should be a walk in the park."

I look at Hap and say, "What do you think? Should we let our new friends go fishing tonight and bring us a nice easy catch?"

Hap smiles and says, "I think it's a great idea, Boss. Crime will never stop, and once we're gone, our young soldiers will need to carry on for us. By all means, let's give them this *mission*.

Chuck, Mike, Angel and Dave all look at me, and Mike says, "Boss, it's funny you thought about us taking over down the road. We talked about that and even expanding our group with other patriot-minded vets from our age group. We know of several solid and loyal guys that would fit right in; all of them, Middle East War vets. We'd be honored to carry on this war."

I smile broadly and tell them, "Guys, you don't know how good that makes me and the others feel. You're gonna be needed after we're done with local operations to keep this neighborhood safer by taking out the trash that keeps coming around. Tonight is your second mission and I'm confident you will do yourselves and us, proud."

Chapter 35

Plans to Nab Roscoe

It's all set. We sit down with our young crew to plan the abduction. I tell Hap and Clint that we'll need to be close by as backup in case any of Roscoe's men pop in while they do their thing. I don't think we'll really be needed. But like I said in the beginning of our New War - we must leave nothing to chance.

The initial plan is for the younger guys to roll up to the building in Kevin's van, wait till 10pm, and quietly break in after Roscoe's men have left; find Roscoe, snag him, and bring him to home base.

Chuck says, "Boss, it might be a good idea to stake out the building before we make our move; to make sure Roscoe's men aren't there."

I agree and tell him and his guys, "That's the kind of thinking you'll need to approach any of the missions you'll be involved in from here on. Okay, you guys get there a bit early to make sure none of Roscoe's men are hanging around. Me and my men will be there around 9:20 or so to observe and to watch your backs."

It's 9:00 pm. The men are ready to move out. Mike and his guys get there by 9:15 to watch and see when Roscoe's three men leave.

As Mike and his guys are on watch, me, Hap and Clint arrive on the scene at 9:25 and quietly come to a stop two buildings away from Roscoe's place. We can see Dave's van with his team inside. They've got their eyes on the main entrance and at 9:30, all of Roscoe's guys come out. They each go to their own car and drive away. That part went smooth. That's good! But the men want to wait a few minutes to make sure Roscoe has gone up-stairs. When they see the warehouse lights go off, they know he's shut things down. They wait to see lights go on in the upstairs apartment before moving in.

At 10:30, they make their move. Figuring the door will be locked. The trickiest part will be, entering quietly. The four are ready for that. It's a good thing that it's an old building with an older door. From the van, Mike checks to see if it's fitted with an alarm system and can see that it's basically just an old decrep-it structure. More than likely, Roscoe didn't spend any money on security. After all, the equipment, installation, and monthly security service fees cost money; that's money out of his pocket. Good thing for us Roscoe is a tight-wad.

Looking at the place, they can see him moving around up there. That's good. It means that if they make a bit of noise when they pry open the door, the sound won't carry all the way up to the apartment. Dave has a crowbar that will pop open the door. They approach, and as luck would have it, there's a nice gap between the door and the frame for the pry bar to get a good grip. Dave inserts it and eases the door open. They're in!

The lights have been turned off in the area where all the stolen merchandise is located; only a couple of small lights are on. This gives our men just enough light to see their way to the stairs that lead to Roscoe's door. Quietly, Dave and Chuck go up while Mike and Angel stand guard below in case one of Roscoe's guys returns. You never know. Not knowing if Roscoe would see them open the door to jump him, they need to make sure he's not in eyesight of the door. They thought about that as they planned this operation and Mike would be the one to cause a distraction. Dave turns on a small flashlight to signal to Mike to go outside and create a racket below the apartment window. Next to the building, he finds an old forty-five-gallon metal garbage can and tosses it in the street. When he does, Roscoe hears the noise and goes to the window to check things out.

As soon as Dave and Chuck hear the noise, they make their move, slowly opening the door, they walk in and sneak up on Roscoe who has his back to them. Chuck zaps him with a stun gun! His body tenses up and down he goes. They tape his eyes, mouth and hands. He's a bit of a fat man. It's gonna be a chore getting him to the van. The good thing for this squad is that they're young and able. With great effort, they drag him down the stairs and to the door near the street. As Mike and Angel saw them carry their prize downstairs, Mike takes off to get the van and brings it right up to the door. He opens the sliding van door, gets out and helps put Roscoe inside. Angel and Chuck put the special shocking headgear on his head. Off they go to our home base. They arrive there at 11:15.

Roscoe persuaded

The young recruits take their catch out of the van and head to the interrogation room. As he's place in the chair, he's pretty freaked out! He's all strapped in and ready for us to get incriminating information from him that will be taped for the authorities.

I step up and tell him, "Roscoe, you've been abducted because you're a criminal and need to be prosecuted. You know what you've done and you will cooperate with us."

At that point, I nod for Hap to light him up with old Sparky; just a quick taste. Roscoe goes wild and does his best to scream through the duct tape over his mouth as he convulses from the shock.

I tell him, "Roscoe, that's just a little sample of what you'll get if you don't give us the information we want. You'll have the night to think about that. Since it's so late, we're going to tuck you in for now and talk in the morning."

I motion for Hap and Eh-Jax to move him out and put him in one of the cages.

As they lock him in, Clint tells him, "We're going to take the tape off your mouth, but if you say ONE WORD, we'll tape you up for the night. And, don't attempt to take off the head gear, it'll trigger a shock mechanism that will hurt more than you can imagine. You can feel around for your blanket on the floor, water to drink and a bucket with toilet paper to take care of your bathroom needs. Sleep tight you low life!"

To separate him and Kevin. They put Kev in a small secure room with the same amenities as the cages. This way, they won't be able to talk. Roscoe has no clue one of his thieves is also in our custody. He'll know tomorrow. As usual, one of our men volunteers to stand watch for the night. The rest of us and the new guys take off. Before we get in our cars, I tell our young troop that we'll meet up by 8am tomorrow. Only Chuck and Dave say they can be there. Mick and Angel have things to attend to.

The Interrogation

The next day around 8 am, everyone shows up and we get right to it. I tell Bull and Clint to fetch Roscoe. They bring him in the room; sit him down and strap him in. He doesn't say a word. He just breathes hard like he's about to have a heart attack and waiting to get a jolt from *sparky*. I back hand him hard enough for him to understand that he'll get more if he doesn't cooperate.

He says, "Please don't hurt me anymore! Please! I'll tell you whatever you want to know."

I tell him, "I'm going to ask you some questions and I want exact details."

He's quick to answer, "I will! I promise I will! Just don't hurt me. PLEASE!"

"Okay Roscoe. How long have you and your band of thieves been doing this porch piracy, and how many men are you working with?" (Hap has the tape recorder going).

He answers, "Me and three of my friends have been at it for a little over a year. We also have five to seven regular younger guys with vans that do the pickups and bring the goods to us."

"That's good info Roscoe. Now then, we need the names of your cohorts in the warehouse. Who are they? I want first and last names!"

He says, "One guy is Sonny Ferrini, the other two are Larry Conrad and Brandon O'Shei."

"Thank you! When do you expect them at your place again?"

"They'll be coming in today around 4 pm. The guys with vans won't be there until the next day."

"You know Roscoe, what you and your misfits have done has caused a lot of people, the UPS drivers and their company, very serious problems. Some little girl probably missed getting her birthday gift from her grandma because of you dirt-bags, or some elderly lady missed getting an order of insulin. You cockroaches have caused incredible hardships for many people including several businesses waiting for critical parts to complete important projects. For that, you and your whole bunch of low life rats are going to do time in a real jail for a long time! Sit tight for a while. I need to speak to my unit."

Since it's now only 9am, I tell Hap and Eh-Jax, "Let's lock him up till around 2:30 pm, then get him back to his warehouse, tie him up and have Hap call his friend at the police station to come see what's in there. When the cops get there, they'll have Roscoe sitting in the middle of all the goods with a note and the tape hung around his neck. We'll also get Kevin and have Dave and Chuck bring him to his house and secure him in his garage with all of the packages he's got stored there. That way, when Hap gives his buddy Shawn at the station the addresses of both our perps, they'll have all the evidence they need to fully prosecute them."

Hap goes back in the interrogation room, unstraps Roscoe and escorts him back to his cage. It's a go. By 2:15, all of the guys are ready to go. Hap asks Boom and Bull to get Roscoe and put him in his van. Bull leads Chuck and Dave to Kevin's lockup; they load him in their van to take him to his house where he'll be tied up in his garage for the police. They'll see what he has stored there and, like Roscoe, they'll find a note pinned on him that will explain everything.

Both teams, each with their prize, leave to secure both men in their respective places; Roscoe in his warehouse and Kevin in his garage. By 3:30 pm, when both crews are done securing their man, Hap calls Sergeant O'Rourke at the station;

"Hey Shamus, this is Hap. We have a couple of bad guys for you and your men to pick up. These perps are all involved in UPS porch piracy. One guy lives at 172 Gavin Street and the other, you'll find in his warehouse at 180 Dingens Street. Both are nicely packaged for you with a note telling you all about their criminal escapades. Roscoe, the guy on Dingens will give you the names of his accomplices and the six other *pirates* involved. When you see where Kevin and Roscoe are and what's around them, you'll know to contact the UPS folks. They'll have their work cut out for themselves making things right for the people wondering where their packages went. Take care, my friend."

Shawn says to Hap, "We've been looking for the creeps that have been doing the pirating for a while now. This is great! Captain Mendola has been on my men's back about catching these low life rats. Thanks! He'll be very happy to hear we've got them. Okay then. You take care, too. I'll be in touch."

All the men return home and wait for word of the next mission. The thought had occurred to me that we older patriots might need to use our younger soldiers to handle more of the future outings to catch bad guys. My plan at the next meeting is to ask my guys what they think. After all, we're not young anymore and this is really a younger man's game.

Arresting the Pirates,

About 3:30pm. Sergeant O'Rourke's men raid Roscoe's warehouse, led by Lieutenant Landry, and Kevin's home, led by a Sergeant James (Jimmy) Rowley. At Roscoe's place, the cops knew to lay low and wait for his three accomplices to show; Sonny Ferrini, Larry Conrad and Brendan O'Shei. At 4:10, Brendan and Larry show up. As soon as they cross the threshold, they're taken down, cuffed and held. At 4:20, Sonny enters and gets the same treatment as his cohorts. All the perps are booked on third degree grand larceny charges. Some of these guys could get up to12 years in jail. Because of the volume and worth of packages stolen, the charges could be bumped up to Fifth Degree Felony theft; a very serious charge carrying jail time up to 20 years in prison. Thanks to our methods of extracting information from our prisoners, we got Roscoe to give up the names of the other six porch pirates. They were quickly arrested and jailed.

Chapter 36

A talk with Captain Mendola

Captain Mendola got wind that his men finally broke the *porch pirate* case and wanted specifics for this latest bust. The way it went down according to arrest reports; he figured it was our squad that made it all happen. Again, he put the word out among his precinct that he wanted to meet with one of the squad members. He made it clear that he was okay with the way it came about and that he just wanted a sit-down with whoever leads these concerned citizens.

He said, "If anyone of you can put me in touch with one of them, contact him and see if he'll meet with me. Tell him, I just want to talk."

That same night, Sergeant O'Rourke calls Hap and tells him what Captain Mendola wants to do. He tells him that he'd contact me as soon as he hangs up to see what he could do to make it happen. Hap makes the call and relays all that O'Rourke told him and gives me a number to call. I dial him up on a burner phone.

As soon as Mendola answers, I ask him, "Captain Mendola, how do you feel about some of the weird arrests your precinct has made lately?"

"First of all, you know me, but I don't know who you are. What can I call you?"

"Captain, you can call me *Friend* for the moment. I want to remain anonymous. Maybe in time I'll reveal to you who I am. So, what can I do for you?"

"I'd like to meet with you to discuss what's been going on in my precinct with regards to people in the neighborhood disappearing and several bad guys getting tied up in vacant buildings for my men to collar. What do you think? Can we meet?"

I tell him, "If we meet, the game is over for me and my men. I don't feel I can give up what we've started so soon. There's a constant flow of scum bags out there that keep popping up and when they're arrested, too many walk free. That doesn't make it for me and my men. Since you know we exist, are you willing to leave us alone to do what we do?"

"Well *Friend*, as a cop with rank, you know I can't just okay that. I need to be the one in charge of bagging bad guys; not every day citizens."

"I get that Captain, but what you don't understand is, we're not your *everyday citizens*; we're a special part of the citizenry. We'll only go as far as needed in getting creeps off the streets. We more than respect you and your men and all they do. All I ask is that you respect what we do. I believe we can complement each other and go on that way until we decide to cut it loose."

"I can accept that. But, please understand that your way of dealing with criminals is not the proper and legal way things are done."

"I understand Captain, but our way is much quicker and the result of our actions puts these social misfits where they belong at a quicker rate than what your department or any courts can do or are willing to do. You know yourself how the courts drag on the whole process of serving criminals their just rewards. We expedite the process. And, if by chance they should get set free, we're here to intercept them and deal out our own punishment. Captain, I respect what you and your men are doing and you have our complete backing, but you know yourself, you can't do it all. And, you have to agree, we've made a huge difference in the short time we've been active. We'll keep doing what we do as long as we can and hopefully have your support and respect, as you have ours."

"Okay Friend, I can see you won't budge from where you stand on all this. I get it. And, I won't interfere unless you take things too far. I appreciate the collars we've made because of your involvement in criminal activities in my precinct. Next time you deal with a bad guy or a group of bad guys, would you do me a personal favor and call me first so that I can be the one in charge of picking up what you leave us to haul in?"

"You got it, captain. You'll be the first person I call. I promise."

"Thank you, my friend. Take care."

Chapter 37

Restructuring the teams

Wednesday night rolls around and the guys meet up at the VFW for a special get-together. Hap made a call to our younger partners to invite them to join us in discussing their future with us. It should be a short and sweet meeting.

My crew is already settled in when Mike, Angel, Dave, and Chuck arrive at 7:30. Hap motions for them over to where my men are and everyone takes a seat in a separate room from the bar area.

I begin by saying, "Gentlemen and Lady Angel, we're going to restructure our operation a bit. By that I mean, me and my men want you to be a lot more involved in taking down the cockroaches in our neighborhood. So far, we've seen a change. Somehow, the word must've gotten out in the streets that there's a group of very scary men taking out 'bad people.' For the next several take-downs, we'd like for you to take the lead in dealing with the trash in our area."

Chuck jumps in and says, "Boss, first of all, we want to thank you for having that kind of confidence in us." Mick, Angel and Dave echo his sentiment.

Mick says, "Me and the others, which includes Angel, already talked about several characters that need to be checked off the 'bad guys list.' We've even come up with scenarios for taking them out of commission and a getting them to the lockup."

Hap tells them, "Fellas, and you Angel - we're glad you're on board and can't wait to see what you come up with. Us older soldiers will be in on the missions you put in motion. Just make sure you run everything by Boss or any of the other men here, okay?"

Dave nods and tells the older guys, "We will make you proud that you opened a door for us to be involved in ridding our neighborhood's lowlifes. Like you, we've seen the decay in our streets and the insane amount of crime that's gone on too long. May I propose a toast to our new alliance?"

He raises his bottle of Coors; all the others raise their glass or bottle, and all the men shout out that famous military war cry, "Hoo-ah!"

Chapter 38

New team talks about new mission, Catalytic converters thieves

The younger guys get together in their own corner of the VFW post to begin hashing out a plan to nab a group of young thieves that have been stealing catalytic converters from cars and pickups in the neighborhood. So far, they've gotten reports that maybe 50 to 70 cars have been hit; maybe more. It's time to bring this to a screeching halt! They know that to replace a Cady's converter can cost up to $1,500 or more with installation. For less expensive cars, the costs are anywhere between $400 and $700. And, for some expensive cars, up to $2,500!

Chuck says, "One of the guys from the streets that's been keeping me informed about crime in our neighborhood says that a twenty-one-year-old punk named Kenny Hunter from Delmont Street is one of four guys doing the stealing. So far, the estimate is that they've stolen close to 80 converters and selling them to crooked car shops around town. We can get him tomorrow night when he leaves his house."

He asks Dave, "Hey Dave, can you still get your brother's van?" "Yes, I can. As a matter of fact, he told me he'd like to get rid of it. It'd be perfect to add to our arsenal to clean up the trash from our streets. He said that since it's twelve years old and has a little over 90,000 miles on it, he'd let it go for $1,000."

Chuck says, "Only a thousand bucks! Tell your brother he's got a deal. I've got it covered. Just get the papers for it. We'll only need liability insurance; no collision, fire, glass or theft coverage. It shouldn't coast much, maybe around $400 to $500."

"Thanks Chuck! We'll have it for tomorrow night's fishing trip. Can't wait to hook this fish! And when we get him, we'll get the names of his cohorts, and nab them too."

The plan is to stake out his house and wait till he leaves. From the info Dave got from his source, he said Kenny usually waits till a little before midnight to do his dirty work; when most folks are asleep. As a matter of fact, these guys call themselves, *'The Midnight Crew.'* They always hit cars after midnight. That works for us too. We'll have the cover of night to sneak up on him, wrap him up, and take him to meet *sparky*.

The next day

The next day, Dave took his brother's van to Chuck's house, gave him the keys and papers. He, in turn, got the paper-work done at the DMV and took care of the insurance. Now that it's street legal, the men are all set. They gather at the Wayside Restaurant at eleven o'clock to do a quick run through for the mission. At 11:20, they drive to Delmont Street, park, and wait.

It's 11:35 when they spot Kenny going to his garage. From what they can see, he's putting tools in his trunk. We figure those are burglar tools. As our unsuspecting thief takes off to make his score, we follow. He only goes a few blocks and parks near a repair shop with customers' cars are being held for the next day. They are perfect targets to get their converters stolen.

We see Kenny getting his tool bag out of the trunk and walk over to a Cadillac. He has a small jack that he uses to bring the car to a level that will allow him to work. He crawls under with his battery-powered reciprocating saw that can cut through the exhaust pipe within a couple of minutes. We don't wait for him to hack the pipe. While our perp is settling under the car, Mick zaps him. Chuck grabs his legs and pulls him out. Dave and Angel are ready with the hood and duct tape. Kenny is dazed momentarily. The guys gather his tools and throw everything in the van along with the creep. Mick gets the thief's car keys so he can drive it to the lockup.

While heading there, Chuck calls Hap to let him know that they're on their way to home base. He tells him that he'll meet his team there. In turn, he calls Bull who is baby sitting at the lock up to get ready to welcome our young squad's catch. Since it's so late, Bull is asked to fit the *new fish* with the usual head gear and lock him up in a cage till morning when some of the older and younger crew members and can deal with Mr. Hunter.

The following morning

By the time I get to our headquarters at 8:30 am, Eh-Jax, Bull, our young troopers; Dave and Chuck have Kenny strapped in the *hot seat*, blind folded, with tape over his mouth. I motion for the guys to go out of the room.

I follow and tell them and tell Dave and Chuck, "I'd like for you two to interrogate this guy; to get any information that would get us the other rats in the theft ring and who the buyer is for the goods."

Since they've seen the older men in our operation interrogate a couple of the perps we've grabbed, they know what to do.

Dave says, "Boss, it'll be a pleasure for me and Chuck to get this creep talking and then have the pleasure of getting the others involved in the thieving."

Chuck is the first to act. Dave has positioned himself at the control of *Sparky* and Chuck shows one finger to signal, one second. Dave turns on the juice, Kenny screams and stiffens up!

They let our guest come down from the shock and Chuck says, "Kenny, you didn't like that, huh? You'll get a lot more of it if you're not honest with us."

Dave jumps in and tells him, "We want the names of the other guys in your little group that have been ripping off hard-working folks' catalytic converters. And, we want the names of the people buying them!"

Kenny answers, "I work alone. I don't know anyone else stealing converters."

Chuck nods again and Dave clicks on *sparky* for a full two seconds! That gets Kenny's attention. Now, not only is he screaming like a dying pig being slaughtered, but he's also breathing heavy like he just ran the mile in record time.

Chuck says to him, "Okay Kenny. Catch your breath and give up everything you've got!"

He blurts out. "Please don't hurt me no more, I'll tell you everything! I'll tell you everything! The other three are; Otis Reed from Okell Street, Tim Jones and Harry Schultz live six houses from each other on Elk Street. The guy who buys the converters is Tom Tillman. Everybody calls him TT. His place is over at Top Care Auto on Farnsworth Street. Depending on the condition, he pays us $25 to $50 for each one."

Both, Bull and me look at each other like we're thinking, *"Well, that was easy."*

Chucks says, "That's real good Kenny. Now then, we're going to keep you here for a couple of days until we make arrangements to put you in the hands of the police that will deal with you and the rest of the people involved in this. You idiots have caused a lot of grief to good people; plus, a huge expense to have their muffler system fixed! Some of them don't have the money on hand to pay for that. You and your scum bag friends are lower than dirt!"

I motion for Eh-Jax to take him to the lock up.

We all gather in a side room. Bull tells our young guns, "Gentlemen, you did yourself proud the way you handle the entire operation. We couldn't have done it any better. Great job!"

Hap adds, "We're looking forward to your next catch, whatever that may be. Do you have one lined up?"

Chuck tells us, "After we get all of the converter thieves in lockup, we plan on snagging some creep that has been spiking ladies' drinks at Joe's Tavern on Lewis Street and then, put a bull's eye on a private contractor that's dumping trash at the end of Erie Street from jobs he does. We also have our eyes on a couple of public nuisance situations we're planning on making right."

Nailing the Other Three Thieves;
Otis Reed, Tim Jones and Harry Schultz

Dave, Chuck, Angel, and Mick have all the info they need to pick up the other catalytic converter thieves. In the cover of night, the team lays in wait on Okell Street for Otis Reed to leave his house. He's parked on the street. As soon as he puts his hand on the door handle, he's zapped and dragged to the *paddy wagon*, and off they go to the lock up where they put him in a cage. Afterward, they go out again to see if they can nail the other two perps.

The plan is to lay in wait for Tim Jones and Harry Schultz on Elk Street. Tim returns first. The men positioned themselves near his house. It takes a while, but he shows up after about a half hour. As soon as he exits his car, BAM! He's taken down; a sack is placed over his head and thrown in the van. Angel and Dave inside bind him up really good as Chuck drives to the warehouse with their latest catch of the night. Babysitter Boom is on night duty and will keep watch over them.

After locking Tim up, the men head out to snag Harry Schultz. They roll over to his house but don't see his car. The wait isn't too long. An hour later, here he is. Perfect! He must have been really busy, because he doesn't get home till 1:30 am. Just like they did to Tim, they hide near where he parks and when he gets out of the car, he's zapped by Chucky. Mick and Angel haul him into the van, wrap him up with duct tape and put a hood over his head. He gets the same unpleasant ride to the lockup and placed in his own little cell. All four rats are in their cage and are told to not to talk to each other - or else! Everyone is quiet. The team has their cars with tools and catalytic converters inside. For any cop having all of this evidence, it's as solid a case as can be. All prisoners accounted for; the young squad heads home to get a well-deserved rest while Boom stands guard.

The interrogation room

The next day while Mick, Angel and Dave are at work, Chuck has the pleasure of being part of the interrogation session with the senior men. He'd like for each one to get a two second taste of Sparky, just to make them pay a bit for the crimes they've committed against the people in our neighborhood. Bull brings out Otis first, sits him down in the chair and secures. This time, Chuck is at the controls of Sparky and lights it up for two seconds. Otis lets out a scream that shakes the walls! His buddies in lockup can hear him and are petrified! They're all freaked out, including Kevin, who's already been introduced to - *the chair*. After Otis calms down, nothing is said by any of the men. They release him and walk him back to his cell.

Next in line for the shock treatment are Tim and Harry. Chuck is enjoying giving each perp the same two second treatment with the same results - screaming and whimpering. Then, they're placed back in their cell for the day. The plan is to let them sit there till all of our young team members can be present later tonight. Then, the rats will be brought back to be dealt with by our young patriots.

Night time arrives

Around 6pm, as planned, the young thieves are marched to the larger room, with the tape rolling to record their confessions. Although everyone knows who's involved, for the sake of taping all four, Mick begins by saying…

"I'm going to ask only once and the answer better come quick, or you will ALL get shocked again; only this time, for a full five seconds instead of two! Who among you is the leader of this idiot crime group?"

Harry, who is the oldest among them says, "I am. I'm the one that came up with doing what we've been doing. I'm also the one that found a buyer for the converters."

For the sake of getting more info on the tape, Dave asks, "And, who is the man buying the stolen goods from you."

"His name is Tom Tillman," says Harry. "He owns Top Care Auto over on Farnsworth Street near Bailey."

Chucks wants to know how long they've been doing the stealing.

Harry tells him, "We grouped up about eight months ago.

All the while, our young team has been processing the crooks, me, Eh-Jax, Hap and Bull give our men a thumbs up to show that we are pleased with their work. That makes me feel confident that our new recruits will be just fine going forward. They've proven that they are very capable.

Notifying Captain Mendola

After Mick and his people leave, Hap does his usual of - *dropping a dime* - to his contact at the precinct and telling him about the catalytic converter thieves.

He tells Sergeant O'Rourke, "We promised your boss, Captain Mendola, that we would give him a heads-up first about any new leads on criminals we bag so he can get the credit for bringing them in. So, make like you know nothing about it and let your boss have his moment of glory."

O'Rourke understands and assures him that he'll play dumb and won't let on.

I make the call and am able to reach the good captain. I tell him, "Captain Mendola, this is your - friend. As promised, I'm contacting you first to tell you where to find the catalytic converter thieves who call themselves, the *Midnight Crew*. We have all four neatly packaged for you and to tell you where they're located; along with their cars filled with the tools, stolen goods inside and a tape that will seal their conviction. They've been secured inside the old vacant shoe store at 180 Kimmel Avenue. Also, you'll need to hit the Top Care Auto Shop on Bailey, owned by Tom Tillman. He's the one buying up all the stolen converters."

Captain Mendola is very pleased, and says, "I'm really happy that you honored our agreement about letting me know of any new take downs you and your men do. It means a lot to me. For that, you have my respect."

I tell him, "I'm more than glad to hold up my end of the deal. Now, go round up those weasels. They've caused a lot of grief and loss of money to people in the neighborhood. Take care."

The conversation ends there. I'm sure we'll get a report from O'Rourke later to let us know how everything went with Mendola and his men.

Chapter 39

Spiking ladies' Drinks

Our young soldiers have another situation to deal with in their neighborhood; creeps spiking ladies' drinks at a local bar then taking advantage of them.

Dave is at the River Inn near the corner of Harding Avenue and spots a couple of dudes trying to impress a young lady named Marie. She's 21. While one of them (Hank) is talking to her, the other rat (Skipper) puts something in her drink. Right away, Dave sends a text message to his buddies to get over to the inn right away. In the meantime, he watches to see what is happening. After about ten minutes, he can see the drug is making Marie drowsy and she begins to sway a bit. As the two punks keep talking to her, Dave sees Chuck and Angel come in the door. Angel tells him that Mick can't make it.

He tells her, "That's okay. We can handle these two monkeys."

He asks Chuck, "Do you have your stun gun with you?"

"Yes! And, I also have the necessary things to tie up these idiots."

"Good! Let's hang by the door and wait for them to make a move to leave. Their little game is most likely, drugging girls, waiting for them to be too out of it to drive, offer them a ride home, and, you can take it from there; taking full advantage of their stupor. This has rape written all over it."

Dave sees them getting ready to escort the young lady out, one on each side of her. As they walk toward their car, conveniently parked in a secluded part of the lot, Hank fumbles with his car keys while Skipper holds on tight to Marie.

Angel walks over and says, "Is she okay? Do you need me to call an ambulance?"

As Angel distracts the perps, Chuck silently comes behind Hank and zaps him. He lets him fall on his face to the ground. Before Skippy realizes what just happened, Dave tases him with the same 35,000 volts which in turn travels into Marie who is being held by Skip. Old Skipper falls and Angel is able to catch Marie before she hits the pavement. She's gently placed in the car while the two scum bags lay on the ground. Dave begins to secure Hank while Angel binds Skippy. As they're doing that, Skip starts coming to. Chuck hits him with another shot of voltage and out he goes. Angel opens the trunk of the perps' car and the men toss them in.

Chuck calls to give me all of the details. I tell him, "Great job!" I'll let Mendola know about this. He'll be sending his men right away. In the meantime, hang around in the shadows to see exactly what goes on when the cavalry arrives and fill me in after they're gone."

"No problem, Boss. Dave and I are interested in seeing how this turns out. We have the young lady lying comfortably in the car with Angel watching over her. She's staying with the girl so she can tell the emergency guys that she found her like that and called 911.

I call Captain Mendola and tell him, "Captain, this is your *friend* again. Listen, two of my men just put a couple of rats inside the trunk of their car. They doped a young lady's drink at the River Inn and tried to get her in their car. A 911 emergency call was placed for them to come A.S.A.P. to tend to her. Her name is

Marie. I suggest you get your guys there right away so they can give these sewer rats what they deserve."

"My friend, thanks again. I appreciate this courtesy to me. I'll send my men to retrieve the rats, as you call them. I'll make sure these sleazeballs are dealt with appropriately; of that, you can be sure. The very same thing happened to one of my men's daughters. She was drugged, raped repeatedly, slapped around quite a bit, and then dumped on some side street. She's still a mess! As you can imagine, he's super pissed! We never caught who did it. Who knows, it could be one, or both the guys your men nabbed. That's two leads in two days. Keep up the good work my friend!"

"Roger that, Captain. I'll be in touch." I hang up and call Chuck to see how things are progressing.

He tells me, "Boss, there are all kinds of red flashing lights in the parking lot at the inn. The E.M.T.s loaded Marie in the ambulance and headed to the hospital. While the ambulance guys and cops gathered to see how the girl was, Angel simply slipped away without being noticed. She's good, Boss."

Taking a lead from Captain Mendola, the cops opened the trunk and pull out our two rapists, stood them up, cut the duct tape that secured their hands and feet, then, pulled off the tape we put over their mouth and eyes. One cop in particular took extra pleasure in slamming one of the perps really hard on the trunk lid of the car before putting cuffs on him."

I tell him, "That may have been the cop whose daughter was drugged and raped; pretty much the same way Marie was drugged. Luckily for Marie, the two deviants you nailed didn't get the chance to rape her. Excellent work, men, and, lady! I'll get Hap to follow through with his contact at the precinct to see what will become of those two cockroaches. Have a good night, guys. We'll see you at the post tomorrow."

They take turns saying, "Good night to you too, Boss."

At the post, next night

The word was out to my squad about our young patriots bagging the two worms that have been spiking ladies' drinks. All the men, and lady, of both crews showed up to hear how Hank and Skippy faired at the station. Hap had all day to get whatever info he could on the case. I asked him to share what he got from Sergeant O'Rourke.

"Well, according to my contact, they processed the two depraved souls. Since one of Mendola's men had the same thing happen to his daughter; raped repeatedly, you can imagine the rage this dad had toward them. The police lab guys got DNA samples of Hank and Skippy to see if there's any match. They put a rush on getting the results. They should know in a few days and O'Rourke promised me that he'd let me know as soon as he hears, either way."

In the meantime, I believe our young troopers are working on another mission. Dave, you want to fill us in about your next outing?"

"Sure Boss. Our next target is a group five punks on a public bus route that are harassing students and older people. Chuck found out from his nephew Billy that these foul-mouth idiots are just rude and crude maggots. They've roughed him up and a few of his buddies a couple times; back handed an eighty-year-old man and make it a game of fondling high school age young ladies. The punks all get off at the same bus stop. Our plan is to zero in on the one that is the leader. Billy told Chuck that he goes by the name of Toro, that's '*bull*' in Spanish; he's seventeen; a mix of Hispanic and American. We're going to straighten him out and his little rat pack very soon."

Update on Marie's rape case

Hap tells the group, "I got the report on that drug/rape case. Marie is okay but still very shaken up after finding out what was done to her by those two. As a precaution, they'll keep her in the hospital for another day to make sure the drugs are out of her system. As for any DNA report on those cockroaches, Shawn said that it'll be another week, at least. I'll keep in touch with him."

Chapter 40

Bad Boys on the Metro Bus

The next day, Dave, Angel and Chuck are in the van waiting for the punks to get off the bus. They all get off at Martin and Towne, then, split up to head home. Chuck was given a good description of Toro by his nephew Billy. He spots him in the group and follows him at a good distance to see where he lives. Half way down Chamberlin Street, Toro makes a right and enters the house at number 54. Good! Now all the men have to do is set things up to grab him. Being that it's only 4:30 in the afternoon, they get creative.

Chuck in disguise, walks up to the house limping; knocks on the door, the mom answers. He tells her, "I have a heavy package in the van for you; do you have someone that can help me, I have bad leg."

"You have package for me. Okay, just a minute I'll get my son. He's a strong kid. He'll get it." She tells her young daughter, "Go get Toro! He needs to help the delivery man."

Toro comes to the door, his mom tells him; "Toro, help this man. His leg is bad and he needs your help with a package he has in his van for us."

You can see his punk attitude by the way he looks bothered that he has to do a little work. That says a lot. So many of today's young people are just plain lazy! Toro fits the bill. He follows

Chuck, and as he opens the sliding side door of the van, he's zapped, and in he goes. Chuck and Angel secure the young buck as Dave drives away. Of course, like most young people, he has his cell phone in his back pocket, to which, Chuck retrieves and looks for his home number. Got it! Apparently, his father is the American side of the family and mom is Puerto Rican. Toro's real name is Archie Nesbit; seventeen years old. Archie! Really?! No wonder he has a nickname."

Chuck calls the house, his mom answers and he tells her, "Mrs. Nesbit, this is the delivery man. Toro needs to go with me to pick up another box that was supposed to go with the one I brought. I forgot it at the distribution center. He'll be home in about two hours; nothing to worry about. He's going to be a great help to me."

She's a bit apprehensive and tells Chuck, "Why didn't he come back in to tell me this himself. I don't like him going off with no stranger like that! That worries me!"

"Mrs. Nesbit, he's a big strong kid and I need him to help me get the other box off a raised dock at the warehouse. We'll be back in no time. Trust me!"

"Alright, but you make sure he's back in two hours, no more! …or I'll call the cops!"

Chuck tells her, "No problem. He'll be home before you know it."

While Chuck was on the phone with Toro's mom, Dave called me to say they were on their way to the warehouse with the "catch of the day." I, in turn, called the others and made my way to meet up with everyone to see how the interrogation will go.

The men made it fast to the interrogation center, maybe fifteen minutes. Toro, blindfolded and mouth taped, is brought to the room, seated and strapped in. Of course, he must get the sparky treatment. Lenny lets him have a quick dose for one second to let him know he's in real trouble. Being that he's only seventeen, the men don't want to hurt him too badly. Toro goes out of his mind when the juice is turned on. He's screaming through the tape over his mouth and begins crying.

Dave says, "Toro, calm down. This will be over soon if you cooperate. You may have some idea as to WHY you've been brought here; you know… bad behavior on the bus. Anyway, we have to wait for a few other men that will want to talk to you, so sit tight! They'll be here in a few minutes; and if you're a really good boy, you can be home in an hour or so…just like I promised your momma."

Since it was Chuck that brought up the bus problem, he tells Toro, "I'm going to remove the tape over your mouth, but I don't want you to say a word, you got it?!"

He nods his head to show he gets it and Chuck says to him, "You and your gang of idiots have been causing serious problems on the bus after school. I heard that you and your goons, while using gutter talk, have been beating up students, beat an eighty-year-old man, threatened a mom that was with her little girl because she yelled at you?! All that is bad enough, but you also think that it's okay to sexually assault young ladies!"

With that said, it sets the stage for punishment to begin. Toro doesn't get a chance to say a word, Chuck cracks him one on the side of the jaw, Dave turns on *sparky* for a second and Toro begins crying out loud and pleads us to not hurt him anymore.

He says, "I'm so sorry! I won't do it again! I won't do it again! I promise you, so help me God! Don't hurt me no more! PLEASE!!!"

Dave says, "For now, we won't hurt you, but you need to name the other guys in your little assault group! Start talking!

He blurts out… "Anthony Bosco, Ray Stone, Kim Miller and James Thomas. That's everyone. Can I go? PLEASE! I won't mess with people on the bus no more. I promise! Please let me go home!"

"Well Archie," says Chuck, "We'll take you home now, but you need to make absolutely sure you behave on the bus and in the neighborhood and tell your four friends that they will get introduced to our *electric chair* if we hear you or any of them screw up. Just know that HELL is coming if you touch even one passenger! Oh, one more very important thing, you and your idiot buddies WILL apologize to anyone you've messed with! Do you understand?"

"I understand. I'll be good! There won't be any more problems with me or my friends. I promise. And, we'll all apologize."

Chuck releases the straps holding him to the chair and helps him get up. He's walked to the van and taken to a fairly vacant street near his house where he's led out of the van and taken behind an empty house. Dave cocks a .38 pistol near his ear so that he gets the message that his captors are to be taken seriously.

Chuck tells him, "Stand here and count to fifty, then, you can remove the hood."

Toro does as he's told. He can hear the van driving away as he's counting. After he gets to the count of fifty, he struggles to find the knot of the hood so he can take it off. It takes him about ten minutes. He makes his way home, walks in his house and just begins weeping. After he calms down, his mother asks him what is wrong. He tells her the whole story. She's thankful he's okay and tells him to make really sure he behaves on the bus and tell his friends to do the same.

The follow up

The next day on the bus is like night and day from previous bus rides for all the usual passengers. Toro and his gang make good on his promise. They even seek out the elderly gentleman and mother with her little one so they can make things right. As for the students and young ladies that have been terrorized, they took care of that, too. All is good. Now, we need to see that they - stay good.

Chapter 41

Private Contractor Dumping Trash

Two days after the previous incident, Dave is at a coffee shop and hears a couple of older guys talking about some contractor dumping garbage on dead end streets recently. They're really angry about this! Dave hears one of them say that there are a few streets where this has happened lately and that someone told him that a home repair guy's outfit named "Dominic" might be the culprit.

He walks over to them and says, "I couldn't help overhearing you guys talking about someone dumping trash in the neighborhood, is that right?"

The oldest of the two says, "Yah! Erie Street has become a main dumping site for this Dominic Company. He has three or four trucks. I figure, they've been doing tear downs in houses in the area and rather than take the trash to a dump where they have to pay a fee, they've gotten the idea of leaving their trash at the end of Erie. It's piling up quite a bit now. It's a real mess!"

Dave says, "Guys like that need to get nailed by the cops and get huge fines."

The younger of the duo says, "I'd like to catch them and fire a salt buckshot round into their butts! That'd show 'em not to trash our neighborhood!"

"Yah, that'd show them alright." says Dave. "I hope they get caught soon. People like that need to be taught a lesson. It's so wrong for them to trash our neighborhood like that. Someday, they'll get caught and get what they deserve. Well, you good people have a great day."

Dave leaves the coffee shop and heads home. As he's driving, he decides to take a ride by Erie Street and a couple of other dead-end streets. It only takes ten minutes for him to arrive at Erie. It's a fairly long street with ten to fifteen empty lots. All the lots were created by homes that were demolished due to deplorable conditions or destroyed by fires. Many of the vacant homes were used as crack houses by local addicts.

Just like the old timers were talking about, Dave could see the piles of garbage and trash in the lots and the end of the street. He sees a ton of drywall and lumber scraps, tarps, and a bunch of empty paint cans as well as joint compound buckets. That's all he needed to see. As he drives away, the wheels in his brain start turning to come up with a plan to nab the "trash perps."

Now home, he calls up his people to tell them that they need to get together tonight to talk about another mission. He sets the time for 7pm at his place.

The Meet

Everyone on the young team is at Dave's by 7pm. They get right into it. He gives them all the info he has on this case. He's already gotten the address of this Dominic character who owns the home remodeling outfit.

He tells them, "I tracked down the garbage man responsible for making parts of our great neighborhood his personal dumps site. His name is Dominic LaRosa. He works out of his house on Elk Street. I have his phone number from the side of his truck. I'll call him to set up a meeting at a restaurant where we can bag him in the parking lot. Danny's Restaurant on Hickory will be the perfect place to do this. There's plenty of room for us to situate our van, lure him close to the side door, introduce him to *Mr. Stun gun,* and bag him. All I need to know is who's free to come with me?"

Angel waves her hand to signify she's on board, and so is Chuck and Dave. Mick looks a little bummed out because he has to be at his daughter's school play. But he lets the guys know that he'll be on the next fishing trip for bad guys. Great! It's a go to get trash man Dom.

After the team leave's Dave's house, he calls Hap to let him know about the new operation. Hap gives him the go ahead and tells him that he'll pick up his crew in his van at 8pm. After hanging up with Hap, Dave makes another phone call, this one to Dominic.

He answers, "Hello, Dominic's Home Improvement, who am I speaking to?"

Dave answers, "My name is Dr. Martin. I was given your name by a friend that had work done by your company. I need to remodel my office on Main Street as soon as possible. It'd be a good size project worth around $100,000. Would you be interested?"

Giving him a dollar amount tickled his greedy bone. It worked. Without hesitation he says, "Yes, I would be very interested in taking on the job."

"That's great! Could we meet tonight at Danny's Restaurant on Hickory at 9pm to go over plans I had drawn up?"

"Absolutely," says Dominic. "I have to work a bit late on a job I'm finishing up and can be there by nine. No problem."

"Good! See you then."

At Danny's Restaurant
Hap, Chuck and Angel - Dominic LaRosa

Hap, with Angel and Chuck got there a bit earlier and parked in back of the restaurant. It's 8:45. Dave drove his own car there and is in disguise. He parks right next to the van. It isn't long before Dominic LaRosa shows up in his company truck. Dave spots him, gets out of his car and waves for him to come over. He situated himself so that their meeting would take place between his car and Hap's van. When Dominic gets there, Dave stretches out his hand as if to shake hands and, ZAP! …he's stunned and drops to the ground. Angel opens the van door; Chuck and Dave quickly toss him up to Hap. Before he comes too, Angel secures him. He's blindfolded and his hands are taped behind his back. Chuck gets Dom's truck keys and drives it to the warehouse.

As Dominic comes out of his stupor, he begins to thrash a bit. Angel gives him a solid right-hand jab to the jaw and knocks him out. She doesn't say a word. She's been told to not say anything to the bad guys they pick up. They don't want anyone knowing there's a lady involved in their neighborhood policing. She's fine with that. She treats her involvement very professionally. She understands that it's a security measure for the sake of the entire group. As the group drives back to the lockup, she keeps a sharp eye on their catch of the night.

At the warehouse where I'm waiting to see our new POW, he's brought in and placed in the venerable *hot seat* and strapped in. He hears people around him but with the hood over his head, and can't see anything and his body language tells us that he's really spooked. He's literally shaking.

He says, "What do you guys want from me?! What's this all about?!"

Dave tells him, "Dominic, you're probably not a bad person overall, but you and your workers have trashed several empty lots in the neighborhoods around here with garbage from your construction jobs. That's unacceptable and folks are REALLY angry!"

Angel raises her hand, ready to let him have it. She looks at me to see if I okay her intention. I wink and nod of my head; she puts on her game-face and lets him have a fairly solid back hand that nearly knocks him over. Dominic lets out a deep moan and snaps back to an upright position. This is her first participation in tuning up a bad citizen. Chuck and Dave give her a thumbs-up as a sign of approval. She smiles, showing that she enjoyed doing it. That tells the men she's going to be a great asset.

Dominic is dazed for a moment, and when he regains his senses, Hap sets his butt on fire with a two second taste of Sparky. That sends him into convulsions and gasping.

Right away, he says, "Please don't hurt me! Don't electrocute me again! PLEASE!"

Apparently, he's been jolted before; maybe while rewiring old houses and is familiar with the sensation resulting from it.

Dave tells Him, "We're trying to come up with the right punishment for you. If we release you with a warning, there's no way of knowing if you'll continue to trash dead end streets and empty lots."

With a sincere voice he says, "I swear on my mother's grave, me and my guys won't do it anymore. I swear it! I SWEAR! Please let me go! Please! We'll clean up the junk we dumped and anyone else's trash we see. Please let me go!"

"Okay Dominic, today is Thursday. If we see that Erie Street and all its vacant lots are cleaned up by Monday, we won't bother you anymore. BUT, if you or any of your crew members do anymore of it, your next session with us will be very bad. We have your name and know where to find you. So, when you do a job; do the right thing and pay the dumping fees at the dump sites. Understood?!" Oh, and spread the word to any other construction people you know that they will get hurt if they leave any trash in fields or side streets."

"I understand. I have a large dump truck that'll be able to handle all of that material. If you see any more trash after Monday, it won't be us. I swear! And, I will spread the word, I promise."

Dave says, "Okay Dominic, it's good that we understand each other. I'll take you at your word. Now, we'll get you back to your truck and you can go home."

They get Dominic to Garvey Street and cut him loose. He's on the next street over from where the restaurant is located. He's led to a secluded spot and told that his truck is in the restaurant parking lot. He's also told to not remove the cinched-up bag over his head until he hears a toot of our horn. Dave drives away. Once he's about three hundred feet from Dominic, he toots the horn. The cord of the hood they put on him is a bit hard to undo, but he gets it done in about five minutes. He finds his truck, gets in, and drives home.

Monday checkup of Erie Street

Friday, Saturday and Sunday, the young team has no new mission to tackle. Late on Sunday, Dave, along with Mick Angel and Chuck take a ride through the Erie Street area to see what it looks like. Lo and behold! They're pleasantly surprised to see a great improvement. Dominic and his guys must've been really busy. The end of the street and vacant lots are cleaned up; at least, well enough that it passes for a "good cleanup" job. For now, the young troopers are satisfied.

Chapter 42

Punks at McDonald'

(Len and Clint)

It seems that today, using foul and vile language has become acceptable for people lacking no basic social skills and having - no class. Decent people shouldn't have to put up with imbeciles that do that whenever and wherever they feel like it.

Well folks. Lenny and Clint met up for coffee at their local McDonald's and had the misfortune of having to deal with such idiots as mentioned above. They're always in disguise when they go out in public, for such a case as this. They never know where or when they'll need to tweak someone or step in to quell a situation.

A group of four young idiots are sitting in a booth talking loudly and spewing out four-letter words; one bad one after another. An older gentleman tells them to knock it off only to receive a barrage of profanities. Clint and Len are sitting in a corner booth listening and observing the low life punks. They walk over to the lads, Clint grabs two of them by the collar, and Len does the same to the other two. They rush them into the men's room and give each one a nasty solid slap across the face. They take whatever I.D.s they have.

All are whimpering and begging to not get hit again. Len says to them, "You punks don't like what we did to you, uh? How about if we broke your jaw so you couldn't use your FOUL MOUTHS to shout out profanities in public for a while?"

One kid blurts out, "We're sorry, we won't do it again. We promise! Please let us go!"

Clint's response, "I don't believe you're sorry or that you'll never do it again! Once we leave, you'll go right back to being PUNKS! We ought to stick your heads in the toilets and flush 'em!"

Clint grabs the biggest of the four by the throat so that he's standing tip toe and having a hard time breathing.

He tells him, "We'll be by here again and around the neighborhood. If we ever hear that you're behaving like you did today, you'll all get more than a slap on the mouth! Do we understand each other?"

All of them nod their heads and say, "they understood."

Len tells them, "We're going to leave but you will stay here till one of you counts to fifty. Then, you'll go to the manager and apologize. After that, you'll apologize to the elderly gentleman and other customers that had to put up with your low-life behavior. You won't see us, but we'll be watching. Do the right thing and you won't get hurt. Do the wrong thing and know that HELL is going get you!"

Lenny takes out his cell phone and takes their photo. He tells them, "We have your I.D.s and pictures. We'll make sure the cops and several of our friends that live in this area have a copy of it and where you live. All of the I.D.s will be mailed to one of you in a couple of days.

Clint and Lenny leave them and exit the restaurant. After a few minutes, they see the four miserable juveniles come to the counter and speak to the manager. They also look like they're making apologies to the patrons. That's good.

Alright! Another group of young misguided brats hopefully got straightened out. Clint and Lenny plan on sending the photo to our younger crew so they can do a follow up. If they screw up, then, we'll need to introduce them all to Sparky. For now, we'll keep a good thought

CHAPTER 43

Car Music's Too Loud!

For some reason, there are idiots that think it's okay to play their tricked-out car sound systems at levels that literally shake the homes as they roll by. They have systems that put out bass sounds to the max causing ear-shattering vibration! That kind of inconsiderate and offensive behavior merits some kind of street justice. It so happened in a town in the south that three young bucks in a pickup truck had such a system. A man in his fifties parked next to it expressed his objection to the deafening noise and asked the driver to lower the volume. He wouldn't do it and a verbal fight erupted. This sent the older guy over the edge and shot one of the kids, dead! It's insane, isn't it? A young man died just because he wanted it his way and the hell with anyone objecting. How foolish! The older guy was arrested and is sitting in jail. That incident ruined two lives, and for what? The man shouldn't have shot the kid, but at the same time, that young punk apparently never learned to show people respect and is now - gone.

Mickey shares his loud noise experience

This brings us to what Mickey shared with all of us at the Post. He said, "I've got a situation on my street where a couple of guys that meet up at one of the houses that have extra loud sound systems in their cars that disturb the entire street when they drive by; not only on my street, but anywhere they drive. I'd sure like to catch them somewhere, where I could destroy their sound systems and even give them a little beating to make sure they get the message. I know that he and a few of his noisy buddies hang out at a bar on Abby Street called My Place"

Bull jumps right in and says, "You know what? There's some idiot that comes by my house with that kind of music setup in his slick Mustang; nice car but, he's dumb-as-a-post! I'm with you Mick. Let's make this our next item for tidying up the neighborhood."

Eh-Jax has a similar story and tells us, "Yah. I've heard a few of those come by my house. I like music, but not that loud. And besides, what they're playing is not music but sheer NOISE! It drives me nuts! Let's do it! Let's quiet down our neighborhood."

The rest of the guys and Angel are all in agreement. I tell them to get plate numbers of the cars and we'll get Hap to have his old partner Shawn at the precinct get us names and addresses. From there, we'll, do that *voodoo* that we do so well.

Everyone laughs at the "voodoo" thing. I explain. "You like that line, eh? It's from the 1962 film, 'Manchurian Candidate' starring Frank Sinatra. It means doing something good or bad to someone. It's meant to bless or to curse someone. In our case, we're definitely going to curse those bad boys. We'll figure out what to do with them as soon as we get their information."

Next day

It's Saturday afternoon and don't you know, Mickey hears that thunderous noise rolling by his house. The guy stops a couple of houses passed Mick's place. He's waiting for his buddy to get in his car so they can drive off together. While one cockroach is waiting for the other, it gives Mickey a chance to take a little walk and covertly get the make of the car and its license plate number. That worked out just right. At least, we'll have two perps to tune up. They both have loud sound systems; and to make things even worse, the punk that drove up also has a really loud muffler that just goes right through you.

The information Mick has is passed on to Hap, and in turn, he relays it to Shawn O'Rourke at the station. In no time at all, Hap gets a phone call and Shawn gives him the names. Mick's noisy neighbor is Kurt Haslet living at 135 Minden and the other rat is Doug Finley at 80 Duffrin Street. It seems both these jerks have been issued tickets for speeding. Their phone numbers are part of the package O'Rourke had on them.

The word goes out to both crews and a meeting is set for that night. Saturday night at the Post is always crowded and we get in early enough to commandeer our private little corner. Hap brings everyone up to speed on the noisy morons.

With that done, Boom tells the guys, "What do you think of warning those two first and see what happens? If they don't mend their evil ways, then, we'll go to plan B or C. Plan B could be to have Shawn get a couple of cops from the precinct to pay them a visit and if that doesn't work, we'll enact plan C; that'll be us doing some *voodoo* on their butts. How's that sound?"

Clint says, "Personally, I'm for doing it all by ourselves. Let's get a message to them by taping a note to their windshields that will spell it out nice and clear that they need to quiet down their sound system and mufflers...or ELSE! I'm sure they've been told by a few people that their noise is offensive. But, being punks, they just refuse to be the kind of citizens their parents want them to be."

I tell the guys, "I can agree with that. There's no need to play around and coddle these mindless morons. They should know better, and I'm sure, even their own parents got on their case about it. Who's gonna write the notes?"

Angel yells, "ME! I'll have them by tomorrow morning. Her, Chuck, Mick and Dave can do the honors of delivering the message."

I tell her, "Excellent Angel. I love your enthusiasm and willingness to get things done. Happy trails to you and your crew as you inform those two fools. We'll see what happens. Maybe one of you can video tape one of them reading the message and see the reaction; that might be entertaining."

Mick says, "Hey Boss, I'm sure the guy on my street would be easy to video tape. He always parks on the street in front of his house where I can see him getting in and out of the car. Since we have his phone number, I'll have Dave call him on his burner phone to tell him that he needs to go see what's taped to his windshield after we do that. That way, we can co-ordinate the call and Kurt coming out to check out his car."

"Sounds like a great plan. Go for it. I can't wait to see the video."

The warning message

Angel wastes no time drafting a clear message to the noise-making half-wits. It takes her fifteen minutes to get the wording right. It reads like this…

<u>Warning!!!</u>

We are concerned citizens and are warning you

about the overwhelming noise you create with your muffler

and car sound system. This letter is to tell you

that you need to keep the volume way down

in your car and you need to quiet

your muffler to a reasonable level.

If you continue to disturb the peace with your obnoxiously loud music and muffler, we will be forced to take action.

There will NOT be a second warning. Do the right thing!

After getting her thoughts down on paper, she runs it by Mickey to see what he thinks.

He tells her, "Good job Angel! It's right to the point. If the guys we tag won't do what's right, then, we'll go to phase-two; whatever that's going to be. We'll talk it over with our older crew and get input from them."

Sending the message

Later, in the cover of night, Chuck and Dave make their way with copies of the message Angel wrote and tapes one to Kurt's car. It's parked in the street across from Mike's house. They then go to Doug's residence and do the same. Lucky for us, both of our new targets get up around the same time to go to work. The plan is for Dave to arrive early, park near Mick's house, and video tape Kurt's reaction without being seen as he reads the note. And, Chuck will get set up to tape the other lad as leaves his house.

Monday - great video

It's Monday 8:30am. Kurt walks over to his car, unlocks it and gets in. As he turns it on and revs up the engine, he notices the note on the windshield. He gets out, snatches it from the glass and looks around to see if anyone is looking at him. He gets back in the car and opens the folded sheet to read what it says.

Dave is in great position to video his reaction. Huh, must be a slow reader. It takes him awhile, but all of a sudden, he sees Kurt looking irate and looking like he's swearing up a storm. He sees him ball up the note and toss it out of the window. His guess is that this idiot will probably not heed the warning. Oh well!

Now, on with Chuck and his covert video-taping of Dougy at 80 Duffrin Street. Around the same time Kurt left for work, Doug makes it to his car and pretty much does the same thing as Kurt; gets the note from the windshield, gets in his car and reads the message. He looks a little worried; maybe the wiser of the two noise-makers. Maybe he's smart enough to realize that his car his too loud. Instead of throwing out the note, he places it on the passenger seat. For now, it's a wait and see situation to see if the message will have any effect on them.

Quitting time

Around quitting time for workers, Angel goes with Dave to intercept Kurt a few blocks before he gets to his house to see if he plays his car system at a max level. Sure enough, he rounds the corner three blocks from his house and he's got the sound pounding out his trash. As he turns the corner for his street, he lowers the volume. It's okay, but still loud enough to bother people. Still, his muffler is offensive; way too loud. Alright! Looks like Kurt's gonna need a talkin' to. We'll deal with him later.

In the meantime, Chuck is waiting for Doug to make his way home. He does the same as Dave, waiting a few blocks from his house to see and hear what Doug sounds like coming down the street. Well, well, well, pleasant surprise. He has his music playing, but at a level that is acceptable. He follows him until he rolls up to his house and just passes by. As he drives away, he can see Doug getting out of his car and walking toward the house. Chuck has a good feeling about him.

Next day with Kurt again

The next day, Tuesday morning, Dave wants to see if Kurt will behave or not. He parks his car about seven houses away from his place, waits for him to pass by as he heads for work. He wants to see if he'll activate his "noise machine." After he rounds a couple of corners and is away from his house, he cranks his music loud enough to wake the dead. Kurt is a bad boy. He's gonna need an adjustment. That will happen tonight.

Here comes the night...

The young crew had time to think about what to do concerning Kurt's bad boy ways. All four are in on this operation with Hap and I being backup. They have it all planned. The good thing about many city streets is that there are a lot of trees that form a sort of canopy that covers most parking spots by the curbs. And, Kurt's car is under one such tree that makes it just right for what the crew needs to do.

Angel has a half gallon of sour milk that stinks really, really bad. She plans on pouring the entire content into Kurt's back seat area. She told the guys that she did that to some woman that wasn't nice to her and her neighbors. She has a funnel with a small enough spout she can insert between the window and the rubber seal to pour out the milk. She makes her move and gets the job done within five minutes. If you've ever smelled really bad, sour milk, you can only imagine what our young punk is in for. It is NASTY!

Next, Dave stays in the van with the engine idling. The next step won't take long. Having done a lot of car repairs, Chuck knows how to get into the car and pop the trunk open. He and Mick will tweak Kurt's speakers so he can no longer blast his - non-music! As the trunk opens, Mick uses a knife to cut the speakers to shred while Chuck locates the wires and cuts every-one he sees. Task done! The men and Angel get back in the van and go home. Hap and I smile as we also make our way back. Tomorrow should be a bit quieter in the neighborhood.

Next day...

The next morning, Dave and Angel watch Kurt as he goes to his beloved ride. The first thing he's met with is this horrendous smell like a thousand babies puked in his car. He quickly rolls down the windows and starts his engine. When he tries to turn on his music - he gets nothing but *pure silence.* He stops the car and goes to the trunk to see if something came loose with the wiring. As he opens it, he almost faints. He sees a sheet of paper with a hand-written note that says,

"YOU WERE WARNED ABOUT THE NOISE. NOW, MAY-BE YOU GET THE MESSAGE. IF YOU BUILD ANOTHER LOUD CAR SOUND SYSTEM, YOUR CAR WILL BE DE-STROYED!"

You can see the young buck is visibly shaken. He gets back in his car and drives off to work. The stereo is destroyed but that horrid rotting milk smell makes him want to puke. It'll be with him for weeks. That's too bad. We'll just wait and see if he's foolish enough to be bad again.

Later that day, everyone from the young crew goes to My Place bar to see if Doug and Kurt will meet up with other guys having the similar loud sound systems. Our young crew of soldiers get there at 4:30 to see who might show up. Since this *righteous evil* was done to Kurt's car, the word got out and 6 of his pals show up at 5pm; all with cars that have evil sound systems, except Doug. He must be the smart one in the group. And, Kurt's system has already been neutered. He rolls in real quiet, except for the muffler.

Dave, Mick, Angel and Chuck wait till the delinquents go inside the bar and attach a small packet to each car's exhaust pipe, except for Doug's car. Those packets were made up by Boom, our explosive expert. Once the boys' cars roll out and the exhaust pipes get nice and hot, it will trigger the pyrotechnic and give them a noise that'll rattle their teeth and damage the tail pipes. Our young crew doesn't leave. Everyone wants to see and hear the outcome of rigged explosives.

After a little over an hour, one by one, the boys come out of the bar and fire up their menacing beasts. Each one of them takes a different route home with music blasting away. Our soldiers want to follow Kurt. He's had the warnings but refuses to heed. His muffler is LOUD. After a mile or so, BAM! He comes to a screeching halt; gets out and looks around his car to see what happened. He gets to the back and notices the tail pipe is gone and part of his bumper is shattered. He looks around to see if anyone is watching him but doesn't see our guys' van where they are recording his reaction. He actually breaks down and cries. He knows he just got dealt with for his refusal to be "nice." He gets back in his car, no music, just a sad ride home where he can lick his wounds. Mick will keep an eye on him from his house across the street.

As for the other six in the group, word got around that they also got the shock of their lives as each packet detonated while heading home. Every one of them suffered damage to their tail pipes and bumpers. None of them reported the incident to the police. What could they tell them?

"Hey man, someone blew up our tail pipes and we're really mad about it!"

They're all driving around with illegal sound systems and loud pipes! HELLO!!!! They are misfits and got what they deserve. We'll see if these guys will give the neighborhood peace and quiet when they drive down the streets of our beloved neighborhood. If not, they'll get hell for it!

Chapter 44

Police Officer - Angel?

It's night time on Alcott Street. Angel is taking a walk by herself with her Pomeranian puppy named Papillion *(Butterfly in French)* and encounters three fifteen to sixteen-year-old wise guys hogging the sidewalk. The boys see her and as she tries passing by, they block her.

She tells them, "Could you please move so I can get by?"

They just ignore her and stand firm right where they are. She picks up Papillion, makes a move to go between two of the young jerks. One of them puts out his arm to prevent her from going through. She's one tough lady and still has that battlefield attitude. She surprises them all by unleashing a bone crushing punch to the kid's floating ribs; knocking the wind out of him and dropping him to his knees. She then leg sweeps the other that is closest to her and knocks him down on his back side, causing him to crash his head on the sidewalk. The third punk backs off; not willing to get manhandled by a woman. They're all in awe of what just happened.

She tells them, "Why do boys behave like idiots?!" She lies and says, "I'm an off-duty detective and can arrest you for harassment! How would you like that?"

None of them answer. They're stunned. They just stand there looking like the dummies they are.

"Alright, you three morons get the hell off this street and go home. If you do this to anyone else around here, you WILL be brought before a judge. Do you understand?"

They all respond with a "yes," shrink back like beaten brats and leave the area.

Angel phones Mick to let him know about the incident and to tell him she managed to take a photo of the delinquents with her cell phone. She plans on getting that in Hap's computer for future use if more needs to be done with these guys.

She's also aware of a few other areas where such callous teen varmints are making pests of themselves and harassing store and diner owners, as well as their customers. It's like there's an epidemic of *teen idiocy* flooding the neighborhood. She'd love to make something happen to remedy the situation. She's so sick and tired of the low-life behavior many of the young people have.

Next day

It's Friday morning, Mick calls Angel and wants to get information about the places where the bad teens hang out and are causing our good people grief. She maps out five different spots in the neighborhood where this is happening. She tells Mick that it'd be great if both the older and younger crew did a one-night *scoop-up* of all the punks and straightened them out.

Mick says, "That's not a bad idea. What we could do is grab one or a couple from each group and bring them in for an *attitude adjustment* with all of us present and introduce them to *Sparky*. We'd release them so they could tell their own crowd what each one will get if they continue to be a problem to local establishments and the neighborhood citizenry."

Angel lets him know that it sounds like a good plan and that they should run that idea by Boss A.S.A.P. Mick agrees and tells her that the men will be at the VFW Post tonight and will give Boss and the others the locations that need immediate attention.

Later at the post

It's 7 pm, and as usual, all the guys are there having a good time talking and downing their favorite brews. Mick has already let Chuck and Dave know what Angel proposed. They're all very open to educating those trouble-makers.

He runs down the list of places for everyone; [1] Sabastino's Pizzeria on South Ridge, [2] Mrs. Bond's Deli on Harding Street, [3] the Deck Restaurant on South Street, [4] the Quick Stop Market on at the corner of Electric and Roland, and [5] Morrison's Wings and Things on the corner of Culver and Smith.

I thank him for the list and say, "Okay men, and Ms. Cruz, we have some planning to do. It shouldn't be too hard with eleven of us splitting up and grabbing up at least one from each group. We should look for whoever seems to be the leaders; bring them in and give each one a session in our *fine-tuning* room."

It's all set. Me and the rest of guys sit and figure out that we can break our ten men and one-woman force into five groups. The plan is simple, isolate one guy from each crowd of bad guys in the dark when they're walking home; use our stun guns to quietly take them down, then, load them in Hap's and Dave's vans and another one Bull uses to do side jobs and two roach cars Eh-Jack has in his yard that run okay. Each crew of two will pick the right time and place to do their mission.

The next night

The best time to snag anyone at the trouble spots will be between 10 and 10:30 pm when the crowds usually start breaking up and people head home. The crews are in position and as planned, each does its job, Hap's, Dave's and Bull's crews grab up three of the local troubled teens and have them on route to home base. The remaining two are picked up in the same time frame. All have been wrapped up and bound, and are sitting in their own cage with the special electric shocking headgear. I want all of these bad actors hear each other scream once Sparky lights them up; hoping it will put the *fear of God* in all of them.

It's 11pm and we need to make an impression quick enough on our deranged young men so we can let them get back home at a reasonable time and not alarm moms and dads.

So far, none of our captured rebels has had any of the unpleasantness we've been dishing out. One by one, they are brought out, placed in the *chair of torment* and given a few fairly solid backhands and a couple of seconds of Sparky. The reaction from each punk is the same; crying, whimpering and pleading for us to not hurt them anymore.

We also are able to get the names and addresses of every bad guy in their respective crowd. That may come in handy if any of them resorts to continuing their wayward ways.

Five different men from our group act as the spokesperson for us all as they read each of the bad guys the *riot act*; to Allen, menace of Sabastino's Pizzeria's clientele, to Frank of Mrs. Bond's Deli on Harding Street, to Bobby of the Deck Restaurant on 2nd Street, to Izzy of the Quick Stop Market on at the corner of Electric and Roland, and to Clifford, menace of Morrison's Wings and Things on the corner of Culver and Smith.

Through voice-modified gadgets, they speak into each perp's cell phone what the first of our crew member says so they can play it back to their friends when they get back to them:

"You're done causing trouble at the place you hang out! If we see you out there again, we WILL get you and give you the beating of your miserable life! That goes for anyone else in your group of misfits! So spread the word. We know where each of you lives. Do the right thing or - get the beating of your life if you screw up!"

With all that said and done, each young man is released in his neighborhood and left to struggle taking the duct-tape off his head while our men drive away. Now, we'll see if those five places of business finally have peace.

Chapter 45

Troublemakers Roaming Kaz Park

There used to be a time when people could walk anywhere and not have to worry about being bothered, harassed, violated or viciously attacked. It seems that today, if decent folks go out on foot, they need to have eyes in the back of their heads wherever they go. They need to mentally prepare themselves for anything when they're out on the streets, in parks, on trains, on airplanes, on subways and in playgrounds; even in their own homes! That's all wrong!

Angel called Dave to tell him that she took Papillion, her dog, to Kaz Park for a walk at dusk yesterday and at a distance, she saw a group of about seven, mid to late teens roaming the park bothering people. She told him that they were belligerent and punched out a couple of younger teen boys that were on the same path.

She said, "I'll bet this is the same group that's been terrorizing people in the park; a bunch of punks that are responsible for over a dozen attacks in the last four months."

"How badly hurt were the two guys they beat up?" Dave asks.

"One boy was able to get away after several punches and kicks. The other wasn't so lucky. As he lay on the ground, one of the perps kicked him in the head and knocked him out. I wanted to yell at them so they'd stop, but you can bet they would have chased me down and ganged up on me. I was really angry with myself that I didn't have my .38 with me. I would've at least fired a warning shot to get them to scatter before they beat him so bad. I didn't see anything on the news about it. See if Hap can get any info from his cop buddy. I have a feeling he could be dead or in a comma; the kick to his head was vicious enough to do that."

"WOW! I'll reach out to Hap right away and see what comes back. Talk to you later."

Hap is contacted

Dave makes the call to Hap and is told that he would get right on it. He also told him that he'd heard something on the news about the park's criminal activities lately and that he meant to bring it up to the others. Hap heard that a couple had been brutally beaten with the guy dying and the girl raped and beat into a comma.

He told Dave, "Man I wish our group had been aware of these cockroaches before now. The punks today are coldhearted. They beat up on people or sexually assault women - just for kicks. It's a really sad and sick world we live in. We're going to take care of these idiots, A.S.A.P.! Get as much information on these rats so we can end their terror."

"You got it Hap," says Dave. "I'll get my crew to scout out that park area to see who has any info that will lead us to the perps. I'll get back to you as soon as I get anything."

Next day

Sgt. O'Rourke is contacted by Hap to see if he knew anything about a couple of teens being beat up with one having received a serious kicked to the head.

He tells him, "One kid that was beaten up has a broken jaw, broken ribs and plenty of facial cuts. He was treated and released. The other kid will have a long road to recovery, but it probably won't be a total recovery. He has brain damage that has affected his walking and speaking ability. His name is Tim Hoats. The rats that did this still haven't been caught. No one in the neighborhood wants to speak up. They're afraid of retribution, you know how it is."

Hap says, "I know. I know. The wheels are already in motion to find these scumbags! Talk to you real soon, my friend." O'Rourke understands.

Two days later

Dave was able to put the word out among his street connections about the park thugs. Two days after talking to Hap, he's able to provide him with real good information. It seems these morons are not only into assaulting and hurting people, they are also into hitting electronic businesses and warehouses to steal and fence the latest gadgets; phones, IPads, laptops, TVs and computers. There's a lot of money to be made from that kind of merchandise.

Hap calls to fill me in on this latest neighborhood problem. I set up a meeting for 7pm. All of the New War soldiers show up at our secured warehouse instead of the Post. We need to be able to talk about our plans without being interrupted and not taking a chance on anyone listening in. Since he has first-hand information on the bad guys' group we need to tune-up, I give the floor to Dave.

He says, "What I got from the street is that there's a group of seven slime balls that have been terrorizing, and in fact, beating up on people in Kashmir Park, better known as Kaz Park. So far, they've put at least twenty people in the hospital; probably more, three with severe injuries. There was a sixteen-year-old that was beat up really bad. The coroner figures the death blow was where someone stomped on his head with a heavy boot. There was an imprint of that on his crushed face. And, one young lady is still in a comma; her boyfriend is in the morgue! They beat him to a pulp. Nine other young teen girls reported being raped and beat up. These injured people and the two dead kids need our brand of righteous justice. Hap is going to check online for any TV coverage for the names of the people that were attacked and also tap into his police friend Shawn for reports filed by officers and detectives that did follow ups on these crimes."

Intel on the research

Hap came up with the name of the boy that was stomped to death. His name is Eugene O'Connor. The girl that's in a comma is Isabel Paczyk and her dead boyfriend was Roman Dolinar. From the TV report he got, they were just about to graduate from high school. Hap's police buddy gave him three names and addresses of guys in the group; Mel Toony, 19, Jack Heinz and Henry Robertson, both 18.

According to Sergeant O'Rourke, the three whose names he dropped on Hap have rap sheets, mostly for robberies and assaults. Jack Heinz was charged with punching a man in the face, breaking his nose and putting a nasty gash on his right cheek. Some pansy judge charged him with a misdemeanor then released him with a $500 fine and restitution to his victim. Shawn didn't know if the punk ever paid the man. He told Hap that he doubted any payment was made.

Zeroing in on Jake and Henry

I ask Boom, Eh-Jax and Chuck to go snag Jack and for Hap, Clint and Mick to go get Henry. It's been observed that most of these rats get home between midnight and 1 am. The men take off to wait on their prey at 11:00. One group will be in Hap's van and the other in Dave's. I ask Angel and Lenny if they'd like to come with me in a separate car to nab Mel, the third monster. Without blinking, both wanted in. Good! We're all set.

Hap, Clint and Mick get to the first pickup, Henry. The plan is to spot him coming down the street and have Clint sneak up on him with a stun gun to take him down. Then, him and Mick will toss their catch in the van and secure him.

Here he comes

It's not much of a wait. At 11:30, old Henry comes strutting down the street. He's alone and that's good. Otherwise, the men would've had to adjust their plan. As he gets four houses from his, ZAP! He goes down and is scooped up and put in the van.

Not long after Henry is bagged, the other crew of Boom, Eh-Jax and Chuck see their man heading home too. It's 11:50. Chuck does the honors. He's waiting behind a tree that Jack will be passing by. As he does, he's zapped; the van pulls up and the men toss him in.

The first crew already has their prize, Henry. He's sitting in a cell, blindfolded and was told to be quiet. No problem with him at all. He was tuned up a bit in the van and knows to, just chill. The other crew is on its way to the warehouse and will arrive in about ten minutes.

Angel gets to shine

In the meantime, me, Lenny and Angel spot our guy, Mel Toony. He's making his way home at midnight. He must be the night owl in the group. We see him staggering; he's a bit drunk. That'll make it an easier snatch. It's one of those *"carpe diem"* moments.

I ask Angel if she's up to nailing this guy.

She says, "Man, I'm more than ready to get this low life. I'll go up to him and ask for a cigarette, and as he goes in his pocket for his pack, I will add one more knockout of my fighting career. I figure one solid right hook to the jaw will drop him like a bag of dirt. If he's not completely out, I'll stun him."

Mel is walking towards us. Without him seeing us, we exit the car eight houses before his and wait. As he gets two houses from where we're hidden, Angel steps out so he can see her walking towards him. It's dark and he can't really make out her face.

Being that Angel is good-looking, and he, being a typical young buck, he says,

"Hey sweet stuff! What-cha doin' out here so late? It's not safe for you to be out here all alone."

"Oh, I'm just out for some fresh air. Say, do you have a cigarette I can bum one off of you?"

He says, "No cigarette, but I do have some real good weed you and me can do. You want to?"

"Sure! That'd be great." says Angel. "I haven't gotten high in a week."

She played him really well. As he goes for a joint in his pocket, Angel's right hand is poised and she unleashes her wicked right hook to his jaw with all of the anger she has for this creep. He doesn't know what hit him. He drops like ton of bricks. Just to make sure he's knocked out, she kneels down, and gives him another blow to the jaw. He's out!

As soon as me and Lenny see the perp go down, we hustle there to cover his eyes and mouth with duct tape and to also binds his hands behind him. While we we're doing that, I tell Angel to get the car. She pulls up and we toss the bad guy in the trunk. Thank God for darkness! No one saw a thing. We were out of there in about a minute and a half. It was a great catch.

Lenny says to Angel, "Hey girl, if you're ever mad at me, don't punch me! Man, you are a killer with those fists. You are a worthy warrior, lady. Proud to know you and glad you're on our side."

She says with a smile, "It's a deal Bufford. I'll go easy on you if I ever have a beef with you. Just don't piss me off and I may just let you live!"

We all have a good laugh and continue in our way to base. We now have the three we went out to get. The next step should be very interesting. I want to know who among our new prisoners caused the most damage. We'll get the information we need by pitting one against the other. After a few backhands, I'm sure the weaker one will break. We'll see.

The next day

The word was spread to those that didn't take part in the latest mission. They all wanted to see what we had. So, everybody shows up early, except Mick, who had to work.

It's 8am when we get the first rat out of his cage with the electric blindfolding headgear on and hands free. It's nineteen-year-old Jack. He's the biggest of the three and I figure him to be the leader; just a hunch. Bull and Eh-Jax sit him the chair and strap him in. Angel, knowing what this punk and his idiot friends have done, looks like she wants a piece of him right away. So, I give her a nod.

She's quiet. She doesn't speak so that he doesn't know that it's a lady that's about to tune him up a bit. She's just following my rule. We don't want any of the cockroaches we catch know that there's female in the group. Anyway, she stands in front of him and punches him right in the forehead; almost knocking him out. That hit put a nice welt on his noggin and drew blood. One of her knuckles cut him. He's dazed for a moment and as he becomes fully cognizance, she back hands him.

He yells out, "I don't know why you have me here! I didn't do anything wrong. Please don't hurt me! PLEASE!

Clint says to him, "So, Jack Heinz, you and your little pack of cockroaches have been robbing businesses, beating up people, raping women and you've also killed two young men. Also, you rats did brain damage to a young man and put a teen girl in a coma. She may never come out of it!"

BANG! He backhands him so hard that he goes to the floor. Boom picks him up with the chair and I get right to it.

I tell him, "Jake, you and your heartless maggots have done a lot of damage and you all need to be put down!"

As soon as Jack hears the part about "being put down," he freaks out and says, "I'm sorry! We didn't mean to hurt anyone so bad. It's just that some of the guys took it too far."

BAM! Lenny slaps him twice; one on each cheek. Now, he's crying like a child and Len says to him,

"Some of the guys took it too far...some of the guys took it too far!!! Are you KIDDING ME! You guys went way, way beyond too far!" He nods for Hap to turn on Sparky!

Jack's two buddies, Mel and Henry in lockup in the warehouse hear the death scream Jack lets out and are shaken up to the point that they begin whimpering silently. They're sure he's being hurt really bad and that their turn is coming.

Well, that shrill Jack let out could have shatter windows. He sits there convulsing for about half a minute. He didn't expect anything like that. As he calms down a bit, Angel punches him in groin; the same part he used to rape the girls. Ole Jack feels like he's going to throw up.

I tell him, "I figure you were one of the guys that raped some of the girls that reported it to the police. Tell me Jack, how many girls did you rape and beat up?"

"I didn't rape any of them, it was the other guys."

I nod to Hap. Sparky is turned on for two seconds. Boy, that gadget really sparks bad memories to life. The punk screams, stiffens up and shakes like a leaf. His two pals in lockup heard him scream again and silently go wild in their minds. They know they're next. They sit there whimpering; unable to see because of the special helmet each is wearing. That makes things worse.

Back in the interrogation room, I say to him, "Jack, you don't want any more of that, I'm sure. So now, how many girls did you rape! And, don't tell me you didn't do any of them."

Trying to catch his breath, he blurts out, "I took part in only a couple. Some of the others guys were involved in at least five or six."

Bull backhands him and says, "You ONLY raped a couple, only a couple, uh?"

BAM! He lets him have another solid one.

"It's not only the rapes you punks did on the girls, one of you slimes did major damage on the kids you beat up. What's more you RAT, one of those young ladies you guys raped and beat up is still in a comma! Her name is Isabel, and her boyfriend Roman is - DEAD! That's called MURDER!"

Jack is speechless. He knows he's in serious trouble and believes his captors might kill him. He's going out of his mind and sitting there weeping bitterly.

Bull continues, "Jack, you and your sick crew are all guilty of everything that was done to those innocent people attacked in the park. You all share the blame for these vicious rapes, attacks and murders of two young men; Roman Dolinar and Eugene O'Connor. Now then, think really hard; name all the guys that did these vile things!"

Barely able to understand him because of his crying, he does his best to talk. He's mumbling but we're able to make out what he's says. Hap is able to record it all.

I step in and say, "Jack, that's great information. Now then, all of you are going down for everything you did as a group, but what I want to know is who took part in that young lady, Isabel Paczik being raped and beat into a comma. Also, who stomped her boyfriend Roman Dolinar to death?"

He's reluctant to give up that information. Seeing that the lad is balking, Hap helps him along with another dose of Sparky. That loosens his tongue.

After he's done convulsing from the shock, he says, "OKAY! I'll tell you. I did take part in holding her down, but it wasn't me that beat her up. It was Henry. She was screaming, so he punched in the head a few times then choked her till she stopped fighting. After he got done raping her and got off; we looked and saw that she had passed out. Henry went too far. We all knew it. It was wrong. As for her boyfriend that died, some of the guys punched him, one guy knocked him down and Mel kicked him in the head. I wasn't part of that, I swear! No one planned on killing anybody."

Angel is biting her lip. She's over the top with this and would like to stomp his head in herself. She wants to yell at him and give him a piece of her mind but knows she needs to stay quiet. Instead, she just lands a mean slap to his face and sees him bring it down to avoid another hit. She takes a step back, balls up her fist as if ready to put a dent in his forehead. You can see the rage in her eyes. She hates this guy!

Eh-Jax motions for her to hold back.

He says to Jack, "I'm sure you and your rat pack watched the news and know about the one teen that survived a severe beating in the park. The one that got kicked in the head during one of your outings to beat up on people, survived. But now, he has brain damage that affects his speech and walking ability. His name is Tim Hoats."

He blurts out, "Mel Toony was the one that did the stomping, and the other kid that died, that was Raúl and Jerome's fault. As the guy lay on the ground after the beating, they kept stomping his face! No one was supposed to take it that far. It just happened. I'm sorry it happened. Really! I'm really, really sorry! Please don't hurt me no more! PLEASE!"

I tell him, "Well son, you and the other cockroaches went way beyond too far. You're all looking at a lot of time in jail."

I motion for a couple of the men to take him to lockup and whisper to Lenny to bring Mel in. Jack still feels the sting of every hit he got as Clint grabs him by the scruff of the neck and has him on his tip toes heading for his cell.

Mel, Angel and Sparky
(Angel's first time at sparky)

Lenny and Clint bring out nineteen-year-old Mel and strap him in the chair. As Clint finishes securing him, he lets him have punch to the gut that has him doing a wicked dry-heave. He can hardly catch his breath. We leave him be for a moment. Then, Angel gets a turn running the switch at Sparky. She gives him a two count. He just stiffens and shakes for about thirty seconds.

She smiles. So do all the guys. This is her first time lighting up someone in the seat of torment. The men near her give her a pat on the back and the others, a thumb's up.

As Mel settles down, he pleads not to be hurt anymore. Lenny knuckles him in the head. This draws blood.

He tells him. "Mel, you're a really evil guy. Besides taking part of the rapes of defenseless young ladies and beating innocent folks in the park, you're the one that kicked a kid's head in and KILLED HIM!"

BAM! Len lets him have a solid backhand to the mouth area; this has him tasting blood.

He tells him. "His name was Roman. You also gave another kid brain damage when you stomped in his head! His name is Tim. And, we're sure you took part in several rapes."

He lets him have a solid backhand to his left jaw and says, "You stomped a kid to death for WHAT?! Just for the fun of it? Is that WHY?! You're going to pay a heavy price for that."

Len nods to Angel who is holding the lever to Sparky. She turns it on with pleasure and cooks him for another two-count. She'd like to keep it on for a count of ten; you know, like the boxing ring, a count of 10 for a *knockout.* She gives him the two second shock treatment. She'd really like to keep in on till his brain is cooked.

Mel goes ballistic with a loud scream and stiffens in the chair so much that he pushes it over backwards. Bull and Hap get him sitting back up.

After about a minute, he regains his wits and says, "Please don't hurt me no more. I didn't mean to hurt anyone that bad. I'm sorry! I wish I could undo what I did; I really, really wish I could!"

Hap says, "You didn't mean to hurt him that bad!!! WHAT?! You just wanted to toy with him in a sadistic way with a few kicks, a few stomps?! You stinkin' MORON!"

BAM! He gives him a crushing shot to the right side of the jaw. This knocks him out.

It's now 9:40am. We're done with Mel for the time being. He'll get more punishment tomorrow. I'm sure it'll include the ball-peen to fix his stomping foot. I motion for Eh-Jax and Bull to put him in his cage. They unstrap him from the chair and drag him to his cell. Still knocked out, he's laid down on the blanket and the men leave. When he wakes up later, he'll find that his jaw is probably broken and will try to remove that special helmet and get shocked. We'll be able to hear him when he screams in pain.

Next, Henry

Our next guest in the interrogation room is Henry. Angel would love to hurt this guy really bad! It was him that raped Isabel. Since she fought him, he choked her until she stopped fighting and passed out. She wound up in a comma due to lack of oxygen to her brain.

As soon as he's put in the chair, Angel doesn't wait for any signal from the crew; she just turns on Sparky and cooks him for three seconds instead of the usual two. WOW! His screams blew the doors off the place and his buddies know he's being handled with extreme vengeance.

Everyone wants a piece of this guy. Angel, being a woman who has experienced bad treatment from men, wants first crack at him. She punches him in the stomach, making him heave and suck in air as if he's suffocating. She back-hands him is knocked over. The men prop him up. He's going out of his mind not knowing how much of a beating he's gonna have to endure.

Between deep breaths, he says, "Please don't hit me no more (deep breath), I don't know why you're hitting me, I didn't do anything, I didn't do anything! Please don't hurt me anymore" (deep breath).

Hearing that, I back hand him right in the mouth causing him to bleed. It's running down his chin and chest.

I commence to rip into him by saying, "You are a worthless rat, Henry! You and your swarm of cockroaches have destroyed lives. And you, you really hurt an innocent young woman when you beat her, raped her and strangled her; putting her in a comma. She may never come out of it! If that happens, you'll be guilty of aggravated assault, rape and MURDER! That's going to be a life sentence, pal!"

Henry doesn't know how to respond. I guess his deviant and mess up mind can't process that information like a normal person would. He just sits there whimpering and sucking in blood from his busted lips.

Clint moves in and puts his hands around his throat and tells him. "Henry, you've just taken a bit of a beating; now, how about I have a couple of the men here rape you; you know, like you did to the girls you raped in the park? Then, how about I choke you till your face turns blue and you pass out; not knowing if - I'll go too far?"

Clint tightens his huge hands around Henry's throat. He tries to breathe, but can't. He holds that grip for about thirty seconds and before the rat passes out, he releases him. Henry takes in deep, deep breaths and begins to weep like a baby. We let him be until he regains his wits, and Lenny knuckles him, putting a good ding in his forehead.

Now, he pleads with all he's got and says, "I'm sorry I hurt anyone. I didn't mean for it to get out of hand. I didn't mean to hurt that girl so bad. I'm sorry! Please let me go! Please, please, please don't hurt me no more!"

Angel is getting pretty bold. She does it again; not waiting for permission. She turns on old Sparky to torment this punk for a count of; one, one-thousand, two, one-thousand, three, one- thousand. No one objects. Henry goes for another terrible ride. He goes wild and stiffens like a steel rod. When the power is shut off, he's breathing really heavy and foaming at the mouth from the excruciating pain he experienced. We give him time to settle down.

Hap says to him. "You know, for what you did, and the others too, you don't deserve to live! You and your little maggots have done incredible damage to innocent people. You've gotten a beating and you will be released, only, it'll be to the cops that will prosecute your worthless ass and put you in jail. You'll be placed in a prison with bad guys that will probably make you feel sorry that we didn't kill you here."

After Hap gives him a solid punch to the gut, he unstraps him from the chair and tells him to not say another word or the other fifteen men will each put a beating on him. He's silent as a lamb. He's led back to his cell and tucked in with all of the pain he's in and to ponder his bleak future.

Rounding up the rest

Next, we bring out Jack again and place him in the "seat of dishonor." This must be a different bunch of young misfits. They don't have wallets where we'd find their IDs, but we do have their cell phones and all of them have money. Out of these three assaulters, we got a total of $456.00 and change. We'll keep that and add it to our - *War Effort Fund*. These guys won't need cash where they'll be going. Jack has a driver's license. Mel and Henry don't; they only have driver's permits. Good enough for us to know how old they are and where they live. According to their addresses, they all live within a half to a mile from each other, and, some live real close to Kaz Park. That means the rest of the bad boys probably live close by too.

I motion for Boom to take the lead in the questioning.

He tells Jack, "We're gonna need you to contact the others in your gang and get them to meet you under the park bridge at 9pm tomorrow tonight. In case any of them can't get a hold of you, Mel or Henry, you'll tell them you three are on your way to Niagara Falls to fence some of the stuff you all boosted; that you have a buyer eager to take the goods off our hands for a good buck. Tell whoever you contact that you'll split up the money you get when you meet at nine tonight."

Jake cooperates. Using his cell phone, he contacts the other four rats; Raúl Ortiz, Joey Reed, Carl Martin and Jerome Jones. He tells them what we told him to say. We can only hope they all show up. If not, it'll mean another mission. That's won't be good.

Next day, hashing out the plan

It's 10:30am and we gather up to plan for the covert capture of the rest of the perps. Since the operation will take place at night, all of our troops will be in on it. That's good. That way, we'll be able to cover every guy with at least two of us on each one. For the rest of the day, everyone goes about his and her business until we need to come together around 8:15. By the time 9pm hits, it'll be dark and the cover of night will be on our side.

It's that time

It's 8:15pm and all of the men and Angel are in place. The idea is that eight of us wearing clear masks will be waiting at the underside of the bridge with stun gun. As the lads make their way down the embankment and under the bridge, they will be zapped and secured. The rest of us will be topside as backups in case anyone of the rats makes a dash out of there. Then, me, Mike and Angel will be ready to take them out.

Later

It's ten minutes to nine and we only see two of the four making their way under the bridge. We later identify them as Carl and Joey. As they round the bottom of the slope and onto the walk-way under the bridge, Boom and Clint nail them with their stun guns. The rest of the guys swoop in and secure them; taping their eyes and hands. They prop them up against the wall and wait for the other to show.

Through the headsets, I hear Hap tell me that they've secured the two that showed up and waiting for the other two. I answer back and tell him that I'll signal him as soon as Raúl and Jerome show.

Right at 9:15pm, the last two arrive and are making their way down. I signal Hap. He, in turn, tells the crew to get ready. Just like the two already captured, Raúl and Jerome get the same welcome. They are zapped, and go down. With our new POWs, we get them to the vehicles and head out for home base.

The first two we want to deal with before calling it a day is Raúl and Jerome. They're the ones that stomped Eugene O'Connor in the head and killed him. Before we put them in their cells, we all want them to know what a beating feels like. We place Raúl in the chair first and nod to our new Sparky operator, Angel, to turn on the juice. She enjoys putting a spark in Raúl for a count of three. Besides killing Eugene, he also took part in rapes and beating other girls. As she pulls the switch, Raúl goes bananas! He convulses like none of the others; must be extra sensitive to electricity. TOO BAD! He deserves it. After he comes down from his *electrifying high*, Boom backhands him hard enough to knock him out. Bull and Eh-Jax cart him off to his cell. He'll wake up in while and will freak out, not knowing where he is, and with the special shocking helmet we put on him, he'll let us know he's awake when we hear him scream as he tries taking it off.

It's Jerome turn

Our next bad boy is Jerome. He's brought in and secured to the chair. He was part of all the mayhem that took place in the park. He and Raúl were the miscreants that took part in Eugene O'Connor's killing as well as raping girls and beating up on people.

It was reported that Eugene had some brain wave activity when they brought him in the emergency room but died after a couple of hours of trying to save him. The head trauma was really severe. That makes Raúl and Jerome murderers.

Now, the interrogation and pain, begin. Angie has her hand on the lever to turn on Sparky. She detests this guy as much as Mel and decides he, too, needs three seconds of the shock experience for his crimes. She does the honors. It takes a bit longer for this rat to recoup. He screams louder than the other guys, who by the way, are shaking in their proverbial boots, in the cells.

I slap him across the face, both sides. He deserves it, and more. All the men want a piece of this action. I know this swarm of cockroaches are all relatively young and may not be up to speed about thinking of doing the right things as members of our society; they should know better! Me and the rest of my crew, and the younger crew were eighteen, nineteen and twenty when we needed to go off to Nam or the Middle East war. We were responsible people, even at that age. There's no excuse for the devastation these devils put on the innocent people they beat, raped and killed! Jerome isn't knocked out like Raúl, but has a very sore jaw from the two slaps I gave him. He's cut lose and taken to his cell. Tomorrow will be especially painful for our last two rats.

It's now 11pm and has been a long day for most of us. I suggest we hold off till tomorrow to wise up Carl and Joey. For now, all seven of the cockroaches will sit out the night thinking about what tomorrow will bring. It should be interesting.

Next day

Bull babysat our group of losers overnight. Most of the men, minus Angel and Mike show up for the festivities of the day. We need to see Jerome and Raúl again. They haven't been properly dealt with for their crimes.

First, Jerome. Eh-Jax takes the ballpeen hammer and smashes his right foot; the one he used to stomp Eugene to death. He goes right off the rails with screams and heavy breathing. The pain is so bad that his heavy breathing has him foaming at the mouth. He's spitting all over himself! The pain is beyond a "ten." We let him sit there in his misery and pain until he begins to calm down.

Eh-Jax isn't done quite yet. Old Jerome also used both hands to choke Isabel and beat her into a comma. He's really evil! Eh-Jax figures he'll be nice enough and won't break both his nasty hands, only one; the right one. He secures the hand on the arm rest and comes down hard with the hammer. Poor Jerome hasn't even come down completely from the foot smashing experience and now, he has to deal with extreme pain to his hand. He cries like a baby. He's in so much pain that he can't speak; he can only sit there and cry. We figure he'll need at least ten to fifteen minutes to settle down enough for us to talk to him.

Boom's been quiet for that last couple of bad guys being tuned up and jumps in. He says to Jerome, "WOW! I've known bad guys in my days, but what you did in the park with the other maggots in your little mentally deficient group is beyond evil!'

Jerome is speechless. He doesn't know that to say. He knows he and his pals deserve to be in jail and realize that the beating they got, they had coming. BUT, too late! I can't imagine how these rats were able to sleep at night after the rampage they took part in.

Boom says "Let me ask you a question. What if what you did to those people and specifically, to that young girl you put in a comma had been done to your sister or mother; how would you feel about that? Would you think that was a fun thing to do?" BAM! He backhands him across the face.

He does his best to talk. "I'm sorry for what I did. Please don't hurt me no more! I can't take this! I can't take this. PLEASE!!! I beg you, don't hurt me no more!"

He goes into uncontrollable weeping with loud wailing. I motion for Hap and Bull to move him to his cell. As they're doing that, I tell them to bring out Raúl for a second turn.

Raúl's turn

Just like Jerome, as soon as he's seated nice and comfortable, Angel positions herself at Sparky's control. She loathes this guy as much as killers; Mel and Jerome. She's sort of become our unofficial "Sparky operator." Raúl has no idea what's about to hit him. She lights him up for three seconds like she did Jerome. Man, he goes out of his mind and screams like he just got his hand cut off. Again, we give this roach time to savor all that pain and when he finally calms down, Clint backhands him in the head with a fairly solid shot. This dazes him for a few seconds.

As he comes out of it, Clint tells him, "Raúl, I'm completely baffled as to how you and the other maggots in your group ever came up with the idea of beating up people; raping defenseless young ladies and stomping someone to death! What sort of depraved, demented, maniacs do things like this?! You and Jerome, stomping a young kid dead and didn't bat an eye doing it! That is really, really sick!" Besides going to jail for a long, long time, you'll probably go to hell at the end of your life. What do you think of that?"

Raúl tries to compose himself and blurts out, "Man, we didn't mean to hurt that kid so bad. We never meant to kill anyone! I swear it. I'm sorry! I'm really sorry! Please don't hurt me anymore!"

That was Boom's cue to take the ballpeen hammer and crush the foot he used to kill young Eugene. BAM! Raúl sees stars and the pain he feels sends him into a wild screaming and crying session. The pain he feels is so strong that he can't calm down. He's writhing with pain and unable to speak. The ballpeen strike was a particularly hard one, one that did a lot of damage to his foot. He'll be a longtime healing before he can walk right again.

Well, we got all of the rats in that terrorizing group, and now, it's time to turn 'em over to law enforcement to Captain Mendola. Again, Hap makes the call to Sergeant O'Rourke and fills him in. Shawn asks him if they'll be contacting Captain Mendola so that he can be in on the arrests. He assures him that it should happen tonight.

Mendola contacted

A few minutes after Hap hangs up with O'Rourke, I phone the good captain as a courtesy to him to honor our agreement of giving him a heads-up for new criminals we have that he needs to lock up.

After three rings, Mendola answers, "Hello, this is Captain Mendola. Who is this?"

I respond, "Good evening, Captain. This is your partner in crime-solving, friend. I have seven very bad misfits that need to be processed vigorously by you and the courts."

"Oh, you do, do you? Where can I gather them up and what did they do to merit *vigorous processing*?"

"How about; multiple assaults, rapes and murders? That's more than enough for vigorous processing. Not only that, but these rats have been busy hitting local electronic businesses for cell phones, IPads, laptops and computers. They are also responsible for raids on area warehouses for large screen TVs. All the information you need to put them away for a long time is on a tape you'll find taped to their leader, Jack. "

Mendola is amazed at the list of crimes these punks committed, and says, "Man, I can't wait to lock up this group. They've been on our radar for quite a while. Thanks amigo! Keep an eye on the Evening News. I'm gonna make really sure they are all known to the public."

"Sounds good to me Captain. I'll call you within an hour to let you know where the perps can be picked up. Have a good evening."

Both men hang up. All Mendola can do is wait for my call while I organize the drop.

Dropping off our detainees

Since we have seven detainees to hand over to Cpt. Mendola, we need to bind their hands, remove their electronic blindfolds while they face the wall; then, wrap duct tape around their head to cover their eyes. With that done, we load them up and head for an abandoned silo near the river.

We load three of the rats in Hap's van with Boom and Lenny, and the other four in Dave's van with Eh-Jax and Chuck. Me, Mick and Angel follow in my car. We head out and make it to our destination in fifteen minutes. Once there, we get them out and tie them to steel girders. I call Mendola and let him know where the 'catch of the day" is located.

The next day on the News

The captain was true to his word about watching the News.

The announcer: *Kudos to Captain Mendola and his men of the 10th Precinct for rounding up seven very bad individuals who have been responsible for unspeakable crimes in Kaz Park. They also face a host of charge for numerous robberies in the south side of the city. According to reliable sources, all of the defendants are looking at many years in jail; for some of them, they will be given life sentences. They are all held in the county jail without bail and are due in court next month to be prosecuted.*

Our next story...

Chapter 46

Worried about Cpt. Mendola

...his Achilles heel!

I'm glad we finally got rid of that batch cockroaches, but now, I'm a little concerned about Captain Mendola. I worry that he just might find out who we are. That could be a disaster! I need to get something on him that would make sure our two crews are never taken down for doing the good work we're doing. The captain works for the city and who knows if he'll ever think of taking us in for political reasons. After all, we're showing him up by all the rats we captured and turned over to him. He and his men haven't come close to doing what we've accomplished in so short a time. I'm betting there's a bit of jealousy stirring in him and he'll eventually want us to stop so that he can be the one nabbing the weasels and rats infesting our community so he can get the glory. Us doing his work surely can't sit well with him and most of his men.

It might be tough to find his *Achilles heel*, but I'm certain we can find something on him that we can use. It's time to talk to the boys, and our Ms. Cruz (Angel). We can't leave her out. She might punch me out.

Next morning

The next day after putting the rats in Captain Mendola's hands, I call Hap to talk to him about my worries of the captain ever finding us out.

I ask him, "Do you have anything on him we could use as our *ace in the whole*?"

Hap says, "It's very interesting that you should mention that. I met up with my old buddy Shawn from 10th a few nights back just to tip a few pints at Floody's Pub and to reminisce about our days of working together. As we talked about the men from the precinct, would you believe that Captain Mendola, Lieutenant Landry and Sergeant Rowley's names popped up. Not surprising, since we all worked together, but, what's surprising is what Shawn had to say about the trio."

I said, "Let me guess; Shawn knows something about those fine officers of the law that might be very damaging to their careers if it ever got out?"

"You got it Boss. Those three have had a thing going on concerning people they arrest; in particular, drug dealers that are caught with a lot of money. They got a really big score one night when they busted a major player in the drug trade at a garage on Chicago Street. According to Shawn's source, the three hulled away well over a million in cash and drugs."

"Let me guess again. The drugs they seized made it to the Evidence Room but the money never got there; it made its way to personal stashes, right?"

"That's right." says Hap, "According to my tech guy, the captain, Lieutenant Landry and Sergeant Rowley stayed behind after the bad guys were hauled away. As they scoured the garage, they came across the cash hidden in a compartment under the floor. Only they, know about this money. Before the dealer could open his mouth about any cash he had tucked away, he mysteriously hung himself in his cell."

"Boss about that cash, it's kind of what we've been doing with the pushers we nabbed and keeping their 'ill-gotten-gains.' It's real dirty money. The difference between our three civil servants and us is that they pocket the dough while we use it for operational costs and to compensate a few of the victims needing financial help."

"Hap, I can understand the cops grabbing a hand-full of the loot they come upon when busting these no-good drug dealers. After all, they have to buy their own uniforms, shoes and bullets. But I also know that it's a really bad department *no-no* and many have lost everything after being caught. Anyway, the information you have on the captain and his ranking officers is just what we need to ensure our survival as we continue policing our neighborhood. What we need now is some kind of proof that will put that proverbial, *nail in their coffins.*"

"It so happens that one of the standup men under Mendola has a taped conversation that incriminates all three. By the way his name is Officer Alfonso Aguzzi. He's thirty-five, with a wife and two kids. His record is impeccable.

"So, how did the tape come about?"

"Well, a while back, him and his partner, Officer Sal Pruitts, were nailed by Mendola for having accepted a gift of a few dress shirts from a men's store owner for nabbing a couple of shoplifters. It was no big deal, but Mendola used this to make a statement to all the men under him that 'graft' will not be tolerated! Both men were put on leave without pay for a month. This really angered Aguzzi. He swore to himself that if the ever got the chance to get dirt on the captain that he wouldn't hesitate.

Alfonzo had one of his closest friends, who's an IT guy, put a bug in Mendola's office. He taped every meeting he and his two partners had. One day, the techie hit it big when the three got together after the huge bust that garnered them all that dough to talk about what they got. If they were ever asked about the bust from the commissioner, they needed to have the same story; that no money was found, only drugs.

So, here we are; he has exactly what he needs. He plans on using it the next time he puts in for the rank of sergeant. If he sees that Mendola wants to hold him back, all he has to do is confront him with the tape. I'd say he's in a very good position to get what he wants."

I ask, "Hap, any chance of getting a copy of that tape?"

"Shawn already gave me a copy, Boss. You can clearly hear the three boasting about the million plus take from that specific raid of a year ago."

"Hap my friend, I hope we never have to play that hand, but keep the tape well tucked in your back pocket for if, and when, we need it. Great job, brother! Hey, is there anything on our 'to do list' coming up?"

Chapter 47

Two pimps

"As a matter of fact, Chuck called me yesterday and told me about a couple of pimps hustling some young ladies a couple of clicks from here in an area bordering downtown. They have six girls ages fifteen to eighteen being forced to work for them, six days a week. The guy got the info from a friend of his that knows about both of the dirt bags."

"Pimps uh? I've always had a real hatred for people doing that to women. I will enjoy putting a hurt on them and freeing those young ladies. As soon as you can get the intel for this mission, we'll nail these lower-than-dirt creeps!"

"Okay Boss. I should be able to get you that information real soon. I'll also see if Sergeant O'Rourke knows anything about it. I'd bet he does. I'll get back to you, proto."

Two days later

Good news from Chucky! Hap calls me to say Chuck has all the info we need to snag the two pimps.

He says, "One guy is known as Ace. He's around thirty-eight and the other rat, in his low forties who goes by the name, Hollywood. Hollywood! Get that! He must think he's some kind of star! We'll need two crews and get them both in one night. They go out each night around 11pm to collect the money at midnight that each girl has earned so far. These sleaze control three girls each and take all they earn; they only provide food, sexy clothes and makeup for the girls. That's it.

They get really treacherous if they think any of the girls has cheated them out of money. Not only that, but some have gotten bad beatings for not earning enough. It's a horrible existence for them. They're treated like property; just sex slaves! By the way the girls are known as; Pixy, Doré, Sasha, Melody, Rosie and Dawn."

He adds, "These two super-rats share an apartment on Reading Street; in OUR NEIGHBOOD! That ticks me off really bad, man! Can't wait to get these pukes! Anyway, I've already done a drive-by to check it out. This should be another easy pickup."

"Chuck, that's great intel! I'll make a few phone calls to put two crews together for this operation. Since Hap is always glad to be part of anything we do, he's the first on the list. Along with me and Hap, I want Angel to come along. I'm sure she'd like to put serious dents in both these worthless worms. Of course, Chuck you'll be part of the second crew. I figure Eh-Jax can handle one of them on his own. We're all going to enjoy tuning up these low life cockroaches. I'd bet Angel would love to let Sparky cook them till they're dead! We'll see."

Chuck says, "I'd back that bet, Boss. She told me that when she was in combat in the Middle East, there were several NCOs and officers that strong-armed some of the weaker female troops to put out or find themselves on the front lines where the action was the worst. The ones that complied got to come home safe. She said all of them hold extreme hatred toward those pigs for what they were made to endure and hoped they'd get shot by the enemy."

She added, 'I came really close to blowing away a few of those scum bags for what they did to my sisters-in-arms. I did the smart thing and held back. They tried to pull rank on me too to make me one of their *play things*. I told them straight up that they weren't going to do that to me. I told them to go ahead and put me on the front lines; that I'd rather take my chances out there than to be made into a *whore*. They put me in some of the riskiest situations, but someone always had my back; that was Mickey. I believe I made it back to the States because of him. I really do.' I owe him."

The plan to bury two pimps

I have a great idea for when we pick up the pimps. Once we have them to our interrogation facility, I'd like to get the ladies involved in dealing with their captors. On this fishing trip, we gotta have all of the guys in motion. They'll need to help gather the six girls so we can provide them with an end to the nightmare they've been living. It shouldn't be too difficult. Boom, Bull, Clint, Lenny, Mick and Dave will each approach one of the girls. They all work the same area of Ohio Street near the wharf. The girls will be told that Ace and Hollywood will no longer bother them and that they need to hear what they've got to say.

Hap, Angel and I make our way to Reading Street to wait for the pimps to drive away. The other crew of Chuck and Eh-Jax wait to tail the second pimp while our other soldiers head for Ohio Street to keep an eye on the young ladies.

Got 'em both

The pimps get in their separate cars at 11pm and head for Ohio Street to collect what the girls have earned up to that time. They've been told to all show up at midnight every night to give up the money they made working the street. Any more money they earn, they'll need to hand over once they're all back at the house they share.

Ace is sitting in his car in the shadows at a distance waiting for twelve o'clock to strike.

In disguise, Hap approach one of the girls (Melody), and begins to get verbally rough with her. Ace sees it. He opens his car door to come and intervene, and - ZAP! He's down. Angel and I quickly bundle up our catch and put him in the van. Angel signals Hap on her sleeve mic that we have our guy. He brings the van around to load up the deviant. The next play is for Boom, in disguise, to walk up to her and explain what she needs to do to be free from Ace and Hollywood. She's hesitant, but is hearing that she'll be free from her tormentor, she agrees to go with him.

As Melody begins to walk away with Boom, the other men in the crew; Bull, Clint, Lenny, Mick and Dave, all disguised, zoom in on the five remaining girls. They're told that they are from the vice squad; that both Ace and Hollywood have been arrested and they no longer need to be afraid of them. They're told that they need to go with them to press charges. All of the ladies are a little leery until they are told that they will be the ones deciding what punishment the pimps should get. With that said, they gladly agree to go with them. The thought of getting even for ruining their lives, spurs them on.

Before all the ladies are whisked away to safety, Sasha and Dawn are asked to stay behind with Lenny acting as a *John* in order to snag the other pimp. Eh-Jax is standing by to wait for Hollywood to show up. He must've stopped off somewhere before getting to the site where the girls do their thing. This works out well for Lenny and Eh-Jax; he didn't see what went down with Ace.

A few moments later, Eh-Jax sees him do like Ace did; parking in the shadows, and checking out Sasha and Dawn. He must figure the missing girls are busy with clients. Lenny, acting as a prospect for the girls, hears a clicking in his ear piece that signals to him the pimp arrived. He begins to make like he's arguing with Dawn; it was set up that way. Eh-Jax who made his way really close to Hollywood's car, gets ready to take him down. As our perp opens the door, Eh-Jax just lands a crushing blow to the side of his jaw and knocks him out cold. He duct-tapes the creep, puts him in the trunk of the guy's own car, then, signals Lenny to head over. He leads the girl to Hollywood's car and Dawn motions Sasha to join them. They all get in. Len drives off while Eh-Jax makes it to his car to go meet with the others at home base.

As Clint is driving Rosie, Pixy, Doré, and Melody to safety, he's filled in by them. They tell him they were abducted, drugged and made to work the streets. If they didn't do as they were told, they'd wind up dead like four other girls who didn't comply. They tell Clint they were raped and beaten by Ace and Hollywood. Rosie and Doré once got broken ribs for not bringing in enough money. Pixy points to a scar she had over her left eye from being smacked around by Ace. And, Hollywood took pleasure in using a belt that left nasty welts on the girls if they came up short in earnings. This told Clint that our cockroaches are sadists, rapists and killers. So, any harsh punishment they get will be well-deserved.

Rosie says that Ace and Hollywood were getting ready to sell her off to a more powerful man in town that's in the prostitution racket and grooms his girls to be high end call-girls. He caters to rich clients for big bucks. She breaks down and does a hard cry.

After calming down, she says, "We were all virgins before those two pigs forced us to sell ourselves. I could kill them! I really could!"

The four dead girls

Clint asks Rosie about the four dead girls that were mentioned.

She says, "All four were killed by Ace and Hollywood. Ace put the fear in us by saying, 'If you girls screw up, you'll get to join Mary, Doreen, Marsha and Terry in that landfill in the Town of Ashbury after we put a couple of bullets in each of your heads!'

We were scared to death they'd do just that. So, we worked the Ohio Street strip and did as we were told. This brings us to, now. Thank you for saving us. None of us chose this life. Those rotten bastards forced us into prostitution. We'll never fully recover from this trauma. Again, thank you so much! You saved us from either, getting killed, sold off to other pimps or sold to some foreign sex trader."

Our two new POWs are brought to home base and put in cages for the night. It's 1:30 in the morning and everyone is tired. We'll deal with those rats in the morning. The plan is to let the ladies dish out the punishment.

The girls are brought to the house where they all stayed under the watchful eyes of the pimps. That way, they can all shower, sleep comfortably and have a chance to get their belongings together for when we get done dealing with Ace and Hollywood, tomorrow. Angel and Clint stay with them to give them a sense of security by them keeping watch for the night. Having a lady there (Angel) makes them feel even more at ease.

Clint did a sweep of the house and found a locked door. He busted in and as he searched it, he found the pimps stash of cash in a box deep in the closet. Ace and Hollywood managed to store up $150,000 dollars.

His thought right away is, *"This will go to the girls, for sure!"*

The next day, Saturday, time for retribution

The pimps are brought out of their cages and taken to a farm that was given to Chuck by his late grandfather. It's the perfect place to process Ace and Hollywood. It's got an old house with a barn; that's where we'll let the ladies have their revenge.

At 9:30. I place a call to Angel to give her directions to where we're taking the two perps and that her and Clint need to get there with all the girls by around 10 o'clock.

Clint and Angel get to the farm at 10:10 and are led in the farm house. They can all see us. Since there's very little to no chance they'd ever come in contact with us again, none of us is in disguise.

When the pimps were searched when we grabbed them, we found they each had a six round .380 pistol in their belt, and cash. Hollywood had $1,800 and Ace, $1,550, for a grand total of $3,350. Along with the $150,000 found at the pimps' house; that makes $153,350 that will be divided among the six ladies. Each will walk away with over $25,500 plus whatever they earned the night we came to save them.

Say good-night Ace and Hollywood

Ace and Hollywood are still blindfolded, mouth taped, hands bound and tied to chairs in an open area of the barn. All the guys showed up and would love to beat them to a pulp. We step outside to talk while our lady guests relax in the house with Angel and Clint.

I ask the guys, "How about we let the ladies they beat, raped and held captive do the honors. That, to me, would be *righteous justice*. What do you think?"

Dave says, "That's a great idea, Boss. I'm sure the girls would love nothing better than to put a whole lot of hurt on these rodents. We can leave their pistols in the room to see if any of them would like to take 'em out like they did the four dead girls they dumped in the landfill. I believe some of them are angry enough to do it."

I ask the men and Angel if they're good with that? They all give their approval.

I say, "Good then! It's a go. "First, let's have a talk with our depraved perps."

Back inside, Hap starts right in with heavy-handed slaps across the face. Then, Angel steps up and puts a solid jab into both rats' ribs to break at least one rib. After her, Hollywood gets a solid back hand over his eye by Clint, giving him a nasty cut. Both punks are whimpering.

We don't really want to talk to them. We know what they've done and their lives will soon be in the hands of our rescued ladies. However, I do want to know who they were going to sell Rosie off to. Maybe we could tag that pig and maybe save a few more young ladies.

I motion Lenny to take the tape off their bloody mouths. I tell them, "Don't talk! Just listen! I'm going to ask you a question and I want an answer. That's all. Who is the man you were going to sell Rosie to?"

Ace starts by saying, "We weren't going to sell her off. I swear it!"

He doesn't get to say anything else, BAM! Angel fires off a punch to his head and knocks him out.

I tell Hollywood. "Your pal here just got knocked out with one punch to the head. Would you like one?"

He shakes his head to signify he doesn't want any of that. Good! I ask him who the big shot pimp is that he was going to sell Rosie to.

He says, "He's the owner of *Club Fantasy*. It's a strip joint on Montclaire Parkway. He provides women for high-paying clients; a lot of them are important men in town. His name is Ivan Petrov."

We throw cold water on Ace to wake him up. What I'm about to say is for both of them to hear.

I tell Hollywood, "Thanks for that bit of information. Now then, I have a question for you both. What if someone abducted your daughters, beat, raped and turned them into prostitutes; what would you do if you found the men responsible for that?'

They don't quite know how to respond to that.

Ace finally opens his mouth and says, "I guess I'd want to get them, make 'em suffer and then kill them! If you're going to kill us, please make it quick! Don't make us suffer! Please! I beg you!"

I tell them, "Me and the other men here won't hurt you anymore. We don't have a beef with you, but we know some young ladies that do. We'll be right back. Hang in there."

We all leave to go talk to the ladies in the lounge. I ask one question, "Which of your ladies would like to give these two worms what they deserve?"

All of them say they'd be happy to hurt those two for what they've done to them.

I ask another question. "Who among you would be willing to make sure they never abduct another girl?" I add, "That would mean, killing them?"

Dawn says, "Me and Rosie were raped the most by Ace and Hollywood because they liked our looks a lot. The others were raped too. But, me and Rosie were raped so often, I lost count. We were made to do disgusting things, more so than the other girls; even after we worked the streets well into many nights. These two guys are rotten pigs and deserve to die!"

I have one more question for our guests and say, "We have their guns sitting in the next room where they are; which one of you would be willing to use 'em to end their reign of terror on young ladies?"

Without a pause, Rosie says, "I'd be more than happy to end their miserable lives!"

Dawn backs her by saying, "There are two guns? Then, that'll be one for Rosie and one for me. I'd have no problem pulling the trigger on those two murdering rapists!"

The ladies are brought into the room where their former captors are held. They stand around their secured abductors and stare at them with extreme hatred. Doré, Sasha, Melody and Pixy have tears in their eye as they flashback in their minds of so many of the horrific moments they've had to endure under these two devils! Rosie and Dawn are looking at them with stone-cold faces and are also remembering the horrors they lived through. Both of them are itching to put a hurt on them and know they won't live to see another day.

I pull Dawn and Rosie aside and tell them, "All of us are going to leave you alone with them. You can do whatever you want. I expect that when you and the other girls are ready to leave this room, these two pimps won't be among the living."

Rosie asks, "We can do whatever we want to them?"

"That's right; anything you feel will be right."

Everyone in our crew leaves the room. Clint is the one last out. He closes the door. We wait to see what will happen in the next few minutes. It should be interesting.

The women don't want to be in the presence of these two monsters any longer than they have to. They make quick work of the punishment. We hear two shots and some blood-curdling screams from the perps that last several minutes. We'd like to see what's going on, but we stay put to respect the ladies' *private moment of vengeance*. After a pause of about five minutes, Rosie and Dawn fire two more shots each with a slight pause; then, six more shots followed by complete silence. Both guns are empty. I figure this signals that Ace and Hollywood have gotten the justice they deserved and are on their way to judgement before their Maker.

The door to the other room opens and all the girls file out; all of them with tears in their eyes; tears of relief and gladness of being free! Rosie and Dawn hand over the pistols to Eh-Jax and Boom who are standing closest to the door.

I tell them, "Ladies you're free to go back home, wherever that may be. Go and start a new life." Hap hands them the $25,500 each they have coming from Ace and Hollywood's ill-gotten gains at the expense of these young ladies."

Each of them tells us where they want to go. Three of the girls want to go to the airport. Doré wants to fly back to Syracuse, Dawn to Cleveland and Sasha to her home in Pittsburg. Hap volunteers to do that. Melody, Rosie and Pixy want to catch buses for Erie, PA. They were all college students there when they were abducted. Eh-Jax says he'll take the ladies to the bus depot in his car. The rest of us will clean up what Dawn and Rosie left for us in the barn.

It's done. This mission was one of the most heart-wrenching one; knowing the inhumanity the pimps poured on these young women. Well, they're free and the two perps have paid the ultimate price for their treachery.

The two bodies

While Hap and Eh-Jax do their taxi service for the ladies, the rest of us go see what kind of vengeance Dawn and Rosie put on Hollywood and Ace. As we look at the two killer/rapists, it's not pretty. WOW! We see that both were shot in the crotch; that's what the blood-curdling screaming was all about with the first two shots. We figured the women wanted to hurt the parts of the bodies these two perverts used to satisfy their unbridled lust. They both bled like slaughtered pigs.

As for the sudden silence after the four shots rang out, that too was significant. The four young girls Ace and Hollywood shot twice in the head was exactly what each of them got; two shots each at the back of the head and the remaining six rounds left in the magazines from both guns were emptied into their worthless carcasses as retribution for any physical abuse the girls suffered at their hands.

Following up on Club Fantasy
A package for Mr. Petrov

Dawn and Rosie really did a job on those pimps, they are a real mess; they're drenched in blood. Boom, Clint and Lenny got tarps and wrapped the rats in them. We don't really know what to do with them.

Then, Dave has an idea and says, "I see there are a few fifty-gallon metal drums with lids in the corner; we can put the bad guys in them and deliver 'em to Ivan at Club Fantasy to Ivan; as a warning. What do you think?"

Clint says, "Great idea! We'll write him a nice little note to warn him he will wind up the same way if he doesn't release the women he's pimping - and stop his human trafficking."

The guys place the two lost souls in the barrels and load them in Dave's van. He drives to home base where the van will be left till tonight. Since it's only a little after noon, Boom drives Dave home and will pick him up later to make the drop at Club Fantasy. Me and the rest of the guys take the rest of the day off.

The plan

The plan is to get back to the warehouse around 1am, then make our way to Club to drop our packages at the back of the place. It closes at 2am. Boom will be placing a small explosive in the dumpster that's about thirty feet from the back door of the club. Besides the surprise barrels for Ivan and his guys, Boom's little dumpster gift will drive home the message we want them to get.

Speaking of the message, Lenny puts a few words to paper. It reads like this:

Ivan, you and your kind ruin lives. I'm going to ruin yours and your family's for being involved in sex trafficking! Your two associates in the barrels got what they deserved. You deserve the same. YOU'RE NEXT! The girls you use and abuse are daughters of caring parents and sisters of siblings. You need to release the girls you're pimping and close down your operation. Your business is EVIL! That makes you and your whole gang, very wicked people!

Next day

It's 4pm when Ivan comes in to open the club. As he makes his way to the kitchen, the bus boy/dish-washer tells him that there's a delivery in the back of the club and a note that says: FOR IVAN ONLY! He hands him the envelope. Before Ivan reads it, he wants to know what's in the barrels. His kitchen help loosens the lid locks; Ivan lifts one of the lids and lets it fall to the ground. As he looks in, he turns a few shades of pale. He tells the boy to get inside and tell his partner Dmitry to come out.

As he's waiting for Dmitry, he reads the note and as we watch from a distance, we can see that he's shaken by it. That's good!

Dmitry comes out and Ivan motions for him to take a look inside the drum nearest them. He says, "This looks like Ace, one of the guys that gets me young girls. I'll bet his partner Hollywood is in the other barrel. Besides getting me girls, these two also did a good deal of drug business for me. That's where they make the big bucks. Man! This is bad, REAL bad! Alright, get some guys and get rid of these barrels as quick as you can!"

As they get ready to walk back in the club, Boom remotely triggers the explosion in the dumpster; thirty feet from them. When it blows, they run inside; falling over each other. Dmitry's so spooked that he goes into a dry heave!

A couple of minutes later, Ivan's cell phone rings. Hap makes the call via the voice-distortion gadget they've used before.

He tells him, *"Do you get the point or do you need a stronger message? If you continue in your ugly and deviant sex business, you and your goons will be visited again; your club will be destroyed, along with your house."*

Two days later

Ivan's crew is told to take the barrels to an industrial dump site and bury them. A couple of days later, Club Fantasy had a kitchen fire that destroyed it completely. We all know what happened there; Ivan and his partner, Dmitry, most likely had it torched so they could collect the insurance. They'll probably get somewhere in the area of half a million dollars or more. Perhaps they'll seek an honest line of business; a pizzeria, maybe. We'll see.

In his travels while doing errands, Bull tells us that he went by Club, just to take a peek at what remains.

He says, "Old Ivan and his partner really torched that place. Man, most of the roof is caved in. I'm sure nothing inside will be salvageable. It won't be long before a bulldozer is needed to completely leveling what's left."

At any rate, all the guys are pleased with the way everything went. For now, we wait for more bad characters to act up so we can straighten them out. The neighborhood is not all cleaned up yet, and will never be, but we're good-to-go for when the next idiots pop up.

Chapter 48

Desecration of veterans' graves

Angel lives near a park called, South Lake Park. She likes to ride her bike there. It's almost a mile and a half around. She usually does the circuit four times; giving her a six-mile workout. Right near the park is Holy Cross Cemetery with a section reserved for veterans of all the wars. As she rides by, she notices a middle-aged woman kneeling next a turned-over headstone and weeping uncontrollably. Angel notices that a whole bunch of stones around the woman, are broken, spray painted, or turned over and potted flowers pulled out and strewed all over the ground.

She peddles over, approaches the lady and asks, "Are you okay?"

The woman turns and completely loses it; throws herself on the ground and says,

"LOOK what they've done to my Anthony's grave!!! Look what they've DONE!"

She screams, "THEY RUINED IT! THEY RUINED IT! THEY DESTROYED IT!"

Angel sits next to her and holds her as she weeps. The woman says that her son was killed in Afghanistan and brought home only two months ago. She came to place flowers on his grave;

only to find the headstone spray painted and toppled over. This ripped her heart apart and sent her into a mind-shattering meltdown.

After she calmed down a bit, Angel tells her that she knows some people that might be able to track down the vandals and bring them to justice. She gets the woman's name and phone number and promises to be in touch soon. Her name is Sandra Mills. As Angel looks at the headstone, she sees the dates - '1987-2010.' He was only twenty-three years old.

This will be a very personal mission for her and the other young patriots in our group that fought in Afghanistan. That stinkin' war lasted almost 20 years; quite a bit longer than the Vietnam War. It began in 2001 after New York City's 9-11 terrorist attack and went on until 2021.

Who done it?

I'm always amazed at how some people can be so destructive just for the fun of it! It's mindless, sub-human, behavior! Our next neighborhood mission will be to find and punish the rats that have desecrated the graves of this young hero and over two dozen other fallen veterans. As a former battle combatant, like Angel and our other young troopers, I'm taking this very personal! Those punks will all get the *righteous indignation* they have coming when we catch up with them! A meeting is set up for tonight at the post.

Later

It's 7pm. Our new war troops gather; me and my crew, and Mick and his young crew. The first order of business is to just socialize a bit before we get down to business. Hap brings up those seven murdering and raping young fools from Kaz Park.

He says, "According to Sergeant O'Rourke, those lads are all awaiting trial. It looks like they'll all do serious jail time. A few will be old men by the time they're released, if ever! The beating, raping and killing they were involved in, is beyond comprehension! It was pure evil!"

New business

Angel brings up the event of the woman she encountered at Holy Cross Cemetery with the men. She's noticeably fuming over what she saw.

She says, "Gentlemen, we need to find these degenerates and make them feel our anger before turning 'em over to the law! Every one of you knows someone you fought next to that is buried in a grave somewhere in this country. Personally, I saw eight of my combat brothers and sisters die out there. I'm really mad! REALLY mad! You guys had to see how devastated that mother was. It was heart-wrenching."

I tell her, "Angel, you're more than right to be angry and so are the rest of us. We'll get them."

I urge our young warriors to put out the word on the street to see what names shake out. Once we know who did this, - then, we go fishing, again!

Word from the street

It's Wednesday. Dave calls Hap to give him the intel he has from his sources on the street about the marauding group that desecrated Mrs. Mills' son's grave.

He says, "Hey Hap, I have the names of the dirt bags that did the dirty deeds at the cemetery. They range from age fifteen to seventeen and all hang out around the recreation building in South-Lake Park. We can find them there most Friday and Saturday nights."

Hap says, "Good! It shouldn't be too hard to snag these low life punks. We need to come up with a plan to nail 'em all at once."

"I knew we'd need a plan, Hap, so I got working on one. It came to me when I saw a good-looking young woman on the side of the road that had a flat tire and some guy pulled over to give her hand. Right away, I thought of our lovely Ms. Cruz. She'd be perfect for the hook. I already spoke to her about it and she's

more than willing to draw those snakes into our trap. She's got a
plain-looking Chevy SUV that'd be just right for our plan."

The Plan

The plan is for Angel to park her van in an area that is
part of a driveway to the concession stand, away from main traffic. She'll be dressed provocatively. This will be a real

draw when she approaches the young rats to ask for help in
changing her flat tire. Young guys are easy to go *gaga* when staring at good-looking girls and women; you know; out of control
hormones and weak minds.

They'll follow her and when they get to the van, she'll tell two
of the boys to open the side door and get the tire. Chuck and
Mike will be inside ready to zap them while Clint, Boom and
Eh-Jax come from the behind and zap the other three. They'll be
secured with tape over their eyes and hands bound before they're
carted off to our detention center.

The Friday night roundup

It's 10pm. Everyone's in place. Angel parks her van, gets out
and does a short walk to where the lads are partying it up; drinking and smoking weed. She makes her plea to them, and just like
the plan we set up, the morons follow; all of them gawking at the
Angel's loveliness from behind, as expected. Now at the van, two
of the young dudes, Richie and Andy, open the sliding door and
get zapped! Just as they go down, Clint, Boom and Eh-Jax come
from behind and, juice the other three, Larry, Toby, and Sonny.

We got 'em all! They're wrapped up, tossed in Chuck and
Hap's vans and taken to home base where they'll be fine-tuned!

It's 11pm in the interrogation room. We have enough time to
smarten up the dummies! Angel is already standing by her friend,
Sparky. She can't wait to light up these bad boys. All the guys get
a kick out of seeing what joy she gets when putting a spark in our
criminals. She's not sadistic. It's just that she has no tolerance for
moronic people that hurt good folks.

Not knowing who did what damage in that cemetery, we're going to treat it like a murder case where in a group, one guy shoots someone to death and everyone else gets to share the guilt. All parties involved become complicit in the murder. Since they didn't stop the crime, it's called "*aiding and abetting.*"

All the young punks are in the room. Bull put them in a line and the rest of the men pulled the tape off their mouth. None of them get vocal. They just stand there scared to death and a couple of them are whimpering; especially the fifteen-year-old lad. They should know better, but having under-developed brains, they couldn't see how stupid that destructive romp through graveyard was. Now, they must pay.

Angie gets first crack at dishing out the punishment. She realizes they're just boys and only gives the first little rat in line a medium slap in the face. This is sixteen-year-old, Ernie. He begins to sob. Then, one by one, the rest are given the same corporal punishment by four different men in the room. It sounds like a chorus of weeping little boys. After a couple of minutes of that, Boom reads them the *riot act*.

"Boys, you're here because you did something that even your parents would turn you in to the police. What you did is beyond words! You desecrated the graves of America's bravest men; probably all of you have someone in your family that served in wars, maybe even died! What you did is almost unpardonable! You are all rodents! One of the graves you demolished belonged to a twenty-three-year-old Marine that was killed just a little over two months ago! His mom came to place flowers on his grave only find it DESTROYED by you mindless hoodlums! You ripped this poor woman's heart apart and caused her extreme grief!"

He adds, "Not only did you destroy that mom's son's grave, but a great number of the other graves of other war heroes buried there - whose families have been devastated by you dumb asses!"

With these words from Boom, the nitwits are all weeping and saying how sorry they are. These boys lack any normal reasoning or common sense. What they did was pure evil!

I ask, "Which one of you in this goofy group is the leader?"

Although he's scared, Dennis says, "I'm the oldest, so I guess I'm the leader."

"Thanks for that information, Dennis. Hang loose while we make your comrades comfortable in our lounge."

With a hand gesture, I motion for the rest of his buddies to be placed in the cages. This leaves Dennis sitting all alone on the hot seat. I nod to Angel to do her voodoo on this lost soul. She turns on Sparky and Denny goes ballistic; screaming like a girl and shaking wildly. His pals in lockup hear him screaming and are frozen with fear. They all start crying. They figure Dennis is being hurt really bad! The sound they heard scares them to death! They know they're next and are going out of their mind!

We let Dennis come down from that very nasty experience and cut him loose from the chair and taken to his own cell. Since Denny got to meet Mr. Sparky, it's only right that all the lads get a taste of it. One by one, they're brought in to have a seat, get strapped in for the ride and as Angel gets the nod, each perp experiences what Dennis did. Each one ends up screaming and convulsing for at least fifteen seconds. Angel would like to give them a second bad trip, but I motion to her that, that will be enough. Although they deserve more punishment, they're lucky and only get the abbreviated version of our hospitality for bad guys. We understand they're not drug dealers or murderers.

Keeping them over night

Being that it's midnight, we put them in the cells for the night. The plan is to get them up while it's still dark, 4:30ish; bring 'em to the cemetery and place 'em in a secure spot where Mendola and his men can't miss finding them. By the time I call the good captain at 7am, it'll be light and the he can order his officers to go fetch the lads.

I ask Hap to call his buddy Sergeant O'Rourke to let him know about the crew that demolished Holy Cross Cemetery, and where they can be picked up. He calls and tells him that Captain Mendola will be notified tomorrow at 7am and told where to send his men to collect the low-life crew.

We do the best we can to get comfortable in the warehouse and get some sleep so we can be up and ready to go around 4:30.

Rise and shine

Angie set her military chronograph wristwatch to 4:30 and is woken right on the button. She in turn, wakes the rest of us. We're all pretty groggy, but we're anxious to get rid of the punks we have in lockup. We're also looking forward to what the courts will do with them. I imagine there'll be a stiff fine and a lot of yelling at them from their moms and dads, especially dads that did military service. Poor parents! They'll all have to dish out hundreds of dollars for reparation. It's gonna be ugly for both, the parents and boys.

We're up and now, it's time to stir the rat's nest and get them up. The boys were fitted with the shocking head gear when they were brought to their cells. Bull goes in and bangs two metal garbage can lids together. They all freak out and stand-up shaking. We get 'em out of their private lounges and walk them to Hap and Dave's vans. They're loaded in and off we go to the cemetery. It's a fairly short ride; fifteen minutes. During the ride, the electronic head gears are taken off and their eyes are duct-taped.

At the cemetery

We're there. It's still a bit dark but the sun will rise shortly. We need to hustle a bit. Angie says there's a grave with a very impressive monument near where the lady's son is buried. The name on it is Albert Worthington. We march the boys to that site and see that we can tie them all together by the wrists around it. They're all scared to death. They don't know what we plan on doing with them. They're freaking out and weeping.

I tell them, "Well lads, we're going to leave you here and hope the rats won't come around and gnaw at your feet and legs. When you're released, if we EVER see you doing anything wrong, remember the slaps and shocks you got. Next time, no slaps but punches instead, and the length of time you get shocked will be much longer than a couple seconds."

They're all sobbing and shaking. That's too bad. Our corporal punishment for these guys may be a bit harsh in the eyes of bleeding-heart people, but I'll bet they won't even think of screwing up again.

It's 5:20am and the sun is peeking on the eastern horizon. With the delinquents tied up, it's time to leave. Where they are, it's unlikely that anyone would be out and about at that hour to notice them. Besides taping their eyes, we also taped their mouth so they can't yell for help. They're all packaged nicely for the captain and his men.

Hello Captain

We make our way back to the vehicles and head back to base where the men get in their cars and go home to get some real sleep; that includes me too.

At home, I lay down on the couch waiting for 0700 hour to strike. Right on the nose, 7am, I phone the captain and tell him that he needs to get to Holy Cross Cemetery and go to the Albert Worthington monument where he'll find the criminals that desecrated numerous graves. There's no conversation between us. After giving him the information, I hang up. He understands.

Mendola gets to the cemetery by 7:30 and finds the five penitent boys still weeping and shaking. He finds a note that was placed in a plastic sleeve and hung around Dennis' neck. The note explains everything and the captain can take it from there. We'll see later if O'Rourke lets Hap know the outcome of this episode. Being under eighteen years old, they won't do jail time, but for sure, life at home with their moms and dads will take on a whole different dynamic.

Chapter 49

Captain Mendola lets the cat out of the bag

At a law enforcement banquet, Captain Mendola shared with nine of his colleagues sitting at his table that his precinct had a "vigilante" group that caused crime to go down by a good margin in his area. All the men were ranking officers and detectives. The feedback he got back from several of the men was positive.

One of the detectives there stated, "All of you know that our hands are tied so often when we're dealing with criminals. When we arrest a perp, seems like the courts are afraid to do the right thing by not levying just punishment. There are too many 'slaps on the wrist' by soft judges and prosecutors. Personally, I'm okay with vigilante groups that deliver swift and right justice on bad guys."

With that information from Mendola, and the detective's comment, the group around the table spread the word among the men and women working the various precincts they work at. Now, we'll see if it's a good or a bad thing.

The spark that lit the fire

Not only did the word spread among the precincts, but it also got out to the people on the streets. Within a couple of days, a few precincts got reports that they had their own vigilante group policing their neighborhoods. The word spread that drug dealers all over either disappeared or got severe beatings. Several got broken arms and/or broken legs and were left tied up in vacant buildings followed by a call to precincts so their officers could scoop them up.

Looks like what we started just might be the way to go in all of the cities to make an impression on the criminals; showing that the people are fighting back! Of course, the politicians and soft on crime bleeding hearts will come against it with all they've got. They are FOOLS! Every time a young person gets shot, politicians and bleeding hearts cry, "SOMETHING'S GOT TO BE DONE!"

Well, going easy on criminals hasn't been the answer, has it? And, it will never be the answer. What our two crews have done so far is put fear in the hearts of criminals. We've made a difference. Other vigilante groups that want to do what we do, believe that it's a good thing. It's a good thing as long as they dish out reasonable justice and not go overboard.

Chapter 50

The Captain and Boss

According to Sergeant O'Rourke, at the next morning briefing at the 10th, Cpt. Mendola let his men know that he'd like to meet with the leader of our policing unit.

He said, "If any of you can somehow get word to the vigilante group operating in our precinct, please do so. I want to have a face-to-face conversation with its leader."

He's figured out that one of them has a connection to us but has no idea who it is among the forty-five officers under him. That conversation should be interesting.

It so happens that O'Rourke isn't at those morning briefings. He's always at the front desk while the captain addresses his crew of officers before they hit the streets. He gets filled in by the other guys there. He needs to be careful not to use the precinct house phones to call Hap. For this new bit of news, he waits till he gets home and informs Hap what the captain told his men.

He calls Hap, "Hey old buddy, the captain asked whoever can get word to your leader that he'd like a pow-wow."

"We were kind of wondering when the captain would be looking for another chat with our crew. I'll pass that along to the right person. Talk to you soon my friend."

At 10am, Hap phones me and lets me know what his pal at the 10th told him.

I tell him, "I'll get right on it. I suppose the *tender-lings* we tied to that monument moved him to seek us out again and he wants to have a talk. I'll let you know later how the chat with him turned out."

On the phone with the captain,
and the favor

I make myself a cup of coffee, sit in my comfy chair and ring up Mendola. It's 10am.

"Hello Captain. *Top of the mornin' to ya.* What can I do for you?"

"Good morning, friend. I hope all is well with you and your men. What we need to do is have a - meeting of the minds. I want you to know that I haven't made any moves to dismantle your vigilante group. Although some of the methods you used to extract information from many of the bad guys were down right mean, I must admit that I actually appreciate the many collars we made due to your work and have put them all away; some, for a very long time."

"Okay. Thanks for the good words. Now then, what do you want from me?"

"Frankly, I need a favor. I'm sure you heard about two of my detectives being killed. They were taken down by two hit men that are tied to a gambling establishment owner. One bad guy is Frankie Durant and the other, Carmen Magio. They hang out at the La Rosa's Bar on Oliver Street."

My men were conducting an investigation in the death of two businessmen that had gambling problems. One man was, Josh Turley. He owned a huge car dealership. The other was Terry Dukes. He ran a fairly large meat packing firm. They were both big losers in high stakes poker games at a gambling joint. It's a former print shop at the edge of the city owned by the one and only, Sonny Murphy; a wannabe mobster. He's just a two-bit wheeler-dealer.

It's a private club with a 'Members Only" policy. That means no walk-ins. Every player is connected to a member and is vetted before he can get in. The joint has dice games on the first floor and poker games on the second and third floor. And, for men looking for sexual pleasures, he has a separate backdoor that leads down to a semi-lavish five-bedroom basement where five young classy-looking women accommodate clients for $200 a pop. Murphy's twenty-five-year-old son Shane is his right-hand man. He handles the hookers and their clients; collecting the $200 fees before any action takes place. At the end of the night, he turns that money over to his daddy. The girls are nothing more than sex slaves."

The captain adds. "I was told that Sonny tucks the profits from the gambling and hookers in a safe at his house. It's real possible that he has a couple of million or more in there. Anyway, the word is that neither of the two dead men could come up with the cash they owed Murphy and were taken out."

"Where are you going with this, Captain?"

"I was wondering if you and your men might be able to even things out for me. Being a ranking lawman, I can't be connected with anything that would bring real justice for my men. Hit men are seldom caught. They hit and then they're gone. I need to send a message to Murphy by having his two bad guys disappear. These two hired guns killed over a dozen or more people that either bothered or were in debt to Murphy. So, the just thing to do is for them to forfeit their lives. What do you think?"

"Well captain, I understand your dilemma and you're right, these are two very bad men that shouldn't be among the living. We're all for that. Going against a man like that can be very tricky. If I decided to move on this, everything would have to be flawless; with no loose ends. We would have to be extra careful how we handle it. I'll get back to you after I meet with my crew. You'll hear from me real soon. You have a good day."

"You do the same, my friend."

I put the word out to both crews that we need to meet tonight at the post.

Preliminary Plans

Around seven, both crews start filing in; they get a drink and settle at the back of the post in our usual spot. I let everyone know what Mendola proposed and what I told him; which was; …no commitment. I want to know what my people thought before we even consider the mission.

Boom says, "A friend told me about those two guys getting wacked and about that gambling house at the end of Sears Street. That's in our neighborhood and shouldn't be allowed. There's some serious gambling going on there with several of high-profile bettors like three local politicians, several lawyers, one judge for sure, quite a number lawmen, lots of businessmen, and a slew of other money men from around here. He also said that a few of the young ladies they used as prostitutes have disappeared; probably for complaining to Murphy about getting cheated out of money they earned. According to my guy, the girls are supposed to get $50 a trick and Sonny, $150. Sometimes, they get less. We can't mess up if we take on this mission. It's all gotta be, covert."

Clint adds, "What's in it for us if we do that for the captain?"

"I take the floor and say to them, "First off, the captain would owe us big time, and we'd be rid of a very foul odor in our neighborhood where foolish gamblers lose their hard-earned money. For some of the less rich among them, it's money needed to feed their families and pay bills. Like the drug problem, some of these idiots are addicted to gambling and only stop when they lose it all; their house, family and job. It's a very bad thing for any neighborhood to have around. Getting rid of it and the men that could care less about people's lives being ruined would be a *noble mission*. They're enemies of the good people around here. The only ones that win are them. It's time they lose everything, too."

Dave says, I agree. I have a buddy who used to go there. He got pretty deep in debt, gambling his money away, thinking he'd hit it big. The problem is; no one beats the house. That's a well-known fact. He ended up blowing all of his savings, had to sell his car and bought a junker. He lost his nice house in the suburbs and is now renting a run-down house in a bad part of town with his wife and three kids. It's really sad, man."

"This is going to be a risky mission, maybe our riskiest," says Hap. "Interestingly, that joint came up one night as me and O'Rourke got together at Joe's Pub on Lewis Street. He told me that he knows of at least a couple of dozen men that went the way of bankruptcy from gambling there. He said that he heard three of them committed suicide over the matter; they all had wives and children. So, this IS an evil we need to kick out of our neighborhood. Wherever these houses of vice pop up, they always bring misery and ruin. Shall we get to go to war?"

Everyone is on board and there's another chorus of, "Let's do it!"

The plan, part one

Lenny says, "If what Mendola says is accurate, high stakes gambling and all that's going on there, Murphy's gotta be raking in a ton of money from a lot of big shots hosts. He just might have a small fortune tucked away somewhere. Wouldn't it be nice to tap into that?!"

I tell the men, "If we can work things right, I'd love to get a hold of whatever cash he has so we could take care of the families that were mentioned; those of the two dead cops, and the two debtors as well as for the families of the three guys that ended their own life."

The plan, part two

First thing's first. Each man, and our lady, need to do his or her job just right. In order to get the feel for the lay of the land, I ask Mick to set up one of his drones with a camera to scan the gambling joint and all of its surroundings. That will show us exactly where to set up and get the best vantage points to do what we need to do.

My thought is that we need to take out Murphy's hitmen and any bodyguards as quietly as possible. We can use some of our sharp shooters with rifles equipped with silencers; no noise! We can't just walk up to 'em and cap 'em. We're going to have to be really slick.

Once we find out where the two hitmen are, we'll get them. Eh-Jax and I will take out one man while Clint and Chuck eliminate the other killer. As for Murphy's bodyguards, that's gonna be a bit trickier.

I ask the crew, "Anybody have any suggestions?"

Angel comes up with a great idea. She says, "How about we grab up Shane, Murphy's son? Once we have him, we contact his dad and tell him he has to pay a price to get him back or, he never sees him again!"

Hap, says, "I knew this little lady was going to be a great asset for *our cause*."

Bull breaks in and says, "What do you mean, "Our cause?" WHAT? Like the *'Cosa Nostra's,* our thing, thingy?"

Everybody laughs and Hap says jokingly, "That's right wise-guy! And, if you don't like it, I'll have Angel Luca Brasi over here whack you and make you *swim with the fishes!*"

The whole gang just loses it and laughs till tears roll down their cheeks. What's a great line; *Angel Luca Brasi whacking Bull and making him swim with the fishes!* That's a classic come back!

After this brief moment of levity, we get back to business. I ask the young crew members if they think they could tail Shane and see if there's a good chance of getting him when he's alone.

Dave says, "My source knows Shane has a special lady called Luci that he takes out to dinner at Sandrino's Steak House on Potter Road; usually, on Mondays and Wednesdays around 7pm. That's a slower time at the gambling house. He won't be hard to recognize. According to my guy, he always wears a special made Irish Tam. You can't miss it."

I say, "Okay, we need to get this junior wise guy as soon as we can. Let's set up the same scam we've used a few times. You know; the parking lot fender bender ploy and have one of us go in and tell him he needs to come out to survey the damage and exchange license and insurance information."

Chuck says he'd do it. Perfect! Today is Tuesday, so tomorrow night, we can bag us a very valuable bait to get Sonny.

Wednesday night

At 6:45, Chuck parks his dark 2007 Tucson in the restaurant's lot to wait for Shane to arrive. Hap has his van there along with Dave, Angel and Mick. They're there to do the honors of securing our target. Once they get him near the mock parking lot fender bender; he'll be stunned and loaded in Hap's paddy wagon and taken to our hoosegow. (lockup)

It isn't long. He arrives right on time, 7pm on the nose. He parks his shiny 2010 Cadillac, gets out and walks his lovely young lady to the door. Good thing for us, he doesn't have any bodyguards watching his back. This will make the grab even easier.

The Maître-d' sits them at a table near a window. That's great! The crew can see them clearly. After being served their usual cocktail and have placed their order, it's show time!

Chuck maneuvers his SUV at the back of the Cadillac so that the bumper dents the lower part of the trunk lid; just enough to show that there is damage. The next play is for him, in disguise, is to go in and have the Maître-d' tell Shane that someone hit his car in the parking lot and that he needs to go out to exchange car information with the person that did it. Chuck goes in and gives the message to the Maître-d'; he in turn, speaks to Shane.

Our young hoodlum is fuming! Besides learning that his Caddy may be damaged, the whole thing is disturbing his dinner. He storms out and walks toward his car where Chuck is waiting. He left his SUV right where he did the damage to Shane's car. This way, it'll make it easier to bag this guy.

"What's wrong with you?!" says Shane, "Are you STUPID? Don't you know how to drive in a parking lot? I just bought this car a week ago and now, look at it! You're gonna pay for this! Alright, show me your license and insurance papers. Man! You REALLY ruined my night!"

Chuck says to him, "I'm really sorry, man! I had a blind spot as I backed up and didn't see your car. I'll get my papers out of my glove box. Hold on a second."

As he goes to his car, Angel walks up and tells Shane that she saw what happened from across the street and that she will wait till the police arrive to file the report, if he wants.

He tells her, "That's okay sweetheart, I got this. But thanks for wanting to help. I appreciate it."

As Shane is busy talking to Angel, Hap maneuvers the van close to where Shane is standing, and at the same time, Dave walks behind him and you can hear that familiar ZAP of the stun gun. Our mark slumps to the ground. Angel, along with Mick and Dave tossed him in the van and make their way to the warehouse to lock up their prize.

As for Shane's girlfriend, Luci, she gets word via a prepared note by us that was left for her with the Maître-d'.

The note simply says; *"Sorry, but I had to leave to take care of something very important. Call my man Jimmy so he can take you home.*

She leaves the restaurant spewing a string of very profanities that would make a sailor blush.

The plan, part three

Shane is all wrapped up in the van. Angel finds his cell phone and looks for his father's phone number. She jots down the number, then, tosses the cell in a field along the road so no one can pin point where he is.

Now at the warehouse, and since it's early enough, using one of our untraceable cell phones, we dial up Mr. Sonny Murphy.

He answers. I tell him, "Hey Mr. Murphy, I have your son Shane in a secure place. Don't ask any questions; just listen if you ever want to see him alive again."

"What do you mean you have MY SON?! Who is this?! You're a DEAD man, whoever you are!"

"You must be a very stupid man! You're in no position to threaten me! You need to SHUT UP and listen or YOUR son is a dead man. Now, SHUT UP AND LISTEN! A man will be in touch with you soon to make arrangements for your son's release. When that happens, you'll need to do as he says or I will send you a piece of your boy one body piece at a time for a month. Think about it; a finger one day, an ear the next... and so on. I know you don't want that. So, just sit tight till I get back to you. If you value your son; and I know you do, you'll gather up all the cash you have so you can save his miserable life. According to your boy, you have well over five million in your safe at home from the eight years you've operated your illegal gambling establishment. If I were you, I'd get it together, real quick like!" I hang up.

Sonny doesn't know what to think. But he has no doubt that getting his son back will cost him most of the dough he's got stashed.

Thanks to Mick's drone footage, we know exactly how to hit Murphy's little domain and where to get his two hit men. We don't want innocent folks to die, so we need Boom to set up a few small explosives as a way to empty the club. Later, a full demolition event will be needed to completely destroy the joint. As for hitmen, Frankie and Carmen, we'll have a couple of our marksmen do that from a distance; like we did with Raptor the drug king; quick and clean hits.

End of the hit-men and the casino

First thing we need to do is set up for taking down Sonny's trigger men. The area around La Rosa's Restaurant was scouted out by Eh-Jax. He found two spots that are perfect.

It's the weekend and both men are there doing their usual carousing; drinking and playing the field with the ladies. It was planned that one of the young crewmen would go and smash the car windows of each of the bad guys, then, have someone go in La Rosa's and tell the door guy that Frankie and Carmen's cars have been broken into.

It's 9:30 dark out. Dave is riding a "crotch-rocket" motorcycle and has a ballpeen hammer in his hand to do the honors of vandalizing Carmen's classic Town Lincoln and Frankie's slick 2000 GT Mustang. He's quick in doing it and as he rides away from the scene, Chuck runs to the restaurant door and informs the bouncer that Frankie and Carmen's cars were broken into. He promptly finds our two killers and gives them the news. They're out the door in a flash with gun in hand and each goes to his car to inspect the damage. As the two thugs stand there cussing away, without losing a second, I squeeze off a shot and hit Carmen. He's down. A split second after, Eh-Jax does the same to Frankie. Now, Sonny's trigger men are no longer part of the equation.

Bye, bye casino

The next thing to do is deal with Sonny himself and any of his bodyguards. Boom, Angel, Mike, Bull, Clint and Hap have already rigged the casino to blow. Sonny, his bodyguards and the clients suspect nothing. It's time to clear the joint. Boom presses the button on his remote detonators and a series of small explosions go off simultaneously. None of the charges are strong enough to hurt anyone; just the right amount to shake the house a bit and scare the life out of everyone in the building. Boom took special care in not setting up charges where the girls in the basement are working.

The place clears out in about three minutes; like rats scurrying out of a rat hole that was lit on fire. Cars go screaming out of the driveway and down the road. The call girls make their way out and get into a van to follow the line of cars. Sonny is also one of the people fleeing. He took a little longer to exit. He got in a Cadillac Seville with three bodyguards. Angel noticed he was carrying a good size bag as he ran from the casino. That must be the loot from the night's take. Well, whatever he has in that bag plus the five million he has at home should be considerable. We'll see.

The job isn't done yet. After seeing that no one is left in the building, Mickey, working with Boom, get ready for the big "finale" using one of his drones. They're at a distance of quarter mile. The drone is equipped with a video camera so we can have a neat souvenir of the event. Boom hooks up the explosive onto the drone that should decimate the casino. Everything is ready. Mike takes the payload above the building, sets it in a gully in the center of the roof; releases it and flies his drone back to himself. Boom is ready to hit the button. He counts it down; three, two, one and, BOOM! The explosion is huge! The roof has a large hole in it and flames spread in minutes to engulf the entire upper section. There will be nothing left to salvage when it's all over.

Since we needed to come onto Sonny's property to take him and his operation down, we had to have our own escape plan. Fortunately, the far backside of Sonny's property, about five hundred feet from his building, through a bunch of trees, there's a service road that leads away from the main highway to an alternate road. It's a perfect escape route. Everyone goes home.

Next day, interrogating Shane

Knowing that the young ladies who were forced into prostitution were whisked away in a van and taken to whatever house they're kept in, we need to talk top Shane and get all the information we can in order to set them free.

It's 8am. He's brought out wearing the special shock helmet. Angel sits him in our not-so-fun chair, and since she's a lady herself, she lays a solid open hand slap across his face. It's hard enough that he nearly goes over. She'd like to punch him out for being the rotten dirt bag that he is, but pulls back as I step in.

I tell him, "You, your dad and his entire crew are done being part of the ugly life that casino has brought. You will give me all the information I want or be beaten till you wish we would just kill you! First thing, where do you keep the young-women you use as prostitutes?

He doesn't hesitate and says, "They're kept at 58 Riley Street on the second floor. The men watching them live downstairs."

"How many men are there?

"There are three men there all the time while the girls are in the house."

"Next question Shane. Besides you pimping young ladies, I hear you deal drugs to your dad's patrons and quite a few street dealers. Where do you keep your products?"

Again, he's quick to answer. He doesn't want to get beat any more.

He says, "Me and the guys at the house have a good size stash in a secret compartment behind the fridge."

"Okay. How much of a stash are we talking about, Shane?"

"We always have several kilos of coke and marijuana on hand."

"That's great info. And, are there cameras surveilling the perimeters of the house?"

"No. No cameras. I just depend on my men to keep a sharp eye on the place."

One more question Shane. "How many of the girls are addicted to the drugs you kept pumping in them?"

He's real hesitant to answer that one because he knows that he's got to take the heat for that, and for any girls that overdosed. Since he balks at the question, Angel who is standing next to "sparky," clears her throat to warn the guys to stand back and turns it on. Young Shane convulses like a thrashing fish out of water. That jolt gave him the incentive he needed to speak up!

Still reeling from the sting of the electric shock, he manages to say, "All the girls got hooked on coke. We didn't want to ruin their appearance by shooting them up with heroin; needles cause ugly scars. The coke kept them submissive. They became dependent on us."

Angel leans over to me and whispers, *"I'd like to keep this rat here for a month and shoot him up with heroin several times a day till he's a stoned-cold addict, then, cut him off completely and let him experience the gut-wrenching withdrawals addicts go through."*

I tell him, "So, all the girls got hooked and that doesn't bother you. And, the ones that overdosed and died, that doesn't faze you! You're a real low-life scumbag, Shane. The pain, misery and damage you've done to these girls are unpardonable!"

He has nothing to say. He just hangs his head down and weeps; wondering if we're going hurt him some more or kill him.

Clint and Eh-Jax loosen him from the chair and bring back to his cell for the night.

Next day, contacting Sonny

I call Sonny at 9am. As he answers. I say to him, "Get your cash ready! There better be at least five million! I'm sure you won't be alone. Just make sure your men don't make any stupid moves. Check out the video on your phone. You'll see that we have Shane all set up to take an eighty-foot plunge to his death in one of six elevator shafts the building has. If you or your men try to get cute, you'll have a dead son."

Sonny looks at the video and can see his boy tied up, blind-folded and gagged at the edge of a shaft. He's shaking with fear!

He tells me, "Okay! Okay! I won't try any funny business. Just, don't hurt my boy!"

I tell him, "I'm glad we understand each other. Now then, here's where you and the money will need to be. Go to the canal. You'll see a very large seven-story building next to a silo marked Simco. Go in the blue door and place the money in the dumb-waiter that'll be on your right. You'll need to press the button that will take the money to the top floor. Once I've verified that it's all there, I'll let you know exactly where in the building Shane is. I'll be checking for any tracking device you might put in the bag. If you do that, so-long Shane! Don't screw up!"

Sonny knows he needs to move on this. He gathers up the money and puts it in a bag. Once that's done, he, along with his main driver, and his two best bodyguards, get into his Cadillac and head for the canal. He has two other men following in another car. They make it there in twenty minutes.

They get out of the cars quickly and make their way into the building. Sonny sees the dumb-waiter, places the bag in it and presses the button that sends the cash up to us; us, meaning; me, Boom and Dave. What Sonny and his guys don't know is that Hap has set up mini cameras in the stairway. There's also one in the freight elevator the bad guys will be using to retrieve junior! Hap will be able to see their every move from his van that's hidden near the silo.

The miss-direction

When I told Sonny that the money will be going up seven floors; that was a plan to miss direct him and his goons. Actually, the money only goes to the second floor where, me, and my crew wait to grab it. At the moment, Sonny thinks I'm alone and will probably send men up the staircase to get me before I can escape. His boy is still at the edge of the empty elevator shaft that's next to a working freight elevator. He would only need a slight push to drop him down the eighty-foot shaft.

As the huge money bag gets up to the second floor, Dave opens it and can see mostly hundred dollar bills. And, by the looks of the cash in there, he lets me know that there should be at least a few million. If Sonny short-changed us a bit, it's no big deal. The amount is good and we have him and his gang right where we want them.

After ten minutes, I call Sonny to tell him that I'm satisfied with the money and that he and his men can come and get Shane by taking the freight elevator that is located fifteen feet to his left. As soon as Murphy gets the go ahead, he sends two of his men to make their way up the stairs toward the seventh floor. As they reach the fifth floor, with two more to go, me and my men have already snuck out another door that is directly connected to the canal where Lenny and Chuck are waiting in a boat to whisk us away quietly.

Sonny and his two body guards pile into the freight elevator and press the button to go to the seventh floor where Shane is tied up. It takes almost two minutes for the tired elevator to reach the top floor. Once there, the two that took the stairs arrive at the same time and everyone rushes to Shane. They're amazed at the amount of duct tape that was used to secure him. He's wrapped up like a mummy!

Sonny is beyond peeved! He says, "Look at the way those bastards treated my boy! I'm gonna make them pay real big for this. Hurry up! Somebody cut him loose!"

Fortunately, one of his guys, Al, always carries a knife. There's so much tape on him that it takes everyone helping, fifteen minutes to cut it all away and peal it off. By the time they're done, there's still a lot of gummy residue all over his face, hands and clothes; not to mention the hair he lost on his head when Al had to cut some of it away to free him from the tape.

Sonny has his boy, but he's way beyond angry! He tells his men. "Whoever this mutt is and any help he had in doing this to me and my boy all gotta be found and made to suffer! Then, just like Frankie Pantangeli said to Michael Corleone concerning mob rivals; *'I want them DEAD! You hear me, DEAD!'* Let's get the hell out of here!"

The last ride

The camera Hap put in the elevator also has a microphone and is close enough to where they worked to free Shane that he heard everything Murphy said to his men. Too bad these menaces to society won't get to follow up on the plan to get revenge or carry on with their life of crime. With all the death, misery and pain they caused people, if anyone deserves to disappear, it's them. They are true enemies of decent folks and must be taken out.

All six men climb into the freight elevator; one of Sonny's men hits the button to go to ground level. Just as it starts going down, Boom presses the remote detonator that snaps the main cable of the elevator. With the combined weight of six men; figuring an average of two hundred pounds per man, it comes to a 1,200 pound plus cargo that makes the fall even faster and deadlier. To be sure the mission is complete, Boom placed an additional charge at base of the shaft that is triggered by the crash of the elevator as it hits bottom. No one survives.

We really don't like taking lives, but all of these men would go on endlessly being criminals; doing killings, prostituting innocent young women, dealing drugs that kill and addict weak people. They contribute nothing good to society, only evil! This is how wars go. As it says in the book of Ecclesiastes 3; "*A time to kill and a time to heal.*" For me and the others in our group at war with murdering criminals, we feel righteous about anyone we've killed that were killers. And as for the word "*heal*" in the verse, we all want to create as much healing as possible for the victims the bad guys hurt.

Freeing the five ladies

As Sonny and his immediate crew are *put to rest*, Angel, Bull and Eh-Jax have arrived at 58 Riley Street where Shane's five young ladies are kept. Angel dressed in a UPS outfit, knocks on the door with a dummy package in her hands; Dave and Chuck are out of sight, hugging the wall, waiting for one of the creeps to open. As soon as that happens, they all rush in and eliminate the rats with silencer-fitted pistols. The girls are all up in their rooms.

They heard the soft pop of shots being fired but don't know what to make of it.

Angel yells out, "Hey girls, come on out. Don't be afraid. You're all safe. We're here to help you."

Sheepishly, one by one, they come out. Angel explains what's happen and that they just need to sit tight for a little while longer. They're told that they should gather up their belongings and be ready to leave that house soon. Angel tells them that she going to work out something so that each of them gets a sum of money to start over. The girls are all weeping and thank her. She tells them to stay put for the moment, that she'll be back Chuck and Dave need to get rid of the bad guys. They toss the three recently deceased down the basement stairs where Mendola's men can find them later. It seems like a terrible thing to do, but when you think about what they've done to those girls and perhaps dozens more, the men don't feel bad at all making the basement their temporary resting place.

Back at the base,
counting Murphy's dough

Back at the warehouse, Clint dumps Sonny's money on a table; Clint, Angel and Dave have the honor of counting it. They come up with $4,950,900.

Angel, right away says, "How would you guys feel if the money was split amongst the four families Murphy and his gang destroyed; the two detectives and the two businessmen - and, for the five girls Shane forced into prostitution for the casino?"

I ask her, "How do you think the split between nine people should be handled?"

Figuring on her cell phone calculator, she says, "The $4,000,000 can be split between the families of the two detectives and two businessmen. That would give each of them $1,000,000, and for the five girls, a lesser split of $950,000 would give each of the ladies $190,000. The remaining $900 could be set aside for some of our expenses. What do you guys think?"

Hap says, "That's good thinking. I like those figures. Sounds like a reasonable breakdown to me as compensation for those folks, plus a small reserve for us."

All the men agree that it's only right that those families and the girls be compensated for the pain and misery they suffered.

I jump in and say to her, "Angel, you are an *angel*. I'm sure it'd be okay with everyone here if we put that job of distributing the money in your capable hands. What do you say?"

With a huge smile, she says, "Boss, I'd be more than happy to make that happen. The girls Murphy enslaved are waiting at the house where they were kept. They're getting their belongings together. Me and one of the men can get over there to give them their share before they take off to wherever they're planning on going. And, I'm sure Haps' friend O'Rourke can give us the addresses of the detectives and the two businessmen that were killed."

"Thank you, Angel. We all value you and your dedication to the group."

"I appreciate you saying that, Boss. And, thanks for thinking of me as an equal in this squad. It means a lot to me."

"Angel, you've more than earned the respect of everyone here. We're glad to call you one of us."

Mendola notified

To finish this, I make a call to Captain Mendola.

"Hello Captain, this is your friend. That thing you ran by me is a done deal. All those involved are history. I'm sure you had a chance to take a look at that facility of *ill-repute* by now. As you can see, that's also history."

"Yes, I did, and, I also just got word about an explosion at the Simco silo where an elevator shaft got blown up and its walls burying the elevator car. Is there anything I should know about that?"

"No Captain, but whatever is at the bottom of that shaft with tons of concrete and steel over it, will only be revealed when the city decides to demolish the building. That could be as long as five to ten years. Oh, and by the way, I want you to know that the families of the two detectives and two businessmen will be compensated, courtesy of the Murphy fund. Also, we got the name of Murphy's lawyer from Shane, a Mr. Russ Callahan. He was the one that drew up the papers that put the car dealership and meat packing owners' businesses in Sonny's name. As we speak, he's being contacted and strongly advised to write up new papers that will return those businesses to the former owners' families. We're sure he'll cooperate, especially after the recent events that befell Sonny and company."

Mendola doesn't need an explanation; he understands and says, "I will consider this case closed my friend. Again, I owe you big time. I want you to know that whatever you and your men do from here on with regards to policing your neighborhood, me and my men will stand aside and won't interfere."

I tell him, "Well Captain, thanks for the green light on that, but even if you didn't okay it, we'd still do what we do. The neighborhood deserves that. Talk to you soon. Take care."

"You too friend, and *tenga buen día*." (Have a good day).

Distributing the money

Hap gets on the phone and contacts O'Rourke. He gets the information needed on the families Murphy destroyed and Angel gets right to work. Since she'll be carrying so much cash, Clint and Dave go with her as backup. The first stop, the five young ladies. Angel goes in Clint's car while Dave drives his van so they can take the girls wherever they want to go when everything is done.

Back at the house where the five are waiting, Angel gathers them in the living room and tells them, "Here's $190,000 for each of you. It's money that was taken from Shane's father. You more than deserve it as compensation for all the suffering they put you through.

She tells them, "I know a couple of you are addicted more than the others in this group; you need to get to a Methadone clinic to get clean. Get cleaned up, then, take that money and go make a life for yourselves."

Everyone promises they'll do that, and thank Angel, Clint and Dave for saving them.

They're all in tears over getting freed and getting that huge sum of money. This will help them get their lives back to normal; and they're so relieved that they'll never have to fear the pigs that enslaved them. All them were abducted from the Virginia University area. Dave takes them to the airport so they can get back there. They're dropped off and wished, "God-speed." Our hope is that they'll be able to live a normal life.

Next, the families who lost loved ones

Angel, Clint and Dave's next move; taking care of the families of the four men Murphy's crew murdered. There's no fanfare; Dave dressed in a FedEx uniform knocks on the door of each of the wives of the deceased, hands them a small duffle bag with a million dollars in cash in it, and leaves. Angel also put a note in each bag to briefly explain where the money came from and to wish them well. What that done, it brings this mission to an end.

Chapter 51

Winding this down

Our two crews have been ridding the neighborhood of trash for a while now and made a huge difference. Us and the good captain can see it. There are still and will always be bad guys and morons around. We can't fix STUPID! Some people just can't seem to think straight; they are stuck in perpetual stupidity!

Since the word got out in the neighborhood about the policing we've done, we don't need to deal with as many situations where we have to step in to tune-up cockroaches or make evil people disappear. We're gonna be around for anything that does pops up. The plan is to let our young recruits take the lead. They're already into it.

So far, Mick, Angel, Dave and Chuck have nailed a few teens that have become unruly on several corners. Some got immediate punishment by being zapped and taken to our headquarters where to meet Mr. Sparky; then, released into the neighborhood as much wiser and respectful citizens.

Chuck and Dave bagged a drug dealer. He'd been dealing on and off on a couple of our streets. The thought is; *we cannot allow one dealer even one day to deal that crap in our neighborhood.* There's to be NO TOLERANCE! The crew nabbed a dirt bag named Tirus. The crew beat him up a bit and Angel, the *electrocutioness,* introduced him to Sparky. Before releasing him to Mendola, they got valuable intel about the perp's drug source; which was passed on to the captain. Tirus caused a lot of people to become addicts and several died from overdose. This makes him a killer. Now, he's gonna do a whole lot of time in jail.

Another mission

Our young justice squad got word about a local area representative by the name of Raúl Sanchez that was put in charge of a major housing project in our district. He'd been heavy at practicing nepotism; taking care of family members and friends by giving them no-show jobs connected to housing projects. He really abused his position and pocketed thousands of dollars.

Angel and the other lads were quick to abduct him and made him pay for his crooked ways and greed. She tightened him up with a taste of Sparky while the men let him have a few heavy backhands that made him bleed and left him with black eyes. They were able to gather great information that got turned over to Captain Mendola. According to the captain, he's looking at seven years in jail.

Chapter 52

Bagging a sexual abuser

Next item, Mike heard of a thirty-eight-year-old dad by the name of Jeff Wilson that was sexually abusing daughters Jessica ten, and twelve-year-old Ana. He beat his wife Shelly when she confronted him after discovering the creep's perversion and wanted a divorce. He told her that he'd kill her if she did that or went to the authorities on the girls' behalf.

The young crew got him while he was coming out of a bar; using the fender bender ruse. He was an easy creep to snag and cart off to the warehouse. Hap, Boom and Bull were there to observe how they dealt with him.

Back at the warehouse

Angel, is at the control of Sparky again. She's taking special joy in cooking this pervert. Instead of the usual two second jolt from Sparky, she gives this-low life three five-second treatments. None of the men object. They all understand her actions. This guy is a supper rat! With the first two jolts, he screams and shakes like crazy. After the third one, everyone thought he was dead.

You can imagine Angel thinking, *"If he's dead, that's too bad. He deserves it!"*

He was only knocked-out. As he comes to, they let him get his wind back. Angel gets the first crack at him. She knuckles him in the forehead; giving him a nice goose-egg. Then Dave, Chuck and Mike each unleash solid backhands that put a cut over his right eye and bloody his nose and mouth. Bull adds one more punishment. He gets Bull and Boom to pull his pants down and gives his genital area a once over with the propane torch; not enough to have them blister; just enough that it sends him into extreme panic!

Since the body part he used to abuse his two young daughters, for who knows how long, is exposed, Angel, who witnessed several of her military friends having to put up with sexual abuse and rape while serving in the Middle East, she wants to cut off this fiend's manhood. Instead, she gets a staple gun that's on a nearby table and puts two staples in it; one for each of his daughters. Man, he goes through the roof! This hurts a lot more than the lump on the head and the blows he got to the face. The sting of those staples aren't going away; they hurt really bad. He sits there weeping and begging for the guys to stop.

Boom says to him, "Jeff, one of the vilest things a man can do to his daughters, is rape them! Besides that, you beat your wife. You're not a husband and surely, not a father! You're the epitome of evil! Your wife and daughters have been permanently scarred. You can see it in their eyes; you've KILLED their souls. That makes you a murderer! You need to go away for what you've done and never come near them again!"

Jeff is freaking out and says in a crying voice, "Please don't hurt me anymore! I'll never do it again! I'll leave and never come near them! I promise! I swear…"

Hap cuts him short and says, "Damn right you'll never do it again! Just sit there and enjoy your pain!"

Very important decision, what to do with Jeff

He motions for everyone to leave and go to the adjoining room. Once there, Hap asks the question; "What should we do with this devil?! I'm for ending his life. Why? Because if we turn him over to the good Captain, his wife and daughters will have to go to court, testify against him, and have to relive the nightmare life they've endured. I don't want them to have to go through that. What do you all say?"

Angel doesn't hold back. She says, "One of the sergeants who repeatedly raped one of the women in my platoon was found dead with a bullet in the back of his head. It happened when we were in a combat."

With a wink, she says, "My guess is that he died from *friendly fire*; probably from my sister in arms he raped. He got exactly what he deserved. Besides her, he did the same to at least five other women in our company. The brass ruled his death as, '*killed in action*.' That was the end of it."

Dave says, "Yah, I agree that turning him over to the law would be very messy and painful for his wife and young daughters; they're just children! I'm sure they would be extremely relieved if he were no longer around to continue raping them and seeing their mother beaten. He needs to make peace with his Maker, and then, be put down."

Angel says, "He ripped the life out of these girls and their mother. This rat's disgusting behavior makes me sick and brings back ugly memories of what went on for over two years while I served."

With that said, Hap says, "Let's get this useless cockroach to the canal."

The men load up their perp and head for the water. As they roll along in Hap's van, there's a flash… Jeff's body goes limp. Without any remorse, Angel put one in the back of his head. Having arrived at the canal, Mike and Chuck cart the body to the water's edge; tie sandbags to his waist and drop him in. Jeff will no longer be a threat to his family. Angel had already thought of his family. Her plan is to give that extra $900 from what we got from

Murphy and another $10,000 gleaned off one of the drug dealers the young crew nabbed; and give it to Jeff's wife and the girls.

Hap says, "As it says in the Book of Deuteronomy, '...*you shall purge the evil from among you!*' Folks, we did just that. Jeff was evil and is purged from our society!"

The crew gets back in the van and heads home.

Next day

Mike drives Angel to Jeff's house; she goes to the door, knocks, and when Shelly answers, she's hands her the $10,900 with a note.

She simply says to her, "This is for you and your girls."

She leaves without saying anything else.

Shelly looks in the envelope, sees the cash and gasps. She takes the note and reads it. *"The man I represent became aware of you and the girls' situation concerning Jeff. Just know that he'll no longer be around to hurt you. He's been relocated to a place far from you. Start a new life without him. God bless."*

As Shelly is reading the note, Angel returns to the car where Mike is waiting. She gets in and they drive off with huge smiles on their faces. That buttons up another fine intercession for innocent victims in our neighborhood.

Chapter 53

Ending of the narration of our "New War"

In wrapping things up, I know that myself and all of my *"new war" soldiers* didn't really want to be involved in the various war tactics we came up with to clean up our part of the city, but the bad people we encountered needed to be dealt with. No apologies made. There's no place for evil people in a society where good and decent folks live. What's done is done.

With the agreement Captain Mendola and I came up with regarding cleaning up our section of town; with him leaving us alone to do whatever we need to do to remove the scumbags, we don't plan on stopping. We'll keep getting rid of the trash.

Also, because of our vigilante activities being made known to other districts, other such groups have taken up the fight and making a difference in their own neighborhoods. Our NEW WAR has proven to be a very good thing.

End